Patchwork People

Patchwork People

D. B. Martin

Published by IM Books

www.debrahmartin.co.uk

© Copyright D. B. Martin 2014

PATCHWORK PEOPLE

All rights reserved.

This is a work of fiction. Names and characters are a product of the
author's imaginations and any resemblance to actual persons,
living or dead, events and organisations is purely coincidental.

Condition of sale

ISBN 978-0-9929961-5-4

'Our main business is not to see what lies dimly at a distance,

but to do what lies clearly at hand.'

Thomas Carlyle

Prologue

'Just(ic)e served at last – but not the final verdict.'

'Crap!' I said aloud after I read it. Luckily no-one could hear me, unless there was already a lurking reporter vying with Ella, my interfering junior, to keep tabs on me. The original cheesy article about my historic revelations in court had sung my praises for the courage to admit to a less than praiseworthy past. Temporarily I was the darling of the courts, but this editorial was bad news. Didactic diarrhoea – but also catapulting me into the spotlight for the caustically curious and enthusiastic mud-flingers amongst the public at large.

> *'Who would have thought it? The white knight of the courts, Lawrence Juste, has a murky past! A family from hell; including an ex-con, a childhood in care and an unusually lucky find in the man originally prepared to fund his studies to get him on to the legal ladder. Lord Justice Wemmick was no doubt an altruist of the first order to bankroll not only Juste's studies, but the charity Finding Futures for Families (FFF) which later came to the rescue of the young client Juste has recently and miraculously cleared of a charge of manslaughter. The boy has haemophilia and so, of course, couldn't possibly have done it – according to Juste. Ironically, we now find that Danny Hewson is also a relative; one of the Juste clan that he's so studiously concealed until now ...*
> *One has to wonder why Juste was originally chosen as the beneficiary of such generosity from Wemmick. So much goodwill flying about – one would think it was Christmas! Will Juste be revealing all about that too? Perhaps not. But however that came about all those years ago, sources claim that it was Juste's deceased wife, Margaret, who put him and the boy together. Sadly*

she's not here to see the happy result after her tragic death in a hit and run accident only weeks ago, but in the meantime we watch with interest the man most tipped for the top to make High Court Judge this year and his erstwhile family, complete with its very own Blackbeard in his brother Winston – amusingly named after one of our greatest leaders, apparently. What will the future now hold for our embarrassingly honest or profligately careless Lord-Justice-Juste in-waiting? Publically acclaimed as potentially one of the most 'squeakily-clean' lawmen of the current legal world, will he become a fighter for the underdogs that he – by his own admission – is one of? Or will he return to his lofty eyrie to continue fighting expensive battles on behalf of the rich and privileged until he swaps his black silk for the scarlet?

As my learned colleague so rightly said, the jury's still out on that!'

Wild was probably behind it – pissed that I'd made a fool of him in court with Danny's dismissal. I flung it down with disgust next to the black-edged funeral card that had been anonymously delivered an hour ago with its own ominous little message. Between them they covered up Danny's case papers, but the problem of Danny was never far from my mind, whether obvious or not. The message on the card taunted me.

'The rat has had its day in court, but now the piper wants to be paid – like with all good business transactions. Honour amongst thieves, Lawrence. I'll be in touch soon. J'

Jaggers. 'J' *had* to be Jaggers; John Arthur Wemmick – rival, enemy, abuser from my days in the children's home, extortionist, and now about to be my nemesis, it seemed. Joining the sarcastic editor in nipping at my heels but in a more sinister way. To everyone else getting my 'nephew' Danny off a manslaughter charge might have seemed like another masterly performance by Lawrence Juste QC, but for Jaggers it was merely the prequel to nuclear war, and only he had the atomic weapons.

The newspaper had nudged the card up against the portrait shot of Margaret that still adorned my desk for appearances' sake. The card was identical in design to the ones I'd had sent out as invitations to her funeral tomorrow. She smiled ingenuously back at me. RIP – gone but hardly forgotten – the tricky little bitch. I knew what Jaggers wanted from me, but Margaret? She'd had a completely different agenda which I had yet to fully ascertain. Ridiculously I suddenly felt like laughing, even though none of it was funny. Who would have believed someone so decorous could be so devious too? My charming spouse; but also my enemy's equally captivating sister, conning me into a trap and still beaming at me as I faced ruin. If she'd been alive and in front of me right now I'd have cheerfully compounded all my other crimes by strangling her.

And so much for my attempt to call Jaggers' bluff with the evidence supposedly showing he'd driven the car that had mown Margaret down. Dirty money was still dirty money when all was said and done – and he wanted what I'd 'persuaded' good old Judge Wemmick (deceased) to part with back at all costs. Perhaps this had all started with defending Danny and unexpectedly running up against my long-lost family, but how this ended was likely to be much nastier. Danny: just over ten years old like the murder case I'd been fixed to prosecute, and won on the same basis. Me: just short of ten years old when I'd been taken into the children's home where I'd met Jaggers and my feet were first set on this path of secrecy and denial. Margaret: first landing up in my office ten years ago to encourage me on this merry dance. There was a lot of coincidence in ten, and what seemed to be as much at the heart of the mess I was now in as Jaggers' demands for Judge Wemmick's money to be returned. And the nasty question of my part in Danny's parentage? That was the icing on the cake. Murder, blackmail and incest – what better way for a middle-aged barrister to start the day?

Tipped for the top, but anticipating the fall.

1: Little Pieces

In life there are days when ebullient optimism makes you hopeful things can still improve, even though you don't know how. Equally there are others when you know it can only get dramatically worse. I was contemplating Margaret and her trickiness, the little black-edged card, the editorial and how things couldn't get much worse when they did just that. My Chambers partner, Heather Trinder, draped herself against my office door dangerously reminiscent of all the mythological harpies she'd ever spouted about when reminding us *plebs* of her *classical* background. Her arrival definitely precluded improvement.

'Ah, so you've read it too.' She gestured to the editorial as I whisked the card into my top drawer. 'When I showed you that press release I'd organised earlier, I had no idea exactly how much shit had already hit the fan. Now I have. So, what are you playing at? You should have run everything past us before you spilled anything in court. Good job Ella has filled me in now. Have you no consideration for what it could do to me, Francis and Jeremy?'

Ella. I should have known she'd drop me in it. When, at the eleventh hour of Danny's case coming to trial, Heather had lumbered me with her as my junior I guessed there was an ulterior motive. She was the spy in the fold. The confession in court had been in order to get Danny off and try to keep Jaggers at bay, not for amusement's sake – but there was no point saying that to Heather. She would simply treat me to a rant about being facetious. The only way was down, but I was determined to make a fist of defending myself. Die trying – better than running away but still dying.

'Heather, I'm the one under siege here, not you.'

'Maybe; but what you do reflects on us too. And I know I might have appeared to have given you carte blanche to sleep with the little social worker to take the edge off things, but I didn't give you leave to confess to the world that you have links to the criminal fraternity via a family that you've kept a guilty secret until now. My God, the press are going to have a field day with you now if you're not careful – and us.'

'But it looks like it could also be a converting zeal field day, don't you think?' I waved the newspaper article she'd originally been so smug about at her. 'I quote, "*certainly, Lawrence Juste can no longer be said to be squeaky-clean, but will he prove to be the most squeakily honest lawman we've come across in a long time?*"' I grinned, hoping it was charmingly. It obviously wasn't.

'And I quote, "*the jury's still out on that.*" You,' she thrust a dagger-like claw at me, 'are going to have to actually *be* squeaky-clean now, *and* squeaky-honest. Make sure publicly you are, whatever you do in private. If I catch even one whiff of anything dodgy finding its way into the open, I'll macerate you. I had to promise all kinds of nasty little favours to make sure that newspaper report was favourable, and now that's all down the pan. Starting with tomorrow, what are your plans minute by minute – and don't even think about trying to give Ella the slip again.'

'Ah,' so my paranoia hadn't been wrong. Ella, the unamiable, was also my minder. 'Is she my little *helper* from now on then?'

'You'd better believe it, at least until you're out of the shit.'

I considered what being out of the shit would require. It was almost too exhausting to think about but I was going to have to address it sometime soon with Heather breathing down my neck and Ella converting it to steam. I inventoried it in my head as Heather tapped her talons impatiently on my long-suffering desk. It was a salutary reminder that one win in court didn't mean victory.

'And her qualifications are?'

'She's my niece.' I'd already guessed as much. It explained the air of hawk lurking within the china-doll.

'And she's my minder too, then?'

Unlike me, Heather wasn't bothered by the niceties of appearance. 'Yes, reporting back to me.'

'Cheers. So where are Francis and Jeremy?'

'Francis is at home and Jeremy is at the bank.'

'Why?'

'Because Francis has been told to stay there by his doctor and Jeremy has been sent there by me.'

'To do what?'

'In case you haven't noticed in your little world of dead wives, lively mistresses and felonious family, Francis isn't well and neither is our bank balance. I said you were walking around blind. What with you trying to ruin our professional reputation, Francis trying to send himself to an early grave with his cigars and Jeremy trying to spend us all there, it seems like I'm the only one holding it together.'

I sighed. I knew what was expected of me. 'Well, drop the scales from my eyes then. It can't get much worse.'

'Francis may have a perforated ulcer. If he stopped puffing those little cancer sticks for five minutes maybe he and we would all be healthier.' She pursed her lips irritably.

'I didn't know you had such a thing about his smoking?'

'Oh my God, Lawrence – you really are blind, aren't you? Do you think I surround myself with flowers for the hell of it? It's to mask the stink. And Jeremy – how do you think he's been financing his lady-loves? Overdrawing on the partners' account.'

I was chastened. What I'd perceived as Heather's permanent air of dissatisfaction was actually the expression of anxiety. Like she said, I really had been blind. We'd all left the administrative side almost wholly to Heather, assuming that as she so relished control, she would enjoy what we loathed: purse-strings and paperwork.

'Are we really in trouble?'

'It wouldn't take much. We certainly can't have any more unplanned expense. Francis may be out of action for some time so his income stream will be nil, and he'll need his account reserve to cover him whilst he's not working, but Jeremy must have been bleeding us for months so it's virtually non-existent. You and I may end up having to bankroll him if he's off for too long. Jeremy's broke – although at least that may make him stay home alone for a while, and you are about to commit professional suicide if you're not bloody careful. I'm just stuck in the middle of it all.'

'What do you need me to do?'

'*Not* commit professional suicide would be a start, and play along with what I thought I'd managed to get set up for you.' She tapped the newspaper article. 'What else is there that might still come out?'

I took a deep breath and began.

'To be honest, Heather, I don't fully know yet. I'm still getting to grips with my family – they may be relatives but I know barely anything about them as individuals, and what I do know confuses more than explains, generally. For instance, I know my sister Binnie disapproves of Win, but not why.'

3

'I would have thought that's obvious.'

'No, it's not just his dodgy background. There's more to it but no-one seems prepared to explain. Both my oldest sister Sarah, and Win, insist I find out myself by getting to know them – and they're probably right – but that takes time, and in the meantime every time I think I've worked something out, I find there's another angle to it I can't even begin to comprehend. Frustrating isn't the word.'

'So how many of them are there? In other words, if you're going to have to take time out to pin them all down, how long is it going to take you away from Chambers?'

'Well, there's Win, Sarah, Binnie, Jill, Emm, Mary, Kimmy – and I haven't even seen Jim yet. He emigrated years ago. Georgie's dead, Win, I don't trust, Sarah is terminal, Jill and Emm make a great double act but aren't exactly easy to talk to, Binnie is positively discouraging and Mary ...' I ran out of steam there. 'Mary is,' I struggled for an appropriate description. '*Different.*' It was the nearest I could get without sounding crass. 'Kimmy – well, you know she's Danny's mother – at a push – but no great role model.' I couldn't keep the revulsion from my voice, no matter how hard I tried. I hoped Heather didn't remark on it and continued swiftly to avoid being questioned. 'Then on top of that, there's Margaret and her connections with the Wemmicks. There have been more name changes than a bigamist would have so far on Margaret's part.' I added what I knew of Margaret's heritage which had taken her from Green, to Juste – legitimately as my wife – and then a month before she died, extraordinarily, to Molly Wemmick. Heather held her hand up as if to fend off further facts.

'Whoa – I think that's enough. I'll let you do the sums. Just don't take too long – huh?'

I grinned – my sentiments precisely. I concluded with Margaret's official position in the triumvirate of power as one of the three trustees of FFF, along with Jaggers, just to emphasise the complexity of the relationship between him and my deceased wife.

'I guess that's his little money-laundering scheme then? But what else aren't you telling me?' I was surprised, then apprehensive. What did she know about Danny? I tried to look blank. 'Oh, come on, Lawrence. I'm not dumb. So, Margaret was playing cat and mouse with some guy who's playing cash for charity games. So what? Not so good if it got out, but she's not you. How does that matter, other than making her a manipulative little bitch? I can't believe she was having an affair with him – not the saintly Margaret. He was targeting you. Why?'

I breathed out. Confession time – some of it, at least.

'That bully is related to a judge who provided me with the money to study for the bar in the first place – as long as I don't discredit him in any way. If I do, the terms of his will enforce repayment with compound interest over thirty years. Move over Jeremy – I'll be bankrupt too.' I didn't tell Heather the reason he'd provided me with it – she might be hard-nosed and pointy-toed in her Manolo Blahniks, but she was also squeamish – and a homophobe. 'But John Wemmick isn't owning up to the connection. Now, I could make it public, but then I would be forcing his hand without knowing why he's keeping it secret, and that may open up another can of worms, with me potentially one of them.'

'Wriggling like bait on a hook.'

'And you too, if I'm to take what you said earlier seriously.'

'Hmm,' she twisted her lips sideways and frowned. I refrained from reminding her it would give her wrinkles. It would almost certainly bring on another rant about how much she'd spent on cosmetic surgery only to have it ruined by the likes of me and Jeremy. I didn't mention the Wilhelm Johns murder case Jaggers had over me either. With things as they were I wasn't sure that decade-old cover-ups might not tip Heather over the edge. 'So it's all just about money?'

'Not *just* about it Heather – it's about *all* my money – and yours too, since we're in partnership. I need to head him off without invoking the repayment clause in the will.'

'Well, keep your mouth shut, then. That would suit the partnership too!'

'But there's also a suggestion that he was involved in Margaret's death. I think he was the one who set Danny up originally, and getting me to defend him was a way to bring this all into the open – to my detriment. It was only having the car that supposedly killed her stashed away that kept him at bay in court.'

'Via your brother, Win?'

'Yes, Win claims to have the car in a lock-up and that a forensics sweep would prove John Wemmick – Jaggers, I mean – was the driver.'

'So what's the problem? The police could take it from there without you needing to be involved at all. We all stay clear then.'

'Win wasn't proposing passing it on to the police.'

'Oh, my God! Who, then?'

'Someone who would want to use it against Wemmick in a rather more creative way, and that might well open up yet another can of worms…'

She stared at me. 'I don't think I want to know what worms they are, do I?'

'No, Heather, I don't think you do.'

'Tell your brother he either hands it over or we hand him over.'

'Well,' I said uncertainly.

'Oh my God! There's more, isn't there?' She stared at me for a while as I debated what else to tell her then surprised me by shrugging her shoulders. 'OK, don't tell me – yet. But you'd better get it sorted then, *privately,* and *without* involving the little social worker. She was a bad idea after all, given how many other complications there are. She makes you think with your dick. Sleep with Ella if you must. At least she won't talk.'

She left as abruptly as she arrived, leaving me open-mouthed, tasting the trace of her perfume as it lingered around the desk. I got up and sat in the chair she'd vacated. The smell and taste were stronger there. I hadn't imagined it – any of it. We were in deep trouble – not just me but all of us. Back to where we'd been just over ten years ago, but worse. Not just failing and broke; failing, broke and fucked. Perfect. If the partnership went under, the personal guarantees we'd each given would be called in. So much for personal assets then! Suddenly the black humour of it got to me. So Jaggers wanted all I had? And my dear departed wife seemed to be helping him get it with her little blackmail list of all the things I wouldn't want aired in public after having slipped covertly into place as partner in shafting me. I wondered what he'd say if he knew it was likely to be nothing!

It was already six o'clock and the clerks had gone home. For once I wanted people around – almost in anticipation of having no-one around – but I still needed to prepare for the funeral, and I should also talk to Kat, Danny's *little social worker*. That was going to be worse than facing Jaggers or Win – and damn it! Why should I pass up what little there was in all of this for me? If my professional life was about to nose-dive, for once my personal one had shown signs of improving. Everyone needs something to keep them going. I toyed with the idea until I was sure Heather had gone home and then I let betrayal find its level. Heather had charged me with not washing my dirty laundry in public by suggesting I sleep with Ella in lieu of Kat but I couldn't believe her principles were so scant she could sanction sex without feeling. And how the hell had any of us got to the stage where principles and preference were traded for public image?

I picked the phone up and put it straight back down. My stomach churned when I started to put together the words and sentiments to walk the fine line I was going to have to balance on with Kat. I already had one set of secrets hidden from her – the possibility of being Danny's father. I didn't add *incestuously* – but there it was, eating away a hole in my brain for my integrity to fall through. Now I would also have to somehow keep from her the fact that she would be a secret herself. After our conversation at the hospital when we first found out about Danny's haemophilia, it had been clear she might want more than a brief affair – a lot more. And so she should.

I picked the phone up again. Damn Heather and appearances. I'd made a promise to myself to be someone my childhood hero, Atticus Finch, would have been proud to call a colleague. To do that I had to be the kind of man he'd be proud to call a friend too. That kind of man didn't lie to the woman he claimed to care for, or deny responsibility for the child who might be his son. Fired up with self-righteous zeal I began to dial her number, only to again falter on the last numeral. But I was still a coward, whether or not I pretended to myself that standing up to Jaggers had made me otherwise. I had to admit it. I was afraid.

I put the phone down again, almost knocking it from the hook when it rang as soon as it made contact. Automatic reaction took over this time. I snatched it back up, cursing even as the caller's voice filtered through the irritation with myself.

'Lawrence, you weren't at home so I wondered if you were there. Can you talk now?'

'Kat.'

My mouth glued shut. What I'd been planning seemed little more than banal cliché and trite promises. The charade I'd been considering playing with her degraded both her and me – but that now left me with nothing useful to say.

'Are you all right?' In the end I managed a kind of strangled yelp in reply to that. 'Oh, have I rung at an awkward moment? Is that woman there again? Your junior?' I could hear the twist of jealousy in her voice and wanted to unravel it, but she rushed on and cemented the deception in place for me. 'I won't be a nuisance then but I just wanted to make sure you're OK and to set your mind at rest that I won't embarrass you tomorrow. I will be absolutely professional at the funeral, but I will have to come because of the work I did with her – Margaret – I hope you understand and that will be all right...' The rush subsided and the hesitation at the other end of the phone was as palpable as my silence. I debated whether to correct her assumptions about Ella, or to tell her about Jaggers' card and Heather's bad news, but a little warning voice cautioned against it. Fledgling emotions don't necessarily grow to flight in maturity. There was still a lot I didn't know about Kat too.

'Of course. Your attendance is very welcome, and thank you for the condolences.' It sounded like the right thing to say if I had an audience. It had almost become second nature to lie, dissemble and deceive. Sometimes I hated myself almost as much as I hated Jaggers.

'OK,' she sounded uncertain. 'I'll see you tomorrow then – at a distance, but call me when you can talk.' She left it a heartbeat before whispering, 'I miss you,' and the little catch at the end tugged at the point under my ribs that was beginning to ache continuously these days. Pragmatism kicked in just in time.

Proximity and appearances: Heather's warning had been as much about them as about my behaviour. If I told Kat about Jaggers or the partnership's difficulties, it increased our proximity. If I increased Kat's proximity, it increased her exposure to Jaggers. Lennox had been right with his assertion to me in the children's home that the elements of life were safer kept separate. Not allowing problems to cross-fertilise was the way forward, and that meant not two, but multiple boxes were required to contain all my potential fireworks. Yet somehow I must also eventually release all of them to get to the truth.

I sat for a while after Kat rang off, consciously stifling the inclination to ring her back purely to hear her voice again. Outside the evening started to draw in and the light was turning a silvery grey. Autumn was approaching before summer had even truly ended. I stuffed the newspaper in the drawer with the card. Danny's case file was still spread out on top of the desk underneath where the paper had been, now more haphazard than it had been before the card and the newspaper had arrived. The neat rows I'd arranged the items of evidence into were scuffed into jagged edges, like my conscience. I started to shuffle them together to put it all away again – the problem of another day – when the photograph of the torn red nail found its way to the top of the John's case notes summary I'd made as a prompt for myself whilst puzzling over how the two intertwined. I hesitated. That was crazy. Surely I hadn't put the photograph in there? It was a close-up of the nail fragment that had been found caught up in the bag twisted round the murder victim's head. It left me as stunned and sickened as when I'd first found it, trying to work who'd set me up with the case that led to Win claiming the woman I'd drunkenly slept with at the post-success party was my sister, Kimmy. Unbeknownst to me then, of course – but nevertheless possibly making me Danny's father.

I wouldn't have mixed the two folders even if I had included notes I'd made of one in the other. Organised isolation with case papers was as habitual for me now as pedantry. Kat had commented on the latter several times and I pulled myself up on the former now. This bit of evidence would definitely have remained boxed in the right place – more so, even, than others, given what it implied. It had to be Margaret's torn red nail; that so definitive red she loved to wear. The conversation about it with Win still rung in my head.

'So who was the real murderer?'

'I dunno, but I can guess. Ask Molly – Margaret, whatever you want to call her.'

'I can't, she's dead.'

'Yeah, and probably best left that way. No-one else gets hurt then.'

It was inappropriate anywhere now she was dead, but infinitely so on the scene of a murder case over ten years old. But there it was – and that made Margaret a candidate for murderer too. I pulled the photo from the run of papers and forced myself to study it properly despite the mental recoil from what it represented. I needed to get used to facing unpleasant facts without repulsion if I was going to get to the truth – a truth which, no doubt was going to be far from pleasant however it panned out.

It reminded me suddenly and painfully of my oldest sister, Sarah, and her unpalatable news the first time we'd met after forty years. Cancer – and terminal. We'd called Sarah 'Little Mother' even as children. She was Ma's substitute when Ma's time was too stretched amongst the others. But I'd had no mother since I was nine when the children's home claimed me. Both she and Ma were lost, or as good as with Ma's death forty years ago and Sarah's now imminent too. My response to Sarah personified my feelings about the past: regret and rage. Regret for what was lost, rage that it should be. I should box this feeling of regret and let it out tomorrow when Margaret was eulogised so credibility could be served. Maybe I wouldn't feel such a fraud then. Margaret and Sarah – too much of one, and not enough of the other. I should go and see Sarah. It would be something I'd done right amongst all the wrong.

The thought made me feel marginally better and I allowed myself to dwell on the visit to Sarah without feeling so guilty for a while. Odd that Sarah and Margaret had known more about each other than I'd known about either of them before I'd even been aware they'd met. Such small, apparently inconsequential things that a husband should know in detail about his wife, and such important, life-altering things a brother should know about his sister.

Fuck! Win had been lying when he implied Margaret could have been involved in the girl's death in the Wilhelm John's case. Sarah had as much as told me that when I'd visited her to re-introduce myself – or rather Margaret had as much as told her when they'd first met.

'She said she were surprised you hadn't hurt yourself like she did when she was a kid. Tore her thumb ligaments, she said. Ski-ing. In a cast for months and missed school because of it. Would've studied more herself otherwise. Even worse than me at carrying the tray.'

How the hell could you hold someone down, bag their head and suffocate them if you didn't even have sufficient grip to carry a tray? And I could attest to that weakness in Margaret too. I'd attributed it to typical manoeuvring of me into the role she wanted me in at the time. Now, I could see my extremely efficient and independent wife for once simply hadn't the capability.

But then how could her torn-off nail fragment have been attached to the murder weapon?

From reluctant consideration my brain turned to furious activity. First things first – prove the nail came from Margaret. It was six-forty-five. The police evidence archives would be closed for the day, but I needed that torn-off nail. I also needed Margaret not to be cremated in the morning until I knew the post mortem samples were adequate to make a match between it and them. Then I needed to check if the tale Margaret had told Sarah was true. Unfortunately for that I needed a witness statement from Sarah and a whole lot more digging into Molly Wemmick's past – and there was someone who really wouldn't like that. The funeral was at eleven-thirty. It was going to be a very early start tomorrow.

2: Delaying the Dead

The coroner was sympathetic but suspicious.

'It's not usual to want to know about samples.' She eyed me curiously. 'We usually expect relatives to not want to know.'

'It's not ghoulishness, I assure you.'

'Oh, I wouldn't have suggested that for a moment.' Her look disputed her courtesy. 'Let me ring the lab and see if I can get hold of someone.'

I looked at my watch. It was already nine-thirty. The Coroner's office kept to its own timings, no matter how early its visitors.

'I don't need to know what the samples are, only that there are sufficient of them to be able to match DNA,' then wished I'd been more vague. I sounded unfeeling – after all, this wasn't merely the victim in a case I was defending. This was my wife. Yet the closer I got to Margaret's life and death, the less intimate I felt with her. In many ways she had become as enigmatic and intractable as an anonymous victim, keeping her secrets closer in life than in death.

The Coroner paused, phone receiver in mid-air.

'DNA? Is there something I should know?' We'd met professionally several times before, but this was the first time we'd spoken about Margaret. She must think me a queer fish. She was probably right.

'At the moment, no, but I want to make sure things can be checked in due course if anything new comes in.' I motioned to the phone. 'Would you mind? Time is rather of the essence. The funeral's at eleven-thirty.'

I could feel the sweat gathering under my arms and round the collar of my previously pristine white shirt and black mourning suit. The evidence archives weren't open until nine-thirty today. 'Part-timers,' the officer on reception had informed me dismissively. That had prioritised the Coroner, supposedly open at nine – but tardy – with Sarah lined up for a visit in the afternoon while she was still 'comfortable'. I wished I'd confided in Kat after all, even if only to have a sidekick. Two people together seemed to make everything easier, as long as it was the right two.

I tried to hide my impatience as she explained what she wanted, got passed onto someone else, explained again, and then hung on the line, waiting. 'They're trying to find the pathologist who carried out the autopsy,' she explained, studying me carefully before looking away as I caught her eye. Professional distance – it made everything easier. I checked my watch again. Nine thirty-five, and it would take at least fifteen minutes to get back to the police archives before I could even check for and retrieve the fragment of red nail. 'Hello? Yes. Fine. Thanks.' She turned back to me, nervous smile in place, hand over the mouthpiece of the receiver. 'They've kept a range of tissue samples, more than sufficient to establish DNA and cross-match to evidence samples. As a matter of course they will retain it all in case there is the possibility of establishing the driver of the vehicle and prosecuting a case eventually. Is that satisfactory?' I nodded my thanks and she relayed them, before putting the receiver back on its hook and crossing swiftly to the door before I could get up to go. I followed her but she stood in front of it as I drew level and deliberately shut the door. 'And now Mr Juste, I think you should tell me why you needed to know that. What new evidence do you have that I should also know about? Apart from the fact of your wife's death, I'm aware your private life has been somewhat in turmoil recently. Is there a connection to this that requires further investigation? Family, perhaps?'

The urge to laugh was almost uncontrollable. I quashed it with difficulty. Family connection, indeed! 'There are some issues with my family – no doubt you've picked that up from the papers, but nothing that is a direct link to Margaret's death at the moment.' Liar! And frightening how easily the lies slipped out. 'However, due to those complexities, in case there are any leads that turn up later I didn't want for us to come to a full stop in the future because we didn't look ahead now.' Gobbledy-gook; crap. She *had* to read between the lines. She looked unconvinced but how can you call someone a liar without proof? My perpetual problem! She opened her mouth to ask something else but I cut across it with, 'And I'm so sorry to have to rush away but the funeral is in less than two hours. I just wanted to make sure everything was in order with this first.'

I reached past her and opened the door. It opened inwards and she had to step aside as I swung it towards us. I shook her hand and marched out. She'd have had to wrestle me to the ground to stop me.

I was lucky none of the lights were against me – or the traffic cops. I must have taken at least three on amber and slid rudely into the parking spot an elderly woman with glasses on a chain and a toy poodle on the front seat was about to claim.

'Yob!' she called after me as I slipped from the driver's seat, rammed some coins in the meter and strode away. The irony didn't escape me – either with reference to my appearance or my behaviour. The car probably didn't help. One of my foibles, but it made me look like the boy racer I wasn't. Freud would have said it indicated a need to go back to my roots. I would dispute that, although perhaps not as rigorously now as I once would. My roots seemed to be nurturing a disconcertingly fertile undergrowth around me these days. It either needed scything flat or nurturing to full height.

The car was a throwback to youth – or childhood, perhaps; an Austin Healey 3000 in racing green. The model was first launched in 1959 and it was one of the highlights of the summer before I'd landed up in the children's home. Unbelievably Michael Thornton – 'Mad Mike' – the landlord's son at the Alhambra, turned up in one on that August Bank Holiday weekend. He parked it ostentatiously outside the pub and it didn't take long for street whispers to reach us in the flats in Queen Vic Road. By midday it was crawling with kids like a magnet covered with iron filings. It can't have been more than a month or so old; sleek, powerful, pristine and so redolent of money I was transfixed. If nothing else it proved to us that Mad Mike really was married to the mob, so the girl friend he'd brought it home to impress had better look out.

'Minding 'er,' he said possessively to Pop, as if the car was a person. Pop nodded as if he understood. Cars are easier to control than women. For me it was the personification of affluence. That evening Pop promised Ma a last night out before the baby was born. No doubt the possibility of mixing more talk with Mike and his mean machine was the lure for him, not altruism, but then I would have swopped a life time of Jamboree bags and any other treats that might come my way just to have been allowed to sit inside it. Of course I wasn't granted that boon, even if Pop was brown-nosing like shit was going out of fashion. Mike leant against the dirty red brick of the Alhambra, pint in hand, thumb in belt like he was lord of the street, eyeing the pretty girls who went past trying not to gawp at the car and assessing the blokes for their handiness in a fight; smug and hard.

He was recruiting. I can see that now, but then it was an event that could hardly have been dreamed of in our world and the shiny green of the paintwork blinded all of us to many things about Mike – not least his calling in life. I spent my allotted minutes peering through the driver's window and trying to store the dashboard permanently in my memory. Win was chief organiser of viewings and he indulged me with a few seconds more than the others, but even then he was potentially a mob's man. Mike flipped him a sixpence later when he stubbed out his fag, dismissed Pop and came over to sweep us off of the car like so many ants.

I couldn't find exactly the same model when I could afford it. I found a 1967 Mk III with more engine power, servo assisted brakes, improved rear suspension and luxurious interior including a wood veneer dashboard. Racing green though. It had to be that or the recreation of memory was incomplete, so Freud was probably right. I remembered it as an alluring target to aim at amidst the smoggy congestion of the bomb-damaged town, still only being haphazardly rebuilt after the devastation of the German V-1 flying bombs and V-2 rockets. It was the future appearing unexpectedly in the ruins of the past. I wanted one. I found one. I possessed one. And now the frustrated mob's man in me almost responded to the irate old dear thwarted of her parking spot in the same way Mad Mike would have done.

I made do with laughing again. I seemed to be spending the whole of the day Margaret was to be cremated laughing. The glorious inappropriateness put me on a high – despite the look of reproach I imagined Margaret would have given me if she'd been alive. Maybe ruin would be preferable to turgid respectability if it brought freedom from expectation too? Perhaps it was anticipation of that which was making me so ridiculously light-hearted when my troubles were clearly only just beginning.

The sergeant on reception was polite but slow. He shuffled the register, checked my entry three times, lost the keys to the door, and then forgot the box number storing the evidence. My high became even higher – verging on hysteria – when we finally located the correct box, retrieved it from the racking and he left me to rummage impatiently through its contents. The nail was right at the bottom in a small evidence bag.

So it was real.

I examined it from every angle, trying to envisage it on Margaret's hand. I fished out the bottle of nail varnish I'd collected off the top of her vanity unit in our bedroom earlier. It looked identical in colour. The pigment and constitution of it, alongside DNA, would either place her finally and inconclusively at the scene, or not. But would that finally and inconclusively mean she was actually there? Appearances. They plagued me – the real ones and the false ones. And if she wasn't at the scene who had so carefully planted evidence to incriminate her there, other than perhaps the person who'd also carefully compiled the evidence to incriminate Wilhelm Johns.

I piled the rest of the evidence back in the box, pocketed the evidence bag with the nail in it and signed myself out, citing Danny's case as the cross-reference and reason for the re-examination. It would have to go back sometime but I wanted to have it tested first myself. No more nasty surprises. It was ten-thirty. That left me only an hour to get from Hammersmith Police Station on the Fulham Palace Road to Highgate Cemetery, in traffic. I'd just about make it. I relinquished my parking spot to the same angry old dear, who must have been circling for the last half hour. The black suit seemed to be magnifying the heat of yet another hot day. It chafed my neck and clung under my arms. I wound the window right down to let whatever air there was to circulate. The fug of mid-morning traffic came with it, grey, and chemical.

'Yob!' the old dear shouted after me again as she ground her gears and claimed her prize. This time I didn't feel like laughing. The little evidence bag in my pocket weighed me down.

I arrived at Highgate barely five minutes before the hearse. The funeral director was pacing anxiously outside the crematorium.

'Mr Juste, I wondered if there was a problem and I was going to have to ask them to go around again.' I almost commented it would be worse than waiting for a hung-over bridegroom and having to send the bride round on another circuit before registering the comment would have been worse than the joke and certain to find its way into the papers and another editorial. *'Un-grief-stricken Juste joshes at wife's funeral ...'*

'Just some last minute business to attend to,' I muttered and took up my position next to him. 'Everything is going to plan, otherwise?'

He smiled mournfully. 'Not that much to organise really, Mr Juste. Don't worry.'

From the number of times I'd used the need to make its arrangements as my excuse for absence or escape, anyone attending could be excused for expecting the funeral to be a grandiose affair. Quite the reverse. I particularly wanted Margaret's obsequies to be observed with the minimum of fuss now. 'Family flowers only' should have resulted in only the mandatory floral cross on the coffin – mine – but I noticed that an enormous tribute stuffed with red roses, arum lilies, and a drift of gypsophilia was also propped against the side of it as the hearse swept majestically up the drive towards us. It overwhelmed one side of the coffin – too bold, too red and too obvious. Scarlet – like Margaret's life seeping through the black and white dress against the grey road, and the lethal crimson of the bagged nail in my pocket. I shivered.

'Unusual arrangement,' the funeral director whispered in my ear. 'I wasn't sure if you wanted it placed on the coffin instead of the cross or wanted to lay it privately later, so we brought it anyway. There were no instructions, just the card.'

'The card?'

'Yes, I kept it separate. I thought it might be too personal to be on public display.' He handed me a small envelope.

'It's not …' I was about to deny ownership but managed a creditable performance of being grateful instead as his eyes displayed intense curiosity. 'It's for later.' I pocketed the card to read at my leisure as the pall bearers shouldered the coffin and invited me to take the lead position.

I'd barely noticed who was present until then, but as we made our way solemnly toward the front of the chapel I scoured the mourners for the face I dreaded. Jaggers. The bold red floral tribute and card had to be from Jaggers. A cruel dig – or another bad joke. The congregation turned, earnest and melancholy, to watch our stately progress. It wouldn't be difficult to weed him out. The gathering was noticeably disparate and equally sparse – again of my doing. FFF and Margaret's various charities were represented by the FFF office manager Kat and I had met, and Kat herself – clearly at pains to sink into the background. Heather, a pained-looking Francis, Jeremy, Gregory and a couple of clerks including Louise, made up the professional contingent. Ella was noticeably absent, thank God – presumably as Heather was taking over being my minder for the day. A select few of Margaret's cronies who I was on nodding acquaintance with formed the only group of friends I'd agreed to. I'd expected I alone would represent family. And indeed I did – other than for Binnie, Jill, Emm and Win all standing off to one side. I wasn't sure how I felt about them being there – or indeed, who had given them the details to enable them to turn up. There was no Jaggers after all. I was relieved, but what had I expected? For him to claim his dearly beloved sister and fall on my neck as his long-lost brother-in-law?

My head buzzed with questions and confusion and my shoulder ached from the weight of the coffin. Dead, she was heavier than alive. The cloying perfume of the carnations and freesias woven into the cross turned the buzzing to a dull ache which transferred to my head. The walk into the chapel seemed to go on forever, like the journey through purgatory for the epic heroes of old. I heard the crematorium doors swish shut behind us and the sunlight streaming in through them was shut out too. Momentarily I imagined being entombed as we steadied and lowered the coffin onto its stand; journeymen to accompany the dead like the Pharaohs had required. I would be one of Margaret's living sacrifices – the one who'd failed to accept the journey she'd expected in life so was now doomed to make it in death.

I sensed Heather's concern rather than heard it. I could see her in the front row, forehead creased. She mouthed something at me. Interpreted, it was probably, 'are you all right?'

I could feel my head nodding the lie whilst my brain continued on its surreal journey, visualising the coffin lid slipping aside and Margaret's bloodied hand, minus the torn nail, gripping the edge of the coffin to hoist herself clear, screaming at me like a harpy and then dragging me back in with her. The organ piece the funeral director had chosen reached a crescendo simultaneous with the screech in my head and then all died away to silence, but still leaving my ears ringing. I stepped back too quickly and perspiration glued my shirt to me. Head swimming, I almost lost my balance, staggering before I regained equilibrium. *And not even a brandy in sight*, the imp in my head whispered to me. *Sober as a judge,* it mocked.

'Steady,' the man behind me muttered as his hand supported me. I catapulted back to reality and my head settled. I turned to nod my appreciation and Jaggers' smiling face greeted me. 'Don't want to give them all cause for gossip, do you?' he hissed. 'Save that for later,' and melted back into the congregation as Heather claimed me and led me to my seat.

'Are you OK?' she whispered under cover of waving the order of service at me like a fan.

'No,' I muttered, trying to see where Jaggers had gone. The organ started up again, melancholy in the gloom and the congregation sat.

'Dearly beloved, we are gathered here ...' I craned my neck to see where Jaggers had gone – swivelling madly to see both sides of the chapel.

'Stop it and turn round,' Heather urged. 'What the hell is the matter with you? You're meant to be the inconsolable spouse, not the lookout bloke.'

'To mourn the passing of our sister …'

'He's here.'

'Who?' Then I remembered I'd declined to tell Heather about my other connection to Jaggers, and if I did, yet another can of worms would be opened.

'No-one. Just a bit shaky,' I muttered back. The chaplain went into full swing and I concentrated on keeping paranoia in check as we made our way painfully through the service Margaret would have thoroughly endorsed and I completely scorned. If there was a God, he'd lost sight of me long ago – me, Georgie, Sarah, Wilhelm Johns, Danny – and even Margaret. I watched the last of Margaret slide slowly into oblivion, feeling guilty that I owed her more than I'd given her. I couldn't give her regret or grief – and certainly not love – now, but maybe I could give her justice, despite my annoyance with her. I rolled the little evidence bag over in my pocket until it settled on top of the bottle of nail varnish, wishing the ordeal over and wondering how imbalanced I already was if I'd imagined Jaggers was here.

Francis went home straight after the funeral, face grey and tired.

'Sorry, old bean,' he said ruefully. 'Doctor's orders,' with eyes rolling toward Heather. 'Dare not disobey if I know what's good for me.' Heather attached herself to my side like a fragrant thorny briar, and directed Jeremy to act as sentry on the other side, forcing the meagre condolences line through like meat through a mincer. I couldn't see Jaggers in it, but my family were. I thanked them for attending without acknowledging names but the discomfort didn't escape Heather. Her meaningful look as Win passed by, nodding mutely at me, warned me that another tirade was probably on its way. Kat temporarily deflected her.

'So sorry,' she gazed anxiously into my face.

'Thank you for coming,' it was automatic – and I didn't know what else to say with Heather hovering around, waiting to disembowel me if I put the slightest foot wrong. I hoped my face expressed more.

'Let me know if I can help at all.' She glanced at Heather, and I wondered if women's instinct was real after all. 'With anything that needs tidying up on the case, I mean …'

'Thank you, Miss Roumelia, but the case is now concluded and Mr Juste has a junior to help him with loose ends.'

She looked from Heather to me. 'I see.' She took a step back and I was irrationally irritated with her for being so unresisting and Heather for being so domineering. Unfair as I was being equally docile where

Heather's manoeuvres were concerned currently.

'*I will* be in touch,' I managed before I felt Heather's nails biting into the fleshy part of my arm, slicing through the fabric of my suit like a knife.

'If necessary,' Heather concluded. 'But it won't be, Lawrence,' she reminded me as Kat walked away, glancing back just once, expression wistful. 'Just like it won't be necessary to say anything more in public about this case.'

'If I didn't know you better, I'd think you were threatening me, Heather,' I replied coolly.

'But you don't Lawrence, remember? You've been walking around blind for ages. Now it's my job to open your eyes – and shut your mouth.' I would have told her what I thought of that but I caught sight of the one person I'd been looking out for since depositing the coffin on its rest and fear did Heather's job for her.

He was near the end of the line, dark and sleek-suited; a cruel black crow waiting to peck out my eyes. He approached as Heather exchanged pleasantries with the mourner in front of him and stepped neatly round, bypassing the obstacle.

'Lawrence, my condolences.' He clasped my petrified hand in his ice-cold one. The iciness of death and disdain. 'The Lord giveth, and the Lord taketh away – is that not so? We must talk again. Soon,' and he was gone before Heather could see his face as she turned back towards me. She helpfully reminded me of the next mourner's identity but it was lost in the melee of obsequious black and doleful grey as the condolence line and my ability to talk dwindled to nothing whilst my eyes followed my tormentor towards the garden of remembrance.

'You look as bad as Francis,' she muttered. 'Have you seen a ghost? Sorry – that was a bad joke for here.'

'No ghosts, something far more real.' I turned to gesture after Jagger's departing silhouette but he was gone. Only the stragglers remained, with no sinister dark form amongst them. I numbly shook the last hand and mumbled the proscribed form of words Heather had primed me with, still scouring the grounds for Jaggers.

'Lawrence?' Heather patted my arm. 'I think maybe it's time we went. You look all in and the next funeral will be arriving soon. Plus we've things to sort out.'

'I know, I know, but …' I could see only my sisters loitering at the exit to the cemetery, but Binnie's demeanour attracted my attention. She was staring rigidly ahead at two figures, one with their back to me, the other remonstrating with the turned back. Win and Jaggers. Win was arguing with Jaggers. Win was talking to Jaggers. Win was shaking hands with Jaggers, and still Binnie stared at them as if suddenly recognising him. I twisted away from Heather but by the time I'd made it through the milling wanderers, ghoulishly admiring other crematee's floral tributes, Jaggers had gone. Win was climbing into a battered grey Volvo but Binnie was still transfixed. She broke her trance as she saw me approaching and tugged at Jill's arm, saying something to her urgently but I was too far away to hear. Jill followed her gaze and then called to Win. He stopped and then jerked his head as if inviting them to get in. Jill and Emm piled into the Volvo but not Binnie. She remained on her own, gazing after them as the Volvo pulled away. I reached Binnie at exactly the same time as the Volvo disappeared through the main exit out of the crematorium.

'Why did they leave so suddenly?' I asked her breathlessly, aware that Heather was only minutes behind me. Binnie turned and stared at me.

'Oh so you want to talk to me now, then?'

'I'm sorry Binnie, it was difficult ...'

She cut me off with a dismissive wave. 'You'd better ask Sarah when you go and see her this afternoon. I ain't got nothing to say about it.'

'How did you know I was going to see her?'

'I know a lot of things, little brother,' she sounded sinisterly like Win had when he'd claimed similar omniscience. 'I just mainly chose not to tangle with them.'

'And how can Sarah help? She wasn't even here to see what happened just then.'

'Happened? What happened? I didn't see anything and she don't need to. Just tell her whatever you want to talk to her about.'

'Binnie, what is going on here?'

She scrutinised me. 'You really don't know, do you?'

'No, I bloody don't.'

'Then I'm not bloody telling you. Go and see Sarah. You're big enough and ugly enough to work it out for yourself after that. And don't believe everything Win says. I'm not saying he lies deliberate like, but sometimes if he don't know everything he adds in what he thinks. Ask him about your dad – not Pop. Both yours' dad. That'll get you started. Only thing I'm saying, though.'

She turned on her heel and headed towards the exit. Her bruiser of a husband idled towards her from where he must have been waiting just outside. I didn't follow, and Heather reeled me back in. Our dad? Not Pop. So Win and I did have the same father? He hadn't been merely winding me up when he'd implied that he, Wilhelm Johns – Jonno to us as kids – and I all had the same father. But that would potentially keep me in the frame for Danny too. Shit, shit, shit! Just when I thought that problem might be out of my way. And he'd been talking to Jaggers – shaking hands after all he'd said about him and the plan he'd had to send Jaggers the same way as Margaret. Appearances – they didn't even appear to make sense any more. All I had to go on was the fact that appearances were very much not what they appeared to be.

3: Broken Promises

Heather finally surrendered the leash at my front door. I promised to go in and stay in. She looked doubtful but my feigned headache made it difficult for her not to allow me some peace. I watched her totter along the mews on her impossibly high Jimmy Choos, ankles wobbling over the uneven cobbles until she disappeared onto the main road, arm already raised to hail a cab before really believing I'd escaped. Nevertheless, I stayed at the window for a while longer in case she changed her mind and came back. After five minutes I assumed she must have been swallowed up by a black beast and been swept back to Chambers or wherever she was off to for the afternoon. Perhaps more cosmetic surgery to hide the fact that she was secretly a gorgon out to feast on my fallibility. No, that was unfair. She was only trying to protect us all when I'd deliberately placed us under fire with my thoughtlessness. And now I was about to do it again.

I couldn't decide who to see first: Sarah or Kat. Reluctantly I decided it ought to be Sarah, for all my selfish desire to have my ego stroked by Kat. Now I had to be an adult, not a juvenile. The living demand comfort, but the dying need it more. I owed Sarah at least as much as I hadn't given Margaret. I let the heavy drapes fall back into place and slipped out of the front door. I'd parked in the garages at the back of the mews and I made it there without any twitching curtains or dawdling hacks spotting me. They must all be out earning a dishonest crust elsewhere. Or maybe they were leaving me in peace today, given its sombre significance.

The address Binnie had given me for Sarah was near Hampton Court. It turned out to be an expensive nursing home with its own electric gates, sweeping drive and extensive grounds. It reminded me of the place Mary lived. The board near the entrance proclaimed it to be part of the Green Healthcare group. I made a mental note to find out which organisation ran the establishment where Mary was resident. Green was Margaret's maiden name, and also – it suddenly occurred to me – the name I'd known Jaggers by at the children's home: John Arthur Green, not John Arthur Wemmick as he now paraded himself. When had the name change occurred for him? I made a mental note to follow that up too sometime. As far as the healthcare group was concerned though, it was a common enough name so it might simply be a coincidence. However, the coincidence of being able to afford a place here wasn't so easily dismissed. Who was paying? There was no way this was NHS-funded.

I gave my name at reception and signed in. I was led along a maze of plushly carpeted corridors lined with fine art prints – many of them limited editions – towards the rear of the building. The place reeked of money, from its ivy-clad Cotswold stone exterior, to its designer furnishings. I asked the attendant who took me to Sarah's room who had booked her in originally, but she merely shook her head.

'Me no unnerstand.' Polish or displaced European of some kind. I nodded politely and gave up. We reached what I assumed was Sarah's door and the attendant bobbed a kind of curtsey and left me there. The nameplate on the door said merely 'Sarah' as if everyone would know who Sarah was. I knocked and waited a moment before going in.

Her voice was recognisable but strained. 'Come in.'

Even though I knew she was terminally ill, I wasn't prepared for the deterioration in her physical condition since I'd seen her last – barely a couple of weeks ago. It must have shown on my face because she tutted gently at me.

'There, there, Kenny – don't look so shocked. I was always gonna get worse before I got better.' She gestured to the visitor's chair closest to the bed. The gardens at the rear of the house swept away in a lush swathe of green, separated by beds of carefully arranged flowers. The last flourish of summer was rampant in them, with their vibrant banks of carefully arranged bedding plants. 'Pretty, ain't it?' she commented, following my gaze. 'Reckon someone's being very nice to me, giving me such a pretty picture to look at. I thought it might have been you?'

I shook my head. 'I wish it was, Sarah – or that I'd thought about it. I've still got a long way to go to remember to think about anyone else before myself.' I sat heavily in the chair and she reached across with effort and patted my hand.

'You'll be OK. Give it time. You only just got back into the land of the living.'

I stared at her. 'I don't understand.'

'Weren't much of a life afore, were it? Now it can be. Now you're free.'

'Free?'

'To choose.'

'You mean free of Margaret?'

She looked surprised. 'I meant now it's all out in the open. I read the papers and saw what you said about your family. It didn't mention Margaret, Molly – whatever she called herself.'

'How the hell did you know that? Her other name I mean. That wasn't in the papers.'

'Win told me, but I guessed there was something going on before then.'

'Win? And did he tell you anything else about her?'

'Only to be careful. He weren't sure whether she were on the level or not, but he said to go along with her for the time being. Had to, you see. Because of the other stuff. Kimmy and Danny, and all that.'

'So what did you tell her?'

'Just kiddy stories. You, Win and the others. She already knew all the facts. I didn't know if you'd told her, or Kimmy had, but she weren't causing you no problems over it so there didn't seem any harm. I thought it might even help.'

'But why did she want to know all of that, Sarah?'

'She wanted to get to know the real man, not the manufactured one, she said. Didn't seem any harm in telling her what you were like as a kid. You were a good kid. It were nice she wanted to know.' I must have looked sceptical, because she laughed, and gently squeezed my hand. 'You were.'

'It's not that. Margaret never did anything out of sentimentality, Sarah. She was business through and through.'

She shook her head. 'I thought it were because she loved you. Weren't it that? I guessed she didn't think you cared that much for her otherwise you'd have told it all yourself, wouldn't you? But it weren't business when we were talking. That's a shame. But if you didn't love her, you're right – now you're free.' I didn't reply. It was a harsh assessment, but she'd got it in one and I was ashamed of myself for what it said about me as a man, content with a love-less union where neither party was fulfilled, and nothing really shared. I'd recreated my marriage in the format of my life. Barren. There was no need for me to confirm it to Sarah, but the idea of being free of someone who'd possibly had more

24

feelings for me than I'd credited her with was disconcerting and a little disappointing. What had I missed? Sarah's expression told me she understood. 'It ain't wrong, you know, Kenny. You don't have to love someone just because they love you, but when you find someone like that you have to do summat about it. Like now.'

'I should have tried harder, shouldn't I? I didn't. And what makes you think it's any different now?'

'Because you're bothering. Now it matters – your family, your life, and what you're doing with them. That happens when there's a reason for it to matter.' She paused and watched me.

I shook my head, not sure whether she was still talking about Margaret or had somehow found out about Kat. 'I don't know Sarah. It's complicated.'

'Then sort it out.'

'I will, but I need to sort out what was going on with the Margaret-Molly mystery first.'

'Oh, I'm sure you will – and then you'll know what to do.' She smiled enigmatically. 'So what else you here for?'

'To see you, of course.'

She nodded. 'And?'

I was embarrassed that I was so transparent. 'Well, there was something you said last time that I wanted to ask you more about.'

She laughed. 'Ask away. But you'd better be quick. I ain't got a lot of time left to answer in.'

Her bony hand was still clasped in mine. It felt tiny; feather-light. I suddenly didn't want it to be this way – losing this sister who I had so little in common with but yet who seemed to understand me better than myself and still not judge what she saw. It was comforting to find someone who saw through me, yet despite that, didn't condemn me. I sensed Sarah would have loved me whatever I'd done, just because for her I was Kenny, the little brother she'd mothered from an infant. That must be why she loved Win too, however he'd turned out. I put my other hand over the top of hers. She looked at it and then at me. 'I ain't going far, you know. And you'll still have your other brothers and sisters.'

'I don't think we get on that well, Sarah.'

'You ain't even tried yet. You might be surprised.'

'Binnie would rather not even acknowledge me; Win I can't trust, and Jill and Emm are so far removed from me, we might as well live in different worlds. Kimmy, I'm afraid I feel like Binnie does about me, Jim is too far away and Mary ...' I let my voice trail away.

She studied me thoughtfully. 'Things ain't always the way they seem, you know Kenny,' she said eventually. 'Everyone has their reasons – like there were reasons for your Margaret and all her names. If you find out the reasons, you'll understand and then you'll understand the people too. And they'll understand you.'

'So tell me some of these reasons.'

'You need to work them out for yourself. That way you'll understand properly. It's like telling kids stuff. They never believe you till they tried it for themselves first.'

I sighed. Win's comment came back to me – *I don't reckon things have been personal with you since you were nine. It ain't real life unless it's personal.* Everyone was intent on being cryptic, right to the last it seemed.

'OK, just Margaret then. I have to ask you about her. I can't ask her myself, can I? Did you believe what she said about injuring both her wrists as a child?'

'Why wouldn't I? Do you mean was she putting it on?' I nodded. 'Nah. She spilt the tea. Burnt herself. Swore like a trooper. That were for real.'

I was silent as I computed what that meant and how unlike the Margaret I knew it was. Margaret never swore. She had a rule – I'd even taunted her with it once or twice, testing to see if she could be pushed far enough to break the *no swearing rule* before admitting defeat. She couldn't and it had compounded the sense of being married to a perfect being, not a person. Perhaps it was that which had switched me off of her – or never allowed me to switch on. The sense of invulnerability or never reaching past her barricades, just as I'd never allowed her through mine.

Sarah broke into my thoughts to answer the main question I kept asking myself over and over again about Margaret now. 'She had her reasons too, you know. Why don't you figure them out for yourself too?'

'Reasons?'

'For tricking you.'

'What do you mean, tricking me? You knew she was going to blackmail me? You said there was no harm in what she asked.'

'There weren't. I only meant about the kiddy – Danny. Not anything else. And she had her reasons, like I said.'

I shook my head. 'Her reasons were that she enjoyed manipulating me, Sarah.'

'She got you to sort Danny's problems out that way though, didn't she? He would have been right up the creek without you. '

'In a way, I suppose so. But she was playing with me too. That's obvious now.'

'If she were playing games, then they was for a reason.' She sighed and painfully shifted position. 'Sent me a nice card for me birthday with some stuff in it.'

'That was Margaret all over – do the right thing in public, follow her own agenda in private.'

Sarah just smiled and shook her head. 'I put it in me keepsakes box for later, like I told her I would. You can have me keepsakes box when I've gone. I told your Margaret I'd give it to you when I went, to make up for all the family things you weren't part of. Give you back your real roots so you could pass them on to your own kiddies one day.'

'Can I see it now?'

She shook her head. 'Nah. It's still my keepsakes box for a while longer, Kenny – and first things first. Make sense of things first. Talk to Win. Sort it out between you. He knows what needs sorting out too. He can tell you what you need to know – maybe even what your Margaret was up to, I expect.'

I took my cue from the mention of Win to press what Binnie had implied, but wouldn't clarify. 'Sarah, who *was* my father?'

She stared at me, surprised. 'Ask Win,' then she leaned back against her pillows, cheeks sunken. I sat breathlessly next to her, hoping she'd add to the suggestion but her eyes strayed to the garden with its riot of colour and stayed there. 'Pretty, ain't it,' she said again after a while. 'And I really thought it were you who fixed it up. It must have been someone who did it for you – knowing, like. I'll remember it all this way – pretty, and you holding me hand like you did as a kid, and everyone back happy again someday.' She closed her eyes and her breathing seemed to fade. 'Be nice to see Ma again too.' She lay absolutely still.

'Sarah?' I shook her hand gently. She didn't respond, so I shook it more urgently.

The ghost of a smile spread across her blue lips, but her eyes stayed closed. 'I ain't gone yet, Kenny. Give us a chance.'

I left Sarah sleeping after I'd cobbled together what I could as a witness statement, getting one of the nurses to countersign it to confirm Sarah appeared to be of sound mind when making the statement. It felt cold and uncaring to force the issue but Sarah had been uncomplaining.

'Do what you must to get yourself sorted,' was all she said after she'd scrawled her name. So Margaret couldn't have been involved in the murder all those years ago, but someone was very intent on making her seem so for my benefit. Yet another mystery to solve in relation to my enigmatic wife.

It was late afternoon when I left, signing myself out like it was a moment to be recorded in history. I drove the opposite way to the traffic escaping London for the suburbs. Pushing against the tide as usual these days. I decided I ought to go home first to make sure Heather hadn't been back to check on me and all hell had broken out in my absence when she'd found the house empty. The approach to the mews was quiet, unusually so for late afternoon when my neighbours were often wending their way home from whatever high-powered positions they held in the city. One of the advantages of wealth was that those of similar means living close by were usually more concerned about hiding their own business than poking their nose into yours – except for the old biddy at number six who silently monitored our every move but never uttered a word about it. Even with her, passer-by conversations were courteous, complacent and curt. They were also regular and commonplace because she manned her post at the window with fortitude, and I was definitely worthy of a conversation today. Yet having parked up at the garages in the rear and made the circuitous trip back to the front like my co-residents were usually doing at this time of the day, I seemed to be the lone pedestrian, as if I was being ostracised. The reason for my neighbour's absence became clearer when I saw the plods heading us off at the top of the road leading to the mews itself. I managed to dodge them but came to a full stop with their colleague who was busying himself threading the red and white crime scene tape across the end of the mews, sealing it off and me out. He was officious but offhand.

'Prefer it if you went another way, mate, unless you've got to go this way. Been a murder. No-one allowed down the mews until further notice unless you're a resident.'

'Well I am. Number five.'

He was suddenly all attention. 'Five? You sure, mate.'

'Of course I'm sure, *mate*.' I bit back the 'you idiot' just in time. 'I'm Lawrence Juste, QC.'

'Have you any ID then please, *sir*?'

'Yes,' I rummaged in my wallet and produced my driving licence.

He examined it and then straightened further. 'Mr Juste, yes.' He handed it back to me. 'You were in the papers with that kid, weren't you?'

'Yes.' Patience was starting to wear thin. 'So where did this murder take place?'

'Well,' he looked awkward. 'I think I'd better get you to talk to DCI Fredriks about that.'

'Why?'

'The body was found at number five.'

4: Patchwork Papers

Instead of ending the day in Kat's bed as I'd fondly hoped might happen, I ended it at Chelsea Police Station. The body in the library turned out actually to be found in my kitchen, and apparently stabbed, but forensics weren't being particularly forthcoming about confirming cause of death. I waited for over an hour in a downstairs interview room for more information before getting fed up with the station's stewed tea and stale air and going to make a nuisance of myself at the reception desk. Luckily the sergeant who'd replaced the cantankerous sod who'd deposited me in the interview room recognised me and went to find DCI Fredriks without so much as a murmur. Notoriety has some perks, it seemed.

Fredriks was thin-faced with wire-rimmed glasses, a beak of a nose and protruding lips. I understood why one of the PCs had referred to him as quack-quack to one of his mates when I first arrived. However, he wasn't squawking much either. He did give me the basics though. He could hardly deny me that even though he would probably have played cat and mouse a little longer with a layman.

'Uhh, I understand you may have known the deceased?'

'Do you? Why's that?'

'A relative of yours, I think?'

The hairs on the back of my neck began to bristle. 'A relative? Who?'

He referred to his notes. 'A Kimberley Hewson.'

I knew I was gaping at him, but I couldn't stop myself. It was the last name I'd expected him to spout. 'Christ! Are you sure?'

'So you did know her, sir?'

'You answer me first. Is that a positive ID?'

'Based on paperwork in her belongings, sir – yes. Mrs Kimberley Joan Hewson. Your sister, I think the papers said?'

'Yes, it would appear so, although I haven't yet confirmed all the details fully myself. I've been busy with her son's case.'

'Ah yes. The mugging kid.'

'Not the mugging kid – he was cleared of mugging, just theft.'

'Well, yes, as you say, sir.'

I was irritated with this lugubrious non-event. 'I don't say, DCI Fredriks. The court said – as of yesterday. So how did she find her way into my home?'

'More to the point, sir – how did the murder occur in your home?'

'That too,' I cursed myself for seeming unfeeling again. Wife and sister – I was doing well.

'We rather hoped you'd be able to help us somewhat with that, sir – for instance, when did you last see her alive?'

'I've been out all day, Fredriks – it was my wife's funeral this morning and this afternoon I was visiting my terminally ill sister. I haven't seen Kimmy – Mrs Hewson – in days, other than a brief glimpse in court yesterday – at a distance. And as far as I know, she doesn't even know my address.' I corrected myself. 'Didn't even know my address.' But Danny did, I thought – and Win. So which of them had told her it?

'I'd assumed she'd been invited there. So you wouldn't know why she was at your home then, sir?'

'Like I said …'

'And can anyone corroborate your alibi, sir?'

'Of course they can. There were plenty of witnesses at the funeral this morning, and my sister and the people at the nursing home can confirm I was there this afternoon. I'm sure even my neighbour at number six could probably provide you with chapter and verse as to my arrival and departure too – if you haven't already asked her. But do I *need* an alibi? What is the time of death?'

He ignored the question and jumped straight to the possibility of corroboration.

'So you didn't go home at all in between attending the funeral, sir, and seeing your sister?' He smiled politely – the alligator waiting to snap its jaws shut round me – not a harmless domestic fowl at all, and he plainly *had* asked the old bat at number six already.

'Only briefly.'

'So you could have seen your sister then? Alone.'

'No, Heather accompanied me home from the funeral – Heather Trinder from my Chambers.'

'And stayed with you until you went out again, sir?'

'Well, no. But I was only alone for barely fifteen minutes …'

'One can do a lot in fifteen minutes, sir.' He smiled thinly at me, duck pout spreading into more of a grimace than a grin. 'But perhaps we should start by corroborating what you've said with Miss Trinder?'

'You still haven't told me the time of death. If it doesn't coincide with the fifteen minutes I was home, I'm somewhat irrelevant aren't I?'

'Somewhere between mid-morning and mid-afternoon sir. We'll have a more definite time confirmed later but for the time being we're covering all bases. May I have Miss Trinder's phone number, please?'

Shit. Heather was going to be incandescent with rage. He left me in the same interview room, but without even cold tea this time. Heather graced me with her presence about twenty minutes later – roughly the time it would take for her to get from Chambers in Lincoln's Inn to Chelsea at a hundred miles an hour. Speed limits didn't exist for Heather – like resistance.

She greeted me with, 'You stupid bastard!'

'Thanks, but I had nothing to do with it, Heather. Do you really think I'm a murderer?'

'No, but it happened in your house, so you're as bad as. Why the hell did you let her in?'

'I didn't. I wasn't even there.'

'Then why the hell weren't you? You promised me you'd go in and stay in. What were you doing out?'

'I went to see Sarah – my older sister. She's terminal, days left now. Is that really so heinous?'

'Oh.' She had the grace to look mollified. 'But you should still have told me. I could have come with you – or sent Ella.'

'Great! I think I'd rather be accused of murder.'

'What's wrong with Ella – or me?' she bristled.

'Nothing, my dear Heather, but there are times when you only want your own company, not that of a warden as well.' She opened her mouth to argue with me, but shut it again without saying anything. Eventually she asked, 'You didn't go to see the little social worker too, did you?'

'No, I bloody didn't. I've told you and Herr Quack-Quack where I was, and it's the truth. I had nothing to do with this murder and I didn't think Kimmy even knew where I lived. Jesus, Heather, she may have been my sister, but have you seen her? She's barely better than a prostitute. *Was* barely better ...' I rubbed my hands over my face, wishing I could clear my head of problems as easily as I could dismiss my unwanted sister from my life. She'd caused enough trouble with her lack of morals and reckless negligence. Why did she have to get herself killed in my house too? Then I felt ashamed. She might mean nothing but trouble to me, but for Win at least, she was family, and for Danny and his siblings she was a mother. And that raised another issue. Now Danny had no mother. 'Oh fuck,' I groaned.

'What?' demanded Heather – as predatory as Fredriks.

'Danny is going to have to go back into care again – and possibly his brothers and sisters too. The father's up for receiving and with previous he'll almost certainly get a custodial.'

'And how does that affect you?'

'She was my sister, remember?'

'So? Ah,' the penny began to drop. 'Well at least it's a reason for you not having murdered her,' she said eventually, a little twisted smile on her face. I wanted to wring it off of her and there was such an easy way to do it.

'Yes, and for having to talk to his *little social worker*.' I grinned at her silent fury.

She didn't have a chance to retaliate. Fredriks came back and told me I could go. I doubted he would have dared asked me to stay without charging me whilst I had Heather as back-up.

'But you can't go home, I'm afraid. Not until forensics have finished there.'

'Not even for a change of clothes?'

'Not today, sorry.' He was suspiciously polite compared to his earlier pugnacious attitude. 'Tomorrow. Call us and we'll accompany you there. We should be almost done by then so you'll probably be able to return then. Have you somewhere to stay tonight?'

'With me,' Heather told him.

'Seems like everyone wants my company these days,' I commented sarcastically.

She ignored the sarcasm and magnanimously added, 'If you'd like to?'

'Thanks – but I had still better speak to the *little social worker* about my nephew first, Heather,' I teased. She coloured with irritation but clamped her mouth firmly shut in a creditable approximation of Mr Justice Crawford's thin-lipped disapproval. Appearances – working for me this time. What a joke! And how close to the edge was I sailing now? As I left Chelsea Police Station, promising to turn up at Heather's later – again for appearances' sake – I marvelled how Lawrence Juste, upright, solid and unremarkably respectable only a few weeks ago, had become the maverick with a murdered sister in his kitchen, skeletons in his closet and a mistress half his age whilst his wife was barely even cold in death. How close? Close enough to fall completely off the edge if I wasn't careful.

I swung past the office to collect Danny's case papers before I drove to Kat's. Luckily for once I'd left them there instead of taking them home with me. The John's case papers were there too, locked safely in my desk drawer. At least that was one secret I didn't have from Kat – my part in its ignominy. I spent the drive reasoning with myself why I hadn't told Heather about the imminent resurrection of the case but still failed to convince myself I was right not to have done so. She, Francis and Jeremy had been just as guilty of acquiescence in the charade, albeit perhaps without realising quite how acquiescent they were being encouraged to be, and quite how much of a charade it all was. But it had been a joint decision to take the case. Why then did I feel so responsible? Because the Wemmicks had only targeted our partnership to get at me. Without me, Heather, Francis and Jeremy wouldn't be in the shit now. They might also have been out of business long ago, but that might have been better than digging themselves out from under now if I couldn't manage to control the other maverick in this case – Jaggers.

I'd only been to Kat's place twice. She lived in Kilburn. The first time was after I'd broken down in the park and confessed some of my past. The second time had been to confess more of it – about the Johns case and my part in the charade. Both times I'd been completely immersed in myself and wholly unobservant of anything else going on around me. It was about time I started to see what was going on in the real world, not just mine – and prove to Heather that blindness could be cured.

I parked by an out of order meter a couple of hundred yards away, congratulating myself on having a lucky break for once, until I realised that most of the houses had garages so the road probably remained clear most of the time and I could have parked for free further along anyway. It was also respectably suburban and wholly dull, so the Austin Healey should be reasonably safe from vandalism. I left it lording itself over a scattering of nearby Fords and Skodas. The road's terraced monstrosities were redolent of the type I remembered from my truncated childhood in Croydon. I could almost see the curtains twitch as I walked the road – completely out of place in hand-made suit and two hundred pound shoes. It hadn't occurred to me until then how much appearance, not manners, maketh the man. We are what people believe us to be. Thank God for illusion or on the basis of current manners and principles I would be in the Scrubs alongside some of my less salubrious clients of former years.

Kat's terraced castle was attached on one side to a garden gnome lover, it's frontage festooned with fishermen, squatting Buddhas and cheeky chappies, all sporting the habitual garb of the gnome fraternity – beard, red hat, overstuffed belly and cheery grin. They nestled comfortably amongst drifts of aubretia. Jesus! Had they sprung up like weeds or had I simply not noticed them when I'd been here before? Next door was contrastingly dour and unkempt, it's paintwork peeling and its windows dark and blank. It was a sad face near a grinning clown. In fact it looked deserted. Placed as it was in the middle of the two, Kat's was the perfect median. Neat, adequately maintained but tired; genteel lace curtains at the windows and a matt blue front door in need of a repaint sometime soon; unremarkable, but respectable enough. A place to live rather than a home. Its single and most striking concession to adornment was the healthy swathe of honeysuckle clinging to the wall around the front door and infusing the air with its heavy perfume. I certainly hadn't noticed that before, but maybe it hadn't been in bloom last week.

Apart from that, everything seemed both bigger and smaller than I remembered it. Bigger psychologically, in the sense that by turning up unannounced on her, temporarily homeless and now 'free' as Sarah had put, I was making a statement as big as the relationship I suspected Kat wanted. The size of that possibility overwhelmed me. Contrastingly, the house itself seemed to have shrunk in size. In truth I probably hadn't really noticed anything the last time I'd been here except for Kat and the effect her body had on me, or my problems and the effect they had on my mind. Now my mind was all on how those problems were going to develop, but nevertheless hopeful that Kat and the effect her body had on me might remove them from it, if only temporarily. Either way I probably shouldn't be here.

I rang the doorbell with a certain amount of trepidation, wishing now I'd rung her before I just turned up. It occurred to me that I didn't actually know a great deal about Kat's life outside of the office. Her involvement with me had been because of Danny, and artfully limited to what I'd wanted so far. I didn't even know if there was already someone in her life that I would be nudging out. Maybe, far from being clear-sighted, I was in danger of repeating the same mistake I'd made with Margaret. Too late now. She opened the door on the first ring as if she'd been expecting me, bare foot and fresh-faced, wearing a gypsy style frilled skirt and loose tee shirt. I could see the outline of her nipples through the tee shirt and immediately my imagination went into overdrive. I consciously talked to her eyes and not her breasts, trying to ignore the remembered sensation of them against my chest.

She seemed unnerved. 'Lawrence, what are you doing here? I mean, it's lovely you're here but ...' she tailed off. It obviously wasn't me she'd been expecting then. I hastily pretended official business to cover our joint embarrassment.

'Hasn't anyone contacted you yet?'

'Contacted me? Why?' Her eyes narrowed.

'About Danny.'

'No. What about Danny – he's all right, isn't he?'

'Yes, *he* is. Can I come in?' She hesitated before opening the door wider. I held back, sure I'd made a mistake now. 'Is it OK? I'm not disturbing anything?'

A door banged somewhere – next door? She relaxed, and laughed. 'Only me and Mr Pizza. Come and join us.' She stepped aside and gestured for me to go in.

'Well,' I followed her in, the perfume of the honeysuckle trailing in behind me as if the suckers had attached themselves to me whilst I'd been standing on the doorstep. 'If Mr Pizza won't get jealous.' She laughed over-enthusiastically and I realised she was as edgy as I was. She led me out to the kitchen and waved a wine bottle at me.

I nodded, relieved to only see one glass out on the counter top. 'Yes please. I need it after today, but only a small one – I'm driving.' The invitation to stay didn't appear.

'Of course, so what's happened?'

'Kimmy's dead.' She froze for the merest fraction of a second and then her arm dropped dramatically in time with her mouth and the wine slopped from the open bottle. I grabbed it before she dropped it altogether, surprised at what seemed like over-reaction to the news, but then, to be fair, I'd had time to get used to it. She remained exaggeratedly open-mouthed as I replaced the bottle on the counter top. 'Murdered, in fact. And just to complete the scenario, it happened in my kitchen.'

'Oh my God, you didn't ...'

'No, Kat, but thanks for the idea.'

'I'm sorry. Of course I don't believe you did. You couldn't. You're not like that.' I wondered how she knew what I didn't. What was I like? 'But how?'

36

'Knifed apparently, whilst I was out. I'm sorry, but I've got to ask you – did you ever give her my address?'

'No, of course not.' She looked offended.' 'And why do you think I would?'

'Danny? He's your case isn't he, and she's one of his parents.'

'Oh, oh – yes. Of course. But I haven't.'

'What about Danny, then? Might he have given her it?'

'Unlikely. He wasn't too keen on going back home but I doubt he'd have given Kimmy your address because of that. He'd be more likely to just turn up on your doorstep again, wouldn't he?'

I thought about that – a complication I hadn't considered until now, but not impossible. 'Then it must have been Win, or Jaggers who told her it.'

She paused uncertainly and then added, 'Or Margaret.'

'Margaret? She's dead, Kat – how could she tell Kimmy anything?'

'I didn't mean now – before. Before she died, I mean.' She retrieved the bottle from the counter and crossed to the other side of the kitchen. She fiddled with a cupboard which proved to contain wine glasses, putting the one from the counter in and taking it back out again; her back to me. Now I noticed there were two used ones in the sink and her shoulders looked tense. I really should have rung; told her over the phone.

'That would have Kimmy and Margaret on very close terms.' I commented into the awkward atmosphere. 'Were they?' She didn't reply, taking back out the two glasses she'd just put in and twirling one by the stem. I thought about Margaret and her closed book of a life – even to me, who she should have been close to. 'I can't quite imagine that, even if Margaret was using her to play out some kind of game.'

'OK, maybe not.' She turned and shrugged, putting the two glasses firmly on the counter next to the wine. She was obviously remembering the same Margaret as me now. Her public image must have been the same as her private one then. What did that say about Margaret and me: us? I didn't want to consider that for the moment. Now she was completely gone, a part of me was unexpectedly regretful it hadn't been better between us, but hadn't I already long accepted there had been very little 'us'? The knowledge had previously left me unaffected, or maybe unaffected emotionally, but with my pride damaged. No-one likes to acknowledge how little they mean to someone else, even if they know inside they've already accepted it.

'You seem anxious?'

'Me? No – just surprised by your news.' She frowned. 'But what would she be coming to see you about, Lawrence?' She paused and studied me speculatively. 'Have you been speaking to her without me knowing?'

'No. Why would I? I've no idea what she was doing there.' It was the truth, if economical.

'Then do you have another mystery on your hands?' I noticed she didn't partner herself with me any more. The investigative team was suddenly made up of only one, it seemed. That would be my fault too. I should have made more of an effort to defuse the two-headed monster Heather and Ella had conjoined to become for Kat's benefit.

'Maybe I do. What do you think?' The issue of our separate or oneness hung between us. I waited, smiling encouragingly. She smiled back, non-committedly and gestured towards the glasses and the bottle.

'I think you need a drink and pizza, and so do I.' I couldn't think of a diplomatic way to return to where we were as a couple without asking outright so I let it go. She bustled around the kitchen opening cupboards and drawers, clanking crockery and cutlery noisily so I had to wait until she'd finished. 'Come on,' she called as she made for her tiny lounge. 'Bring the wine and the glasses, will you?'

'You don't seem very upset about Danny,' I commented as I set the bottle and glasses down next to the plate of pizza on the coffee table.

She poured two large glasses and handed me one. 'He's not my child.'

'Pardon?' I struggled to reconcile the Kat who'd urged me to consider adopting him simply because of the family connection with the one who seemed completely unconcerned now that he was almost an orphan.

'I don't mean I don't care, I just can't. I've been told very firmly to back off now he's home with his parents with a detention order, and the case is closed. Officially told. I've been told to back off you too, haven't I?'

'Who by? Heather? She's not my mother, you know.' I was already planning what I was going to say to Heather later.

'No, by my line manager. A stickler for red tape. I'm not surprised really. I'd rather been expecting it. They always tell you not to get too close – maintain a professional distance. I haven't done that. Now I'm doing what I'm told.' She wouldn't meet my eyes, deliberately toying with her slice of congealed pizza. 'Anyway, it's clear I was being told the same thing by you too.'

'Why do you say that?' I asked quietly.

'Well, your *assistant* – and the fact that you were so cool with me after the verdict and on the phone. I guessed you were having second thoughts.'

'No, Kat. I was just in difficult situations where I couldn't be forthcoming. Haven't we had this conversation before?'

'Have we? Then maybe I need to have it spelled out to me more than once, Lawrence. Or be able to believe it.' There was more but she obviously wasn't going to share it with me for the moment.

'Shall we start again?'

'How many starts do we need Lawrence?'

'I think you said as many as it took, last time.'

She didn't say anything for a while, just watched me, expressionless. If it came to a battle, I knew I could win in the non-commitment stakes. I'd been doing it for years.

'And who *is* the officious little bitch?'

'Ah. Ella. Heather's niece, and my Heather-appointed warden. Where I go, she attempts to follow, and I work like hell to stop her.'

'Heather Trinder? I'm surprised, but I think I see now. Well, you seemed to make quite a good team when I was there so maybe Heather is doing you a favour.'

'Really?'

'Well, it was certainly a team I was no longer part of.'

'Unintentional. And I've still got a mystery on my hands …'

'And the reason you're really here now is to ask me to help with it, not to tell me about Kimmy.' She shrugged irritably. I tried to look as sheepish as I could but with no mirror to check the result in, I probably just looked dumb. 'And you know I will,' she sighed. 'But you have to be honest with me – and trust me.'

I moved over to her side of the settee. 'I will. Are we on a truce yet?'

She made a face at me. 'You know we are, Lawrence. One crook of your little finger ...'

'Good, so shall we eat some of this unspeakable pizza or do unspeakable things to each other instead?' She gazed at me, clearly debating the question in her head, then giggled and the pizza was forgotten, but her initial reluctance wasn't. I went to sleep later pondering that.

I didn't make it back to Heather's after all. I went straight to Chelsea Police Station the next day to regain entry to my home, leaving Kat stewing over her coffee as I left.

'Lawrence,' she called me back as I made for the tiny passageway she called a hall. 'If I'm going to help you sort this all out, you'll have to tell me the rest of what's going on, you know.'

'The rest of what's going on?' What makes you think you don't already know all of it?'

'Because I don't. I've met one of your sisters, but she was crazy and I didn't understand a word she said. I know a bit about Win and how you let him down. I know about the murder case that you should have enquired into and Jaggers obviously set up. I know your wife was Jaggers' sister and must have been playing games with you. I know Jaggers may even have killed her to stop her from talking to you about him. I know you're worried about Danny's parentage and touchy about Kimmy – I suppose because she was hardly the type you'd want to admit was your sister – but what I don't understand is why you should be the reason for the storm. Because you are, aren't you?'

'No, I'm just in the middle of it, Kat.' I shook my head, apparently ingenuous. She didn't look as if she believed me. Something was different about her since a few days ago. She had acquired an edge – one than questioned rather than simply accepted. She didn't disagree, just carried on looking at me, dark eyes reflective.

'And will you always tell me the truth?'

'Of course – what kind of silk would I be if I didn't?'

'That's not at all the same.'

'You know everything you need to know, Kat.' And she did. The rest could stay boxed.

* * *

Scenes of crime hadn't quite finished in my kitchen but I removed kettle, mugs and coffee to my study and left them to it. I created my own scenes of crime across my desk with the two case folders I'd brought home. The clues to the mystery had to be in one of them somewhere, and a part of me relished the challenge of finding them. Maybe I was a frustrated detective, not a silk after all. I laughed quietly at the juxtaposition of myself next to Fredriks and wondered what nickname they would give me if I was in his place.

There was nothing I hadn't already pored over time and time again in both files, but the nagging in my gut told me the answer was there somewhere. I tried a linear approach – one item flowing on to the next. The original murder had all the signs of something Jaggers might have done, yet Win and the red nail tip had convinced me until recently that Margaret was the culprit. But Margaret couldn't have done it. Sarah had proven that. Margaret had an inherent physical weakness, so someone had deliberately planted evidence implicating her at the scene of the crime. Margaret and Jaggers were unacknowledged brother and sister so maybe someone was intent on either making the connection, or for one to be seen to be covering for the other. Who would do that? There were two alternatives. Jaggers – although that didn't make a lot of sense, and Win. That did make sense.

Win had implied that Jonno was Danny's father, but subsequently it seemed that all of our parentage was far more complicated than I'd assumed, and Win was the one who seemed to know how it unravelled. Sarah had said Margaret was playing games, and Margaret had obviously known far more about my past than I had at the time – and been plotting with Win. So what games was Margaret playing and how was Win aiding and abetting them? Win. I kept coming back to Win.

Strange he hadn't been breathing down my neck since the trial. In fact he seemed to have gone completely off the radar; unless he'd been at my house yesterday, with Kimmy, because Win *did* know my address, and also quite probably that I was going to see Sarah in the afternoon. Binnie knew, and if she knew, Win could easily have prized the information out of her. Win Juss gets what he wants – even no doubt from his reluctant sister. So it all came back to Win again. Now I was getting somewhere.

5: Past and Present

Obviously I should talk to Win. Equally obviously, I couldn't. I might have been given the run of my home again but the eyes of law were still upon me, and so were the press. The murder was spread all over the front page of the newspaper one of the scenes of crime plods had left on the hall table – maybe to remind me they would still be watching after they'd gone. The one advantage of having them there was that the hacks who'd clamoured to interview me when I arrived there under escort had been bluntly told where to go and I'd made it into the house unmolested. I was under no illusion I'd make it back out again the same way.

They removed their palaver by late afternoon, leaving only chalk traces outlining where Kimmy's body had lain on the grey slate floor. I perched on the stool Danny had chosen when he'd run away from the hospital and sat in my kitchen eating peanut butter and jam sandwiches, and stared at it. That day seemed a lifetime ago now, but it was barely a couple of weeks. In that time I'd regained and now, it seemed, probably lost again, the principles and high aims Atticus would have endorsed. How could I sit here, unmoved by the deaths of both my sister and my wife, other than to view one as an unwanted and annoying complication and the other as an enemy still battling me from the other side, and call myself a man; a man worth calling a man?

I'd felt somewhat the same at Kat's when I left. It was clear she guessed I was still holding out on her but I was relieved she allowed me to, albeit dark-eyed and broodingly. Was I still so much the cold-hearted, self-seeking automaton Margaret had seen me as? The body that could satisfactorily complete the most complex of tasks as long as it was programmed to do so, but without understanding how they related to the greater whole – the soul. Deep down, there must be some vestige of regret for losing my sister – for the death of a human being – the same way that I should be grieving for Margaret. I trawled the depths, willing myself to face the feelings I had about first Margaret, and then Kimmy. They both fell into a black hole of bitterness. Margaret for manipulating me, and Kimmy for – what? Being manipulated, I suppose. How could she not have seen that Jaggers was bad news? How could she not have considered what kind of mess she was allowing Danny to be dragged into? How could she have been so unmotherly as to be prepared to hand her child over for adoption? How could she slept with me if she knew who I was? Why was she born at all unless to push us all out, and herself to grow up worthless and unworthy of usurping my place in my home?

That was the crux of it. Not blindness to potential danger, or lack of maternal concern. I was angry because of what she'd done to my childhood. She'd taken it away from me. If she'd turned into a 20th century Einstein or Florence Nightingale, my ejection would have had meaning – logic. Nurture the best at the expense of the worst. As it was it had no sense and no recompense. She was the root cause of all the troubles now sprouting like weeds around me. Bloody bitch. Bloody useless bitch! She should have never been born, never existed at all, even as an atom or a strand of chromosomes waiting to line up with their pair.

But then Danny wouldn't have existed either.

And I disgusted myself.

The brandy in the study called but I steadfastly remained where I was. Too easy to lose myself in that, and losing myself wasn't the way to find solutions, or to deal with what was. Face it. You feel nothing for her; you hate her. She was your sister, kith and kin, flesh and bone, blood and body, and you hate her. Even dead, you hate her because she has left you a lasting legacy – if not a living child, a lost past. One you can never change, never hide, never ultimately deny. You were abandoned and never reclaimed. You lived your childhood out in a children's home where your soul was abused as cruelly as your body, and that's why you can feel no remorse, no regret, no pity – nor love. It doesn't exist in you.

The black hole engulfed me. With no love there could be no Kat – like there had been no Margaret. Whatever Margaret might have offered me, I hadn't had the eyes to see it or the will to accept it. Maybe that was what Kat had been seeing in me and the dregs of her coffee. The man who gave only what enabled him to acquire what he wanted back. It was all going to slip away again and I was unable to stop it. My work – under threat from Jaggers and Heather; my liberty – from Win and whatever he was up to, and the chance to live – through Kat.

She'd shown signs of disenchantment with me last night, and why wouldn't she? Her initial infatuation had made me ridiculously

43

complacent, and fatuously miserly with what I gave back. No-one could live on a beggar's diet forever, and that was what I'd been offering her. The same as I'd offered Margaret. Get real, man – you're pushing fifty and she's almost half your age. You have to do the running after her, not the other way round. You have to give to receive. But I had nothing to give.

I scuffed at the chalk marks and went back to the study, taking the pile of post some helpful detective had left on the end of the counter. I added it to the pile I'd left there the day before, but couldn't be bothered to deal with. I knew I should pull myself together but now I'd finally recovered peace and privacy, I lacked the equanimity to enjoy it. I picked up Margaret's photo and studied it, then laid it flat again, uneasy. She looked exactly the same as she always had in it but now I fancied I saw recrimination in her eyes. Times past. No point in becoming maudlin. What could I do to change it? Nothing. Face it. You don't know how to be a decent man. And without being a decent man, you can offer nothing to anyone, Kat included. Do something about the future instead.

Yet I couldn't shake the lethargy of misery brought on by the acknowledgement of my feelings. I slumped in the chair and idly shuffled the case papers I'd been looking at on the desk. *The devil makes work ...* Miss Liddell intoned. *Piss off*, I replied. Kat's brooding eyes and Margaret's reproachful ones lingered with the phrase in my mind, together with my inability to give either of them what they deserved – the truth.

I sorted the post desultorily. I ought to at least open it. It split easily between professional and personal with the leaning towards personal. None of it looked urgent. I had almost reached the bottom of the pile when I found the card. At first I thought it must be a mistake and I'd invited myself to Margaret's funeral. It was identical to the cards that I'd sent out. I turned it over and it became quite a different beast.

'Time to focus. What do you think of the exciting new artist I've discovered? Words and images – a powerful combination. Let's start with the images. The words will follow.

Be in touch soon – J'

My chest lurched. Again! 'J' – it was obvious who it was. He wasn't leaving me on the loose for long then, but what exciting new artist was he talking about? I turned it over and over, examining the post mark, and the smudged hieroglyphics in one corner that looked like an inverted capital L with a circle attached to it, but there were no clues to the reason for it or the 'artist'. It was posted in central London the day before, and other than that, nothing. Typed, anonymous – apart from the obvious connection I'd made – and cryptic. Another nail in an already hammered coffin, no doubt. Twisting the knife until I bled whilst my tormentor enjoyed the joke. Fuck him! I was about to give in to the brandy when the doorbell rang. Another of Margaret's choices, a shrill alarum echoing through the house with an insistence that couldn't be ignored – strange because it was so contrary to her usual guileful methods. It made me jump and the sensation of being on edge without knowing why intensified. I almost didn't answer, thinking the hacks were probably planning to reassert siege mode now the police had gone, but peering out of the study window, I could see only the postman.

The parcel was small, and carefully sealed. About the size of an A4 letter – but thicker. It was addressed neatly to me in small black print and sent recorded delivery yesterday. It had obviously been planned to arrive today. I took it back into the study, trying to decipher the postmark but that too was smudged.

Stupid. It was recorded delivery. I turned it over to read the sender's details and almost dropped it. Kimberley Hewson.

'Bloody hell!' I put it on the desk and studied it as if it were as explosive as the revelations I'd blasted the court room with. Should I call the police and hand it over to them, or open it and claim over-enthusiasm as my excuse once I knew what was inside? She must have sent it before her death, therefore she'd intended me to have it. It was only right I opened it. Or had it been sent on her behalf? I squinted at the franking again. It had come from a post office in Croydon but the time stamp was unclear. I hesitated. Maybe it had been sent *after* her death – after all, if she'd been coming to see me, surely she'd have brought it with her? Exactly! She would have brought it with her. So someone else had sent it in her name and the game looked set to change again.

I went round to the other side of the desk and sat down, still debating what to do. I rubbed my hands over my face but the parcel was still there when I looked – a time bomb, quietly ticking. What I did was instinctive and should have told me something else about myself. I rang Kat. I was still lacking foresight – as Heather so rightly pointed out. Kat wasn't in so I debated ringing Heather, but knew she would advise handing it over to the police and I now had no intention of doing that. With no accomplice to help me, it had to be my own decision.

I leant across the desk and pulled it towards me. The hand writing was nothing like Kimmy's – or at least not like any of it I'd seen. I could compare it. There was a signed statement from her in Danny's case folder. I rifled through the papers and found it. She'd helpfully filled in the top half of the witness statement form. The handwriting was sprawling and badly formed. Not neat regulars and carefully coached print like Margaret's. I traced my name across the front of the package. No need to consider fingerprints. Half the Croydon sorting office would have handled this, including the ones who'd peed without washing their hands afterwards or picked their nose whilst tossing post into pigeon holes. Margaret would probably have been disgusted if I'd joked about it to her whereas I imagined Kat would laugh and make a wry comment in return about life and letters being a dirty business, or something comparable. I wondered why she thought she wasn't smart. Indeed ironic if this had been a package from Margaret. This *was* a dirty business, and she'd appeared to have more than soiled her hands already.

The decision had to be made. I pushed Kimmy's statement back into the folder and it displaced Margaret's post-it note about the adoption papers. I disentangled it from its claimed position to re-insert it and had to eat my words. Not ironic at all. I stuck the post-it next to the address. A handwriting expert would confirm it but the similarity was obvious even to me. *'Insert Adoption Papers here'* and *'Mr Lawrence A Juste, 5, Atherly Place Mews, Chelsea'*. The same A, curling slightly at the end, and the P with a tiny embellishment where the pen slipped across the upright to end just beyond it.

And the list – I could compare it to the list she'd left me. Christ, where was it? I rummaged wildly for the key to the top drawer of my desk. I'd stuffed both Margaret's and Win's lists with my family's addresses at the bottom of it in the same envelope. I spread Margaret's list out next to the package and the game changed a second time. Impossible though it was, Margaret had addressed the parcel to me.

There was no decision to be made then. The recovered letter opener was in the same drawer. Apt. I carefully sliced through the tape at the ends of the package and smoothed the wrappings apart, curious what other nasty little surprises my enigmatic dead wife had in store for me. Inside was a bundle of papers enshrouded in a plastic wallet. They mainly looked old, but one stood out fresh and startlingly current in its brash colours. It looked like a child's drawing – an older child because the figures had defined characteristics, and a body shape consistent with reality. Of the three figures, one was clearly male and the others probably female. The male figure looked on with a rabid grin as one of the women – the one with the distinctive red fingernails – bent over the other. She appeared to be lying on the floor with a circle like a halo round her head. At first I assumed the recumbent figure was meant to be an angel, but I puzzled over the angel's face. It was leering and unpleasant, the tongue hanging lasciviously from the side of its mouth as if about to slather over a lollipop.

Then I realised what it was and wanted to retch. It wasn't a halo. It was a bag. It was the depiction of a murder scene, one in which the unfortunate victim had been suffocated by a bag secured over their head. Whether the second lady with the red nails had been putting it on or taking it off, wasn't clear, but who she was could hardly be in dispute for me. Even the shade of red was almost perfect. The only questions lay in who the victim and the watching man were. My initial assumption was that they were Win and Kimmy. I dismissed that almost immediately. Kimmy had been stabbed not suffocated. Then it occurred to me they could also be Jaggers and the 1988 murder victim. There was no clue to the artist, but if this was present-day, I was afraid it could be Danny, the only child I knew involved in this mess. If from 1988, then someone else was potentially at risk as well as him. No-one could have witnessed this, recorded it and expect to remain alive.

Underneath the picture were other documents, detailed on another list in the same neat and dainty hand. Margaret had liked her lists. I compared it to the items filed neatly underneath it. And she was efficient.

'28th May 1988: In the wars. Crashed my new blue car. Broke my pretty little arm. Check Brights of Crawley and St Helier hospital for the repairs.' It was a blurry photograph of what looked like a young Margaret, right arm in a sling and face swollen.

'29th May 1988: John Arthur Wemmick and Maria Flowers.' It was a photocopy of a photo of Jaggers and a pretty girl – not unlike Margaret, but blonde – arm in arm in a nightclub. His arm was proprietorially round her waist and because she was so slim, his hand extended beyond her side and across her hip. A large fob ring of a tiger's head with stone eyes adorned his little finger. Maria Flowers; the 1988 murder victim.

'29th May 1988: What the detectives didn't see.' A photocopy of a photograph of the dead girl close-up, and not included in original evidence. A graze in the shape of an animal was clearly impressed in her neck just under where the bag must have been twisted tight. The blood spatters around her reminded me of the brutality of the crime, and the bag

of Jaggers' modus operandi in the children's home. I gagged.

'*30th May 1988:* The Daily Express. *Grim Bank Holiday for Good-time Girl.*' A clipping of the newspaper report of the murder at the Gods and Gargoyles Club, Soho, giving the victim her stage name too – a goddess of course. Aphrodite.

'*Papers: Deed of Ownership of the Gods and Gargoyles Club.*' A photocopy of the partnership deed between John Arthur Wemmick, Wilhelm Johns and Winston Juss, devolving all interest in the club to Wemmick if Johns or Juss were ever charged with criminal acts, but otherwise allowing Johns to front ownership and Juss to partake in the profit share. I whistled. I hadn't known the three of them were *that* close then. Win had said he'd done some work at Jaggers' club – not part-owned it.

'*The ring.*' A photograph of the ring, lying on top of a privately commissioned forensics report identifying the DNA on the ring as belonging to the murder victim, one Maria Flowers. In close-up the claws holding the stone eyes in place looked tarnished – old blood.

'*The certificates.*' The place of birth was our flat in Croydon, the mother was Ma but the father's name was absent. The child's name; Kenneth, Lawrence and Winston all figured in them – both of them; smudged, partially obliterated and randomly ordered so they were almost interchangeable between us. Ma had bestowed all the names on both of us, in a different order – as she had with Georgie too. Her attempt at attaching us all to Pop? His name included some of them as well. Lawrence George Kenneth – but not Winston. That had been Ma's commendation for our wartime leader.

I almost wanted to smile as I read the names – so many of them, jostling on the certificates like naughty children playing tag. Margaret had laughed at them when I'd had to list them for the registrar, alongside the deed to change my name. The only time I'd admitted my real identity to her and I'd assumed she'd dismissed it as her only comment at the time – more piquant than usual was, 'aren't just a couple of forenames enough?'

'It's tradition,' I'd replied brusquely to avoid elaborating on my family. 'And law requires traditions to be upheld – even marital law.'

The second certificate was identical to the first apart from the alternative version of the name, juggled into a different order. So was the original Win's birth certificate; or mine? If it was mine, the other can of worms involving Danny's parentage was clearly about to be opened and the wriggling mess of degradation and scandal exposed for the world's appalled fascination.

At the bottom of the list, still in Margaret's hand, but longhand this time, flowing gracefully across the page, was presumably what this was all about.

'The verdict: Ah, life! So many things in it needing to be done or undone. Remembrances remembered, wrongs righted, displacements replaced. A little patchwork to recreate in the right pattern but with no threads left to fray this time. Always a problem if you don't get it right first time, isn't it? The abandoned ends unravel, and then you have to go back and make reparation – don't you, Lawrence?'

I went back to the drawing, utterly bemused. The parcel could hardly have been compiled by Margaret in partnership with Jaggers. Some of the items were positively incriminating – if not admissible in court. He'd hardly hand the means of his own destruction over to me, unless they somehow enabled my ruin too. No, this was from someone else – someone with an axe to grind and who wanted me to help them grind it. Even though it was clearly some form of blackmail, yet it was but blackmail with integrity. Justice? That didn't smack of Kimmy, or Jaggers, but it could of Margaret, self-righteously pompous about justice for all. And if this was intended to reopen the Johns case and lay the blame of a wrongful verdict at my door, ruin was assured. I tapped my fingers on the desk top, simultaneously angry and afraid.

'You tricky bastard! What are you and your sadistic cronies playing at with me now?' Margaret's perfect social smile seemed to widen in the photograph that lay facing heavenwards. 'That includes you, you bitch,' I added. A sense of pointlessness replaced the confusion then. To hell with it. I'd spent a life hiding and now, as the note said, it was all coming undone. I couldn't stop it. I'd have to make reparation somehow for my part in the past – perhaps this was the way? 'I'm done. If you want to ruin me, go ahead - take the lot. At least you can't take any more from me when it's all gone.'

The brandy won then. I poured myself a whole glassful, and sprawled back in the chair with it. I downed it in one and got myself another before the burn of the first had left my throat. The next one went down more slowly and blurred the edge of rage. I let it spread to my brain. It didn't matter if I got pissed now. A clear head wasn't going to make any difference to the mess. I poured another, but sipped this one, letting my sordid past and pointless future combine at the mid-point of helplessness.

Alcohol allowed lethargy to invade again. I studied the drawing and the papers as if from far away, and they no longer seemed so terrible. The ring winked at me from the photocopied photograph. They'd lied about that, I thought inconsequentially. If Margaret had been a party to preparing the parcel before her demise she couldn't actually have had it. *One time you're wrong, smug cow.* I'd seen it – or its twin – on Jaggers' finger when I'd visited him with the birth certificate of her alter ego, Molly, to face him out. This was simply more of their games; their devious little games – albeit games with a purpose. And so very Margaret's style – to be abstruse. Perhaps Margaret Juste or Molly Wemmick – whichever name she wanted to go by, didn't like having evidence in place which incriminated her and had played her own little double cross; the nail clipping countered by the ring – impasse. Margaret: always perfect, always reputable and always hypocritical it now seemed – and maybe playing all sides off against each other before fate caught her out.

I dwelt sourly on Margaret and her hypocrisy for a while longer. Bitch for messing with my head even when she was dead. Then another thought burned through the blur of the brandy like a fireball. I paused, mid-sip and put the brandy glass down heavily. The contents slopped drunkenly from side to side and my brain mimicked them. To send me the parcel herself, or put any of it together, Margaret had to have been alive.

I pulled myself upright, desperately trying to marshal logic. Idiot! Margaret was dead. She couldn't send me anything. Kimberley was dead too, so neither could she.

But one of them had.

My head pounded and everything fell back into the black hole as the brandy achieved its end and the room swum. The bright red claws in the drawing leapt off the page and grabbed at me. The figures seemed to dance a deadly tarantella before distorting into a series of jagged lines and leering faces. Inside my stomach the warm pool mutated into a gurgling pit. There was no doubt about Kimberley's death, but Margaret's? She'd been unidentifiable apart from her wedding ring, the dress I knew she'd worn out that evening and the things in her bag. All easily swopped. All easily transferred onto another body for me to identify as Margaret whilst Margaret slipped away to plague me later. You're paranoid, I told myself – drunk and desperate.

Or maybe inspired? If Margaret *was* still alive, then Margaret *could* send me a package full of evidence. And Jaggers and Margaret could still be playing a nasty little game together with me as piggy in the middle. But if Margaret was alive enough to send the package to me, who the hell had I just cremated?

6: Trade-off

It would have been too easy to expel my self-abuse by throwing up. Instead I suffered the consequences of stupidity with something approaching equanimity – and a blinder of a hangover. I staggered out to the kitchen and filled myself with black coffee, burning my hand on boiling water in the early stages of detoxification. I could imagine Sarah chiding me. '*You can't go on ignoring it, Kenny. You gotta face it – put it straight.*'

Or like Margaret's note had observed about life – 'S*o many things in it needing to be done or undone.*'

The anonymous sender had become unequivocally Margaret to me by then, even though there was no proof or logic to the belief. But DNA – that would nail it. Yes – the coroner had samples. Logic started to tackle absurdity. But how would I explain away wanting to prove my wife was my wife? The impossibility of that suddenly struck me. There was no way to determine whether the woman I'd just cremated was or wasn't Margaret from the DNA. There were was nothing to compare the samples the coroner had kept to. Her sister was dead, her parents were dead and she'd had no surgical procedures requiring blood tests that I knew of. The DNA the coroner had could prove nothing. I laughed aloud. Priceless – and very clever. So what else was there to address that I could do something about?

Reparation. There was plenty of that to make. Where did I start?

When the coffee had completed half a job, I took a mug of it back to my study and forced myself to sit in front of the package again. Sobriety was bringing a mother of a headache with it and someone had set up a brass band in my head to boot, drums pounding out a rhythm that the trumpets gaily echoed every few seconds. I decided I might try a list of my own while the band settled into a rhythm. Maybe some of Margaret's organised ruthlessness would rub off on me through it.

The protagonists in my little tragedy fell neatly into three camps – the

Wemmicks, the Juss family and the undefined. They didn't encompass all of the issues I had to 'sort' but they pretty much created them between them. Murder, blackmail, family and future – or lack of it. I sat back, head full of wool but at least it was muffling the brass band and cushioning the headache. It made the groups blur and merge as well, and it occurred to me that maybe I hadn't got the groupings right after all just before I drifted into sleep. I woke up the next morning with a mouth full of sludge and a head probably the culprit for putting it there. The pounding and the band were back, but this time I tackled them with painkillers. And Kat.

She appeared at my door just as I was making my way unsteadily to the bathroom. I peered through the spyhole in the door, anticipating press and was briefly relieved it was her, before groaning at how I must look. I opened the door a fraction, mindful that the press might still be lying in wait behind her.

'Oh.'

'Don't say it.'

'I wasn't going to,' she smirked, 'but you do.' I opened the door wider and gestured weakly for her to come in before shutting the door quickly behind her. 'You'd make quite a good reverse Dorian Gray, if that's any better,' she added. She was dressed in a tailored suit and it hugged her rear like they were having an affair. The stirring in me was automatic, and irritating.

'Thanks.' Even to me it sounded withering, but she seemed unconcerned. The edge was still in place then.

'You're welcome.' She stood hesitantly in the hall. 'You called me last night?'

'Ah.' The door to the study was open and the dishevelled package spread across both case folders, with crimson-taloned Margaret still lying on top of them. I crossed to the desk and shoved the black-edged card underneath it and flapped the packaging shut while Kat lingered by the door.

'Have I disturbed you from work?' I was about to exit the room and usher her away, closing the door behind me but I stopped myself. What the hell was I doing? Last night I'd called Kat to help me decide what to do about the package after promising to tell her the truth only hours earlier. Now I was about to hide it all from her. She was looking at me curiously, expression slowly transforming to disappointment.

'No, not really work, but yes.'

'Now you're starting to sound like your sister, Mary.'

'Sorry.' The warring parties in me went back into battle. *You're no good at this.* Here's your chance – tell her everything. *Everything? That will include Danny too. What do you think she'll make of that?* She asked you to trust her – tell her the truth; all of it. If she meant it, she'll stick by you. *Would you stick by someone who's lied and manipulated their way to the top, and possibly slept with their own sister?* She knows about the lies and manipulation, it's only the last bit she doesn't know about. *The worst bit* ... I couldn't avoid the evidence on my desk, so I made a deal with myself; the last deal, I insisted. The last bit of my secret life. I showed her what had arrived the night before, including the card, but not the certificate with my name on it. I palmed that and stuffed it in the top drawer as she sifted through the rest of it piece by piece, face becoming more sombre as she worked her way through the pile. She paused at the birth certificate I'd left in the papers.

'Win's?'

I nodded. 'It would seem so.' I waited for her pass on from it, heart thumping.

'Lawrence and Kenny. He's got the same names as you.'

'Yes, I think it was probably a common theme then – pass them down the line.'

'How odd. But you've done the same with your new name.'

'Only Lawrence.'

'Lawrence A Juste. What does the A stand for?'

'Just a foible of mine.' She waited but I didn't elaborate. This was why I was no good for her. Why not simply tell her I'd chosen the name of my boyhood hero as my middle name? If I couldn't share such an insignificant fact about myself then how could I hope to share deeper secrets? *But you have*, the little voice taunted. *You told her who you really are. Isn't that a deep dark secret? Or is who you are deeper and darker?* Lawrence Atticus Juste, but not just, and not the kind of man Atticus would have lent his name to.

She shifted her gaze back to the certificate. 'Funny kind of order it's in. Has it been doctored?'

'Doctored? What do you mean?' I looked over her shoulder, uncomfortably conscious of the rich musky smell of her skin compared to my two-day-old sweat and brandy. I tried not to touch her as I pushed the copy certificate around so she could get a better view. She twisted round to look up at me and I held my breath, partly to stop myself breathing rancid alcohol fumes over her and partly because that was what she did to me physically. I concentrated on focusing on the certificate and not her. We needed to move on from this before she made the other connection between genetics and their role in Danny's heritage. She was right though. The certificate looked authentic at first glance, but the names were oddly arranged. The order was that of Win's name but they weren't all in sync. Kenneth and Lawrence were aligned but Winston appeared to have been written a fraction lower, as if the names could have been taken in blocks and dropped there to create a whole out of a number of parts.

'See?' she said softly, pointing to the misalignment, her breath touching my cheek like a warm summer breeze. She waited whilst I froze, afraid to move in case I gave myself away. 'Lawrence, I'm here to help. Please let me.'

'I don't think I should, Kat. I don't think I should have asked you to the other evening either. I shouldn't be dragging you into this. It's my mess.'

'You're not dragging me into anything. I'm volunteering.'

'Margaret volunteered and look where that got her.'

She withdrew, offended. 'I didn't think you considered us similar.'

'I don't. But you were right. I am the centre of this storm, for a lot of reasons.'

'Then tell me what they are so I can help.'

'I think I'm past help, Kat.' I pulled up a chair on the other side of the desk and sat opposite her. 'Remember how we discussed personal involvement when I first took Danny's case?'

'Yes.'

'I warned you then things were complicated for me. Since then they've become far worse.'

'I know. You've told me about them. Your family and the Wemmicks.'

'Kat, you wanted the truth. The truth is that they're just the tip of the iceberg. Now you've seen it do you know what conclusion I've come to about this little bundle I've been sent?'

'That Kimmy knew more than was good for her and it got her killed. It's dangerous. I understand that.'

'No, far worse than that. Probably Kimmy did know more than was good for her, and possibly it did get her killed, but it wasn't her who sent me this.'

'Who then?' She frowned and I noticed for the first time she wrinkled her nose when she was perplexed. I wanted to reach across and stroke the wrinkles smooth and then kiss the tip. It steadied my resolve – the fact that I could feel an emotion for her that was unrelated to sex or merely getting what I wanted. If I wanted anything from this it was for it to be merely a good moment between two people. No devious relatives or undead wives, no blackmailers, no threats, no promises, just a woman and a man and a future – in which I might finally get it right. But it wasn't. It was merely another phase in another deceit and I owed her more than for her to become entangled too. Margaret was right. I had a lot of sorting out to do before I had a life to lead.

'I think it was Margaret – and that makes it more than dangerous. It makes it deadly, and we're the little pawns being used as bait for the kill and I don't know whether it's Jaggers, Margaret or both of them together manoeuvring me. I can't let that happen to you too. I can't let you wind up the way Kimmy did and therefore I can't let you help me in this other than for one thing.'

'What's that?' She looked mutinous – the kind of look that had been on Danny's face when he thought he was being taken straight back to hospital after he'd run away. My gut twisted for both of them. No I was a man, I just had to learn how to behave like one.

'To keep yourself and Danny safe.'

'But how could it be Margaret?'

'It's the same handwriting on the package and on her list– and I should know my wife's by now.'

'But you've just been to her funeral, Lawrence – and she was formally identified. It must have been put together before her death. Maybe it was why she got killed too?'

'Maybe,' I conceded, but I still thought my first idea was the more likely, unlikely though it was, and all those little details of identification easily arranged if you were a clever arranger.

'And what about helping you work out what's going on?' You promised you'd ...' she broke off as her cell phone rang. She made a face at me. 'I'm at work, officially. I have to.' I nodded and hunched over the desk, feeling frayed and exhausted, wondering how to put my other request to her. A night slumped in a chair, too much alcohol and no food had ground the last ounce of energy from me. I'd made a decision as I'd been talking to Kat. There'd be no handing anything over to the police until I'd solved this myself. The sooner it was sorted, the sooner I could pick up where I'd left off. Maybe Kat would still be around then, and so would my life. She cut through my thoughts. Her voice was scratchy and shocked. 'Danny's gone missing again, and as he hasn't shown up here, it's not just a case of truancy.'

'Missing? Since when?' A shiver of fear ran through me, sharp icicles of foreboding. The drawing was sticking out from under the birth certificate.

'Since he should have shown up for breakfast this morning. He's probably just expressing his disgust at being back in a children's home, but ...'

'Children's home?'

'Sorry I didn't tell you earlier. My line manager rang me about Kimmy soon after you left yesterday. Because I know more about him and his problems than anyone coming into it fresh I was re-allocated to his case. The other kids have stayed with the father pending his own court hearing, apart from the two littlest ones, but Danny was felt to be at risk because of his condition. He went back to the children's home he was at before he went to the remand home whilst awaiting trial. I went to see him there yesterday afternoon.'

'Were you there when I rang you?'

'Yes, and into the evening. By the way, neither he nor the other kids know their mother has been murdered. They just think there's trouble with her again. We thought it best for the moment until the case is more resolved – too upsetting for them. I did ring you back when I worked out the missed call was from you, but there was no answer so I thought I'd better not interfere. I didn't know if you might have had company.'

I sighed. 'Company? I thought we'd done that.'

'I know. I was being silly. That was what I'd decided by this morning so I came to see you. Anyway, Danny seemed fine last night. A bit put out at being back in the home, and annoyed about Kimmy, but glad not to be with his Dad. He doesn't like him much, I don't think. The two little sisters were put in the same place as him so he didn't feel "shoved out", like he said before. In fact he was quite enjoying playing big brother. Told me he was going to show them the ropes there.'

'Poor kid. He's having a rough ride of it. Looks like it's about to get a lot rougher – but they can't just leave it. With all this turning up, and Kimmy's murder he's at risk even if he's merely taken it on himself to run away. Is anyone out looking? The police?'

She shook her head. 'They will be, but a missing persons report has to be filed first and the children's home aren't keen on doing that until they've exhausted other options. It looks bad on them otherwise.'

'So what can we do?'

'I'm going to go over there and see what I can find out.'

'Then I think I'd better come too.'

She raised her eyebrows. 'But you're not his brief any more.'

'I know. Do I have to come as his brief? What about a concerned relative?' The eyebrows went even higher, but she looked pleased.

'OK, but not like that. They'll think I'm bringing a very well-heeled tramp with me!' I laughed, but the bite in the reply didn't miss me.

'Have you been eating lemons since I last saw you?'

'No,' she shook her head, bewildered. 'Why?'

'No reason. I'll go and get showered and changed if you can give me twenty minutes?'

'OK.'

'Help yourself to coffee – it's in the kitchen.' I took the stairs two at a time, cursing when I reached the top for having left her with the whole muddle spread out across the desk in the study and just begging for her to sift through the puzzle pieces. With time might come clarity; too much clarity. I debated going back downstairs and tidying it all into the drawer but that would be like slamming her nose shut in it too. No recovery from that, even if there might be from complacency and reserve. I made it back downstairs within fifteen minutes, to find her not engrossed in the case papers or Margaret's evidence pile but browsing my bookshelves. The desk drawer was shut, although not fully and the papers looked as they had when I'd left them and her. I couldn't remember if I'd shut the drawer completely or just pushed it to.

'They say possessions tell you about a person,' she commented as I joined her.

'And what do mine tell you about me?'

'That I don't know you at all,' she replied pointedly. She gestured to the case papers on the desk. 'Don't you need to put all of that away?' She smiled archly at me. 'You don't know who might look – I didn't, by the way.'

'It would have been all right if you had,' but I shuffled the papers into the drawer with relief and this time turned the key in the lock.

'Oh, I don't think it would, Lawrence, but one day you might decide to show me of your own accord and then it would be.' We faced each other at the door to the study. Her expression was challenging – as it had been when we'd first met. 'How shall I introduce you at the home? The concerned relative?' A fleeting expression of mistrust passed across her face again, like a shadow. It irked me.

'His uncle.'

She raised an eyebrow again. 'OK,' and the expression faded away.

Surprisingly we made it out of the mews without apparently being noticed by anyone – expect perhaps the biddy at number six. I was relieved. The murder was bad enough, but Kat's visit would draw even more unwanted attention my way if she'd been spotted. Lawrence Juste, secret past, recently dead wife, murdered sister and lascivious bastard. The press really *would* have a field day if I had a young mistress to focus on too.

The children's home was so unlike the one I'd lived in, it could have been another world. It was in New Southgate on the way to Enfield. It reminded me of a secondary modern with dorms, but a fraction of the size. No greenhouses out the back to sift for treasures, no dank cellars for initiations or bullying, no charts or black dots overlaying the yellow stars. Most of the children were at school when we arrived, but the few residents around seemed happy enough. A handful of boys, between about six and ten, were kicking a football around on the grass at the back and three girls were making daisy chains on the edge of it.

'Why aren't they in school?' I asked Kat.

'Probably waiting placement. If they've come from another area, a place has to be organised at a local school. Bureaucracy means they often have to wait five days before starting there.'

'That's ridiculous.'

'Admin, paperwork, rules. Everywhere has them – not just court, or hadn't you noticed?'

'Have I done something I've missed?'

'Why?'

'The lemons.'

'The lemons?' She looked mystified.

'I asked if you'd been eating lemons earlier.'

'I know.' She shook her head, still bemused.

'Sharp.'

'Ah, you mean I am?'

'Yes. I thought we had a truce?'

'Yes, but not peace in our time – yet.' She buzzed reception.

'Yes?'

'Kat Roumelia here about Danny Hewson.' The door whirred and she pulled it open. I held it for her, wanting to say something in response that might tame the beast, but suddenly had nothing to say. She slipped past me, all tight black skirt, sensual wiggle and fresh as juice.

Danny's room was pleasant but bare. The bed cover was probably too childish for him and I could imagine what he might have said about it. The little steam trains it depicted puffed happily along their tracks and over the edge as they headed for never-never land and the small window looked out over the back where the boys were still playing football. The curtains matched the cover. Kat twitched the cover straight.

'And when did you say someone saw him last?' she asked the dorm parent.

'He got up for breakfast, but just didn't turn up for it.' She looked more kindly than Miss Liddell but still had something of the no-nonsense about her. Or maybe she didn't like being questioned.

'How do you know he got up for breakfast?' Kat queried.

'I called him myself. We always check on the new ones more often over the first few days.'

'And there was nothing out of the ordinary this morning?'

'No. Absolutely nothing.' I watched Kat's eyes stray around the room and stop on a pile of papers by the side of the small desk unit under the window. 'He didn't go to a club or classes or anything last night after I left, did he?'

'Classes? What like evening classes? We don't let the children out after seven, unless they're over fourteen and it's an organised activity, Miss Roumelia. Danny was only ten – and had only just arrived here.' She frowned and I was surprised Kat hadn't already known their rules. 'No, I think he spent the evening with his little sisters and then in his room until lights out.'

Kat went over to the desk. 'Did he draw these last night then?' She picked up the top two or three and I went to join her. She put the drawings back down on the desk and was about to turn over the top one when I stopped her. It was of a woman with blood-red fingers. The dorm parent joined us.

'Oh, maybe. Or perhaps the last time he was here and he brought them back with him. I recall he loved drawing, although not usually quite as much as this.'

'Were you his dorm parent when he stayed here before?'

'Yes. Nice kid. A bit rough round the edges but a soft side to him. He was good with the little ones, getting them settled.' She picked up the top drawing and studied it. 'He even entertained one or two of them once by telling a story and drawing illustrations to go with it – a bit like these, but much nicer. One of the stories was obviously going to turn into a horror story though and I had to get him to change it so he didn't frighten them. I suppose this could be something similar.' She turned another of the drawings over. 'The witch with the magic nails. Bit odd though.'

'What would she do with them?' I wondered, and then realised I'd asked the question aloud. The dorm parent and Kat were both eyeing me curiously.

'I have no idea,' the dorm parent replied, 'but I stopped the first story anyway. No matter how nice these kids seem, they're here because life has turned on them one way or another and that can find its way out in unexpected ways at times. Never assume with a child in a children's home. Assumptions can produce unpleasant surprises.' I stared at her but the use of the phrase seemed to be mere coincidence.

'So why did you think it was going to turn into a horror story then?'

'Oh I just knew – the way you do sometimes. Instinct. You get to know working here – what's good and what's bad.'

'And what's your instinct about Danny's disappearance?'

'Not good,' she said dourly. We all considered that in silence for a while until she broke it with, 'I've got to call those kids out there in to lunch. Are you OK here for a moment? You're making the report so it'll give you time to check out his things here.'

'Yes, fine,' Kat answered for us. She waited for the dorm parent to go and then cut across my question about her making the report by waving the picture at me. 'It's like yours.' I took it from her. It was similar, but not identical. It could have been the scene ten minutes before the one I'd received through the post, with the red-nailed woman apparently arguing with the other woman and the man in the background holding the circle – the bag – out ready to use. 'Jaggers?' She asked, pointing to the man. He had a blob on his hand, which could have been the tiger ring or could be a flaw in the paper.

'I don't know. But whoever it is, they weren't there to help.' I handed it back to Kat and looked at the sketches underneath. They were again spaced at time lapse intervals, and all of a size. A thought suddenly occurred to me – a game we'd played as children. 'Kat, if we put these all together and flicked through them, what do you think we'd see?' She shook her head. I took the top drawing from her and put it together with the others to create a booklet. Holding it tightly on the left hand side I flicked the right hand side to make the pages splay open like a run of cards. It created a patchy moving picture show. Kat clapped her hands.

'How clever!'

'We used to do it as kids with scraps of paper – making our own cartoons because we didn't usually have the money to buy comics. We used old envelope backs and that sort of thing. Watch carefully.'

It took a while to master but eventually I had all the drawings pinned tightly together and completed the display. We watched in silence as the figures acted out what the drawings had been trying to illustrate in isolation. I knew what the drawings were depicting straight away. An eleven year old murder – or a one day old one, minus the bag. It was only missing the final image because that was locked in my desk drawer.

'A bit sick, isn't it?' Kat commented after a few moments of silence.'

'They're telling a story, like the drawings I've been sent.

'Ah, and you have the last one,' she added quietly.

'I do, I think. But how could Danny draw them?'

'And who sent them to you? Surely it makes more sense that it was really Kimmy who sent you the package now. Danny only recently drew these so they would have been done after Margaret died, even if Kimmy somehow got her to address the envelope and write the list beforehand.'

'Kat, do you really see Kimmy as the mastermind behind that package of evidence and Danny's disappearance? Especially since she was already dead by the time Danny took to his heels.'

'No, I suppose not. But then who is?'

'Someone who's playing possum – and that's why this has become more than just complicated. We're back to Margaret – and before you remind me she's dead too, may I say again I think that still remains to be seen.'

Kat stared at me. 'But if you think she's still alive then the body wasn't …'

'Yes.'

'But you identified her.'

'I identified her personal effects but those kind of things are easily organised, like organising adoptions of orphan kids who still have both parents around.'

'Ouch.'

'I wasn't actually having a go at you. I was thinking about my so charitable wife.' I put the booklet of pictures down. 'And this means that Danny's whereabouts are of even greater concern. After all, someone must have told him about this for him to be able to draw it. He wasn't around eleven years ago, was he?' Kat picked it up and flicked through it again. There was no doubt what story it was telling.

My mobile phone rang and I answered it without thinking – too late to stop Heather's tirade which ended with 'back here immediately unless you want me to dissolve the partnership right now; the back way – the hawks are already gathering, including that swine of an editor ...'

'Kat, I've got to go. That was Heather. I need to get back to Chambers before she implodes. There are things I have to sort out there too.'

'Don't you mean people?' I stared at her and she visibly wilted. 'I'm sorry, I didn't really mean that. It's the jealous bitch in me.'

'There's no jealous bitch in you, only a jealous beast that needs subduing. Perhaps we can do that together when we've found Danny and shut Heather up.' She smiled, and the acid lemon become golden sun on a burnished lake. 'Let me know if you find anything else.'

'I'll pass these on to the police.'

'For the moment, no.' She looked surprised. 'They need the full set, don't they? The other one will need to be repatriated but that's going to require some explaining from me.'

I felt guilty leaving her with a lie, but I still needed the time I thought I'd bought with the manslaughter dismissal. That time was rapidly running out before the clock had even started ticking. No matter how much I disliked the idea, as soon as I'd defused Heather, I was going to have to seek out Win. He might be playing a double game himself, but I didn't think he was a murderer, nor that he would want to see Danny at risk. All things considered, he was probably our best bet for finding Danny now – before it was too late.

7: Preceding Priorities

I was smugly congratulating myself for having dodged the press at the front door and Ella in the clerk's office, when I fell foul of a worse fate. Heather was lying in wait for me when I arrived back at Chambers – the back way. Her room was empty and I was about to sneak into Jeremy's office to see if he could fill me in first but she pounced before I made it through the door.

'He won't help. He's back down at the bank trying to buy us some more credit.'

I turned on my heel and saw her across the corridor, leaning against my door, leg carefully arranged in front of her like a hooker touting for business. The toe of the Manolo Blahnik completed the pose by pointing at me like a shiny pink knife. I guessed the impossibly high heels of the shoes had something to do with the way Heather was standing but nevertheless the impression she gave was of a disconcerting cross between seducer and assassin.

'What was so urgent I had to come back straight away? Danny Hewson has gone missing again.'

'I'm sorry to hear that, but it's probably going to be the least of your worries by the end of today.'

'The reason being?'

'For a start we're broke, Lawrence – and the bank is about to shut us down.'

'What do you mean, we're broke? Jeremy can't have been spending that much on his girlfriends.'

'It's not a joke, and it's nothing to do with Jeremy – or Francis, come to that. It's you. You've cleared the account over the last few days.'

'Me? I've done no such thing! I haven't even touched it, in fact. I've had far more important things on my mind than to count partnership pennies, if you remember.' I walked towards her, conscious that Gregory was probably hovering at the bottom of the stairs, sweatily enjoying the piquancy of our troubles without having to listen at keyholes. 'Shall we talk about it in here?' Reaching past her, I pushed the door open, breathing in her heavy perfume as I did so. No Francis and his cigarillos currently here to warrant it but old habits die hard. I was more aware of that than most.

She hesitated on the threshold. 'That's not all.'

'It's enough for us to be talking in private and not in front of the whole world,' I nodded towards the stairs. She followed my gaze and my suspicions were rewarded by the shifting of light across the bottom of them as someone moved swiftly away.

'OK, but I think I'd rather keep the door open, even so.'

I walked in and sat at my desk, determined to maintain control in my own space this time. She sat uncertainly on the visitor's chair. The door remained ajar behind her.

'Perhaps you'd care to explain that comment?' I asked snappishly. There was a pile of rubbish on my desk, presumably Louise's offerings from the post room.

'Well,' she looked awkward. 'I find it hard to believe but there's something else apart from the money.'

'What?'

'I haven't passed it on yet – well not to the police.'

'The police? What the hell are you talking about Heather?'

'Your sister,' her nose wrinkled as she said it.

'What about my sister? Or maybe I should ask which sister?'

'The one who's been murdered. The boy's mother.'

'Yes?'

'A package arrived from her the other night – the night you didn't turn up.' Her nose wrinkled again. She wasn't just disapproving. She was downright condemnatory. Heather would never risk exacerbating wrinkles unless moved beyond habitual control. 'I suppose you stayed at the little social worker's place instead?'

'She has a name, Heather. It's her job, but she's a person, and hardly deserving of censure.'

She backed off marginally. 'Maybe not, but you know what I think about the inappropriateness of the liaison.'

'About as inappropriate as the liaison you suggested between your niece and me?'

She waved the comment away. 'That's purely business. This is personal, Lawrence – and at the moment you can't afford personal.'

65

'Sounds like I can't afford anything from what you say! What *is* this all about?'

I hadn't noticed until then that she'd been holding a folder behind her. Maybe the Blahniks had been less architects of her unnatural posture than its contents. She slapped it on my desk and it spread another cloud of her perfume on impact, as well as scattering the pile of unopened correspondence. The combination of sound and smell made my head spin as the dust on my desk rose in a small tornado, backlit by the sun streaming through the windows. I looked at her unsteadily through the haze, aware there was something else that was turning my stomach at the corner of my eye.

'It's all in there,' she announced testily. 'The withdrawals from our account were on Margaret's bank card – which of course is in your possession – not Jeremy's. Then there's the drawings, and the birth certificates. It's obvious what was going on Lawrence. She was blackmailing you and you were having to pay her off.'

'Who was blackmailing me?' I reached across to open the folder. Underneath it the corner of a black-edged card poked two fingers at me. On the top of the folder was a drawing similar to the one I'd been sent, but with major details changed. The woman with the red finger nails was being attacked this time, and her attacker looked remarkably like me, complete with wig, gown, winged collar and silk bands. The onlooker appeared to be a child.

'Pretty obvious from that I would say,' she commented, looking over her shoulder shiftily, presumably to make sure the door was still open. 'And what happened to her because of it. I would guess you know exactly where the boy is now too, despite the self-righteous show. It looks as if he probably did the drawing. Ironic since I don't suppose he's studied the old masters to understand the conceit of including oneself in one's work of art, but there you are. It obviously works in ignorance too. ' The sarcasm seemed to have settled her. She leaned back in her chair and crossed her legs, swinging a pointed toe at me.

'Christ almighty! You think I murdered Kimmy?' I stared at her, aghast.

'Well, I find it hard to believe but that rather suggests it, doesn't it – red hooker nails and all?' She looked slightly abashed. 'Odd its Margaret's colour, though – I never did like that colour she wore; so un-Margaret, yet so apt as her signature note now, turning tricks on all of us.'

'And what if I were to tell you that I'd also received a drawing like this through the post yesterday, depicting quite a different murderer, victim and onlooker?'

She studied me for a moment. 'Did you?'

'Yes, as a matter of fact I did, and Kat and I. The *little social worker* and I,' I corrected myself nastily, 'had just found a whole fistful of drawings like these in Danny Hewson's room at the children's home when you commanded my presence here – all showing a similar scenario to the one in the drawing I was sent.'

'Oh,' she was taken aback now. Briefly I relished the moment. It wasn't easy to catch Heather off-balance. 'Who sent you them?'

'Supposedly Kimmy herself, but I rather doubt it – not from the way the package was addressed.'

'What do you mean by that?'

'It wasn't her handwriting. I compared it to paperwork she completed for Danny's trial. It was someone else's altogether.'

'You say that as if it was significant.'

'It is, especially in view of what you've just told me about the account withdrawals.'

She waited whilst I thought about how much to tell her but obviously lost patience before I'd decided. 'Oh for God's sake, Lawrence, we're in enough shit already. Don't go all strong and silent on me now.'

'It sounds crazy.'

'And this isn't?'

'OK, I think it was Margaret.'

She considered me for a moment. 'You're right. It does sound crazy – good attempt if you're thinking of pleading temporary insanity because of grief though.' She paused. 'She's dead, Lawrence. She may have been a lot of things whilst alive, but now she's dead.'

'That's something I'm not so sure of, Heather.'

Her pointed toes could probably have cut the air between us, two equal slices of disbelief and incredulity. 'You mean it, don't you?' she said eventually.

'Yes, I mean it.' I said heavily. 'It's a long story and I thought Danny's case would close it all down, the funeral would wind it up and life could start again with it behind me. Quite the reverse, it now seems. I think the case merely set the scene and the funeral was the opening act.'

'So if Margaret is alive – only *if* mind you – who the hell did you have cremated?'

'I don't know.'

She put her hand over her mouth and spoke from behind it. 'This is bad, Lawrence – and dangerous.'

'I know.'

'I think you'd better tell me what's going on, not the other way round.' Of all the people I wanted to not have to tell the whole story to, Heather came only one behind Kat, but in this instance there really was no choice.

'Before I do, have you still got the packaging all this stuff came in?' I tapped the pile of paperwork on the desk.

'It's at home.'

'It was sent to your home address – not here?'

'Yes, why?'

'No reason, just trying to get a picture of what's going on.'

I spread the paperwork so all of the pieces could be seen, but the black-edged card was completely covered, wondering if I would have to tell her all or only as much as I'd told Kat. At least I wouldn't have to own up to the charade that had first got us all into this ten years ago. My own birth certificate stared back at me – or rather a duplicate of one out of the two I'd been sent; the one with the names positioned so they read Kenneth Lawrence Winston Juss. I couldn't stop the expletive.

'What?'

I pulled it out from under the other papers to examine it better. It was identical to the one I'd received, and attached to it was Danny's. The same name had been clearly inserted in the 'father' section. 'Is this what you meant by certificates?'

'And the other one.' She shuffled the drawing aside and at the very bottom of the pile was another. Kimmy's, tying in exactly with the mother's name on Danny's certificate. 'If I understand this right, it suggesting his father is you, isn't it?' She said. 'Danny Hewson's father and his uncle, one and the same.'

'Yes, so someone wants me to believe,' I agreed reluctantly.

'Well, you're named as the father on the birth certificate.' Her nose wrinkled again.

'Yes, that would seem so too.'

'There's no seem about it, Lawrence. Tell me; is it true?'

'Is it likely?' But now I understood why she'd assumed I was being blackmailed by Kimmy and when the money had run dry, had killed her instead. She stared at me, eyes piercing my nonchalant attempt at deflection.

'Oh my God, he doesn't know!' She flung out of the chair and paraded around the room, hands gesticulating as she mimicked my *is it likely* over and over again. I'd never seen Heather in court but I suspected I was being treated to her version of dramatic irony as it would have been displayed there. Incongruously I wanted to laugh. Her display of sanctimonious repugnance was so at odds with the cynical suggestion I sleep with her niece I could have been in the middle of a scene from a restoration comedy. Briefly the possibility of actually being Danny's father had its humorous side. It didn't last. The show ended with a more serious issue. 'How are you going to find out?'

'I've had a blood test.'

'And the results?'

'Inconclusive – they've got to redo it. Sample cross-contamination, apparently. But really Heather, it's all part of the game, isn't it?'

'Maybe, but in the meantime, this little bundle of joy is going to land you right in it with the police.'

'Only if you hand it over, Heather.'

'You're suggesting I shouldn't? Give me one good reason for that.'

'Because unless I can find out what's at the bottom of all this, that money won't ever find its way back into the partnership bank account and that case which first provided us with the wherewithal to earn it all ten years ago will keep resurfacing until we go under with it.'

'What do you mean?'

'I think it all started with that – the Wilhelm Johns case.'

'The Wilhelm Johns case?' She looked mystified.

'Our big break, remember?'

'I remember the case, yes. It was a bit cut and dried but there was never anything controversial about it, just brutal – so why would it take us under?'

'Oh, Heather. Didn't you ever wonder?'

'Wonder what?' She came over to the desk and peered at me, forehead wrinkling as she scrutinised me. The glasses she should wear were probably snug at the bottom of one of her drawers like my secrets were at the bottom of mine.

'Why we got it, and won it so easily. The evidence was so shaky the whole thing clearly a sham. It only passed muster because Johns wouldn't give evidence so everything that was thrown at him stuck – like shit on a fan that had been turned off. Surely you could see that as well as me –

and so must have Jeremy and Francis, but we all acquiesced. We're all guilty.'

She slapped me round the face. It stung and one of her nails scratched my cheek. Now I saw Heather how I'd never seen her before – incandescent with rage.

'Don't you ever accuse me of a cover-up again; I would never do that.' She didn't shout but the volume seemed to have gone up suddenly. I wasn't letting her off the hook so easily.

'And what about Alfie Roumelia?'

'That wasn't a cover-up either. It was a clean verdict.'

'Really? Kat wasn't so sure and she's his sister.'

'Margaret assured me everything was absolutely above board. All I had to do was present evidence – and I did.'

'So, exactly like I did in the Johns case. I expect Margaret would have assured us that was squeaky clean too if she'd started work here a year earlier. As it was we only had her family's word to rely on then.'

'Her family?'

I sighed. It had gone far enough. Heather had already seen what I wanted Kat to never know. Someone had been very determined to make that happen. Perhaps I could count myself lucky it had been Heather they'd nominated to be present as I faced my nemesis, and not Kat. Heather would no doubt survive it but obliterate me. Kat I had my doubts about – or doubts that I would be able to protect her whilst facing it. I might as well enlist Heather's help rather than her enmity now. She'd make a formidable opponent. Maybe she'd be an impressive ally too.

'Let's start at the beginning. Meet Kenneth Lawrence Winston Juss – me. And how I came to be here and who I am isn't particularly clean or nice – like my adversary.'

'I know. When Ella showed me your notes I thought you were on speed, but as you didn't admit to the worst parts in court I waited to see what explanation you cobbled together instead. The papers didn't of course, but that's a problem we'll have to deal with later once we've got this one straight. Go on, I'm all ears.'

By the time I'd taken Heather through the whole history, including Margaret's alter ego as Molly Wemmick, Win and Margaret's plan to set up Jaggers by faking her death – now in some doubt, Jagger's objective of recovering the old Judge's 'investment' in me and how the Johns case was the way he had set me up for the sting including the drunken after-party, it was early evening. I wondered what else Kat had found out in my absence. There hadn't been any calls from her, but that didn't necessarily mean anything, as disinclined as she was to contact me at Chambers. Heather's reaction was curious. She was neither shocked, nor judgemental. She was perplexed. That made me more anxious than ever – Heather not on the attack.

'I don't think you've even scratched the surface of what is going on here, Lawrence,' she said at last. 'It's not just what is going on now, either – that's a by-product of what happened in the past. It's the past itself – and all the constituent parts of it you've been side-stepping all these years. I think it's the case you need to focus on – the case and the money. Whether you were entitled to the money or not, you've got a potential criminal miscarriage of justice to refute here. Hadn't you better sort that out first? Prove the verdict either right or wrong – and get the evidence to back it up. Someone has it.' She flicked the birth certificate. 'I reckon this stuff has all been tampered with – and this paternity thing is just a red herring. Nothing that you've seen or been told so far is the truth, but someone's absolute priority seems to be for you to establish the truth while someone else's is to distract you as far away from it as possible. Find out what's going on between your warring family members, by all means, but get to the bottom of the Johns case first. Then, if there's a link between it and the rest of the crap, you'll find out what it is.'

'Oh I know what the link is, Heather – the Wemmicks – but not the reason. John Wemmick – Jaggers – could have simply gone after me for the money in the will, and it would have been a straight out dirty public fight – him trying to get me to discredit the old Judge and him turning the terms of the will back on me. But he hasn't done that. He set me up instead. Ten years ago. It's only now coming home to roost and that makes no sense.'

'You're smart. Work it out, like you would a brief.' She was right, of course. But whereas with a brief my thinking was clear and precise, here my guilty conscience threatened to engulf me. No matter how much I analysed and categorised, with this I wasn't smart at all. I was dumber than the school dunce. She must have seen something of the sort in my expression. The efficient business partner gave way briefly to the sympathetic friend. 'Try and step back from the personal, even though it's difficult. Being impersonal helps you see more clearly. That's why I suggested you slept with Ella not Kat – if you have to sleep with anyone. Jesus, I would have thought you'd have learnt your lesson there by now, though.'

'I really don't believe I could have ...' I started, but Heather's expression told me she wasn't interested in what I believed. I concentrated on the bigger problem – in her eyes; the Johns case and how it related to now. 'But so much of it is depends on now – for instance, Margaret; is she dead or alive? What does she know that would help me?'

'True, but I think you need to decide on priorities – what is the most important issue to solve first. The other issues will probably resolve themselves out of it, including this parentage nonsense. Shall I tell you what I think is most important right now?'

'What?'

The business partner had returned.

'To get hold of that bloody bank card and stop your ghostly wife cleaning us out. *Then* figure out who's behind the murder eleven years ago, and bomb-proof the partnership against someone trying to re-open the case and claim conspiracy. *After* that you can sort out your tangled personal life – but preferably without including the little social worker.' She ignored my exasperated expression. 'Well, haven't you potentially got enough on your conscience to be going on with already? Do you really need to be accused of cradle-snatching as well as cradle-filling? Anyway, it sounds like your sisters and brother would probably know far more about all of this than they've told you so far. They'd be the ones to help you get to the bottom of the boy's origins. And when you find out what really happened, then you might also be able to square your conscience over the rest of it – rejecting your family, I mean. That's what they're playing on too. The fact that you already feel guilty. Even if you did sleep with Kimmy – and it doesn't sound certain you did by any means – you can't change it now. You have to learn to live with yourself sometime, Lawrence. And even if you don't come to your senses beforehand, the little social worker will wonder why you hate yourself so much if you don't. Then she'll hate you too.'

'I think she'd hate me more if she knew what I might have done.'

Heather laughed. 'You really don't know much about women do you? I'm going to keep all this stuff for the moment – somewhere safe – so don't even think about trying to find it. I'll see what more I can find out about the Johns case for you but you get that bloody bank card stopped and then go and do some digging.'

'But what about Danny?'

'Isn't your little social worker on to that?'

'She's hardly a match for the mob, is she?'

'Oh, I don't think the mob's involved where he's concerned. More like the mob's Moll – and that means he may be absent but I doubt he's at risk. She seems to have had quite a fixation on him, didn't she – Margaret? I would never have had her pegged as maternal – but then I didn't have you pegged as stupid until now. Concentrate on the things that are most at risk – your livelihood, for instance.'

Danny with Margaret. I hadn't considered that before. Maybe he wasn't so at risk then? Heather got up to go, sweeping the papers on my desk towards her into a neat stack. The black-edged card went with them and I was about to protest, but decided silence was the better part of valour for the moment. At the last moment it dropped back onto the pile and I silently buried it as she straightened her skirt so it was as crisp and creaseless as the moment she'd leaned warrior-like against my door. 'But don't think I'm going to back you up if you get burned.' Something about her expression belied the statement.

'Heather?'

'Yes?'

'Thanks for the vote of confidence.'

'Vote of confidence? I just don't want to have to groom another suitable business partner. Christ – men! Talk about pricks, pants and pussies. You need to learn the alphabet better; they all come after 'm' for marriage. By the way – take Ella with you if you go off to talk to anyone. Especially the little social worker.' She walked away, wiggling her ass as if it was 's' for sex, whilst I concentrated on 'w' for Win. I dug his card out of my wallet. *Win Juss – gets you what you want when you want it.* This time *I* was going to get what *I* wanted.

8: Non-disclosure

And there again I was wrong. I couldn't get hold of Win. My call went straight to answerphone and I didn't want to leave a message so I moved on to the next job on my list. Cancel the bloody bank card. It was too late to do it over the phone. I would have to make it the first port of call tomorrow. It was only then that I remembered the black-edged card, now shuffled to one side of the dishevelled pile of post. Heather had completely distracted me from it. It was identical to the first one; typed, again with a patchy sketch of what now looked like a hanged man in the corner with the base under him underscored, franked but with the print smudged, the day before – presumably the same time as Heather's parcel had been sent – and otherwise innocently nondescript.

'Costs such a lot to stage a story, doesn't it? I think I will have to look into financial funding first. People so often presume only to get caught out when the bottom line is drawn – like curiosity and the cat.

Be in touch soon – J'

Clearly blackmail, then, and perhaps a veiled threat too, but still not really explaining the reason for the packages being addressed from Kimmy unless she was involved in Jaggers' schemes. But then that called Margaret's place back into question. My head ached and my brain stopped working altogether. I shoved the card in my top drawer, cursing that I couldn't find the key to it. No matter. The message was cryptic enough to be lost on anyone but me.

Give up – give up and leave it until tomorrow. You can't do anything more tonight.

That left what to do with myself tonight. I wanted to seek out Kat, and also find out the latest on Danny but was afraid of confronting either and of the possibility of the press following me. I left Chambers via the back entrance again and wandered back to my car, aimlessly taking the longest route because I wasn't sure where to drive to once I got there and hopefully it would throw off or allow me to spot any hacks that might be tracking me. It was warm enough to walk around in shirt sleeves and I slung my jacket over my shoulder as I strolled the early evening streets of the city, apparently relaxed, but inside screwed tight like a ball of paper. The usual hardened drinkers were clustering round the most popular bars having their 'quickie' on the way home, which would extend to three or four before they finally headed dishevelled and fume-laden to the Tube and their homes in the less exciting suburbs.

The third bar along was a Chambers 'local'. The Grape Vine. Its name worked equally well for the bar as for the other service it provided after office hours – keeping Chambers' staff informed of the in-gossip. I usually tried to stay well away from it, especially currently when I was just as likely to be the source of the current gossip as a partaker in it. I could see Jeremy propping up one of the chest-high tables nearest the window and some of the clerks on the far side of the bar, Ella amongst them even though she was senior to them. Usually ne'er the twain would meet. An unwritten rule in Chambers. Perhaps Heather's spy was working in more than one camp. I hoped to make it past the window without Jeremy spotting me but he waved furiously and I reluctantly had to poke my head in.

'Lawrence, old chap – come and join us!' He waved a half-empty bottle of red at me and the blonde on his right smiled flirtatiously. She was in a tight black two piece work suit, but the skirt managed to make it look more like the prelude to a party than a day at the office. 'Meet Melinda. We've been talking about the future of Chambers and my part in it. Melinda's going to be looking for somewhere shortly, and I think she'd fit in rather well if Francis has to stay off-piste. Don't you think so? Smart *and* sexy.' He leaned in toward her and patted her ass proprietorially. She giggled, then smoothed her skirt and smiled alluringly at me again. He sloshed the bottle of red at me again but I declined.

'I'm not sure Heather would be too keen on you handing out places at Chambers when Francis is still very much on-piste, merely walking wounded temporarily. But talking of off-piste, won't the lovely Lizzie be expecting you home soon? Isn't that her name? The most recent one? Don't want her ringing Chambers to find out where you are and getting Heather on the prowl, do you?' It elicited the right response – affront from Melinda and fear and trepidation from Jeremy – as I suspected it would. I was glad to see the mention of Heather obviously did it to everyone, not just me.

'Oh, no – too right, old chap; got to keep the home fires burning.' He put the bottle down with a bang and Melinda blinked. 'Sorry Melinda. Must talk again one day. Very interesting. I'll leave you the rest of the bottle.' He followed me out, leaving Melinda tight-faced and even tighter-skirted, glowering after us. 'You won't tell, will you? Old habits and all.'

'Just go home, Jeremy. I'm in enough shit myself to want to drop anyone else in any.'

'Good chap!' He clapped me on the shoulder and wandered off towards the blue and red Tube sign in the distance, leaving me outside the bar dithering where to go myself since home offered no comfort. I sighed. Tonight all of life in the city felt choking and grimy, not lively and buzzing. The green of the countryside was where I wanted to be – fresh air and sap-filled swathes. For all her closeness to death, I envied Sarah her pretty vista, and suddenly there was only one place to be that made sense – with my dying sister. I stepped up my pace and made it back to my car in less than fifteen minutes despite my off-route dawdling. Me and my racing green needed space.

Leaving the smog and heat of the city behind me was like entering a different world. Hampton Court could have been a thousand miles away, not a mere handful. Even the crackle of the gravel as I drove up the sweeping drive to the nursing home was satisfyingly crisp and the immaculately tended grounds were as lush as the last time I'd visited. It was nearly seven. Entering the sleek reception hall the place appeared deserted. The distant clatter of crockery accompanied the smell of stew. Perhaps all life here had been temporarily funnelled into the stew pot. I laughed involuntarily. Whilst the unlucky had nothing but the indignity of death to look forward to, only the evening meal was uppermost in mind for the ravenous hordes of the living. Life went on and some things never changed.

The same little Polish assistant took my name and led me along the maze of corridors to Sarah's room.

'How is she today?' I asked.

She smiled and shook her head. My heart plummeted until she followed the shaking head with 'not unnerstand,' again and an apologetic grin. We stopped at an unfamiliar door with no name on it. She gestured for me to enter.

'She was in another room last time.' I objected. 'Sarah Juss.'

'Yes, missus Sarah. Here.' She frowned and gestured again. I knocked and pushed the door open. It was the chapel. Sarah's coffin was on a side table, and she looked like she was merely sleeping inside it. She was dressed in white silk – her shroud – yet she looked like a small shrivelled bride, face now devoid of the creases of pain or the ravages of illness. The smile on her face was barely discernible but to me it was clearly there, reminding me of Ma indulgently watching from a distance as Georgie, Win and I raced up and down the mound of the air raid shelter in front of the flats. It had claimed us as hers, and yet also simultaneously released us into the world. Sarah's smile blessed me whilst releasing herself from the woes of the world in the same way.

Someone had surrounded her coffin with pastel blue flowers – forget-me-nots – making her appear to be sleeping in a drift of colour. They had no smell but in the low-lit room their colour reminded me of lavender and I immediately imagined its scent, sweet and slightly smoky, filling the room. I looked back at the little Polish assistant.

'The flowers?'

'Yes,' she nodded. 'Missus Sarah love flowers.'

'Where did they come from?' The sheer volume required to surround the coffin as they did was mind-boggling.

'Lady. Nice lady. Missus Sarah love flowers. I…' She made small picking gestures to indicate she'd arranged them around the coffin. 'Like?'

I looked back at the coffin and Sarah floating away to heaven on a sea of blossom. *I'll remember it all this way – pretty, and you holding me hand, and everyone back happy again one day.'* I nodded and looked quickly back at Sarah to hide the tears that had welled up. I wondered if she was with Ma as she'd imagined. The lump in my chest hurt – for both of them.

'When did she … go?'

'Last night.' I could feel the woman close behind me and a gentle touch on my arm. 'She happy. No sad. You happy too.'

'It's hard to be happy when someone you love dies,' I said, aware of the gruffness in my voice and wanting to clear my throat but unable to do so. Realisation of love too late to share it with the person who prompts it is almost crueller than death itself. The question of love and what it meant had been one I'd barely considered until Kat and my discarded family had appeared in my life. I still couldn't answer it, but the ache in my chest seemed closer to love than anything else I'd ever experienced.

'She know.'

Despite her well-meaning sentiments, I wished the little Polish woman would go. There was nothing I wanted to say out loud to Sarah, but a part of me wanted to be alone with her and think all the things I might have said if I'd known what they were and could find the words to voice them. She must have read my mind because she whispered, 'I go,' and I sensed rather than heard her leave.

I stood alongside the coffin and touched Sarah's hand, cold and waxy, clasped around a pink rose. Had she liked roses best? I should have known. There was so much I should have known about my dead sister and now never would. All the years I'd not known – or wanted to know, and now I would have replaced all of them for just one in which to have got to know who my big sister, Sarah – my 'Little Mother' – had become since we'd left childhood behind. They say you should never regret what you haven't done because that is a life lost; not lived. Better to regret what you have done – mistakes and failures included – because that is a life savoured. I regretted my lost life bitterly as I held Sarah's hand the way I should have held it when she was alive. The twilight drew in as I stood there, remembering every detail I could of her. A half-man remembering a half-world. I scrutinised her carefully from head to toe and ended there, surprised. Shoes; she wore no shoes. Her small bare toes pointed delicately towards the heavens. I knew why. The memory flowed over me in a wave of sadness. Polished soles. *'Keeps them waterproof,'* Ma urged. *'Don't want wet feet on a rainy day.'* True enough, although we boys didn't really care. One of our favourite games was to stamp in the puddles to see who could make the water splash highest and furthest. If we could soak each other – or better still – one of the girls and make them shriek, it was perfect. What I remembered was Sarah's turn to polish shoes – and the soles - the first time she'd been asked out by the boy down the road, Harry Thompson. A date, it would have been called now. Her friend Glynnis Jones had been assigned to walk part the way with her 'for propriety's sake' but Glynnis was anything but that. Glynnis had high hopes of her own. I'd heard her say more than once that she only needed one bang with Harry Thompson and he'd be hers for life. I hadn't told Sarah that because I didn't know what a bang was and whether Glynnis needed a gun for it. Whenever Glynnis came round I made a point of hanging around in case she let slip any clues. She never did, but her burgeoning breasts were enough to make my eyes pop so I kept my counsel and simply observed.

Unfortunately it was Sarah's turn for the hated shoe polishing and Pop was a stickler for routine with us, if not for himself. Sarah was already in her best dress – white like her shroud, but with pink rickrack binding round the hem and neck – and Glynnis was hassling her to hurry up, anxious to get away. I was drafted in to help by Glynnis. You didn't argue with her – big, brassy and bossy, the oversized antithesis of Heather Trinder, but just as intimidating. She thrust a shoe at me and I cringed.

'Don't forget the sole,' Ma called from the steps. 'Waterproof it, Kenny, there's a good lad.' I did as I was told and passed it timidly onto Glynnis. She took it gingerly, careful to avoid the sole, and passed it straight on to Sarah.

'Go on. That one's done. Only needs buffing on the top.'

Sarah took it and although I wanted to warn her, my puny voice was never more than a whisper when Glynnis was around, afraid I might fall foul of her bang. The shoe with the polish-laden sole landed in Sarah's lap and the best white dress with the pink rickrack was ruined by the smudge of red-brown stain. Sarah burst into tears and Glynnis rounded on me.

'Kenny what you do that for? You spoiled Sarah's dress. Now she'll have to change.'

I was incensed, but you didn't challenge Glynnis. The soft breasts hid a hard heart. But there was no dress to change into and Glynnis left without Sarah. She probably got her bang with Harry Thompson that afternoon because the talk shortly afterwards was all about her being 'so-so' and she went to live with her granny by the sea-side. The bang eventually turned out to be the prelude to a shot-gun wedding and Harry to be a cad, according to Glynnis, so perhaps Sarah had a lucky escape although at the time it hadn't seemed so. However, she never complained at or blamed me. Little Mother had done what mothers generally do – forgive and forget.

It made me regret all the more knowing nothing of her life in the intervening years. Had she been happy with the man she'd eventually married – albeit without any children of her own – a childless Little Mother. Would it have been different or better for her if the white dress with the pink and white rickrack hadn't been spoilt and Glynnis Martin hadn't had her bang? It *had* been my fault. I should have piped up, shouted out, stopped her – like I should have done with the Johns case. As usual I'd done what I always did. Kept quiet, turned a blind eye, kept myself safe. I was a coward. I was still a coward. It was time to change.

The door opened and shut behind me, letting in a chink of light with it. The little Polish attendant was there again, whispering, 'Missus Sarah's brother?' I turned and faced her, now barely seeing her in the gloom. All of life seemed to be lived in it currently – my life, anyway – gloom.

'Yes, I'm her brother.' The lump in my chest swelled again, but it was no longer painful, it was sweetly sad.

'She left thing for you. At door.'

'At the reception?'

She nodded enthusiastically.

'Thanks. Can I stay here a bit longer?'

She nodded again. 'In dark?'

'No, in the light please.'

She flicked the light switch and a soft glow suffused the room. Sarah looked alive again in its mellow warmth.

'Has the time for the funeral been set?'

She shook her head. I wasn't sure if it was an answer in the negative or indicating she didn't understand. Another reason to have to talk to Win. She melted away and I stayed another ten minutes or so, remembering the Sarah I'd met over the last few weeks and attaching her to the girl I'd known in childhood. Yes, they were the same. I could see that now. The curve of her cheek, and the set of the chin. It was evident even in the mask of death – the family I'd had once and needed to rediscover.

I left the lights on when I left. It didn't seem right to leave her in darkness. In reception, I was asked for ID and then given what I assumed must be the keepsakes box Sarah had referred to when I'd last visited. I'd almost forgotten about it until the sleek receptionist handed it over. It was about the size of a shoe box, but covered in red velvet and gold braid – the kind of thing you'd find in a market. A bit gaudy, but lavish enough to imply it contained something of interest to someone. I debated settling in a corner and opening it there and then, but the open plan arrangement of the reception area wasn't conducive to opening what could prove to be full of secrets I preferred not to be aired in public. I tucked it under my arm and carried it away to the car where it sat next to me all the way back into town, gently teasing. It was almost like having Sarah with me, nudging me in the ribs and winking like she used to as a child when she knew I wanted to know something but didn't dare ask – like about Glynnis and her 'bang'.

I parked up, noticing the petrol was almost on empty just as I switched off. I would normally have used Margaret's more modest VW, as I had been doing until the day before yesterday, but the tax had run out and without her around to see to the more menial parts of life, I'd overlooked renewing it. I should go and fill up now whilst the engine was hot and before the last dregs in the tank evaporated, but I couldn't be bothered to set off again in search of a petrol station. And the red velvet box was too enticing.

I'd go in the morning on the way to the bank to cancel Margaret's card. How I'd missed that was a mystery. I'd cancelled everything else within days and the bank should really have automatically put a stop on it anyway. The vague recollection of having already dealt with it bothered me, but if Heather said it had been used and had the statements to prove it, it must have been. My memory must be unreliable at the moment. I hadn't remembered Kat's house clearly either.

I took the box straight into my study and put it in the middle of my desk. Margaret's picture had been righted again and appeared to be looking at the box with interest. I couldn't recall doing that. Maybe I wasn't merely forgetful. Perhaps my mind was wandering and Heather was right – I could make a case for temporary insanity. I badly wanted to examine the contents of the box but not knowing what had happened about Danny bothered me too. Perhaps ownership of Sarah's treasures was facilitating her morals rubbing off on me too.

Duty overcame inclination and I dialled Kat's number instead of opening the box. It was on answerphone like Win's. I felt vaguely irritated to not be able to raise either her or Win now I actually wanted to talk to them. I rummaged in my wallet for the piece of paper I'd scribbled her mobile phone number on and tried that, but it was turned off. No reason not to open the box now, then. I lifted the lid just as my own phone rang. I grabbed the receiver. It was Kat, ringing me back, and anxious.

'Did you get my message?'

'What message?'

'You didn't answer at home so I had to leave it at Chambers – with that officious bitch – Ella – sorry I know I shouldn't call her that, but she is. She said you were in a partners meeting and couldn't be disturbed.'

'Ah well, that wasn't entirely untrue, but it was more of a dressing down from Heather than a partners meeting. What was the message?'

'I've received a parcel too – same writing on the front as yours, and supposedly from Kimberley Hewson. I thought you ought to know – and maybe be here when I opened it.'

'You don't know what's in it yet, then?'

'Hardly. I've barely had time.'

A small cynical part of my brain wondered why she'd barely had time when she'd told me about it some while earlier. It was a strange sensation.

'Wait there, then and I'll come over.''

'OK.'

'By the way, Kat – is there any news on Danny?'

'No, nothing.' She sounded tired and worried. There was a fraction of a second hesitation before she continued, 'I looked through everything in his room. There was nothing else except for the drawings you saw – well, a few more of them, that was all – odd ones.'

'Has the missing persons report been filed now?'

'Yes, the children's home has done it. Twenty-four hours and it becomes active. Until then we're all trying to rack our brains. It's odd. There was nothing else there, but he did take something with him – and if he'd been abducted we doubt he'd have been given the opportunity to collect it.'

'What?'

'His sketch pad and pencils. I wondered if he wanted to go somewhere and make more drawings, but privately.'

'Has he got a hiding place there?'

'I don't think so. I did suggest that but you saw the place – there's not really anywhere to hide. It's quite, quite – clinical.'

'OK, I'll be with you in about twenty minutes.'

'I'll wait. I don't think I want to look at this stuff on my own anyway. After you put all those other drawings together I realised Danny was telling us a story, but it hadn't reached a conclusion. I don't think I'm going to like the conclusion.'

Reluctantly I decided to leave Sarah's box until later. Without knowing what its contents comprised, it was too much of a Pandora's Box to open in front of Kat. More important than reliving past failings right now were the delights Margaret or her sidekick had prepared for our delectation in Kat's package. I left it on the desk, intending to come back to both it and my own parcel once I knew what was in Kat's. Sneaking out of the front door, I dodged what could have been a loitering reporter at the head of the mews and made it clandestinely back to the garage. I turned the engine over and it coughed and died. I tried it again before cursing that I hadn't gone and got petrol after arriving home from the nursing home after all. Now I'd have to take the Tube or find a taxi.

I opted for a taxi but being a Friday they were all busy transporting revellers to their end of the week social life. After the twenty minutes I'd claimed it would take me to get to Kat's had already long gone, I gave up and walked to Earls Court to pick up the District Line. The nearest Tube stop to Kat's was Kilburn Park. I fed the remaining coins I had in my pocket into the machine and it spewed my ticket out at me, dirty yellow with an unpleasant plasticised black back. A single. I couldn't afford a return as I'd left my wallet at home in the rush. I cursed and then retracted it. I'd ask Kat to give me a lift back. It would make her feel needed.

The stale air was more rank than usual on the Tube, with the aftermath of a hot day sucked down into the earth by us the human ants, swarming into its guts. I stood well back from the edge of the platform, neurosis making me even more sweaty and uncomfortable. I'd never liked the Tube. It reminded me of the cellar. No vermin, of course, but too many people all crowding into the same small place until it became impossible to breathe or escape. It recreated an identical level of panic as the imagined rats in the cellar had unless I consciously assigned the bodies surrounding me names and menial lives to distract myself. I did that now as the doors closed and I and a few hundred or so of the said bodies were transported along the District Line to oblivion at Paddington where I would change lines.

The bloke nearest me had halitosis, pungent and reminiscent of garlic even from where I was standing several paces away. The woman clutching the rail on the other side of him had a pimple on her temple just about to burst. It looked like a ripe mistletoe berry, tinged green at the base burgeoning to a white pustule at the peak. I looked away, disgusted, and tried instead to summarise in my head what was going on around me. Rolled up and squashed into the pocket of the man next to the woman with the pimple was today's newspaper. My face peered obliquely back at me, nose curving bulbously with the fold in the paper. Shit! I studied my shoes and hoped no-one else had noticed it, not even looking up when the doors opened at the next station and the influx and exit of passengers shunted me further along the carriage.

Someone was as intent on reopening past wounds as the young woman with the boil would be on bursting it when she saw how large and protuberant it had grown over the course of the day. When she left home in the morning it was probably no more than a red bump. It had fermented and matured as the day had progressed, just as the rancid facts of my situation had over the previous weeks. I was convinced the person responsible for ripening my particular problems was Margaret, but not why. Heather had been right about the priorities though. The more I considered the various issues, the less important the current nonsense and its potential damage to my reputation seemed, and the more important solving the original reason for the drama became. That was the swelling pustule of venom that could kill all of us simply because I was equally sure that Jaggers was the irritant causing the canker. That only left the other man I couldn't trust, nor pin down currently – Win. And with Win, the other confusion over parentage bubbled back up to consume anything that survived Jaggers' poison.

The woman with the pimple got off at the stop before Paddington and I was relieved because the thought of it was starting to make me feel nauseous. I changed lines and completed the journey jittery, but without further issue, bursting out of the station at Kilburn Park gasping for air and with sweat snaking down my back and soChapter 9 starts on page aking rings under my arms. I felt as if I was covered in a layer of grime and faeces. It always did that to me. I decided I would walk home later, if I went home at all.

The gnomes were still out in force in the next door neighbour's garden, and the other side still looked abandoned and depressing. I knocked on Kat's door after finding the bell had stopped working over the last day or so. Mrs Gnome herself poked her head out of an upstairs window.

'She's out love. Been out ages.' I looked at my watch. Ages could be anything but thirty minutes ago was precisely the time Kat would have been expecting me to arrive, not already have gone out – and before then had supposedly been ringing me from home to arrange it with me. My jitters turned to apprehension, and then after a moment, annoyance. So what game was Kat now playing?

9. Deceit

I loitered on the doorstep, wondering what to do. I was irritated that I'd rushed over here at Kat's invitation, rather than delve into Sarah's box, only to be stood up by her. I looked at my watch. It was already nine-thirty and the light had almost gone. The ghostly gnomes next door peered at me through the murky twilight. Where the hell was she? The scratching of a sash window opening overhead signified the re-emergence of Mrs Gnome.

'I told you she's out, love.' She had a scarf round her head, moulded into nodules and spikes. I guessed she had curlers underneath it, but with only a modicum of more imagination she could have passed for an alien. Once again I was straight back to childhood, and the Saturday morning glamour of half our neighbourhood. If you were female and under forty, the possibility of a night out meant curls if you could manage them – even Ma did it from time to time if Pop could be persuaded to take her down the Alhambra for two halves of stout. Sarah and Win would be left in charge of us, scrubbed, topped, tailed and barefoot in our winceyette pyjamas that had been washed so much their softness had long since disintegrated to hard nodules of fluff which scratched rather than soothed. But it had been a treat for us too because it was the one time we'd have been given some coppers from Ma's thin purse to get sweets from Old Sal's.

My choice was always to share a Jamboree bag with Georgie, in the hope that it would contain the coveted toy parachute alongside its assortment of Black Jacks, Fruit Salads and sherbet dip. It never did, but it didn't stop me hoping each time the possibility of a treat arose. Win always chose gobstoppers and humbugs – Jamboree bags were too childish for him by then. Sarah wanted love hearts and Parma Violets, and Binnie, Spangles, aniseed balls or liquorice laces. Jill and Emm were too small for sweets – and already in bed by then. Mary wasn't bothered. She would absent-mindedly eat whatever Binnie or Sarah sent her way, gazing into the distance and humming tunelessly to herself. It's surprising we had any teeth left after the onslaught of sugar and no regular teeth brushing routine until it was imposed at the children's home. However sweet those memories though, Kat's neighbour didn't belong with them. She leered rudely down at me, sticking her head forward and her chin out like a tortoise peering out of its nobbly shell. It was difficult not to laugh, despite the disapproving set of her face.

'I know, thank you.'

'Well, yous can't wait there all night.'

'What makes you think she'll be out all night?'

'Why do say that?' The Irish accent was thickened by hostility.

'I didn't, you did.'

'Oi never said she'd be out all night. What you trying to make me out to be? Oi don't speak out of turn.'

'I'm not saying you do. I'm simply waiting for her to come home.'

'Well you can't wait there. Ain't right. Making me nervous.'

'I assure you, I'm entirely respectable and there is no need for you to be nervous.' I sighed. This was all I needed. The window slammed and I hoped she'd given up. My temper took a turn for the worse when Mrs Gnome appeared at the front door.

'She's out oi tell yous. Can't yous go away and come back later? Oi don't like all these comings and goings. '

'Really, how is my waiting for her bothering you?'

'It just is. Oi want yous to go away or oi'll call the police.'

'And say what?'

She stepped up to the picket fence dividing the two front gardens and leaned over it. 'That yous harassing me.' She breathed heavily into my face – a mixture of sour breath and temper.

'Oh for God's sake, I'm merely waiting on your next door neighbour's doorstep for her to come home. How is that harassing you?'

'Yous arguing with me. That's harassing. Oi know me rights.'

I'd never felt so inclined to punch a woman as I had then. I consciously uncurled my fists and tried to calm myself. *Don't draw attention to yourself, you fool. That's the last thing you need now.*

'Lawrence,' Kat's voice cut through our animosity. She sounded bright and brittle and out of breath, walking briskly up the path. 'I'm so sorry. I had to dash out. I have all that paperwork you need to see inside.' Mrs Gnome squinted over my shoulder.

'Oh, yous back. Yous should keep better company, dearie. Are yous sure yous want to let him in? He's been harassing me.' I stared at the mean face under the alien scalp and felt as much desire to annihilate her as I felt towards those I encountered like her in court. Kat got there before me.

'Oh Mrs Tooley, I'm sure he hasn't. He's a lawyer. He wouldn't harass anyone, and certainly not one of my lovely neighbours. It's fine, really.' She smiled sweetly at her. '*Really*,' she said again and nodded meaningfully. I watched the horned spikes disperse and Mrs Alien Gnome become simpering charm for Kat's benefit.

'Oh go on with yous, oi've got me curlers in. Can hardly call me lovely.' She looked at me and her face hardened again like setting cement. 'See, she's a nice girl. Respectful. Not at all like yous been saying. Should be ashamed of yourself.' She turned on her heel and slammed the door, leaving me open-mouthed. Kat walked towards me, face quizzical as she drew nearer the overhead light.

'I said absolutely nothing about you,' I told her, mystified.

She laughed lightly. 'I'm sure you didn't. People, Lawrence. They all have their own agenda – like you have yours.'

'Ouch. And you don't?'

'Well, I have mine too, I suppose.' She reached past me to put her key in the lock.

'So what was it on yours that took you out just as I was due to arrive, I wonder?'

She didn't answer, disappearing into the kitchen. Her muffled voice floated back, cool and business-like, as I stood uncertainly in the hall. 'On the table in the lounge. Do you want alcohol or coffee?'

I walked into the lounge debating whether I wanted anything at all at the moment, other than an answer. The package she'd received was lying already open on the table.

'So you didn't wait for me after all?' She appeared at the door between the kitchen and the lounge. The place reminded me even more strongly of a rabbit warren than the last time I'd visited.

'I did.' She paused, surprised.

'Well, it's already opened. I thought you wanted me to look at it with you?'

'I do.' She came over to the table and flicked on a side lamp. 'It was all intact when I went out.'

'And unopened?' She didn't reply, just fingered the package nervously then looked over her shoulder.

'So? Is there someone else here?'

She cast around the room melodramatically. 'Does it look like it?'

'What about upstairs?'

'Oh, an intruder, you mean?' She moved closer.

'You want me to check?'

'We-ell,' she was hesitant, but clearly that was exactly what she wanted me to do. I noticed how small she felt against me whilst also for the first time wondering how good a psychologist Kat was. Recently the voluptuous queen of social rights seemed to be able to transition seamlessly from wronged lover, to sharp investigator and now to vulnerable little woman, evoking an amazing diversity of emotions in me with one thing in common – all of them had me wrong-footed. Whilst Margaret hadn't played on my emotions, the ability to manipulate me suddenly seemed to be as suspiciously present in Kat as it had been in Margaret. My instinct for a liar jarred. She was sweet, and nice – but she'd already prised more from me in a few weeks than Margaret had in all the years she'd known me. And lately she could also be sharp and secretive. Play along, my gut said. Play along and see where this goes, but be careful.

'OK, stay here, and don't move.' I went out via the kitchen, collecting a carving knife from the block on the counter before returning to the hall. Lingering traces of last night's pizza followed me out of the kitchen and up the stairs. I edged up them, back to the wall and knife held out defensively in front of me. From memory there were only two bedrooms upstairs. Kat's, which of course I'd sampled, and the spare room. Other than that there was also a tiny bathroom with clanking pipes and an ancient cistern. Instinct was telling me there was no-one there, yet I hoped there was, otherwise Kat was lying about the package being opened in her absence. That meant she could also potentially be lying about a lot of other things too.

Reaching the top of the stairs, I kicked her bedroom door open with my foot. The door swung back easily with a soft creak. Knife still poised in front of me I felt for the switch with my left hand and the room flooded with a harsh white light. It was empty, bed neatly made and paisley cover smooth across it. I noticed it matched the other soft furnishings but it didn't seem Kat's style. Indeed, what was Kat's style? As I scoured the room for anywhere an intruder could hide, another part of me was straining for any sounds from downstairs, and yet another was questioning what I knew of Kat. All drew a blank. Comforting in one way, yet disconcerting in another. In less than a half hour the woman I'd assumed I knew intimately had abruptly transformed into a stranger. I left the light on and skirted the landing to check the spare room. There wasn't much to check. The door was locked. I kicked the bathroom door open and it bounced back on its hinges. Pulling on the light cord, its aged porcelain monstrosities were thrown into stark relief as the light clicked on. There was nowhere to hide in there either, unless some clever contortionist had removed the bath panel, secreted themselves behind it and screwed the panel back on from the inside out.

There was no intruder. Therefore Kat must have been lying. Before making my way back downstairs I lingered in her bedroom, stealthily opening the wardrobe door. It was full of clothes – Kat's presumably. I pulled some of the dresses aside to look at them. The first specimen was dark blue and sheer – an extravagantly detailed cocktail dress. It would look spectacular on her, the net hugging her curves and accentuating the ripe fullness of her body, but when would a social worker wear a dress like this? The dress next to it was plum-red and plush – devoré velvet and silk, and the others nestling alongside them lavishly sequined like the Moulin Rouge dancers would have worn. As with my uneasy emotions, the dresses had one thing in common. Their wearer was a seductress.

Further along were outfits more akin to the sort I'd seen Kat wearing in working mode. In between them were casual tops, skirts, jumpers, slightly ethnic, but all expensive. Even I could recognise designer labels. I'd seen them often enough on Margaret's clothes. So Kat had expensive – and exotic – tastes, and presumably a bank balance to afford them. That didn't fit with a social worker's role either.

'Is everything all right?' Her voice drifted querulously up the stairs. I quietly closed the wardrobe door and went out onto the landing. The old floral carpet felt sticky underfoot, as if it had borne too many dirty feet across it. The wallpaper was faded and out of date too. Kat stood at the bottom of the stairs looking anxiously up at me, straining to see. I realised I must be silhouetted by the landing light so she was unable to see my face clearly. I took advantage of the fact to study her.

'I'm fine and there's no-one here.' She visibly relaxed. 'Unless they're behind the locked door.'

'Locked door?' Her posture stiffened. 'Which locked door?'

'The spare room, presumably. Not your bedroom.'

She made an exclamation of annoyance and started up the stairs towards me. 'It's not locked. It's open. I put some washing over the dryer in there before I went out.' I remained where I was, watching her as she approached me, the knife now hanging loosely by my side. She was very good if she was acting. I stood aside when she reached me, thankful the wall steadied me. Her perfume and proximity made my head spin as usual. She carried on past me without stopping. The spare room door was painted mint green and chipped where the panelling met the beading. I wondered how I hadn't noticed the general air of impersonality and neglect before. Heather called me blind, but I wasn't completely oblivious, surely? Maybe the rosy glow of presumed intimacy had masked it. The whole place now seemed as dejected and abandoned as the place next door. It could even be the place next door. Unloved. *Temporary lodgings*, the little imp inside my head whispered. Paranoia draped itself round my shoulders like a cloak. *It's another façade*, it teased, *like Margaret's.* Did Kat really live here after all?

Kat was wriggling the door handle to and fro as I battled the mantle of insanity. It gave suddenly and burst open, taking her and her surprised, 'Oh!' with it. She turned the light on and even from where I stood I could see two things: the outline of the clothes horse draped with damp washing, and the fact that it was blowing gently in the breeze from the open window.

I pushed past her and entered the room, slashing irritably at the fluttering underwear and blouses on the clothes horse. It reminded me of the contraption Ma had sometimes used when washing day was too wet to get the essential things dried. Then it would stand in state in front of the coal fire and none of us – apart from Pop and the washing – would get warm. In the morning it would still be hogging the dregs of heat as we shivered, thin-ribbed and blue-skinned in our over-scrubbed cotton vest and pants as Ma doled out something temporary for each of us to wear until the rest had fluttered dry on the line in the yard or hung out of the window. The sheets usually took the window space and the clothes the yard. There had been times when the block of flats had looked like a patchwork itself when it had been a particularly wet wash day the day before. Then everyone's ma would have festooned their windows with an assortment of sheets, towels and tablecloths, turning the drab brown brick building into bunting. I pushed the distracting memory away with Kat's real time clothes horse. Apart from it, an unmade bed and a stack of unopened boxes, the room was empty. No assailant here either. I swung round and started back towards her at the door.

'Oh my God!' She backed out of the doorway, eyes on the knife as she recoiled. 'Don't, please don't …' her voice was high and panicky. I stopped.

'Don't what?' I asked.

'Nothing,' she mumbled.

I finished it for her. 'Don't hurt you.'

'No, no – just nervous because someone might have been in here.'

I retreated to the window and looked out, as much to cover my dismay as to examine what was outside.

'Did you leave the window open when you went out, Kat?' I asked, still offended.

'I, I can't remember …'

The back garden gate was hanging on its hinges but whether because it was broken or it had recently been flung open, I couldn't tell. There were scuff marks on the window sill and the drain pipe led straight down alongside the window. I leant against the wall next to the window – both her and the swinging garden gate within my peripheral vision. There was a certain similarity between the pair of them.

'Or the back gate?'

'I don't know.' She looked sheepish.

I put the knife carefully down near the foot of the bed.

'How about these? Were they here earlier?' I pointed to the marks on the window sill and waited for her to join me. She didn't move, just stood awkwardly in the doorway. I sighed and pushed the knife to the far end of the bed and out of my reach.

'Better?' I asked sarcastically.

'Sorry, I didn't mean … I just don't like knives.' She reluctantly moved close enough to examine the scuff marks, still eyeing the knife. 'I don't think there were any marks there before,' she added doubtfully.

'But you're not sure?'

She shook her head. 'But I'm sure now that I didn't leave the window open though.'

I studied her, sceptical she could so suddenly, and conveniently, remember now what suited the explanation that there had been an intruder. The sash window was old and heavy, catching on its way down where the wood was rotting away. It took effort to pull down and it made a grinding noise when it reached the sill. Unlikely anyone could have opened it quietly, but Kat was adamant she hadn't done it. My inner demons growled wildly at me – the same ones I'd heard regularly in the children's home. The ones that advised against sharing trust and confidences. The ones that cautioned me to self-preservation. Kat, for all her artless naivety and seductive simplicity, seemed anything but innocent now. The facts lined up in my head – conveniently the responsible adult for Danny, unexpectedly responsive to my inappropriate overtures, appealingly confessing her own sins so I reciprocated with mine, and suddenly tart and incisive once I'd allocated her a position of trust. And she'd come my way via Margaret.

Maybe paranoia made me wary, but instinct was suddenly telling me loud and clear she wasn't to be trusted for the moment. The over-reaction with the knife had been designed to make me feel awkward. Even the little charade on the doorstep could have been planned to do the same. I concentrated on extracting what I could without giving anything away myself.

'Well, whoever it was – if there was someone here – has gone now. Let's go and see what's left of your package.'

Kat looked at me suspiciously. 'You don't believe me, do you?'

'I don't disbelieve you Kat. I just said whoever or whatever is gone. I deal in facts, remember. The only ones we have at the moment are the ones downstairs on your table.'

She preceded me out of the room and I pulled the door to, taking the knife with me back to the kitchen.

'Sorry about your knickers.'

She burst out laughing. 'That's one for the court annals.'

'Don't quote me,' I quipped in reply, but nevertheless was disconcerted by her sudden change in mood. She lounged against the worktop, giggling, and the Kat I'd assumed I knew was back. How could she fear me one minute and then joke with me the next?

She opened the fridge and produced a bottle of wine, already half empty.

'Would you like a glass or are you driving?'

Everything went back on alert. She must have noticed my car wasn't outside when she returned from wherever she'd been. Through the kitchen window I could see her car parked directly in front of the house. The space either side of it stretched across the front of both neighbour's places, significantly empty. If I'd been driving it was obvious where I would have parked.

'A small one is fine.'

'You're not driving then?'

'Is that relevant?'

'No, not really.'

'Why ask then?'

She looked surprised. 'Are we arguing?'

'No, not really.'

She grimaced but filled two glasses and put the bottle back in the fridge. I watched, trying to determine which Kat had the upper hand now. I'd been aware of nuances and ambiguities in her before – I'd even remarked on the fact that she'd deliberately lied to me once and withheld what she knew another time but I'd discounted both occasions and tried to trust her implicitly – until now. My altered perception of the house could be explained away by immersion in self and focus on other concerns, but it wasn't simply the disparity between real and assumed. No, it was down to Kat herself. There was something inherently different about how she was behaving with me – in fact how she'd been behaving with me ever since the dismissal of Danny's case. Ella was just the excuse, it was Kat who was orchestrating the distance. Now it felt like she could be playing as complex a game with me as Win, Jaggers or Margaret.

I pointed to the doorway back to the lounge. Might as well see what had been sent to her whilst I figured out what was going on.

'Shall we see what they left behind then?'

She nodded, apparently not picking up on the trace of sarcasm I hadn't quite managed to suppress.

'Well, it looks untouched,' she commented innocently.

'Did you check what was in it before you went out, then?'

'Only cursorily.'

'So you *did* open it before I arrived?'

The naïve little girl reappeared. 'But I didn't look properly.' My alarm system screamed full alert. I flipped the top of the packaging aside with the end of my pen. 'Why are you doing that?'

'Caution.' She frowned. 'In case there's something I won't want to touch in there – or in case there's something I *shouldn't* touch in there.'

'*Shouldn't* touch?'

I studied her. She appeared genuinely bewildered.

'Kat, has it not occurred to you that someone is doing an elaborate job of muddying the waters with all of this, and possibly setting me up? My wife wanted to blackmail me. My sister was murdered in my kitchen. Very apposite of them to bring the dirt to my door, don't you think?'

'That's not a very nice way of describing your sister.' Her expression was openly antagonistic. 'She was a person, not a piece of trash. Why are you always so contemptuous of anyone who isn't the same social class as you? You're the only the same as them underneath – and look at your brother. He's not exactly to be trusted but you were happy enough to go along with him, weren't you?

I stared at her. 'Is that what you think of me?'

'Well, you were being rude to Mrs Tooley as well. Just because she wears curlers and lives in Kilburn – like me.'

'You don't wear curlers do you?' It fell flat. She glared at me. 'Kat, I'm not a snob.' She didn't reply, just fiddled with her glass. 'So since when have you been thinking this of me? I seem to have missed something fairly significant here at some point?'

She sighed. 'I don't really think you're a snob, Lawrence, but you're so, so … self-assured. Always know everything. I suppose it makes me feel inferior, and when people like that bitch you tell me is now your junior orders me around and you let her, or you'd rather confide in Heather Trinder, who also made it very clear you were out of my league, well …'

I allowed myself a brief moment of wry amusement at my own expense. *Always know everything.* Most of the time currently I felt completely in the dark and ignorant, but the old Lawrence automatically kicked in – the one who never admitted to failings.

'I think this is more your problem than mine, Kat.'

And I was irritated. We'd already done this one only a day or so ago. Why should everyone else's behaviour always be laid at my door? Ella was rude and supercilious. Kat projected it onto me. Win was shifty and obnoxious so Kat likened us because I'd had to agree to his way of dealing with Danny's problem until I'd found my own solution. Now she attributed Heather's heavy-handed methods to me too.

She shrugged, and took a slug of her wine. I watched it take effect. I had long acquaintance with the undesirable effects of alcohol and the bad ideas it encouraged. I put my glass down on the table. One of us needed to be sober, and for novelty's sake, if nothing else, tonight it should be me. Besides, it looked as if I was treading a tricky path all of a sudden. One false step would take me over the precipice with her – and not in the good way it had done before. 'I know you don't know me very well, but...'

She snorted at that. 'I don't know you at all, Lawrence. That's very clear now.'

'I think you'd better explain that.'

She put her glass clumsily down on the table next to mine, clinking them together. 'Cheers, Mr Juste. *To family likenesses.*'

'Family likenesses?'

'I know.'

The back of my neck tingled. 'You know what?'

'Do I really have to spell it out? The birth certificate. I figured it out.'

'What did you figure out?' I could feel the hot and cold of apprehension prickling across my skin.

'All this crap about making sure you don't carry the faulty gene along with Kimmy and Win. You're just trying to prove you're *not* related.'

'Why do you say that?'

'Because both yours and Win's birth certificates say father unknown. You're trying to prove you're not related to Kimmy so you don't get lumbered with Danny simply because you're his uncle and the only respectable one in the family.'

The relief swept over me like a cocaine rush, followed by shock waves of indignation and anger.

'I wouldn't say I'm the only respectable one. Emm, Jill and Binnie might dispute that assumption,' I said coldly.

She stared at me. 'I didn't mean they're not decent,' she looked shamefaced, 'but you're … Oh dear, I'm making a mess of this.'

I ignored the little girl lost look. 'And if you didn't look at anything in my office, how could you know about a birth certificate which I'd already put away in a drawer?'

Her jaw dropped. The booze had blurred logic for her and she'd made a fatal mistake. I realised too late I'd just admitted to a similar one but she was too loaded to notice. I could guess where the first half of the bottle had gone.

'I, I didn't mean to, but you never tell me anything. I didn't know if you were lying to me about it all. I'm sorry.'

We were back to where we'd been in the café, and her eventual admission of knowing about Margaret and the proposed adoption ruse, the complication of the stage-managed case against her brother and stalking me. I didn't know whether to set this indiscretion aside too or whether it was one too many amongst all the others. One thing at a time.

'So you had a look through my desk whilst you had the opportunity?'

'I'm sorry – and it *was* open. Wide open. I pushed it shut when I heard you coming downstairs.'

'And who do you think is Danny's father then?'

'Win,' she said quietly. 'That's why you're shielding him – and he's blackmailing you.'

'Jesus, Kat, I'm not shielding anyone, least of all Win. How have you come to that conclusion from what you've seen anyway?'

'Because of the birth certificate you had and the association between him and Kimmy. He was always being mentioned but his connection never explained. Then you wanted to go along with his suggestion for getting Danny off, awful though it was. It was like he had some kind of control over you, and now there's the drawings. Anyway, she explained it all to me.'

'She? Who's she? And what have you had explained to you? Christ if Heather is meddling in this too she can dissolve the partnership with my blessing!'

Kat laughed. 'Not Heather. Why would she be involved? She just told me you had other things on your mind when I rang the day after the funeral. It was obvious by things she meant *people*. Her.' She picked up her glass and drained it. Enough Dutch courage for both of us.

'If by her you mean Ella that's ridiculous. I spend my time in Chambers dodging her.'

'Well,' she sounded mollified. 'OK, but ...'

'Go on.'

'You're not going to like this.'

'I don't like any of it, Kat. What's one more thing?'

'Kimmy. Kimmy told me.'

'She's dead.'

'She told me before she died. That morning.'

'Why the hell didn't you tell me you'd seen her?'

'How could I? I was going to but then you told me she was dead and I couldn't say anything could I?'

'I'm not the Gestapo,' I paused, 'or the police,' I added as an afterthought.

Her eyes opened wide and momentarily I could see the whites encircling the darker iris.

'It's complicated.'

'You're telling me! So where did you see her and what did she tell you?'

'I met her in a café – but it doesn't really matter where. She didn't want it to be official but she told me to be careful of you. That there was more to you than met the eye. There were things about your past I didn't know. That you weren't telling me.'

'Oh, I get it. And did she tell you what they were?'

'No, but ... it's true though, isn't it Lawrence? You go so far and then you clam up. I only ever get part of the story. I've sensed it all along. You told me about the children's home, and about being bullied but not by whom to start with. You only told me that Wemmick and your childhood bully were the same person after you realised he and Margaret were linked. You told me Win was your brother, but not that Kimmy was your sister until you couldn't avoid telling me. You drip feed everything and in between the drips I don't know what the truth and what the lies are. Why wouldn't I believe her?'

'I might well ask *why would you*? If I don't tell you things it's because at the time you don't need to know them or maybe it's safer you don't. I'm not the only one to do that, though am I?'

'That's not fair. I didn't do it to trick you.'

'And neither have I – to trick you.'

She grimaced. 'We're not very good at understanding each other are we?'

'I'm beginning to see that understanding someone takes time and a lot of effort. It all depends how much of either you're prepared to put into it.'

It was as much a criticism of me as of Kat. I'd applied virtually no effort to understanding Margaret. If I had, perhaps I would have a very different perspective on things now.

'I'm sorry, Lawrence. You're right. Can we start being completely truthful with each other from now onwards?'

In my defence, I agreed with good intentions. It's just it's not so easy to tell the truth when it's wholly unacceptable is it? I didn't correct her assumption that Win was potentially Danny's father. For the time being it was as close to the truth as either of us could get. Win said he wasn't but I might be. Jaggers had implied I might not be but not who was. Kimmy had remained significantly silent about it, even hours before her death, and now could no longer be asked. There wasn't a truth to tell yet, so I didn't. I did want to know about Kimmy's other assertions about me though – and what or who had prompted her to share them with Kat.

'All right – so why tell me why Kimmy thought you should be careful of me?'

'Margaret,' was her one word reply, as if it explained everything. It probably did – everything and nothing. 'Before she was run over, of course. She told Kimmy to be careful of her brother, apparently. That's what she said. *"She told me to be careful of me brother – he ain't what he seems and he'll blow everyone out of the water one day."* She did a creditable imitation of Kimmy's Croydon twang, and shrugged her shoulders deprecatingly at my mock applause. 'My friends used to get me to mimic the Corrie characters when I was at school. I went into the wrong profession.' She picked up her empty glass and made unsteadily for the kitchen. 'So now do you see? I'm going to have another after that confession session – what about you? You're not driving, are you?'

'You already know I'm not. Where did you go before I arrived?'

Her full mouth twisted into a wry smile. 'Down the road, to watch.'

'Watch?'

'You arrive. See if I could figure you out.'

'And did you?'

'No.'

'And what prompted that? You seemed fine on the phone – *asked* me to come over, in fact.'

'What was in the package ...'

'You said you didn't look.'

'No, I said I *hardly* looked. It didn't take much to set me running.' She disappeared behind the door and I could hear the glug of the bottle as she poured another glass of wine. She reappeared at the door. Red this time. 'It's on the top.' She looked older and more world-weary; shadows I hadn't noticed before blossoming under her eyes. The crisp professional of earlier had become jaded. It was what alcohol did to you. I pushed the top flap of the wrapping aside and saw what she meant. The same picture as in Heather's parcel. Me attacking the unknown woman.

'And this is why you thought Win was blackmailing me?'

'Well, wouldn't you?'

'No, but then I know I didn't do anything of the sort.'

'I don't now ...'

'Now? Implying you did then?'

'No, I didn't really believe it but I wondered why anyone would want to make it look as if you had. And you'd told me about the case ten years ago, and how you turned a blind eye. It all started to make sense – Heather warning me off, that supercilious bitch warning me off, Kimmy warning me off. I thought it might be a threat – what would happen to me if I didn't keep clear of you. So I ran away. Then I felt silly and came back.'

'I don't think it's you being threatened, Kat.' I turned the paper over, not bothering with the pen now. There wouldn't be any prints on it. The sender was far too clever. 'On the contrary, I think the victim about to have the life squeezed out of them is far more likely to be me.'

10: Faith

The sex was exceptional. Maybe because for once I was sober and Kat was drunk. I didn't have to worry about hiding my feelings and she didn't worry about expressing hers and then regretting it later. And by the time she'd finished off the rest of the bottle of red, the little imp who liked to plague me at times like this taunted me she probably couldn't even remember who I was. I ignored it. I needed the fix of being wanted. Neediness is such a divisive emotion. If she'd been sober she would have seen how easily she could have controlled me through that need, without any manipulation at all. None of the sugar and ice, sweet and sour to keep me on my toes. Good job she wasn't. Afterwards I watched her sleep as I had the first time we'd made love. She was less dusky goddess and more fallen angel now. It made no difference to the uncomfortable lure she exerted, or whether I trusted her or not. But love had to be built on trust, didn't it? And trust was something I didn't seem able to find anywhere, or in anyone currently.

I couldn't sleep even though I was dog-tired. I lay next to her trying to mimic the regular movement of her breathing and listening to the gently snuffling snores alcohol produced, but that merely agitated me more. The furniture loomed unfamiliarly at me in the dark. I imagined the contents of the wardrobe again. It probably had a rational explanation, but the glitzy outfits at one end of it still needed explanation. How to approach obtaining it was a problem. It should be the least of my worries, but it nagged me as one I should give priority to. Appearances – it all kept coming back to that, and the versions of themselves the people I was dealing with allowed me to see. In the end I gave up and padded downstairs naked to make myself some coffee, knowing it would only exacerbate the insomnia, but feeling bloody-minded enough not to care. I would normally have put something on but my clothes were tangled into a mound with Kat's and I couldn't be bothered to attempt disentangling them in the dark. I amused myself by thinking that if Mrs Tooley peered in the window – and I wouldn't have put it past the nosy cow – she'd get a nasty surprise and have to rethink her designation of Kat as 'a nice girl'. In defiance I even deliberately stood in front of the kitchen window as I waited for the kettle to boil.

Mrs Tooley stayed in her bed, no doubt weighed down by her curlers and mean thoughts and I wandered back into the lounge with my coffee. We'd briefly looked at the meagre contents of Kat's package before allowing desire to take hold, but without enthusiasm. Kat had clearly been too drunk to focus and a quick review of them had led me to the conclusion they were only copies of a mix of what had already been sent to me and Heather. Nothing new. So what was the purpose behind them? I sat at the table, unpleasantly aware that the chair was covered in vinyl and sticking to my ass, but too lazy to find anything to substitute for it. The same defiant part of me that had posed in front of the kitchen window relished the inappropriateness of sitting naked in someone else's lounge in the middle of the night and looking at pictures of myself suffocating someone. How the mighty are fallen – or the timid grown fierce. I was glad, however, that Atticus was merely a character in a book, and unable to observe me in life – only in my mind.

I sorted the papers into piles. The drawings, of which there were three, were the same. The official paperwork – one – was the doctored birth certificate for me, and apparently inconsequential, but new was a list of three names; Emilia Juss, Kimberley Hewson and 'J'. How were they linked? I puzzled over that but couldn't think of any connection other than the obvious – me.

I set it to one side and examined the drawings first. I was sure the top one of me was identical to the one Heather had been sent – or as sure as I could be. The man wore the same wig, gown, winged collar and silk bands as had been depicted in it, the onlooker was still a child and the victim still had red finger nails. The only difference was that it was marked '3' in the top left-hand corner. The next one was a variation on the theme, and marked '4' in the same place. In this one the child onlooker was gone, but what looked like a piece of paper and a pencil were abandoned on the floor near the two scuffling figures – murderer and victim. The paper was covered in lines – like print – but too small to read, if indeed it was anything more than artistic licence. The third picture was of the wig, gown, winged collar and silk bands, drawn as if left in a neat pile on the floor, and a sprinkling of red droplets lying around them. The 'paper' had gone, but the pencil remained, with an arrow rising up from it. The drawing itself was labelled '5'. I puzzled over them. The first thing that struck me was that drawings number one and two were missing. So this package wasn't as intact as Kat had pronounced it to be – or she had already removed them. The arrow on drawing number five was emphatic. It made me want to turn the page over and see what was on the back. I did. Nothing – a complete blank. I turned it back again. If it wasn't pointing to something overleaf then maybe it was indicating there were others to follow, or that it should be viewed as part of a series, '*keep going*'. But there was nothing to move on to.

Or maybe it was cyclical – *go back to the start?* But I didn't have the start. The first two drawings from the start, in fact. I examined drawing number three again, trying to imagine what might have preceded it. Impossible to say, given the enigmatic identity of the artist. I placed three, four and five alongside each other, looking at them episodically. What were they saying? What had happened? Murderer and victim meet, plus witness; then the 'murder' occurs and finally the artist leaves but the props are left behind.

Shit! I had it. Props. Someone was orchestrating this and Margaret's finger nail fragment was a prop in the play. That meant she hadn't necessarily even been where it implied she'd been. Someone had placed it at the scene of the crime in order to incriminate her, but she was no more guilty of that crime than I was of the one in the drawings. We were both allocated roles in a play, but who was the playwright – and to what end? Margaret might have been inserted into the evidence of the Johns case but no-one was seeking to pursue it other than me. It was closed, filed away and forgotten. I'd only resurrected it because of the connections that defending Danny's case had kept making to it. It didn't make sense, but I was definitely missing two of the clues – drawings one and two. They'd either been omitted on purpose or had been taken out. There were two possibilities for the latter. Kat, and the unknown window opener, but I didn't believe her claim that she hadn't opened the window, so it boiled it back down to one possibility. Kat was lying to me.

I shuffled the drawings together again and turned my attention to the birth certificate. Nothing new on that either – for me – but for Kat it should have rung all sorts of alarm bells. If she'd drawn the inference that Win was Danny's father from the version of the certificate she'd seen in my package, how could she have missed the possibility that I could equally well be it from this? She hadn't even commented on the similarity between the two. She'd had a lot to drink by the time we'd got to this particular page but she hadn't been blind drunk by any means. I left it to one side and placed the list in front of me. Emm, Kimmy and 'J', whoever 'J' was. I considered the possibilities for 'J'; Jaggers, John Wemmick, Juss – Win, Juste – me, Johns – the case, Jonno – the man, or 'J' my black-edged card sender. It could refer to any of us – or be something completely different.

I gave up then, exhaustion finally catching up with me despite the coffee, half of which I'd allowed to grow cold and congealed in the mug. I had the presence of mind to fold up the birth certificate and shove it inside the packaging. If Kat hadn't remarked on it yet, I wasn't going to leave it under her nose. The part of me that tipped the wink at fair play accepted that she might still undo the packaging and find it. Far more likely she'd simply bundle it up and throw it away, or ask me to in the morning. Then I would remove it. I didn't even attempt to rationalise it in terms of principles or honesty. It had none of either to it.

I left the rest of the papers strewn across the table and slipped back into bed beside her. She stirred and rubbed up against me. The dying man made his last request and feasted like a king, principles entirely abandoned. In the morning it would be very different, I mused as I rolled away from her later on and allowed sleep to finally take me over the edge and down, down into the precipice full of bloodied nails, muffled accusations and a tapestry woven from twisted and broken bodies.

Kat woke me just after ten with more coffee.

'I take it you couldn't sleep?' She put the mug clumsily on the bedside cupboard next to me. It spilled and left a dirty brown ring around the bottom. I rubbed my face and struggled to make sense of my surroundings. She went round to the other side of the bed and dragged the curtains open. The sun streamed in, waxy and golden even long before the day had reached its peak. The curtains hung limply either side of the window, the vivid paisley pattern dull against the greater brilliance of the azure sky outside. I pulled myself up and leaned against the pillow. It sunk under my weight and I slid back down with it. Pretty much how I felt now – deflated. 'The papers from the parcel are spread everywhere,' she explained. 'I assume that was you?'

'Oh, yes. I thought a bright idea might be born in the darkness of night.' I struggled out of the collapsing pillows and sat upright, the head board cold and hard against my back. That was vinyl too. I leaned forward and it peeled away from me, seeming to take a layer of my skin with it. I stuffed a pillow behind me and leaned back again. I picked up

the mug to drink and it dripped on my naked stomach. It was too hot but I
didn't care. It woke me up, but one sip was enough; bitter as well as
boiling.

'And did it?'

'No, other than we're being fed clues to follow. Are you sure
everything that was there when you first opened it was still there when we
looked at it together?' She cocked her head to one side and looked
strangely at me. I silently cursed myself. Jesus I needed to think this
through better. I'd just primed her to question where the birth certificate
had gone. 'The drawings,' I explained hastily. 'They're numbered, but
one and two are missing.'

Her expression cleared. 'Ah that explains it. I *was* thinking there was
more there yesterday than today.'

'So you think there were more drawings there when you first looked,
and less now?'

'Maybe. Five drawings you say?'

I hadn't, but clearly she'd checked for herself. 'It looks as if there
should be, unless they were deliberately left out to make you wonder
about them.'

'Me?'

'Well, the parcel was sent to you, so its contents were intended to
pique your interest, weren't they? Whoever is sending them had already
got mine.'

'Oh, I see. Yes.' She sat on the side of the bed and studied me. She
looked fresh and unaffected by the booze of the night before. Youthful
constitution. I envied her it. She was wearing the same peasant blouse
she'd worn the last time I'd been there, hanging loose at the neck so I
could see the suggestion of cleavage where the tie was barely knotted.
Christ, she didn't need to try to seduce me. I could already feel my body
responding under the bedclothes. I thought of ice and Judge Crawford and
Margaret, and the erection collapsed. 'But why are they trying to get my
attention?'

'As back up? If you're involved, I have to be too.'

'Do you?' She tried to hide the pleased little smile but it crept across
her face nevertheless.

'Kat, you know I do.' She grinned. She reminded me of a child with a
treat, eyes wide, cheeks stained apricot blush under the brown.

'Well, I didn't think so last night – or not to begin with.' She winked
and the inference was lewd. 'I thought I was going to have to do the

dance of the seven veils to seduce you at one point, you were so cool with me.' I was surprised. Something dispassionate and objective inside me kicked in and crushed the neediness of the night before. It helped with broaching the subject of her unusual wardrobe of clothes.

'Have you got anything that would do as a costume then?' I nodded towards the massive cupboard. She half turned and laughed. 'Oh probably. Don't all girls?' I didn't reply. She swung round suddenly and studied me. 'You've looked, haven't you?'

'For mysterious intruders,' I agreed.

'They're not mine. Mine are the boring things up the other end.'

'Whose are the rest, then?'

She chewed on a nail. 'Oh God, this just gets worse.' She paused, eyeing me over the bitten finger. 'It'll sound weird.'

'Weird is becoming the norm for me. Fire away.' I settled more comfortably against the pillows.

She hesitated. I waited. 'OK,' she said defiantly at last, 'they're your wife's. Margaret's.'

'Margaret's?' I was incredulous. 'Why the hell have you got a wardrobe half-full of Margaret's clothes? And why the fuck that sort?'

'I don't know why, Lawrence. Suppose she asked me to, OK? Yes, that was it. When she was sorting out the case for Alfie, she asked. I was indebted to her and there didn't seem anything wrong with it. A little strange maybe, but that was all. People have strange sides to them they want to keep to themselves sometimes. I assumed she felt she could trust me because I had to trust her over Alfie.' I pictured my mouth hanging open with shock and tried to shut it, only to find it was already clamped into a grim line. 'And actually, the boxes in the other room are hers too,' she added nervously.

'Jesus, Kat, what the hell is going on here? Last night you wanted complete honesty and now I find out you've been storing my wife's possessions.'

'I am being honest. I'm telling you now, aren't I? I could lie or say anything – I'm a drag artist or I have a sequin fetish. You wouldn't know if it's the truth or not.'

'No, I wouldn't – not about anything. Why haven't you told me any of this before?'

'I didn't know how to. I thought you would think I'd been targeting you; stalking you or something kinky. I wanted you to get to know me before I told you about it.'

I was hardly in a position of strength, naked in her bed, having hidden the birth certificate from her and withholding my potentially more personal involvement in Danny's creation from her, but none of that registered then. Only the squirming in my gut that I'd felt the night before when I wondered whether she was playing games with me. The prop master might indeed even be Kat, with her ready supply of other surprises to hand. I put the coffee carefully back onto its ring on the bedside cupboard.

'I think, Kat, we need to establish some guide lines where honesty is concerned. Firstly, honesty means telling the truth,' She wasn't fazed by the sarcasm.

'Like you said to Danny – that sometimes means only telling what you want someone to know, not everything that you could. We can all play that game, Lawrence.'

'Honesty does seem to be a problem between us.'

'Doesn't it!' She flared. She got up off the bed and the springs bounced, taking me with them. I rolled onto my side and out of the bed with as much dignity as I could and looked for my underwear. It had been kicked under the bed. She watched me from the door and I felt uncomfortably exposed, every slack muscle mocking me. By the time I'd found my trousers and was buttoning my shirt, she'd softened. 'But it shouldn't be,' she added quietly.

'No, it shouldn't be, but maybe we need to find out our own truths before we try to understand each other's.'

'What does that mean?'

'It means I have a mystery to solve and you would seem to be part of it.' I found my shoes and pulled them on. She watched me silently. I straightened my tie. 'For a start, there's the names on the list. You were sent them for a reason.'

'In the package?' She paused as if considering whether to tell me. I nodded. 'If I tell you can we stop arguing?' I stared at her. She could have been Danny, childishly plea-bargaining. Her quixotic nature confused me.

'I didn't think we were – arguing. I was merely considering what to do next, since every day seems to bring a new revelation about you and my wife.' She flinched but said nothing before eventually grimacing and shrugging.

'It's a list of Danny's visitors the morning before he disappeared. I worked that out straight away.'

'How?'

'The children's home has to keep a record of visitors. I asked about it after you went back to Chambers. Those are the names on the list.'

'And "J" is?'

'Well, you.' She was surprised. 'Or I assumed it was you – it merely said "Juste" in the book at the children's home. Who else could it be? And I'm not the only one with secrets to confess, Lawrence. You're far better at keeping them than me!'

She flung out of the room and stomped melodramatically downstairs. She was right on both counts. We were having an argument and keeping secrets was definitely my forte at the moment, even if they were also revelations for me. It didn't seem a good time to ask to look in the boxes she was storing for Margaret in the spare room, but later on ... I added them to my own list of things to pursue.

11: Hope

Hope is a small time shyster, goading you into committing to more than you should. I'd thought I was getting somewhere with Kat, only to be thrown back into the pot of pretence. Who was hiding what from who, and who was doing it best? The revelation about Margaret and the secret wardrobe of call girl clothes Kat kept for her made my stomach turn, but Kat's would no doubt be turning over and over too if she'd made the connection the doctored birth certificate I'd hidden could have provided her with. I swept the packaging and it up as I left, telling her I'd put it with mine but not to tell the police about it. She began to protest and then clammed up, plainly trying to avoid another 'argument' between us. I couldn't decide if that was a good or a bad thing. Good in as much as she was trying to stop us from tearing each other to shreds, which must mean she wanted us to still be on speaking terms, at least – or bad because she had more to hide and didn't want to risk me probing.

She shoved the rest of papers into her own drawer as I left – in the fifties style sideboard at the back of the lounge – but agreed I could claim Margaret's boxes when I could get back over in a re-fuelled car. The sideboard was the one thing I'd remarked on each time I'd been at her place and which hadn't changed in my perception. Maybe that was because it looked so similar to the one we'd had in the flat when I was a child – so much so I could almost envisage its contents. Of course the contents would be Kat's contents not my childhood ones, but nevertheless it made it real – solid, when everything else seemed to be shifting. Perhaps last night I should have examined what Kat's version of the contents were but I'd been riding on the high of sex and misconception. It was only this morning that I'd reverted to suspicion. Too late now anyway as I was striding self-righteously out of her front door, and realising as I did so that I had no change on me after feeding the Tube machine nearly all the coins remaining in my pocket last night. Damn! I decided to walk, even though that would take almost two hours. It would clear my head and give me thinking time. I could lose myself more easily in the steady flow of pedestrians on the street than in the huddle on the Tube where I risked being scrutinised and matched to another newspaper spread merely because of the obligatory proximity. I also had to stop off and cancel Margaret's partnership bank card. It nestled in my pocket alongside my redundant car keys and two ten pence coins – inert, but mysteriously active even though it had apparently been in my possession ever since Margaret had 'died'. One for the bank to solve, not me for once.

I made my way toward Kilburn High Street. It was a tired affair filled with ethnic clothing shops, out-of-date electrical retailers and sprinkled with small grocery shops. I hadn't eaten anything since yesterday, or drunk much of Kat's slopped coffee this morning. My stomach growled irritably. It matched my mood. I put my head down and ignored the temptations of the café that I passed frying bacon and allowing the aroma to escape the half-open door by trying to piece together where the contents of the packages might be leading.

Cancelling the bank card was simple. No questions, no comments. I handed it over. They cut it up. They promised to make enquiries and report back. I promised to make a complaint if they didn't. At least the partnership bank account should be secure now. I left the bank and set off in the direction of Chelsea. The pavement thickened with passers-by the further into the centre I got, and the traffic built, adding more expensive cars to the throng of beaten-up Fords and the ubiquitous white vans. I lost myself in trying to piece together what Margaret or Jaggers might be planning next to make use of otherwise wasted time. It wasn't until I nearly stepped in front of a sleek black Merc with opaque windows that I dragged myself back to the real world. I waved an apology and waited for the pedestrian crossing to indicate I could walk. Three blocks further on, what seemed like the same Merc cruised past again. My attention caught and snagged on it. Coincidence. I trudged on, a blister bubbling up on my right foot, and my feet beginning to ache. The Merc stopped at the lights just ahead. I made to cross, belatedly following the crowd, but it revved, making me step back abruptly. The lights changed from red and amber to green and it swept away, hooting at me. Arrogant bastard!

My mood changed from reflection to irritation. The blister on my right foot was sore and I still had another couple of miles to go before I reached the mews. The Merc idled past again. Where the hell had it come from this time? It slowed as it drew alongside me, appearing to kerb crawl and holding the traffic up behind it. It stayed there, keeping pace with me for several minutes. The hairs on the back of my neck started to prickle. I slowed. It slowed. I broke into a half jog, and it sped up. I detoured and it reappeared at the end of the side road I'd shortcut down, loitering at the far end as I hesitated half way along the road. It was waiting for me. Stupid! Now there was no-one else around. I should have stayed on the main road. At least there was some protection from the crowds there. I waited, at a stand-off as the Merc idled. I could feel the sweat forming under my arms, sticking my shirt to my jacket and both to me. My heart was racing. Was this it? Was this going to be another hit and run, even though Jaggers hadn't recouped his losses from me yet? I debated running in the other direction, but I guessed the Merc would reappear at the other end of the road just as quickly. What now? Panic churned my stomach over until a group of three Asian women, clad in brightly coloured headscarves and pushing a pushchair with a variety of other errant children trailing after them, unexpectedly turned down the road and overtook me. I speeded up and followed, staying within mere paces of them, using them as cover. One of the women turned and gave me the once over but my dark suit and tie saved me from being labelled a pervert. The Merc pulled slowly away as we reached the end of the road and I completed the rest of the trek home along the main roads without sighting it again, but still nervous of every dark car passing me by.

The blister burst just as I opened my front door and stepped inside, relieved the mews had been empty of passers-by. The carpet of rubbish from the postman didn't include anything black-edged or parcel-shaped and I relaxed. I hadn't managed to put anything into a good order in my mind during the walk, but there was something I knew I should do. The list of Danny's visitors that had been in Kat's package worried me. She obviously hadn't been concerned by it because she'd assumed 'J' was me. I was because I knew it wasn't. I also had my suspicions who the exciting little artist 'J' enthused about was now, and that either meant Danny was with them, or Danny had given them the drawings. Either way, there was contact between the Wemmicks and Danny, and that made me afraid for him. After all, his mother had only recently turned up dead and all she'd apparently done was have her name used to send the parcels. The little artist was helping create the contents of them – a dangerous and expendable position to be in once the job was done, surely? I couldn't do much about that for the moment but I could do something about the list. Why Emm? Surely the rancour she'd expressed when we first met and she described how Kimmy had stolen Jonno away from her would preclude her from wanting to visit the boy she thought of as his son, even if Kimmy was now dead? As strong as the ties of family might be, some emotions were still stronger.

I showered, changed my clothes, and went to fill a can with petrol. It took a further two hours to get the car roadworthy by the time I'd taxied to the nearest petrol station, filled the container and taxied back. As I steadied the container whilst it emptied it into the tank, I surveyed the car with my usual sense of satisfaction at its solidity and worth. Its tan leather interior was as plump and luxurious as it would have been new, marred today only by a dark-edged blot on the driver's seat. It didn't register fully until I was tipping the petrol can almost vertical to drain the last dregs. I put it down with a jolt. Habit alone made me delay long enough to screw on the petrol cap before bolting round to the driver's door and unlocking it. The card sat smugly and at a gently rakish angle in the middle of the seat, but it had none of the rashness of something thrown hastily down. It had been carefully positioned there. On top of my copy of *To Kill a Mocking Bird*.

But I'd given it to Danny! My stomach turned over. Danny wouldn't have parted with the book voluntarily. He took it everywhere. It had even accompanied him into court, according to Kat. What had happened to him that he and the book were no longer together? Christ! Maybe he wasn't with Margaret after all. Panic took over where complacency had been before. I'd assumed. I had a habit of assuming, even though recently I was realising most of my assumptions were wrong. I unlocked the car and grabbed the book, heart pounding. Maybe there was ransom note inside or some other demand? I was taken aback. Just the book. Dog-eared and roll-edged, it looked like my copy but it wasn't. Mine had my name carefully inscribed on the fly leaf. Danny had insisted on writing his underneath when Kat and I had returned him to the hospital after our trip on the big wheel. I'd considered it as claiming ownership at the time – his first 'real' book. Or perhaps it was a statement of intent, as it had been for me – to be another Atticus Finch in my own small way. This copy had no names inside it, just a cryptic little note. *'To help you find what you're looking for.'* All the things I was looking for tumbled though my head – Danny, absolution, forgiveness, understanding, escape from Jaggers. I could sense the mischievous enjoyment of its donor, anticipating what it would do to my peace of mind. This mockery of my deepest held belief wouldn't help me find any of them. I turned to the card instead, to see what my tormentor had to prod me with this time.

'Such an inspiring story. The truth is indeed sometimes stranger than fiction if you get past the plotting. You never really understand a person until you consider things from their point of view, do you? Can you do that Lawrence A Juste? Find the right page so you can right the final chapter.

Be in touch soon – J.'

In the top right-hand corner the tiny hanged man dangling from a noose was almost complete, now missing only his arms. We'd played it as a child; drawing in the gallows, the victim and their appendages as we won or lost elements of another game. It implied an impish sense of humour – in the hanged man, the cat and mouse game the sender was playing with me and their play on words. 'Right' not 'write'. And the A of my adopted middle name was outsized compared to the rest of it – taunting me. *Mocking me.* The corner of one of the pages of the book was bent over. Turning to it I found it was in chapter three; Atticus explaining to Scout how to understand others and their motives by pretending to climb into their skin and imagine she was them. Mocking me again, because it was the one thing I seemed completely incapable of doing.

However, satirising me was one thing but this was in my bloody car! I flung the card and book onto the passenger seat, sliding into the driver's position and slamming the gears angrily into reverse. The clanging of the metal container as I collided with it reminded me I hadn't moved it out of the way. I stopped and got out, tossed the container into the boot, slammed it shut, mentally apologised to the car for taking out my fury out on it, revved and made my way more slowly to Emm's place on the Fulham Road. It was now nearing three o'clock and I hoped she'd still be there – not taking the afternoon off. I guessed she would. She'd struck me as the kind of business owner who kept everything very firmly under control.

I found a spot on a meter and fed it with coins. It allowed me two hours. Long enough to find out what my sister had gone to see my nephew about, I imagined. Sure enough Emm was hovering beady-eyed in the shop as two women collected an armful of clothes and an assistant dragged around behind them. She eyed me equally beady-eyed as I entered. At least I looked the part. Margaret had dressed me well whilst refining me to her requirements.

The shop was as unlike my roots as I was now: sophisticated, expensive, elitist. This year's designs only. Definitely Heather, and probably Margaret if she were around. The window was framed with white ostrich feathers and crystal glass cut into diverse shapes hanging amongst the waving white fronds. The feathers gave it the effect of a window full of flying diamonds. Mary and her origami birds. I wondered if Emm had got the idea from her.

'Hello Emm, is it all right for me to drop by like this?'

She looked down her nose at me. 'Two visits in almost as many weeks? I am the lucky one.'

'If it's inconvenient ...'

She shrugged. 'No, they won't buy anything. They never do when they want to try so much on. Just have to watch none of it goes walking out with them when they go.'

'Oh.' I considered the two women with the armfuls of clothes. They looked chic and well-heeled. Chelsea set. 'Do you get much shop-lifting?'

'Do you think I do?'

As a business woman she would have made Heather's twin. 'No.' I said decisively with a small laugh.

'One thing you're actually right on then.' She rolled her eyes towards an elaborate white panelled door at the rear of the shop. 'If you want to talk in private, I'll turn the sign over and we can go and get a cuppa in the office. Katy can mind what the *could I justs* are up to.'

'Could I Juste?' I wondered why she was using my surname.

'*Could I just* try this on...' she completed sarcastically. 'Oh I'm charm personified to them, don't worry.' She went over to the shop door and flicked the sign hanging on the back of it over with her left hand as she slipped the bolt with her right. It read *open* in elegant script slanted at a jaunty angle on the side facing into the shop. 'I'll just tell Katy – but go on through.' She gestured to the panelled door.

Beyond the door was another Emm; an office as immaculately arranged as the shop was tasteful. Box files lined the shelves on one wall, with year ranges written neatly on their spines. Next to them a range of catalogues displayed brightly coloured text – Vogue, Designers Guild, Peekaboo. I went over to take a better look at the kind of merchandise my younger sister regularly sold.

'Peekaboo is underwear. Please don't tell me you're like all men and a fetishist about it.' I heard her push the door shut behind her and we were engulfed in silence broken only by the edge to her voice. I spun round. She had her hands on her hips. She obviously intended looking fierce but ironically she looked small and vulnerable to me. A pink Barbie doll with flaxen fair waves and a frown.

'I have no idea. I've never even thought that much about women's underwear. Margaret sorted her own out.'

'Oh my God. That's even worse. How old are you? Victorian era?'

I laughed. 'Just not a very womanly man, Emm.'

She made a moue of dismissal and went to perch by the window. In my curiosity over the catalogues I'd failed to see the bay window that faced onto the back garden had been turned into a window seat. Emm had style as well as perspicacity.

'None of you are really. What have you come to see me about?'

I adopted the same business-like tone as her. 'Danny. You went to see him a couple of days ago.'

'Who says so?'

'The list of visitors at the children's home.'

'Oh. OK. I did. Why do you need to know? I thought he was off the hook now. You aren't still acting for him.'

'I am in a way – now he's a relative. I'm acting in his best interests – and he's gone missing again since Kimmy died.' She'd been fiddling with a tassel on one of the cushions, paisley like the curtains and spread at Kat's but classier – exclusive as opposed to mass-produced.

'Kimmy's dead?' She was open-mouthed. 'When?'

'Two days ago. Didn't you know?'

'No, Binnie didn't tell me.' I digested that. Did it suggest Binnie was the lynchpin between siblings in Sarah's absence, or just for Jill and Emm?' I wanted to ask but her closed expression implied I'd be wasting my time. It was the sort of family politics you learned about through being part of it.

'Oh. Well … perhaps she was thinking about Sarah's arrangements more.'

'Sarah's arrangements? What arrangements?'

'Her funeral.' I watched Emm's face crumple in on itself. 'I'm sorry. Didn't you know that either?'

'No. I knew it was imminent but why did no-one tell me? We weren't close but she was my sister.' The way she said it made me feel like Sarah hadn't been my sister. On reflection I was struck again by the fact that in many ways she hadn't. Do blood ties surpass distance, or do they need to be continually reinforced by presence? The little I knew of emotional ties suggested they grew from continuity and familiarity, not because of a similar name or a common ancestry.

'I'm really sorry, Emm. Two bits of bad news in one day. I would have broken it better if I'd known.' She sniffed and produced a tissue from her skirt pocket. It had a pastel floral design printed on it. Fleetingly I marvelled at how the poverty-grown girl from Croydon was design-coordinated even down to her disposable commodities. The effect was stunning, even to my unappreciative eye. Appearance, as I'd remarked so often recently, was what made you what you were. The memory of the hangers full of gaudy costumes in Kat's wardrobe – all ascribed to Margaret – tagged along behind it. The alternate persona they suggested for the Margaret I'd known was curious in the extreme.

'It's Sarah that upsets me – and not being told. So how did it happen?'

'Sarah or Kimmy?'

'Don't be daft. Kimmy of course. I know what was what with Sarah.'

'She was knifed it seems.'

'Where? On the pull?'

'No,' I replied sharply, feeling an unexpected burst of indignation on Kimmy's part. 'In my kitchen, actually.'

'Oh my God, you didn't, did you?'

'You're the second person whose automatically assumed that,' I paused, thinking that maybe I ought to amend that to third, given Fredriks' pointed look when he suggested I stayed close to home. 'Why does everyone think I'm a budding serial killer?'

'Well they say most killings are domestics, don't they, and if she was in your kitchen … I wouldn't blame you, if you had. Nasty piece of work, she was. Fine with you one minute and then slagging you off like a fishwife the next. A right bitch. Shame about the kid, though. He seemed OK.'

'Danny.'

'Danny, yes.' Her face over-shadowed.

'So why did you go to see Danny?'

'Well like you said, he's kin, isn't he?'

'I didn't think that bothered you where Kimmy's side of kin was concerned?'

She fiddled with the cushion tassel again. 'God, I need a joint,' she announced suddenly. 'I don't suppose you do too, do you? Smoke, I mean.' My face must have been one of those pictures Heather found so illuminating. Emm found it amusing. 'Of course you wouldn't,' she laughed. 'Far too improper for such an upright legal eagle as you. The kind who sleeps with his juvenile client's responsible adult, and hides his unsuitable family from the world.' She was openly mocking me, mouth twisted into an angry little half-smile. I attempted court cool, even though she was niggling me.

'Is that what Danny told you when you went to see him?'

'Oh for God's sake, Kenny – Lawrence – whoever you want to be; can't you ever let the front down and react? I'm trying to needle you and you stay as cool as a cucumber. Jesus Christ, you've just told me two of your sisters have died – one stabbed in your own kitchen. I'm accusing you of gross impropriety and all you can do is question me like I was in the dock!'

'Why are you trying to needle me?' Like Kat did. Was it something women did? It was one female characteristic that had been absent in Margaret then. Or maybe she had, in her own way – subtle, understated and sly – and I'd been too obtuse to see it. That seemed now to have been a feature of our relationship; her manipulating and me blind to it.

'Because I'm trying to find out about the man who suddenly turns up out of the blue, announcing he's my brother, directly preceding my family collapsing around me. Like I was trying to find out what kind of child Jonno produced, and if we'd stayed together whether he would have been anything like the child I would have liked to have had.' She flung off the window seat and rummaged in her desk drawer. She produced a half empty packet of cigarettes and threw the rest of the drawer contents onto the desk until she found a lighter. The tang of cigarette smoke made my eyes smart as she inhaled deeply and then blew it out with an 'ahh'. 'There, that's why I went to see him, sad bitch that I am. You asking all those questions and Jill telling you about Jonno and me, and how Win split us up brought it all back. I had to see what the kid was like, that was all.'

'And what did you make of him?' I asked quietly. She dragged hard on the cigarette again and exhaled, talking through the smoke. She did it exactly like Kimmy had when I'd interviewed her.

'He's a nice kid.' She flicked ash into a coffee mug that had been left on the edge of the desk. I watched, taken aback by what seemed so out of character for her. She noticed my pointed look. 'Katy will think its Jill,' she commented. 'Jill's slovenly habits are very useful at times when I can't be bothered to be *naice*.' She grinned, and it was the first genuine smile I'd seen on her. 'Don't you ever do things you shouldn't?'

I immediately thought of Margaret's pet hate. 'Like leave the toilet seat up?' She burst into a belly laugh and it was infectious. It felt as natural as the childish enjoyment of tickling her and Jill into writhing heaps when they were toddlers. 'Don't all men?' Recklessly I added another confession, 'Or pretend I'm unavailable if there's something Margaret wants to do and I don't.' She raised her eyebrows at me. 'I work a lot of evenings,' I added, noticing I'd slipped into present tense. '*Worked* a lot of evenings.'

'Ooh, bad boy!' She made a mock disapproving face. No, it wasn't bad at all really. It was more a sign of the dull self-imposed repression of our lives together. The part of me that had spent a life observing and not living in case living revealed something of me to anyone else observing. Margaret and I lived in mutual co-observance at an agreed distance, neither touching each other's lives other than from necessity. I'd never tried to appreciate her, and she never insisted. Emm didn't comment. She concentrated on dissolving distance – and formality.

'Have you ever done something really mean?' I shrugged. Being inconsiderate was bad enough, wasn't it? She giggled. 'Like stayed in the loo when you know someone's busting …' she winked, and I recoiled at the implied turn to vulgarity. Not something I was used to or allowed. Margaret would have made it very clear she disapproved – but then rebellion took hold. If Margaret had secretly maintained a wardrobe full of tart's clothes, why shouldn't I now savour a ribald joke? I no longer had to temper my behaviour to meet her requirements. I'd certainly done that more than once to Gregory, as he waited patiently but desperately outside the gents at Chambers. It had made up in a small way for the many times he'd watched me squirm as he wilfully brought a client through when he knew I was unprepared for them and mournfully enjoyed my discomfort as he left me to it.

'Maybe,' I admitted.

'Me too,' she grinned conspiratorially. 'I used to do it all the time to my boss at work before I got the shop. Just to see how long she could last. She could be a bit of a bitch, but not when she was jigging around outside the loo.' I found myself suddenly wanting to laugh out loud. The urge triumphed and I surprising even myself with the gusto of it. Emm raised her eyebrows and then joined in. We laughed until absurdity exhausted us.

'That's the man I wanted to meet,' she said when the laughter had subsided.

'And what do you make of him?'

'He's probably OK too.' She pursed her lips and cocked her head to one side. Distantly the shop bell tinkled. 'They'll have gone without buying,' she commented. 'Katy will be asking about the closed sign in a minute.' Katy's head appeared around the door seconds later.

'They've gone – didn't buy anything. Do you still want the closed sign up or shall I turn it round again?' Emm made an *I told you* so face at me and smiled wryly.

'No, it was only so no-one else came in whilst you were keeping an eye on them. Business as usual now.' Katy nodded and disappeared.

'You know your staff and your clients well,' I commented, impressed.

'I know people,' she replied. 'You can't watch them day in, day out as I do and not know what they're thinking even when they don't think they're thinking. Everything someone does tells you something about them – even down to the way they pick things up and put them down.'

'Really? So what have you picked up about me?'

'You're afraid.'

I thought about that for a moment. 'Afraid? I don't think so. Pissed off with a variety of things at the moment, and anxious about some, but I don't think I'm afraid.' She observed me wryly as I spoke, allowing a short pause to settle between me talking and her replying in which we considered each other.

'There are different kinds of afraid, Lawrence. There's gut-wrenching *I'm gonna shit myself* – the type you get when you're watching a horror movie. There's *oh my God, please don't let that happen to me* – like if you think you're going to get mugged. And then there's yours. Afraid of living. Or of what happens to you if you *do* live – the things that go wrong, or make you feel bad, or don't work out. Failure. Pain. Disappointment. That's being afraid too.'

'I hadn't thought of life that way before.'

'Hadn't you?'

She was right. She did know people. Disconcertingly, she'd described the hidden part of me – without even knowing me. When I thought about Kat, that was how I felt – exposed and afraid, whilst simultaneously longing for what she offered. Perhaps that also explained how I felt about Danny. And Margaret.

'I hadn't really come to talk about me.' She looked disappointed. 'More about you.'

'And Danny?' she added.

'Well yes, but in some ways he's incidental because I wanted to know about why you went to see him – and this divide between all of you; Win,

Binnie, you and Jill. Sarah seemed to be your only common ground.'

'All of *us*, you mean. *We* include you, whether you like it or not.'

'Binnie implied otherwise.'

She was dismissive. 'Binnie's just pissed at everything.'

'Why? It was such a long time ago.' I thought of Kat and her fresh starts. 'Isn't there such a thing as forgive and forget?' Then I wished I'd held my tongue. Forgive and forget must be the most difficult issue for Emm. I expected a cutting reply but yet another version of Emm responded.

'I guess you do. That was the other reason I went to see Danny. I needed to see what might have been mine, and let it go, because it wasn't and never would be. Forgive and forget, like you say. I did a lot of thinking about Jonno and me, and what happened. You're right there too. It was a long time ago. I wouldn't be here doing this if it hadn't happened the way it did. Spurred me on to go to college and the like. And actually I'm happy. All that stuff about men and what arseholes they are – it's more for Jill's sake than mine. She's had a shit time. After Jonno, I didn't bother about men much. I just got on with this. You change. Things change you. The more people I watch coming through the shop, and find out about their life, the more I realise that.' She laughed. 'I could write a book, me!'

'So that was all? All you went to see him about?'

'Yeah – and I felt sorry for him, being in there again. Poor kid.'

Something else suddenly struck me. 'But if you didn't know about Kimmy, how did you know he was back in care?'

She stared at me as if I was mad. 'You told me.'

'Me?' I was incredulous.

'Yes, you sent me this.' She rummaged in the remaining contents of the drawer she'd half-emptied to find the cigarette lighter and produced a black-edged card, now folded in two, but otherwise exactly like the two I'd received. 'I did think it was a bit morbid, using the funeral invitation cards, but I assumed you'd bought too many and were being a scrooge.' I held out my hand, feeling one of the other types of afraid she'd defined for me. After a moment's hesitation she handed it to me, watching me curiously. I took it and spread it out flat, seeing the 'J' before anything else on it.

'I didn't send you anything, Emm. Someone else has a very black sense of humour.'

It read, *'Could you check on Danny Hewson? I think he might need to*

*see you – or you him. He's in St Alexander's Youth Care in Maida Vale
whilst things get sorted out re: his mother.*

Be in touch soon – J'

'Oh,' she looked bewildered. 'I just assumed "J" was you – and with
the card, of course. So who is "J"? And why did they send this?'

'I don't know. I am beginning to think we're being marshalled in
some carefully planned campaign though. Kimmy's played out her part,
you've probably just played yours and I'm still being primed – along with
a few others.'

'Well, thank God I only seem to have a bit part – and I'm not the
body in the library like Kimmy,' she grimaced ruefully, 'or the kitchen.'

'Yes, but *why* were you sent to see Danny?'

'I see. Well someone obviously thought he needed to see me as much
as I needed to see him.'

'So did he say anything significant whilst you were there?'

'No, but he did give me a drawing. Hang on, I'll go and get it. I stuck
it up on the fridge in the kitchen. I live upstairs – over the shop,' she
added by way of explanation. She paused in the doorway leading out of
the back of the office and I could see a flight of stairs carpeted in plush
cream pile through the open door. 'I think that's what mums do, isn't it?
Put their kid's drawings up on the fridge.' The Barbie doll re-emerged,
pensive and vulnerable this time. I felt like putting an arm round her and
comforting her as I might have done when she was tiny and I was her big
brother, but maybe we hadn't moved on far enough from repression for
that. She turned to go upstairs and the moment was lost by the time she
returned with the drawing.

I examined the office room in more detail while I waited for her to
return. I thought about what Kat had said about possessions telling you
about a person and what Emm had said about actions doing the same.
Manners maketh the man indeed. When I looked more closely at the
components a different kind of Emm began to emerge to either the Barbie
doll or the business bitch I'd categorised her as originally. A gentler,
more reflective woman, matured by life. In amongst the catalogues there
was also an exhibition programme for Japanese silk embroideries at the
Ashmolean Museum in Oxford. The filigree patterns and designs it
featured were exquisite. Other similar leaflets and handbooks were tucked
alongside it, as well as flyers for forthcoming exhibitions at the National
Gallery, the Tate and other the more obscure small galleries around
London. My younger sister was a woman with a fine eye for detail and a

refined taste. The open desk drawer was higgledy-piggledy, and I liked the fact that the cool businesswoman also had a scatter-brained element hidden under the efficient exterior; one who secretly still relished the child within and being impish.

The furnishings were elegant and carefully co-ordinated to contrast in an aesthetically pleasing but unique way, colours almost clashing so the effect was striking and vibrant. The desk was old, burnished wood like mine, and the chair behind it upholstered in rich brown leather, pleasant to the touch. I sat on it and it moulded to my contours as if welcoming me. Yes, the room was very much Emm as I was beginning to see her. Beneath the obvious, the underlying woman was diffuse, varied, intriguing. I could like this woman now I took the time to know her better.

'Comfy?'

I'd been so deep in thought about Emm and the reason for the card I hadn't heard her. I jumped out of the seat, embarrassed. 'Don't worry. It's fine. I rather like my window seat, actually.' She handed me the drawing with a grin, and went back to the window. The light fell from behind her, shadowing one cheek so it looked bruised. I hadn't noticed the discolouration before. A trick of the light, or a real injury? I must have stared.

'Does it show?' she asked.

'I, er...'

'It's a burn scar. I can usually cover it completely with make-up and by pulling my hair forward but sometimes the light catches it. You have to use green to cover red but it's all to do with perspective whether it works effectively – as with life.'

'I wouldn't have noticed it, not until you sat there. How did it happen?'

'When I was a teenager. Just before I met Jonno. I guess that's why he was so important to me. He didn't recoil with horror when he saw it. Life is ugly sometimes.'

'Emm, I ...' but I didn't know what to say. Probably something like I should have been there, I should have helped, should have stopped it happening. The words merely dammed up in my throat and stayed there.

'It's OK. No-one can protect everyone they care about all the time. You weren't around. Maybe that can be different in the future.' I nodded silently, thinking of Sarah and how I'd failed her too. I hadn't even managed to say goodbye to her until she could no longer hear. 'We're all human, Lawrence. That's why we're *all* afraid of life and what it can do to us. Living's all about being brave despite that. What do you make of the drawing?'

I was relieved I didn't have to reply to her homily on life. There was little I could say in return. I was still trying to live – somehow. I studied the small sheet of paper she'd given me – half the size of the ones I, Heather and Kat had been sent. It had been torn along one edge leaving it feathered. It was labelled '2' in the top left-hand corner and I immediately wondered if it was half of one of the drawings that had been missing from Kat's parcel. It depicted part of a house, roughly sketched and the features indistinct at first glance, but yet reminding me of something I couldn't quite place. Something hovering at the back of my mind.

'It's been torn in half.'

'Yes,' she agreed. 'He said as I'm a twin I should have half and Jill should have the other. Twins together make the whole story. Odd thing for a child to say, don't you think? He was most insistent I had it, like he was under orders to give it to me. I was going to ask Jill about hers but she's been in a paddy with me for the last couple of days because I won't go to Blackpool for a girly weekend with her and her gang.' She looked apologetic. 'Some things I won't do even for my sister.'

I laughed. I could see now how Jill and Emm's ideas about a girly weekend would differ. 'Yes, odd – and not very Danny. Like the pictures – none of them seem very Danny, even though he seems to have drawn them.'

'Pictures?'

'Yes, there are more. In his room at the children's home and sent to me.'

'Oh,' she sounded disappointed. 'I thought it was special – for me.'

I looked at the picture again and the memory coalesced. One I didn't want. 'It is – because it's brought us together, hasn't it?'

'Yes, that's true.' She smiled.

'And I think I might know where this is.'

'Where?'

'Somewhere you, Danny, and definitely I, don't want to visit.'

12: Charity

At the time I'd been terrified, and the angle in the drawing was oblique, but there was no doubt in my mind that the door in the half of the picture Danny had given Emm could be the one to the cellar at the children's home where I'd first encountered the thing that scared me most. What had obscured the memory – apart from fear – was perception. I'd approached and entered the door terrified. Danny – if he'd been drawing it from life – had drawn it as it was. To me it had been huge, sinister and dark. Danny portrayed it as dilapidated and with the air of the forgotten that abandoned buildings have.

'Where is it?'

'I think it's the children's home I was in.'

'It looks pretty run down, but then I suppose it would be now.'

'I think it was pretty run down even then. This is the cellar door.' I pictured the back of the building as it had been, with the black iron fire escape stairs dangling from the brickwork like strangler vine, and we the imprisoned, inside and choked by it. The brickwork had been crumbling in places and you could chip your initials into it if you were diligent enough – or wanted to. Win had. Win had always needed to make his mark on things – and people. I realised then that Emm was watching me carefully.

'You had a rough time of it there?'

'Pretty much.'

'Do you want to talk about it?'

'Not really. That would make it still real. I've left it so far behind me sometimes I think I can even imagine it didn't happen – until now.'

'The picture has brought it all back?'

'No, it has been steadily gaining on me since before Margaret died – if I'd but known it. Danny has merely brought it into the open.'

'Because of the family connection?'

'Oddly, no. Because of the similarity to what happened to Win.'

'Win? Now you've lost me.'

'We were in the home together. It was complicated – and brutish. If I think about it now we were both victims, but in different ways. He got sent down whereas I've lived my sentence out in open prison. I'm not sure which one of us did worst out of it. I thought I was the winner, but I've been changing my view on that recently.' She still looked mystified. 'He's never told you?'

'No.'

'Or Binnie?'

'She won't talk about then. I was so little, I can barely even remember our mum or dad, let alone you. Jill and I were fostered. Not quite the same as real parents, but they were kind. We still stay in touch although they're both in a nursing home now.'

'You were antagonistic when we met.'

'I know. I'm sorry. It was a bad day, and I kept thinking about what happened with Jonno. As soon as Win told us you'd been in touch my hackles were up. Not so much with you, but with him. You simply got mauled by association.'

'You really hate him?'

'Hate is too strong a word. But he's one person I won't forgive and forget – simply for not giving me the choice of whether I ballsed my life up or not.'

'There may be another side to the story you don't know about. There are quite a lot of them, you know.'

'Tell me.' She rested her chin on her hand and waited. I hesitated. If I told her about Win and Kimmy I'd have to tell her the rest of it too. The light from the window behind her slanted off the scar and I remembered her face as she'd told me about Jonno. Trust has to start somewhere. Of all people, the one person I felt right now I could trust – despite having known her for no more than a few hours in all those lost years – was my little sister. I told her about the initiation in the cellar right up to the last conversation with Kat, but skirted round Danny and his potentially closer link to me. Her expression didn't change. Only the scar seemed to darken.

When I finished she remained quiet for a few minutes, before commenting, 'I don't think I should write that book, brother mine. I think you should – but you'd have to classify it fiction because no-one would believe you.'

The truth is indeed sometimes stranger than fiction ...

'And nor do you.'

'Oh no, I do. It explains a lot.'

'Such as?'

'Binnie mostly.'

'Binnie?'

'Why she's so insular, I think. She's spent the last ten to fifteen years afraid she'll get eaten up by the acid between us all. Crazy, because if she'd told me about our dad and your dad I'd have understood – or at least accepted what Win did where I was concerned. Although it still doesn't excuse Kimmy.'

'Maybe Binnie didn't know? I don't for certain. I'm only going on what I've been told but Binnie warned me once not to believe everything Win told me.'

Emm laughed. 'Oh, she knew, all right. That's why she's kept us all at odds. So we didn't.'

'That needs explaining too.'

'I think Win's your man for that. He's the one who's always been trying to pull us back together over the years – while Binnie kept resisting. Not at first. To begin with we had this spell when Win was sweet-talking Binnie, you see. We met up lots of times then, all of us – including Binnie. I got to know Kimmy a bit and she was OK then, although I didn't like her friends much – and then Binnie became difficult. But it was later on, after Jonno, that things really changed for me. Win was always snap-happy, taking tons of photos. I once joked to Jill that he was trying to make a family album out of a few days. Shame that's how it's been for us.'

'He showed me some of them. Even Pip and Jim were in them. You all looked happy, actually.'

'Yes. We probably were. You would have liked Pip and Jim. They were a halfway house between you and Win. I was seeing Jonno then and it looked like one day we might actually become a real family, albeit a bit unusual. The Addams family in real life! Then all of a sudden it went pear-shaped. Binnie told me Win had warned Jonno off me and then Jonno went off with Kimmy. I was furious. I stopped talking to all of them then – apart from Jill. I didn't even follow the trial when Jonno was charged with murder. None of us did, apart from Binnie, I think – ironically. Story of a family feud, huh? How to do it, step by step.'

'More like a family mishap. Win was trying to protect you, you know. He didn't anticipate Jonno would latch on to Kimmy, or that Kimmy would encourage him. I suspect Kimmy had her own agenda.'

'I can imagine that. I know I'm biased but Kimmy could be a real bitch, especially round that friend of hers. One minute nice as pie, the next like she'd didn't even know you. Cut you dead. Men like that kind of thing, I'm told – the chase.'

I was doubtful. The chase seemed like a lot of hard work to me, but it occurred to me that there was an element of it playing out between myself and Kat – cat and mouse, except just recently I always felt like the mouse.

'I still don't understand why Binnie is so insistent on keeping us at a distance.'

Emm shrugged. 'Sarah probably knew. She seemed to know everything about everyone.' A side of Sarah I hadn't considered before – the repository of all secrets. And I still hadn't looked in her keepsakes box. Fate seemed to be keeping me away from it, just as surely as Sarah had kept things in it. 'Or Mary – when she makes sense,' she added. I laughed but it sounded more like a grunt. 'Oh, I see you've been to see Mary then,' Emm grinned. 'Bertha Mason, without the aggression.'

'We're all pretty dysfunctional, it would seem.'

She gazed at me, expression reflective. 'Yes. One wonders what we might have been like if Kimmy hadn't been born.'

'I've wondered that too, many times – as a child, anyway.'

'But it's irrelevant, actually,' she added. 'Going to see Danny made me realise life can't be about what could have been, but what is. What we make of what we have.'

What we make of what we have – or had. I hadn't made anything.

We sat in silence for a while, each lost in our own thoughts. She cut across mine eventually with, 'You need to talk to Win. He'd know about your dad, and all that stuff. I always thought the baby must be Jonno's even though Kimmy never admitted it. I did the sums and figured it out. He was premature, wasn't he – but I worked it out anyway. She was married off to the bloke she was with until she, well – you know – by the time Danny was about three months old. Talk to Win – and tell him I'll talk to him too – one day.'

'One day?'

'Soon, probably.' She indicated the drawing. 'You can take that, if you need it. I don't think I do anymore.'

'Do you think Jill has the other half of it?'

'I'll find out for you, if you like.'

I left her my phone number and address and wandered back to the car, weighing up what I'd found out about family politics. Not much – other than that Sarah had seemed to understand all of them whereas Binnie avoided most of them. And yet while Sarah and Binnie had stood diametrically opposed within our family, they didn't seem to have been at odds with each other.

I'd been blocked in by the car in front of me parking too close so I had to sit and wait for the Renault driver in front or the Ford driver behind to arrive and let me out. I felt like Emm's shop – designer chic sandwiched between utilitarian daily bread. I leant my head back against the soft leather of the car and allowed the thoughts wriggling like eels in my brain to have free-flow. I was suddenly very tired. Lack of sleep at Kat's was catching up on me, and the emotional stress of the last few days was compounding it. I should go home, but Emm was right. I needed to talk to Win. If Danny had drawn the picture of the cellar door, I was more concerned than ever who he was with and where he was. It didn't bear thinking about that he could actually be behind it, in that tumble-down and decrepit hell hole of my worst nightmares.

The Renault driver arrived first – a twenty-something, all tight pencil skirt, too much lipstick and too many teeth. She got in and then proceeded to fiddle around with things for another five minutes – make-up, hair, radio. The eels completed their invasion without any good result. None of it made any more sense than when I arrived. Kat, Margaret, Binnie, Sarah – even Kimmy – they all seemed to have an agenda I couldn't understand. And the more I found out about them, the less I understood them. Indeed, finding the people around me were strangers seemed to have become a theme recently. *Mockingbird* taunted me from passenger seat, now lying on top of the black edged card. It still all came back to that old chestnut: appearances, and what lay beneath them.

Eventually the red Renault pulled away, creating a gap for me to escape through into the nearly rush hour traffic. I drove aimlessly, letting the traffic flow force me along like meat through a sausage machine. It gave me time to decide what to do next. To cope with Win, I needed to feel abrasive and angry. For the moment I merely felt raw and confused; sad. I also wondered what life could have been like if events had been the smallest part different. The alternate possibilities spiralled into a whirlpool of what ifs. What if Kimmy hadn't been born? What if I'd gone to the same home as Pip and Jim, or we'd not accepted the Johns case? What if I'd not met Margaret … They stopped there, and reversed. But I had, and once again the pivot between future and past seemed to be Margaret. Maybe it was time I started getting to know my wife – and whether she was really dead.

I was sandwiched mid-flow by then, circling Hyde Park. The next logical stop en route would have been home or Chambers, but ironically neither would tell me much more about Margaret. There was somewhere that might though. Louise hadn't found anything concrete on Molly Wemmick, but I needed to know more about her – the one who'd apparently been created only a month before Margaret 'died' but I'd not had the time to pursue before Danny's case was heard. Now I could. I slipped into the filter lane leading off the main road, intending to make my own search at Kew, then abruptly changed my mind. It was already four-thirty and with the density of London rush hour, I'd be unlikely to get there before they shut for the day. It would have to be a job for the morning. In the meantime that left three options – Win, Kat or – finally – Sarah's box. Of all of them, Sarah's box seemed the least challenging and most inviting. Exhaustion had something to do with it too. The box had only been relegated to later because of the steady incoming wave of crises that had been accumulating ever since I'd been given it. Perhaps it would contain something more illuminating than the half-truths I'd extracted from Win and Kat so far, but even if it didn't, I suddenly felt like I needed to talk to my older sister and looking through her treasure box was the only way possible now.

I allowed myself to be nudged around Marble Arch until I reached Oxford Circus and then headed back past the Ritz. In bygone days it might have occasioned one of the sequined affairs secreted by Margaret in Kat's wardrobe. The Molly Wemmicks of bygone years would no doubt have frequented there if the family had been moneyed then. I passed it with a salute to bygone glitz and headed on through Knightsbridge towards the Fulham Road and home. I passed Emm's shop, now permanently closed for the day. The brief glimpse in passing of its stylish feather-white window dressing gave me an idea.

I parked the Austin Healey in the garage behind the mews, and locked it, taking the book and card with me and making sure the padlock was also on the garage door. *Try and get through that, you bastard*, I thought as I tucked the keys in my pocket, knowing it was pointless. The book and card on the seat had been to make a point, not gain possession of the car. *I can get to you, wherever, however, whatever.* That was what it had been saying – but frustratingly I still didn't know who was saying it.

Everywhere seemed unusually quiet and I wondered if I was being paranoid about the press trailing me, or whether the police were still seeing them off. I walked the short distance to the mews nevertheless still uneasily imagining being stalked. The mews was empty, not even a twitching curtain at number six. I considered ringing her bell and asking if she'd seen anyone hanging around recently, but no doubt the police had already done that when they'd been house to house after Kimmy's body was found. They would have flagged up anything unusual with me then. I resolutely passed the yellow front door and headed for my own, an intriguing idea quickened my step.

I turned the key in the lock at exactly the same moment as the tap on my shoulder. Swinging round, heart plummeting, I was face to face with Win, sweating and angry. After the initial surprise I found I was angry too, even though I'd wanted to speak to him. Why couldn't he just ring like anyone else?

'You seem to make a habit of this,' I replied drily.

'Huh! You avoiding me little bruv?'

'No, I've been busy.'

'Visiting your girlfriend and riding round in your fancy car?'

'Trying to establish what's going on actually.'

'I'll tell you what's going on. You shafted me in court, your sister's got murdered in your kitchen and her kid's gone missing. Have I missed anything?' Behind him the curtains did now twitch at number six.

'Come inside.' I gestured for him to enter. 'I know we need to talk about what happened in court, Win, but like you say there's been other more pressing things happening since then. Margaret's funeral too.' I tucked the card and the book under some unopened letters on the hall stand after he'd pushed past me. I had no intention of sharing them with Win right at this moment.

He walked testily ahead of me, filling the hallway with his bulk. 'Yeah, did you invite him? I wondered what the hell you were up to if you did.'

'Jaggers?'

'Yeah.'

'I thought you were pals again.'

'Pals? Don't be daft. Slimy bastard!'

'You were shaking hands when I saw you together.'

'Never curse your enemy to their face. He's why I took off sharpish, and took the girls with me.'

'Does he know Emm and Jill then?'

'Course. He knew Kimmy and me – so he knew them too. He ain't one for being kept in the dark.' He eyed me as if I was an idiot.

'And so that's how he found out about me as well – through you?'

He shrugged. 'In here again then?' He indicated the study. Without thinking I nodded, forgetting I'd left Sarah's box on the desk. He pushed the door open and stomped in. I followed him, belatedly remembering the box and wondering how to get to it before he did. I needn't have worried. There were surprises in store for both of us of far greater magnitude than what might be in a box full of memories. We both stopped in amazement on the threshold. The room was filled with bundles of woody green herbage covered in needle-like leaves, and tiny bluish-white flowers. The scent was overpowering in the heat of the enclosed room.

'Rosemary!' I exclaimed.

'Christ is that what it is? Smells like snuff. Gonna make me sneeze!' Win barged past me and I could hear explosive sounds from the hall, which I assumed were him doing what he'd threatened. It didn't bother me. I rather liked the smell: tangy, reminiscent of loam and herbs. The only good bit of the children's home was the herb garden that the cook had maintained – probably for herself as I was sure none of its flavourings had found their way into our slops.

The bundles were tied with lengths of rye grass, dry and straggly. The walls were lined with them – and the sparser patches on the bookshelves where I was awaiting updated editions of law manuals or hadn't yet completely filled the shelf. A small sprig was tucked impishly into the gap that Atticus and *To Kill a Mocking Bird* had created when I'd donated it to Danny, as if the floral decorator had known the significance of its absence. The desk was clear of it apart from a jam jar with a small sprig like the one tucked into Atticus's home. It stood solitarily next to Sarah's box, but the box appeared untouched. Propped against the jam jar was the missive I was beginning to dread. A black-edged card.

'Some facts about rosemary:

The Virgin Mary is said to have spread her blue cloak over a rosemary bush, and it changed the colour of the flowers to blue. The shrub became "Rose of Mary".

Its leaves are similar to hemlock leaves. It is said by mystics to ward off evil, and by herbalists to aid memory.

What do you remember now that might have been transformed under rosemary's cloak? Or should be seen differently? A cupboard full of secrets.

It's a sin to – you know …

Be in touch soon – J'

The little hanged man in the top right-hand corner now had a left arm waving maniacally at me. Virtually complete. Did that mean I also had almost everything to complete the puzzle, or that I was one arm away from being completely fucked? A sin to what? Commit incest? I was aware of Win blundering into the room behind me and tried to snatch the card up before he could see it but wasn't quite quick enough.

'Nice,' he said, peering over my shoulder. 'Someone telling you they know you've been up to no good, then?' He was right – they – whoever 'they' were, must mean Danny and his parentage with the reference to sin. 'That'd have you well and truly by the balls – but then you wouldn't want to risk using them again now anyway, would you? Might as well chop them off and be done with it!' He laughed offensively, but I couldn't object. His interpretation might be crude and simplistic – but probably accurate. 'Who's J?' He added before sneezing again. Some of the spray landed on the back of my neck. It connected with the shiver running down my spine.

I picked up the card. 'I don't know.'

'Jaggers. Gotta be. "J", see?'

'I don't think this is Jaggers' style. And I don't think it's to warn me that I'm about to be hung, drawn and quartered either. I think the meaning is far more metaphorical.'

He wiped his nose on the back of his hand and shrugged. 'Whatever. Can we get rid of the crap and then talk about it?' He sneezed again and this time the spray caught me full face. 'Sorry,' he added as an afterthought.

We cleared the bulk of it, me more so than Win. Eventually I got fed up with his explosions of snot and sent him to the kitchen to make coffee. I piled the rosemary outside the front door and opened the study window. By the time he came back with two overfilled mugs the room was cooler, fresher and filled with only the merest hint of woody top notes. I kept the two small single sprigs – the one filling Atticus's shoes and the one in the jam jar next to the card. They were the ones carrying the message, the rest of it had simply been to make sure it got my full attention. The more I thought about it, this message was key – unlike the others, although apparently from the same sender.

Key. Secrets. Kat's cupboard full of Margaret's clothes.

No postmark on this card – it was obviously hand-delivered, and clearly also reminding me that they had full access to me whenever and however they wanted it. The audacity of filling my study with the herbs indicated a perverse, or perhaps more accurately, a wicked sense of humour – and how the hell had all of this got past the old biddy at six? No, this was definitely not Jaggers' style. This had an elegance and a wit far more eloquent than his, cool and clever as he was. This had the marks of another 'J'.

'Wait here – but don't touch anything,' I instructed Win as he arrived with the coffee. 'There are coasters over there,' I indicated one of the now empty book shelves. 'Put the coffee on them and don't wreck the surface of my desk. It's antique.'

'Yes, master,' he sneered at me, but I noticed he did as he was told nevertheless. I went upstairs leaving him juggling the mugs and coasters.

In Margaret's dressing room – created by her out of the smallest of the spare rooms – was another cupboard she'd always kept locked; the intriguing idea that had been starting to take shape when Win surprised me on the doorstep and even before I'd seen the card.

'My secret treasures,' she'd explained once when I'd asked her why. *'Vivien Westwoods, Alexander McQueens – not day jobs, Lawrence. The stuff of dreams. That's why I keep it locked away. In case dreams get the better of reality.'*

It had sounded like nonsense at the time – and strange coming from Margaret, the most pragmatic and least flighty woman I'd ever met. Secret treasures – yet I'd always known where she kept the key to the cupboard. I'd seen her put it in there a thousand times and ignored it. I'd even been sent to get it occasionally yet denied access whilst she chose her 'treasure' for whatever event we were attending that evening. One of her foibles I'd noted and simply ignored. My disinterest in my wife had been sublime and absolute. Viewed from a distance, I could see now she wasn't always the dutifully diligent but unremarkable woman I'd labelled her as. There were times when she was an unusual and potentially fascinating enigma and yet I'd completely overlooked them. The blindness Heather accused me of seemed to have affected me for a very long time.

The key was where it had always been, in the top drawer of her vanity unit. I'd not even looked in her vanity drawer since she'd died – putting off the chore of clearing her things from the house because doing so sealed the deal for me. Lawrence Juste, single and free to do as he pleased again, but unsure what that was. Whilst Margaret remained officially inhabiting the house with me, time could stand still a while longer. The strands of a different life that had already begun to invade me from both the past and the future could be delayed from knotting together to form a new kind of patchwork whilst that was so. I was afraid of life, as Emm had said, but now I also found myself – oddly – missing Margaret, with her pragmatic efficiency. She might have represented repression at times, but she'd also provided structure, whereas now there was only chaos.

The drawer was another revelation all of itself. I backed away from it, shocked. The very blatancy with which its contents were displayed caused me to wonder if Margaret had actually planned for me to look in it and be aghast. The vibrator took pride of place in the centre. Outsized, disconcertingly life-like and loudly active when I flicked the switch. It buzzed vigorously at me and I almost expected it to light up and take off like a spaceship. I hurriedly switched it off and stuffed it back into the drawer, embarrassed and ashamed – although I wasn't sure what of. It was Margaret's sex toy, not mine.

'*Yes, but that means she wasn't satisfied by you,*' the demon whispered.

My shame doubled. I cautiously pulled the drawer out to its full depth but there were no other sex toys hidden behind the vibrator, not even lubricant. Next to it, and to the right, was a card advertising a night club. 'Gods and Gargoyles', the night club Jonno had been made a partner of with Win and Jaggers. It had an address in Soho. A bunch of keys nestled on top of it – not ones I'd seen before. They had no identifying tags, but two were definitely front door keys, one small and analogous to all the standard kind of travel locks and keys, two were bunched together on a separate ring looped into the main key holder and the remaining one looked like a safety deposit box key. It had 119 stamped into it. On the left hand-side were a bottle of the iconic red nail varnish, the wardrobe key and a letter still sealed in its envelope. *'To be read in the event of my death'.*

Christ, how could I have missed that?

'*Because you didn't care,*' the little imp whispered. '*If you'd cared about her, you would have wanted to linger over her possessions to keep her close to you.*'

I was about to tear the letter open, but Win's blundering downstairs reminded me I'd have to share the contents with him, or cover them up until he went. I hesitated and my own boxed secrets pressed in on me. The book and the other card were still in the hall too. Did I trust him yet? No. Not yet. He might even take it upon himself to see where I'd found it, knowing how naturally crass he was. That made me cringe with embarrassment. I tucked the letter back into the drawer and picked up the wardrobe key instead. I'd work out what the reference to the cupboard meant first and get rid of Win, then see what Margaret wanted to share with me. Better to tell Win later if appropriate.

The key fitted neatly into the wardrobe lock and turned easily. The room was very public persona style Margaret. Understated, elegant, sparse. The wardrobe was all clean lines and sharp angles. Had she always been like that, I wondered? Inside was a complete disappointment. Precisely what she'd said was in there – her collection of extortionately expensive designer gowns and shoes. Her perfume seemed to have been confined with them because with every lungful I breathed in Margaret. A smell I knew intimately and not at all. The only disparate note amongst the opulent formality was the little suitcase sitting in the corner underneath the trailing lace and chiffon.

'You ever coming down?' Win called plaintively up the stairs. 'Or shall I come up?'

'I won't be a minute.' I called back hastily. I pulled out the suitcase. 'Don't touch anything,' I reminded him. Margaret's design plan for the room had included a suitcase stand, as if it would be a regular feature of its use. I laid the suitcase on the stand. It was dark brown and battered on one corner. Unpretentious – completely at odds with the contents of the cupboard. I flicked at the catches but it was locked. The small travel key on the ring. I dashed back to the bedroom and the still open drawer to grab the bunch of keys.

'You can't avoid me forever, you know,' Win's voice floated up to me. 'And your coffee's getting' cold.' I smirked at the ludicrous inappropriateness of the two comments in juxtaposition. Anyone would think Win was an old woman, not an old lag.

'Be right down,' I repeated and returned to the locked suitcase. The key was a match. I slipped the locks back and opened another kind of Pandora's Box. This one contained a dark blonde wig, stage make-up, and a number of prostheses, including false teeth. It also contained what looked like fake blood, some small vials of rusty brown powder, nail clippings, mid-brown hair strands and some kind of wax impression kit. Jesus, this was becoming surreal! A cardboard folder lined the bottom of the case. I slid it out from under wig and make-up tubes. It contained a series of photos of a crashed car, and a tailor's dummy arranged across the road in front of it with measurements and markings scribbled across them, with names and the roles assigned on the back. Win's, and Margaret's. The dummy was wearing a black and white dress, like the one Margaret had been wearing when she was killed. I put the folder back in the suitcase and shoved an errant velvet jacket back into place so I could shut the wardrobe door. One edge of the hanger banged against the back panel, resounding hollowly. Funny kind of construction – another Margaret foible, no doubt. Downstairs I dumped the suitcase on the desk, next to Sarah's box. The lid on the box had been moved out of position but that was the least of my worries. Next to it I placed *Mockingbird* and the other card. That intriguing idea I'd first thought of as I'd walked back to the house from the car had its place here too, only barely displaced by whatever might be in Margaret's letter. Win raised his eyebrows.

'So, rather than bollocks me about you being shafted in court, why don't you tell me why you are shafting me out of it?'

13: Connections

'OK, you got me.'

'No, I don't Win. That's the problem. I don't get you or any of it, but there's something damn funny going on and you're up to your neck in it, aren't you? Let's start with Margaret's accident. Was it real or a put-up job.'

'It were meant to be a put-up job but I don't know now.'

'What do you mean, you don't know. She's either alive and the dummy in these pictures replaced by some other poor bitch; or dead, and we have still to nail her killer.'

'We was never using a real live body. Jesus – you really think I'd do that? No, I know someone who could get us a stiff from the morgue. We was gonna use that – dress it up like, smash her up so she couldn't be identified. Put her in Margaret's gear and with her jewellery like and then you were gonna identify her and it would be done.'

'That begs two questions to start with – why, and did you?'

'Why? 'Cos Margaret had a plan. She was gonna get Danny out of it and have summat to hold over Jaggers. We'd have her dead and the car, with his fingerprints all over it and his hair and things in it, so he'd be stuffed. He would have to back down and lay off Danny or we'd have him. What else she had planned after that she didn't tell me.'

'And what about Margaret? She'd be "dead" – how would that work?'

'She'd be Molly till it suited her not to be.'

'Molly Wemmick.'

'Yeah.'

'Blonde Molly Wemmick,' I added thoughtfully. 'But how would she get past the fact that Molly Wemmick and Margaret Juste looked identical?'

'They didn't – that's what the teeth and wig an' stuff were for. If you'd seen her done up as Molly I don't reckon even you'd know her. Still hot, but different. Posh tart – well she had to be at the club. More like Maria used to be.'

'The Gods and Gargoyles Club.'

'Yeah.'

'The one you owned a share in.'

He stared at me. 'How'd you know?'

'Let's say I can also get hold of information when I need to.'

He shrugged. 'Fat lot of good it did me. I had to sign it over when Kimmy got herself into trouble – just to make sure there was money and stuff to see her OK. I only ever really skivvied for him anyway – even before that.'

'So how long had my wife been leading a double life?'

'Years, bruv.'

'And how did I not find out before?'

'Dunno. Must say I wouldn't have let my bird outta my sight, looking like she did. I always wondered why you weren't bothered. Finding out about that stuff when you was a kid explained it for me. You were either gay or you've been put off sex for life.'

'I'm neither,' I said coldly.

'That case you're bloody blind.'

'That I might be,' I acknowledged. 'So now explain the rest of it – and why you don't know if your little plan played out as it was meant to or not. In other words – whose funeral have I recently attended? My wife's or some "stiff" you roughed up to look like her?'

'I don't know 'cos Margaret took it outta my hands that night. She told me to get it all set up then sent me off on some wild goose chase to see Sarah. I got back just in time to see it all happening in front of me. I watched it from the end of the road – the car, her lyin' off to the side of it and blood everywhere. The car reversed up, passed me and he were in it like we planned, then he shot off and the sirens went. I made myself scarce then but sure enough – like she said he would – he rang me about half an hour later asking me to come over and sort out *a little mess,* as he put it, for him. Margaret were gone and so were the suitcase.'

'So if the case is back here, someone must have brought it back. Surely that could only have been Margaret?'

'Or your girlfriend. Margaret had her jumping around too sometimes.'

'Kat?'

'Yeah, the little brown bint.'

I aimed the punch at his jaw – the best right hook I'd ever managed. It found his left cheek and eye. He reeled and steadied himself, hand to eye.

'Jeez! I always thought she were trouble. You've just proved it. No offence, bruv. It weren't meant that way, but I had to know where your loyalties lie before I told you anything else.' I nursed my knuckles, ready to swing again. His face looked lopsided and the skin was darkening round his eye. His last comment took me aback.

'What do you mean?'

'She were supposed to be helping Margaret, but Margaret told me she couldn't be trusted. That's why she set up your lady partner with your girlfriend's brother and his little problem. See if your girlfriend would follow through – or go running when Jaggers applied a bit of pressure. Jury's still out on that, I reckon, but she's been doing quite a number on you since Margaret's not been around, ain't she?'

'Christ, is there any one of you I can trust?'

'Maybe you don't believe it at the moment, but, yeah – you can trust me, and your sisters.'

'Really? So far you've let me believe I'm potentially Danny's father, that my wife's dead, that Jaggers killed her and you have my best interests at heart – despite trying to drag me into a scam to land Jaggers in the middle of some kind of gangland payback with that hit and run car. The Flowers family, I believe, although you didn't tell me that at the time, did you?'

'How'd you …?' His mouth opened and shut like a fish, then clamped shut.

'I *prosecuted* the case, remember? I can trust you, Win? I can trust you like Jesus could trust the devil!'

'It's all been for a reason. You wouldn't have found a way to get Danny off otherwise, would you? Or seen Sarah before she died.'

'That's not the point. You lie to me at every turn to manipulate me into doing what you want me to. That's not trust, that's megalomania.'

'No it ain't, its good business sense. Look there ain't much love lost between you and me, so I gotta get you to do stuff other ways. Like Margaret did. She knew you didn't care about her, but she had to get you on her side somehow too.'

'Am I on her side?'

'You're on Danny's side – and you ain't on Jaggers, so I guess you are.'

'OK, I can see I'm not going to get to the bottom of this in one sitting, so let's at least get some facts straight. Who is Danny's father?'

'Dunno. Might be you, might be Jonno. Might be some other bugger.

Margaret'd know, but you can't really ask her, can you?' He sniggered. 'Sorry bruv, you might be the hot-shot lawyer with an antique desk, but you can't always get a straight answer to a straight question. Sometimes you have to wait for the angles to play out.'

I was irritated but tried to control it. He was right. The more complicated the case, the longer you had to wait for the strands to unlace before you could knot them together again – round your intended target.

'OK, what was Margaret doing all this for?'

'Get at Jaggers? Get Danny off? There was stuff between her and Kimmy. They go back a long way.'

'I didn't know that.'

'You don't know lots of things, little bruv. That's why you have to talk to people and find out for yourself. You ain't done enough of that yet, but there's still time.'

'Before what?'

'Before they take you in for Kimmy's murder. That was what I really came here to tell you about. I wanted to have a go about the court stuff too, but that's by the by. I wanted you to find out the truth for Jonno, but that weren't a priority for you. Seems like someone's thought of a way to make it one by killing Kimmy right under your nose and the pigs don't like the smell of it or you at all. Now you've got to find out who fucked both of them over, or it'll be your head in the noose.' He pointed to the black-edged card. 'That's what that means. One limb left. It's code. No limbs means four days, one is three day's grace, and so on. You got a day before they come for you.'

'Thanks, that's just great. Why is it me with my head in the noose?'

'Well, it happened here. Makes sense don't it? I'm not saying the cops are big brains. They usually look for the obvious and you're it.' He laughed. His eye had swollen and he reminded me of Quasimodo in one of the nineteen-forties' screen versions I'd seen on late night TV when there'd been nothing else on. I would have liked to have punched him again but I wasn't sure my knuckles would take it – or that I'd manage to hit him a second time. I'd taken him by surprise the last time. The wary look in his eye told me he was anticipating trouble now. I made do with clenching my fists and trying to contain the anger into a little ball the way Margaret had shown me to do when stressed. *You only lose it if you let yourself,*' she'd said. *'Just don't let yourself – put it somewhere else instead.'* Mentally I threw the balls of fury into the corner of the room and thanked her for that, at least.

139

'You want me to help you?' Win asked at length, picking up his coffee and sipping it. He made a face. 'Fucking awful. It's cold.' I went round to the chair and sat down, taking the black-edged card with me.

'Why would you?'

'You're me brother. Kimmy was me sister. You think I'm an unfeeling bastard, but I ain't. Just because we're different and grew up to do different stuff, don't mean we don't have the same feelings. We're just the same, you and me. OK, you look like a smooth bastard and talk proper. I smell like shit and can't string me vowels together. People is still people under what they look like, Kenny. Time you started to see that and work out which ones are OK, and which ones are bullshitting you. Take your little girlfriend ...' I squared up again. 'No, no, don't get all arsy with me. I weren't being rude about her, but you've been setting her up in your head as a Miss Goody-Goody 'cos she's a social worker, haven't you? It's natural. We all do it. We have stereotypes and think everyone's the same.' He laughed at my expression. 'Did I get the word right?' I nodded. 'There you are. Just proved it for you. You think I'm stupid 'cos I'm a bully-boy.'

'No, I don't think you're stupid, Win,' but I knew he was right. I had been stereotyping. I'd been hovering around the truth with my pithy little mental notes about appearances but not getting to the meat of it. I'd cast him as the villain because he looked like one; Margaret the same because she was making life difficult for me and Kat as my saviour because – like Win astutely observed – she had a background which automatically put her on the good guy's side, the side of the underdog. And she was desirable, even though I seemed now to be regularly coming across elements of her that were less so. 'What do you suggest I do, then?' I asked heavily after a while. He pulled the chair from the corner of the room toward the desk and propped his now completely asymmetrical face on his cupped hands.

'That's better. You can start by explaining the rest of that to me.' He nodded awkwardly at the black-edged cards and the book, 'and not going to have it out with Jaggers.' I was about to protest, but that has been at the back of my mind as a last resort.

'Are you a mind-reader?' I asked, laughing involuntarily.

He sighed. 'Naw, I just know people.'

'That's what Emm said. She said she talks to you sometime too.'

'Did she?' He looked pleased. 'Now we're really getting somewhere then.' He pointed to Sarah's box. 'So shall we let the cat out of the bag?'

14: The Box

I still would have preferred to have opened the box without Win around, but he made it clear he wasn't going anywhere if I wanted him to help me. It presented a motley collection of mementoes – the kind I would have expected of Sarah: a photo album, some birthday cards, seashells, a small amethyst coloured perfume bottle, a locket and a rose-petal print covered box tucked into the corner. Win picked up the photo album and flicked through it. He shouted with laughter.

'Us – as kids! I never even knew there were any.' He showed me what had occasioned the amusement. Georgie, Win and I standing in a line, a feather stuck in our hair – mine pointing sideways – and makeshift bows and arrows tucked under our arms. Our knees stuck out like small pebbles under too-long shorts and Georgie's socks hung round his ankles like shrivelled balloons. We were grinning. The Juss boys. Red Indians for the day. Happy. 'I remember that. You fell out of the tree with the crooked trunk. Big baby. You hollered for Ma until Georgie made you Big Chief Kenny, bravest warrior of the tribe.'

I laughed despite myself. I remembered it too. Georgie had a way of righting things, when he decided to join in. Brave Big Chief Kenny couldn't cry, could he? If Georgie could see what others needed to set them right, how could he have got so lost himself? My throat closed over with grief for Georgie. Win surprised me by voicing my feelings.

'He were good at sorting us out. I should've been able to help sort him out too, shouldn't I?'

We spend our lives apportioning blame without realising we are doing it. Until then I'd apportioned all the blame for Georgie and his descent into the abyss to Win. When I'd heaped it on him at our first meeting in Chambers, he'd accepted it. He'd been the one to allow introductions to the seamier side of gangland business – the drugs and alcohol abuse that slithered just below the surface of repression. I'd allocated myself the role of helpless observer, but I wasn't. Not then or now. I'd chosen the role because I'd been afraid to do anything different – just as I'd chosen to go along with what was presented to me in the Johns case. I could have done something about both situations. The blame wasn't only Win's, it belonged also to me and everyone else who'd turned a blind eye.

'*We should have*, Win; but we didn't.'

He scrutinised me, lopsided eye squinting moodily. 'You changed your tune,' he commented.

'And no doubt I'll change it again sometime, but for now, maybe it's time I saw this all as a joint effort – including the fuck-ups.'

'I'm with you on that,' he laughed. 'Always happy to share a fuck-up. How about this one?' He waved the photo album under my nose and I took it from him. There was a different kind of family photo in there. A photo from the children's home. Me, Win and Jaggers, uneasily comradely.

'How the hell did that get in there?'

'More to the point, how'd Sarah get hold of it?'

'Didn't Sarah know about him and us? She implied she knew all about what happened when I went to see her the first time.'

'I guess.' He seemed reluctant to go on, yet the inflection implied he wanted me to prompt him.

'What?'

'Binnie, I guess. She knew – about him. She must have told Sarah. She disapproved of me getting us together in case I were a bad influence on the girls – Jill, Emm and Kimmy. Dunno where she could have got the photo from though. '

'Is that's why she's so antagonistic?'

'Naw, it's the other stuff too. She didn't agree with the club, but I had to work or I'd be back in clink. Didn't want anything to do wiv it and didn't like me risking involving the girls – Jill and Emm. Sarah didn't say now't so I thought that's what she knew – now't.'

'She must have known a lot more than now't to have that photo, Win.' I handed him back the photo album.

'Yeah,' he studied it reflectively. 'Or Binnie did and Sarah were looking after it for her. They did that sometimes.' He frowned but didn't say any more.

A quick scan had shown nothing else particularly revelatory. A wealth of memories, which I would have to come back to later, but no more surprises. They were reserved for the petal-print box. I opened it, anticipating more sentimental treasures like the seashells and the perfume bottle. I couldn't have been more wrong. It contained a stack of paperwork, neatly bundled together and secured with a thin pink ribbon. It fluttered jauntily at me as I lifted the papers out of the box, reminding me of the pink decorations on the case folders in Chambers archives. I suppose part of me knew what to expect then. The association created its own assumptions. Win and I exchanged glances. I wryly imagined his expression superimposed on my face, thinking of Heather's comments about me and my inability to control my face out of court – although that had been in connection with Kat. Out of control. But now I felt out of control too. I wanted to laugh at the result – the monster surprised by his own monstrosity.

The papers comprised a number of legal documents. A deed poll name change – Margaret Flowers to Margaret Green, dated 1989. Was that my Margaret? But she was also Molly Wemmick if I was to believe the other name change. A stillbirth certificate for 'Baby Flowers', 9th July 1989, mother Maria Flowers, but registered by Margaret Flowers, being *'present at birth'* as well as Danny's birth certificate, dated one week later, father unknown, mother – Kimberley Juss, and again registered by Margaret Flowers, *'present at birth'*. Tucked into the middle was a photo of three lanky schoolgirls. I didn't recognise any of them because it was taken from a distance and their faces were indistinct but the similarity between two of them was obvious from their posture and general air. Twins. They looked a little younger than the other girl. I handed it silently to Win.

'That's Kimmy,' he said immediately. 'The one on the right. At school in Bromley where she were fostered.'

'You had contact with her right from the start then?'

'Yeah. When I got out I got us all together. Seemed the right thing to do, somehow. I didn't get very far to begin with – well, I weren't exactly *suitable* company for kids, were I? I had to get Sarah and Binnie involved to get anywhere to start wiv – respectable family, like – and it were fine, until it all got messy.'

'Who are the other two girls?'

He peered at the photo. 'Binnie would be better at that than me, but I don't s'pose she's talking to me at the moment.' He frowned and opened his mouth as if to add to it and then shut it again. He reminded me of a gulping fish again.

'Go on.'

'Naw, can't really say.'

'Yes you can.' He stared at me defiantly. I stared back. It was plain he knew precisely who the two girls were. 'You were supposedly going to help, Win. Lying doesn't.'

'It's habit,' he said at last. 'I got used to it. You have to sometimes. Only safe thing to do.'

'Not to me. Not if we're brothers.'

He digested that, moody deformed eye watering as if he was crying. 'We are.' He agreed eventually. 'It's the Flowers girls. They were twins.'

I picked up the deed poll certificate, an unpleasant vat of acid bubbling up in my stomach as I connected the dots of the unknown artists yet to be discovered final masterpiece. 'Margaret Flowers and Maria Flowers?' I passed him the deed poll. He glanced at it cursorily and handed it back as if he already knew what it said.

'Yeah.'

'You know the murdered girl well then. Do you want to tell me the rest of it?'

He looked uncomfortable. 'Don't think I need to from your face, do I?'

I shook my head. 'Margaret Flowers is my Margaret. A bit of an enigma.'

'Could say that.' He looked doubtfully at me. I wondered if he understood what I meant but his next comment made it clear he did.

'She'd explain it better – leaves me standing most of the time. But whatever you think about her, she ain't bad. She were trying to get things set right.'

'And it was her sister who was murdered?'

'Well, maybe murdered.'

'By Jonno?'

'No – he weren't no murderer. I told you – if she were murdered, it were someone else who did it.'

'And Kimberley and Danny?'

'Like I said, reckon your Margaret were trying to protect them.'

'And who are you trying to protect Win?'

'Apart from myself?' He laughed. 'I run out of space on me own list …' He picked up the last item of the paperwork and gave it to me. 'She were on it though.' A doctor's letter diagnosing Kimberley Joan Juss with Bipolar Disorder. 'Now do you begin to see? Same as Mary.' I read the list of symptoms associated with the diagnosis: manic episodes, periods of disassociation, social phobia and issues, substance abuse, eating disorders, hyperactivity, depression. 'Mary were always weird so she didn't have the chance to get into most of that. Just stayed in her own little world. Kimmy were better at hiding it – or maybe fostering and swapping around left her more open to it not being noticed until it were a real problem. That Maria were a bad influence. They were at school together. The twins were a bit younger'n Kimmy, but you'd never have guessed it when you saw Maria all dolled up. I suppose it were my fault for getting Maria a job dancing at the club to start with, but I didn't know she'd take Kimmy there, or about the rest of it until it were too late. Best we could do was cover it up. Jonno brought Kimmy back home for me a few times just after Binnie'd told me about Pop and Ma. I steered him away from Emm 'cos of it, but Kimmy latched on to him. Couldn't do right for doing wrong.'

'So how does it all relate to this?' I flipped the black-edged card that had been left on the desk across to him. 'And to Kimmy's murder?'

He read aloud. 'Bit weird, ain't it? Who wants to know about flowers changing colour? Prissy. More your kind of thing than mine.' I bristled but managed to contain my irritation this time. He rubbed his hand over his face and winced. 'I don't know. You got any ice? Or a steak? That's meant to be good for a black eye, ain't it? Though I'd rather eat it than wipe it over myself.' He laughed.

'I'll get some ice,' I offered coldly. I collected a bagful from the freezer and handed it to him. He took it without thanking me, arranged it across his cheek. *The ice man cometh*, I thought whimsically but without humour.

He spoke from behind the ice mountain, 'Summat to do with sin and flowers?'

'Rosemary. It's the herb the room was filled with. Someone cloaked the room with rosemary like the card mentions. *The Virgin Mary is said to have spread her blue cloak over a rosemary bush, and it changed the colour of the flowers to blue. The shrub became 'Rose of Mary'.* It's to do with memories – or remembering something.' I paused, something tangential slipping in next to my own memories. 'Or maybe remembering things that have been perceived differently in the past – the cloak. What am I missing, Win?'

He shrugged. 'Beware your sins will find you out? You know what they are,' he added meaningfully, and grinned from behind the ice pack. I ignored him. It started to melt and dribbled down his cheek and onto his chin. He put the ice bag down to wipe the trickle away and the two-faced man faced me again. Win on one side and the deformed beast on the other.

And then it came to me. Two. Appearances. Two sides to everything. Margaret Flowers became Margaret Green. Transformation – the herb's flowers changing colour. Same woman – two different identities. She did it again when Margaret Juste also became Molly Wemmick. Playing a very duplicitous double game. Kimmy was bipolar. Margaret had a twin who was murdered – or maybe she wasn't – by a man we'd got convicted by closing our eyes to the truth – two visions. One clear-sighted, one blind. Even Win and I potentially had a different father to the one we'd assumed we had. And Danny – might be my son or he might be – whose? Something about the two birth registrations bothered me too. Why would Sarah have the one for the Flowers baby? And why had Margaret registered them both? However it all fitted together, it was all about separating the sides and then putting them back together again differently. Even the herb itself had two appearances ... *its leaves are similar to hemlock ...* '

'I need to talk to Margaret.'

'She's meant to be dead.'

'Then she needs to come back to life.'

I put everything back in the petal-print box, tucked it back into the corner of the red and gold braid affair and secured the lid. My life might be unravelling, but old habits die hard, and they dictated I kept the evidence where it belonged. Apart from which, if I ever got my hands on my wife, I wanted everything in the right place to confront her with.

'And how the fuck is that going to happen if you neither of us know where she is?'

'That's where the book comes in – I think. And these.' I gestured to the cards.

Be in touch soon – J.

Or the letter.

Twenty-four hours, Margaret. You had better be.

15: The Vanished

In my immersion with Win and the events of the day, I'd temporarily forgotten about Danny. Kat reminded me of him just after Win left so the letter remained upstairs in the drawer, taunting me. It was nearly nine by then and we'd examined the contents of the box several times over in the interim. No matter how dire the present circumstances it's a fact of human nature that we'd rather remember good times past than face bad times to come. Perhaps it was also necessary for us as brothers to remember what we'd shared and set aside for a while what we clashed over. And there *were* good things between us. For all the bad blood that had followed at the children's home, our childhood before we'd been sent there had been filled with genuinely happy times.

The Red Indian phase had been preceded by Viking marauders, and the chiefdom of Big Kenny later gave way to invasion by the aliens and their star ships, with the launch of the Project Mercury spaceship programme by the USA between 1959 and 1961. When, in May 1961 Alan Shepard became the first American in space, chasing hard on the heels of Yuri Gagarin one month earlier, I was nine – a few months short of becoming almost an orphan – and completely star struck. There was a photo confirming that too – an old Tommy's tin helmet with foil adaptations to make it my astronaut's helmet, and Pop's stained white boiler suit transformed into my space suit. Georgie held a makeshift clipboard, checking the ship's instruments and Win had obviously assumed the role of President Kennedy, announcing lift-off was imminent.

There were also more images of other residents of the flats. Even big-busted Glynnis showed up in one of them, face like a squeezed lemon around raspberry lips as one of the boys was caught on camera in the act of pinching her ass. Our enigmatic relationship had resolved to uneasy truce and tentative examination of each other as people by the time Win and I had laughed our way to that one. I was accepting of his distrust of me and he was accepting of my animosity towards him with an equanimity approaching comradeship. The sensation was odd, disconcerting and encouraging.

However, my twenty-four hours grace were rapidly dwindling. Apart from the rest of the mess to sort out, I still had Chambers' disappearing bank balance to account for. I took a last look at the cryptic card that had accompanied the rosemary, closed the study window and went out to the kitchen in search of the steak Win had optimistically hoped for to soothe his black eye after I'd seen him safely off the premises. There had still been no-one around to see him go and the very absence of press was starting to worry me now. My luck had to give out with the hacks soon. I fried and ate the steak with a mixture of salad leaves and olives, twisting a small sprinkling of the rosemary from the jar onto it in defiance. It gave the meat a strangely herbal tang, redolent of an apothecary's or what I imagined an alchemist's lab to smell like. It felt apt. The blending of the conventional with the anomalous was entirely representative of life currently. I also liked the idea of metaphorically eating 'J's words.

I couldn't finish the steak though. The strange taste palled about halfway through and I wandered back to the study, too wound up to sleep but too tired to do anything rational or useful. I idly shuffled the papers together. Margaret was rapidly becoming my lynch pin again, and I had little doubt now it was her behind the black-edged cards. They didn't strike me as Jaggers' style – and anyway, it seemed obvious they were inciting me to action and justice, not torpor and dishonesty. The latter would have been Jaggers' intention, surely? I wondered why he'd been so significantly silent since the funeral. The calm before the storm, perhaps?

That was certainly how it felt that evening in late July. I'd told Win the way to find her was via the book, but I'd been bluffing. I suspected the way to find her was through the book, but I wasn't sure precisely how. I leafed idly through it, trying to make links between its themes and my predicament. I couldn't – other than appearances being deceptive, but now I looked at it closely, the book was more worn than my copy had been and the pages marked by turning the corner down, irritated me. I flicked through to the first of them and forgave the defacing of the page. It was an iconic passage in the book: Miss Maudie confirming Atticus's assertion that it was sin to kill a mockingbird. I turned to another: Atticus explaining to Scout the importance of seeing both sides of an argument.

The last I turned to was at the beginning – Scout's atmospheric description of her hometown from the first chapter. I revelled briefly in re-reading the text after so long but couldn't see any link to my situation at all. I went to bed, putting the nagging sense of missing something down to apprehension over Jaggers' silence, which had to break soon. I was almost asleep when I remembered the letter still nestling in Margaret's vanity drawer. I could dimly see the outline of the front of the drawer in the gloom but even the lure of finding out what secrets Margaret was prepared to share with me after her 'death' couldn't beat exhaustion. My last conscious thought was of getting out of bed to collect it. My first one the next day was the same, interrupted by Kat's phone call. Her tone was simultaneously icy and sarcastic.

'I thought you might be interested in an update on Danny. I assumed all the phones in your home and Chambers must have ceased to work or you to have lost the power of speech so I'm taking the initiative for you.'

I was about to flip an equally sharp reply back but managed to hold my tongue. I deserved the criticism.

'Kat, I'm so sorry. It's been one thing after another – more situations; more surprises. Tell me what's happening, please. I was kind of relying on you here.'

She seemed mollified. 'Well, he's back, but under sedation.'

'Where?' it came out like a strangled yelp. So had he been with Margaret or not?

'Back in hospital. Don't worry. He seems fine, just confused. They thought it best to sedate him until he settled down. He's got a whole sheaf of new drawings with him though. All of the same place and just one person. It looks like an angel. Big halo round her head.'

'You're sure it's an angel?' I thought about the alternative version.

'Oh yes – a shiny yellow halo and red finger tips.' I didn't answer. 'Lawrence? Are you still there?'

'Yes, yes I'm here. When can he have visitors?'

'Not yet. I'll let you know. We've put Terry Hewson down as next of kin. Well, he is until acknowledged otherwise, isn't he?' The rhetorical question was more than that. We both knew it, but I declined to answer.

'Any more intruders? I asked lightly instead.

'No-o.' She sounded like lemon juice again. 'Why?'

'No reason.' Impasse.

'Lawrence,' the sharpness had gone, replaced by persuasive tease. Kittenish. 'About Margaret.'

'What about her?'

'You do understand, don't you?'

'Not really, but that's nothing new. I feel as if I haven't understood much of what's been going on around me for weeks now. What's a few more years between friends?'

'Oh, I knew you were pissed with me!' She sounded peeved.

'I'm not pissed. I just don't understand why everyone has so many secrets they don't own up to.'

'Pot and kettle?' The waspishness was back again. I sighed. She was right, but I was becoming tired of having to apologise for it. My secrecy hadn't been to deliberately deceive for deception's sake. It had been to start afresh. There was a difference ...

'You remember that thing about arguing?'

'Not arguing,' she corrected me.

'Exactly.'

'Oh.'

She rang off, the argument still potentially about to simmer. I replaced the phone on the hook and padded out to the kitchen for coffee, avoiding the area on the floor still lightly outlining where Kimmy had lain. Bloody police marker chalk. I'd have to get a cleaner in to get rid of it. The phone rang again. I hoped it wasn't Kat back for round two. It was Louise, the Chambers clerk currently allocated to me.

'Mr Juste, could you possibly see a new client later on today? I know it's not a good time, but he was quite insistent about talking to you, and Ella said you were looking for new briefs now.'

A new client and their problems was the last thing I wanted to take on but given the dire situation of the partnership bank account I couldn't very well refuse. Damn Ella and her interfering. I must have a word with Heather and tell her to call off her hound before I turned pitbull and savaged her. I hesitated before replying. Louise – smart girl – immediately homed in on my reluctance. 'Or I could see if Mr Squires might be free – he sometimes takes this kind of case?'

'What kind of case?'

'Fraud and demanding money with menaces.'

I sighed. More Francis's cup of tea, really but he was still off the radar. Maybe getting his teeth into a new case would keep Jeremy out of The Grape Vine and Melinda's arms.

'If he can take it that would be better. Tell him I'm available to consult though.'

'Oh that's good. Mrs Trinder told me to diary you as in, but I wasn't sure if I should.'

Little choice now, then.

'I'll be in shortly, Louise – no problem.' I thought of the letter, waiting in the upstairs drawer and cursed. Heather would have my guts if I was needed to back up Jeremy. I dare not take time out now. The letter would have to wait until this evening. Whatever storm it was brewing would have to break then.

'Oh and by the way, Mrs Trinder says to look at this morning's *News Today*. Apparently there's an article in it she wants you to read. I've left a copy on your desk for when you're in.'

The storm, gathering nicely.

* * *

I slipped into Chambers virtually unseen, keen to avoid Heather and any more reviews of my current status as unsuitable business partner. I determined to rectify that before I faced the newspaper report, grimly checking through my post and relieved to get to the bottom of the pile without any familiar black edges peeping out from it. There were only two new briefs allocated to me to consider. Louise had obviously been successful fending off the masses in the run up to the funeral and while I was involved in Danny's case, but although I was grateful there wasn't more to have to apply myself to, it maybe also suggested the need to get properly back into harness given our current embarrassing financial situation. Briefly I regretted batting the new client Jeremy's way, knowing I would probably make a better fist of it than he. My conscience was salved marginally when my phone rang and the caller display showed it was from Jeremy's extension.

'Old chap,' he greeted me with effusively. 'Got an interesting case here, which I know Louise was going to pass your way, but things are a little difficult for you at the moment, are they not?'

'Well,' I hedged.

'No problem at all, but as the chappie's in later on this morning, would you like to come and give us the benefit of?'

'Of course, I told Louise I'd be happy to consult if needed. When?'

'About half an hour? I'll get the facts off him first and give you a buzz then.'

'OK, fine.'

'And, er, Melinda…'

'Do I know a Melinda?'

'Exactly – cheers, old chap!'

I put the phone down and pushed the pile of post around lethargically next to the newspaper, unable to muster enthusiasm for anything despite my good intentions. It was no good. The newspaper was nagging at me. I'd better get the bad news out of the way. I flicked through it, looking for yet another report on the murder that no doubt Heather had meant me to read. I still hadn't found it by the time I got to the sports pages. I frowned. Had I flicked straight over something? Ah, the sarcastic little editorial had been in the *News Today*. I found the relevant page and sure enough, there it was; my brewing storm, leading on from savaging one of our more lax politicians.

'White knight turned black?

And about another man of the moment, interesting times continue for Lawrence Juste QC as his recently reclaimed family starts to decrease, following the recent murder of his sister, Kimberley Hewson, in Juste's own kitchen, no less! What a stew he's cooking up for himself. The police haven't pressed charges yet and Mr Juste has been significantly scarce – without even the chance for a 'no comment' yet. So, with his wife's recent murder and now this, that's two down and how many to go?'

'Bastard,' I said under my breath. I could almost have him for libel, but not quite. He hadn't actually accused me of anything, only implied. I wondered whether it was going to whittle away my remaining time before the almost-hanged man got completely hung by the police. At least it helped in one way. Lethargy had no place in any part of my day now.

Heather didn't seem to be in so I prowled the corridor, enjoying the temporary freedom of being the naughty boy not caught playing truant. I checked in on Francis's room as well as hers before returning to the problem of the partnership bank account – and my own. The assistant manager was unavailable but his secretary promised he would ring me back later. It was all 'in hand', she promised.

'Yes, someone else's hand,' I grumbled.

'Tracing misplaced deposits sometimes takes a while,' she explained smoothly.

'These aren't misplaced, they're misappropriated,' I replied.

'Oh, but it says your wife withdrew the sums.'

'I know – my *dead* wife.'

'Ah …' and then we were back to the promise that the assistant manager would be in touch with me later on. I put the receiver down heavily, and walked over to the window to stretch my legs and let the activity dissipate some of my frustration. The street below was quiet and empty apart from the same black Merc that had followed me parked insolently on double yellow lines outside the building. Jeremy's new client? I went back to my desk and buzzed Louise. There was a short delay and then Louise's voice came through breathlessly.

'Mr Juste, sorry.'

'Are you all right, Louise?'

'Just a small misunderstanding here, that's all.'

'Misunderstanding?'

'With Mr Tibbs.'

'Is that Mr Squire's new client?'

She giggled. 'Oh no – it's the cat – remember? The one Mr Gregory got to keep the archives mouse-free.'

'Oh, yes – but I thought you were taking him – or was it her – home?'

'I did – but she tends to follow me into work sometimes. She's in my bottom desk drawer now though, Mr Juste – you won't tell Mr Gregory, will you?'

I shook my head in humorous despair. At least Louise's secrets were innocent ones.

'I won't say a word.'

'Oh, thank you! Were you after Ella?'

'Good God, no!' She giggled. 'But can you tell me if Mr Squires' new client has arrived yet, and what his name is? Rather rude if I can't address him correctly when I meet him.' There was rustling at the other end and I wondered whether it was Louise or the cat.

'It's a – oh, I'm so sorry – the cat's knocked my coffee over and it's gone all over the diary.'

'Never mind,' I cut her off. Jeremy's light was buzzing on the phone. I switched lines, but his had gone dead by the time I disconnected from Louise and her coffee-cat disaster.

'Lawrence old chap! Couldn't stand on ceremony – he's an old pal of yours. Such a small world, huh?' Jeremy was beaming at me from the door, and just behind him the last face on earth I wanted to see at that moment grinning malevolently back at me.

'What a surprise, indeed.' Jaggers' hand was outstretched but I couldn't bring myself to shake it. He smiled wryly and sank into the guest chair nearest me. 'Jeremy tells me you are the expert on fraudulent dealings and I have a tricky little situation myself to get sorted. Maybe you can offer some suggestions as to how I resolve it?

Jeremy folded himself into the accompanying guest chair.

'Definitely more your forte than mine, old chap, although I know you're very busy with personal stuff at the moment.' He turned to Jaggers. 'Lawrence's wife was killed a short while ago, I'm afraid – hit and run. Bad business.'

Jaggers nodded politely. 'That is indeed unfortunate. So many careless drivers on the roads these days – with so little consideration for the safety of others. My condolences.'

I opened my mouth to reply but no words would come out. The effrontery of the swine! Jeremy filled the awkward silence with his embarrassed babble.

'I'm sorry, old chap – the funeral was only a day or so ago, wasn't it. Probably not at all the right time to be asking you to figure out how to nail someone for fraud and misrepresentation where a will is concerned.'

Jaggers stood up, as I sat down. For the few moments before I scrambled to my feet again, he towered over me – a vulture eyeing its prey.

'I agree, and certainly we can't presume on your good will now. I will consult with Jeremy but in due course would be delighted if you would look the papers over. The names have been blanked out for confidentiality's sake until I know if you can take the case but I'm sure you'll get the gist,' and that cruel smile at me again.

Jeremy was nodding like a toy dog as Jaggers slipped past him. He paused at the door and ushered Jeremy past as if he was the brief and Jeremy his client. Jeremy hovered obsequiously behind him, grinning awkwardly and no doubt anxious his faux pas would now change my mind about not mentioning Melinda.

'Again, so sorry for your loss, Lawrence. Let's hope things don't go from bad to worse as they sometimes do in situations like this. I mean too much prying interest and business being adversely affected as a result.'

I was painfully aware that my hands were balled into fists and my shoulders rigid, but I could do nothing but wait for him to go. My tension wasn't born out of anger, but fear. The editorial was a storm in teacup compared to the storm he'd made it so clear was coming, whether I liked it or not.

I left Chambers, feeling nauseous and ill shortly afterwards. There was no point pretending I was doing anything useful there now. I was on the look-out for press and Jaggers on the way back to the car, but I didn't expect Heather. She was waiting for me behind a pillar in the car park as I unlocked the door of the Austin Healey. I wouldn't normally have risked leaving it in the car park, home of the local vandals and graffitists, but I was starting to take a more pragmatic view of life and possessions these days, along the lines of *enjoy it while you can*. There had been little of that so far today.

'Christ, are you stalking me?'

'Do I need to?'

'Pretty much everyone else seems to be!'

'Well I'm not, but I wanted to catch you away from Chambers and not at home. I feel pretty much the same way. Apart from that editorial which I presume you've seen now?' I nodded glumly. She pursed her lips, 'Well, yes – I've also had a visit from a friendly policeman last night, very interested in you and your family background. Your brother's unwholesome past was prime topic to begin with, but you kept cropping up in connection with it. We can deal with rumour and malicious editors but we can't displace fact. So what I want to know Lawrence is this: what is your connection to your brother's gangland friends? It seems to be extremely close and very long-standing from what Detective Gestapo was implying. No, don't worry, I didn't say anything to him, but I can't keep it quiet for much longer if the police are snooping about. Your private past is going to become a very public one soon. That editorial was a tap on the shoulder. The next one could be from plod. And Gregory tells me you've had a letter. That might change things somewhat too.'

The last question hung in the air between us, apparently harmless but I knew it meant trouble. Her expression was ominous.

'How does he know? He wasn't even around when it arrived.'

'Jesus Christ! So you have, and you didn't tell me – or anyone! What the fuck do you think you're playing at? I keep covering your ass and making excuses for you and you just keep pushing it a bit further. Are you making fun of me?' She stamped her foot and I thought for a moment the spiked heel of her stiletto would pierce the tarmac or break in two. It did neither. The reverberation as it impacted the ground travelled the length of her body – either that or she was trembling with rage. This time I *had* gone too far.

'I didn't know what to do, Heather. I'm sorry,' I mumbled pathetically. 'How can I take it with everything as it is – and how can I not take it?'

'What you do about it is neither here nor there. The fact is you didn't tell me about it. You're meant to be dealing in honesty and truth, Lawrence.'

'I'm not sure they always go together, Heather – or whether they ever have.' She looked at me as if I was one of the aliens Win, Georgie and I had been about to battle the summer before we were sent away.

'If that's what you truly believe Lawrence, then you shouldn't have been called to the Bar at all. What we do is put the truth right out there, honestly in open court.'

'I beg to differ, Heather. What we do is put the truth *as we present it* out there in open court. What we should do is put the truth out there, *honestly*, in open court.'

We examined each other like pugilists spoiling to fight.

'So what are you going to do next then, Lawrence?' she asked at length.

'I don't know. Things have moved on rather since we last talked.'

'That was only a day or so ago.'

'I know. Life moves fast in the fast lane. I've had something else sent to me, and Kat has had a similar parcel sent to her.'

'Meaning?'

'Meaning that what has been presented so far has been a version of the truth and the actual truth has yet to be discovered. I think Margaret is behind it – or at least central to it.'

'Bloody Margaret again,' she exclaimed bitterly. 'I rue the day ...' she paused waiting for my reaction. I waited too, for the usual rant, but it didn't come. She looked at me strangely. 'You've changed your tune.'

I did a double take at her repetition of Win's words. 'But I haven't said anything.'

'No, exactly. Once upon a time you would have been heartily agreeing with me. Denouncing Margaret for meddling, manipulating and messing you around. Now you're saying nothing.'

'Maybe there's a reason I haven't seen – still don't see – but should, for what she's been doing. Maybe it's time I found out what should be presented in open court, and then did it.' The passages in *Mockingbird* began to draw into focus.

'Jesus, you *are* going to ruin us,' she breathed. 'You're a maniac.'

'I won't do anything to harm you or the partnership, Heather. I promise that, cross my heart and hope to ...'

'You bloody will if you do.'

'It's all about me, and if it affects you at all, I'll make sure I tell you about it far enough in advance for you to do a PR job. I can't change facts though – once I know what they are.' I debated telling her about Jaggers' appearance in Chambers but there seemed little point. The warning shot was across my bows, not hers and it would only set her more firmly on my case.

She rubbed the toe of her shoe across the tarmac. The sole made a light grey scratch on it. She shifted her weight to the other leg and traced the scratch line with the other toe, considering. Eventually she said, 'This is the last time I cover for you, Lawrence. And God knows why I'm doing it this time.' She looked up and stared me full in the face. I tried to withstand the scrutiny without flinching. 'You need to decide where things are going with the little social worker too. It's not just about being blind to everyone and everything around you, Lawrence. It's about being blind to yourself. I said you'd changed your tune about Margaret, and that means maybe you're changing your tune in other ways as well. Don't fall down the well there – ding dong dell, remember? Pussy's in the well.' I shook my head, mystified. She recited, *'Ding, dong, dell, Pussy's in the well. Who put her in? Little Johnny Flynn. Who pulled her out? Little Tommy Stout. What a naughty boy was that, to try to drown poor pussy cat, who ne'er did him any harm, but killed all the mice in the farmer's barn* [1]. My Mum used to sing it to me as a kid and it kind of stuck. Your little pussy cat could get drowned alongside you if you're not careful.'

'Duly noted,' I nodded. She was right. She was always right about Kat and I kept acknowledging and ignoring her.

'Off you go then.' I must have looked surprised. 'Well I didn't really think you'd be coming back to Chambers later. Go and get this sorted so you can start working again. We've a bank account to put back into the black, in case you've forgotten.'

I didn't risk her changing her mind. I climbed quickly into the Austin Healey, only to be pulled up short when she rapped on the window. I wound it down.

'By the way, you asked me who sent me the parcel.' I was all ears. 'Margaret. Your dead wife sent me that lovely little package. I'd know her handwriting anywhere. All those cryptic little notes she used to leave me on the Roumelia case. She'd have known I'd recognise it straight away. I had words with her about that damn violet ink she had a fad about once. Used to make my eyes water. Still does. Remind her about that when you run her down – and I do mean literally,' she added nastily. She didn't wait for an answer. I watched her totter purposefully down the slope towards the exit. Even on heels as high as the Eiffel Tower, she looked like she meant business.

I put the car into gear but didn't move off straight away. I shifted back to neutral and the car idled as my mind raced. So Margaret had sent Heather her parcel too? That meant she positively wanted to be identified. Seen to be alive. It wasn't just a message, it was a downright war cry. Seemed like having the name Wemmick, either by inheritance or acquisition, went hand in hand with mortal combat. I debated whether to go home to read the damn letter she'd left, or to follow up on the deed poll certificate for the original Wemmick name change that I hadn't got to yesterday. It barely seemed necessary now. It had been superseded by the earlier name change and what that implied, together with the information Win had reluctantly shared – that Margaret was apparently the sister of the 1988 murder victim. If it was true, it most certainly explained the motivation and zeal for justice to be done in connection with the crime – and that also militated against the correctness of the conviction. If Wilhelm Johns – Jonno – was the murderer, then there was no reason to get the case re-examined. Logically, then, clearly he *wasn't*.

But surely Margaret could have simply told me her background and asked me to seek reopening of the case? The little voice which accompanied reason argued back. *Of course she couldn't. You helped cover it up.* The voice carried on, a*nd of course you wouldn't because you didn't love her.* Win had nailed that too.

'*She knew you didn't care about her, but she had to get you on her side somehow.*'

Oddly enough, she was arousing stronger emotions in me now, absent, than she had present. Frustration, irritation, admiration, regret, nostalgia. The last one took me by surprise? Nostalgia? For what? You felt nostalgic about things you'd treasured but which had since been lost. I'd felt nostalgic as Win and I had relived our childish role-playing – a lost world of innocence; some-when I wished I could recapture. What of Margaret did I want to recapture?

It had been a business arrangement for me – *the suitable wife*. I had never really considered the woman I'd been married to, been intimate with, had devolved part of my life to – and relinquished control of the rest of it to now, it seemed. When we married she effortlessly slipped into the role of organiser and pattern-maker, taking the frayed edges of my life and cobbling personal and professional together into a *suitable* style for success. I thought of her impassive dark-eyed gaze. Occasionally the dark would flash, signalling depths I hadn't plumbed and which I'd wondered about, but only idly. Mainly she'd been a cool, soft skinned Madonna, quiet, dignified, organised and unassailably complete within herself. The outer casing of serene calm rarely displayed any of the layers that I now suspected stretched beneath. Now, Margaret was calmly, quietly and efficiently unravelling them, and me, so I had to take notice or I would disintegrate altogether.

I was just laughing silently and insanely at my stupidity when Fredriks rapped on the car window in exactly the same way Heather had. I swung round ready with an 'OK, OK, I'm going straight back home, if that makes you any happier,' assuming she'd returned for one of her habitual, 'and another thing ...' which generally followed a good punch line, completely taking the punch out of it. 'Oh, Inspector ...'

'Detective Chief Inspector,' he corrected politely, smiling good-naturedly.

'Detective Chief Inspector,' I agreed. 'What can I do for you?'

'Well, sir, probably get out of the car and come down to the station with me.'

'May I ask why?' I didn't really need to. I guessed my twenty-four hours had run out early after all. Sod Win and his code. He couldn't even read a card right, let alone the time.

16: Misrepresentation

'Do I need representation?'

'Entirely up to you, sir. I wouldn't presume, given your profession. We just have a few questions we'd like to ask.' I turned off the engine and sent out a silent threat to the local residents, detailing all the things I'd do to them if one inch of the car was damaged in my absence like a reverse law of attraction request. 'Is your car all right parked here, sir? Lovely vehicle. Would have one of them myself if money allowed.' He made as if to usher me towards the panda car.

'It had bloody better be.'

'If you like I could get one of the men to bring it down to the station for you.'

'Or I could simply drive myself down there in it?'

'Ah, well, that's the problem.'

'If you're bringing me in, you'd better charge me, Detective Chief Inspector.' I was surprised at the potential technical error – with me of all people.

'I don't really want to do that sir, but it would be extremely co-operative of you if we could take a look over your car too. Both of them. The other one – Mrs Juste's – where would that be?'

'In the garage – out of tax. I don't make a habit of breaking the law. And may I ask why you need to look at it – and this one?'

'Damage sir – the kind a hit and run might cause.' He left the implication hanging in the air.

I laughed. One problem solved at least. Innocence had some rewards at last.

'So what – or in respect of whom – do you want to question me, Detective Chief Inspector?'

He smiled again, apologetically this time. 'The deaths of Mrs Margaret Juste and Mrs Kimberley Hewson.'

'I see, but you aren't charging me with either?'

'Not yet, sir.'

'But you may?'

'Not yet, sir.'

I sighed and handed over the keys to the Austin Healey. I knew enough about the ways of the police to know that to challenge them outright was to make a rod for my own back. Besides they wouldn't find anything on the car, and it would be safer at the station than abandoned here all day and possibly into the night.

'Thank you, sir. Very helpful.' He beamed at me and I was reminded of not the Donald Duck icon of his nickname, but a grinning crocodile.

I sat for what seemed like hours at Chelsea Police Station, in a room virtually identical to the one where I'd interviewed Danny, even though it was a different station. The sergeant had smiled knowingly as he'd recorded my name in the register. I imagined what was on the tip of his tongue. We'd met a few times before on different cases I'd taken. He was a slobby bastard, foul-mouthed out of public hearing, and downright belligerent at times; the sort that got the profession a bad name – deserved or otherwise. I'd taken him to task about his attitude once. I wished now I'd kept my moment of reforming zeal to myself. Normally it was incumbent on the sergeant to ensure interviewees had refreshments and adequate opportunities to relieve themselves – comfort breaks. For me the service was as dry as the Sahara and as uncomfortable as the weekend in Blackpool that Emm had refused to go on with Jill.

At just after twelve Fredriks reappeared. He slipped into place and his short fat sidekick settled next to him. He arranged a pile of papers in a buff folder in front of him and smiled politely at me; the tease. The sidekick was sweating but Fredriks was ice cool. He silently handed me back the Austin Healey keys with a 'thank you, sir.' I wondered if he'd sat in the driver's seat as I'd wanted to as a child when I'd seen the one Mad Mike had brought home to show off, and revelled in the idea of driving it himself. The air clogged with unspoken accusations. Fredriks slid the tape into the machine but didn't turn it on. We both eyed the tape recorder. Its green light glowed: ready.

'I don't suppose you have the keys to the other car – Mrs Juste's – on you, do you, sir?'

'No, Detective Chief Inspector, I don't. And if you are wishing to search my property, shouldn't you obtain a warrant?'

'Oh, not search, sir – merely take a look. Is there anything we shouldn't see?' I balled my fist under the table. *Throw it away, throw it away.*

'No, not at all, but I've now been waiting here for several hours for you to interview me, I've let you inspect the car I'm driving and all without being charged. I think now ...'

'Yes, sir, of course. You're absolutely right.' He pushed the pile of paperwork in front of me on the table. With one fluid movement he flipped the top of the folder open like a magician completing a trick. I recognised the papers immediately. They were from the parcel that had been sent to Kat. Fredriks tugged at the bottom of the pile and the bottom section divided from the top. He placed the pile of drawings we'd found in Danny's room next to the contents of Kat's parcel. I remembered now I'd forgotten to ask Kat what she'd done with the drawings after I'd rushed away to Heather's summons. 'It's most definitely time to talk, I think.'

'And it looks like it's time for me to make my phone call.'

'By all means, sir.'

I rang Heather.

'I knew you would do this to me,' she fumed. She sent John Norton. Stoic, poker-faced, softly-spoken and lethal. I was glad he was on my side, and not intending to assist the prosecution. He was an old-school solicitor, practised at passing on just the right amount of information and no more. They gave me twenty minutes with him before starting the interview. It consisted mainly of him needlessly lecturing me about saying nothing unless he gave me leave, me outlining the rudiments of my predicament, and him repeating his lecture again.

'Miss Roumelia passed this information on to us this morning, Mr Juste. Have you seen it before?' Norton nodded to me. I had leave to speak.

'I have.'

'And what did you advise Miss Roumelia to do with it?' Norton's head twitched again.

'Take care of it. When she called me over to look at it with her, she was concerned that someone might have broken into her property and removed some of it.'

'And was that so?'

No movement from Norton, but I knew I needed to answer. I gave a typical hostile witness response. An answer with no information.

'I didn't find an intruder.'

'And you didn't remove any of it yourself?'

'I saw what you see.' Norton smiled and Fredriks shot me a sharp look.

'And what do you make of it? It appears, at least in part to relate to you.'

'Someone's idea of a sick joke?' Norton's expression cautioned me.

'So it means nothing to you?'

'I have no idea of its purpose.'

The sidekick got up to answer a knock on the door. A WPC poked her head round it and they whispered together. He came back to the table, beads of sweat gathering round his hairline. He must have a medical condition, I thought inconsequentially. Fredriks and he exchanged glances. The sidekick nodded. Fredriks studied me, and stopped the tape, stating the time he did so carefully before asking us politely to remain where we were whilst he took an important message. He and the sidekick disappeared, leaving Norton and me considering each other.

'Heather says you're in the shit.' The mournfully disappointed tone made me want to laugh, but it was hardly funny.

'Heather would, but she's probably right. Someone's definitely trying to set me up.'

'Well for God's sake don't say that to them. That's the best reason for them to charge you that I can think of. If someone's trying to set you up it's because you know something – ergo you can tell them something they want to know too. Just keep it sweet, to the point and don't volunteer anything.' He frowned at me, 'And don't be a smart ass. You're not in court now – or maybe I should say *yet*.'

'I thought you said don't be a smart ass?'

'It doesn't apply to me.' Suitably slapped down, I told him the rest of the details our twenty minutes hadn't given us sufficient time for earlier. His eyebrows gradually rose, and then dropped back to noncommittal again. No wonder he was so good. He really was the wooden man. 'Heather *was* right,' he commented at the end of my monologue. 'You are in the shit. Why the hell didn't you turn it all over to them when it arrived?'

'What do you reckon they would have made of it?'

'A damn sight less than they're going to make of it now. Where's all yours?'

'On my desk at home.'

'Then we'd better hope we can get to it and come up with a plausible reason for you withholding it before they get a warrant.'

'They've nothing to get warrant for.'

'They hardly need probable cause. The murder happened in your house, was a relative of yours, they now have evidence that suggests there may have been reasons for you to want to suppress personal information she possessed about you, and you deliberately didn't tell them about it. They've pretty much got a case already. Is there anything else you haven't told me?'

'I think I cremated someone who wasn't my wife.'

It was worth it just for the reaction. If I'd had a camera I could have sold the photograph for a fortune. I could even imagine the newspaper caption – *no-comment Norton nobbled!* I wanted to laugh even though it wasn't funny. The whole of my life seemed to be descending into sick black humour.

'I don't think I wanted to hear that,' he said eventually.

'Neither do I, but you asked.'

'Have you any proof?'

'No, it's a suspicion, but I think she's the one behind the parcels too.'

'Why?' I'd never heard so much disbelief and dismay put into one word before.

'Because she wants to force me into re-opening a case that was a miscarriage of justice over a decade ago.'

'Why couldn't she just *ask*?'

I shook my head. I hadn't the time, or even the clarity myself to explain before Fredriks came back. The door opened with a silent fanfare. Sweat bucket turned on the tape and mumbled the time the interview recommenced. Fredriks waited for him to finish and then raised his eyebrows at me whilst simultaneously smiling, close-lipped. How the hell did he do that? He look like a grease-painted clown, with arched eyebrows and exaggerated mouth.

'Mr Juste, we now have a warrant to search your property. We believe there may be evidence there linking you to the death of your sister Kimberley Hewson. Is there anything you would like to tell us before we do?'

Norton made a sound like a strangled frog as I considered my options. There weren't any.

'You wouldn't believe me if I did.'

'Try me,' Fredriks said, the clown grin turning triumphant.

17: Manipulation

By the time I'd related highlights of my story to Fredriks, the evidence was on its way back from my house. Norton and I were left to consider the error of my ways whilst Fredriks considered the errors of my life. I had to admit there were many, and unfortunately what Heather had assumed from the items in her parcel was close to what the police pieced together from mine. They gave me one get out possibility. Kimmy's killer could be me, or my brother – Win. Either of us had a good enough reason to get rid of her – me: blackmail, Win: a contract job, given his sleazy CV so far. The potential link of Win to Kimmy via Danny didn't escape the police either. Nor the possibility that he'd been my henchman, ridding me of a meddling wife and a threatening sister as part of the same deal since I'd been spending so much time with him and his known links to other criminal elements. That put me firmly in the frame with him even if I didn't actually do the deed myself. I wasn't sure which was worse. Me in the frame, or Win. At least I knew when to speak and when to be silent. Win seemed to have no such understanding despite his years at crime school.

Fredriks was sufficiently courteous to give me a chance to explain before charging me. He spread all the evidence out on the table in front of Norton and me again. It presented me with a new perspective on it, seeing it all together like that. Each item was marked with a small flagged note, obviously tagging which source of evidence it derived from, but Fredriks wasn't content with possession. He wanted to play. He set the tape going again and recorded the interview start time and then proceeded with his own form of solitaire.

The birth certificates naming myself and Win went onto one pile, multi-coloured red green and yellow with their relevant tags. Next to them the piles of drawings, arranged in four piles – red, green, yellow, and black too, now. The chart in the children's home materialised before me, with its preponderance of black and minimalistic yellow. I deduced from the proliferation of black that the drawings from Danny's room in the home were tagged black. Kat's items were tagged yellow, mine red and the others green. I couldn't identify what the green item was, or where it had come from as it was buried under the black, red and yellow. Fredriks started another pile; photographs this time. Only tagged red. The final pile was an assortment of items and colours, topped with the newspaper article from the parcel I'd been sent. *'Grim Bank Holiday for Goodtime Girl'* stared back at me ominously.

'Interesting, isn't it,' remarked Fredriks, following my gaze. I wasn't sure whether he was referring to the newspaper photo or the array of evidence against me and its multi-coloured associations – a colourful patchwork of damnation. 'I wonder if what we have here is really three crimes, but one criminal.'

'And who do you think the criminal is?'

'Well, perhaps that's open to philosophical debate. Who is the criminal? The man who commits the crime, or the one who induces him to?'

'In law it is both.'

'Ah then, I beg to be corrected. Three crimes and two criminals.'

'Neither I – nor my brother, as far as I know – have committed any of the crimes which you would appear to be referring to, if that's what you're implying.'

'Ah, so you acknowledge yours and your brother's involvement?'

'Reluctantly, but not in the way you are suggesting. Someone was responsible for the death of Maria Flowers in 1988, someone clearly murdered my sister, and my wife apparently died in a hit and run – which, if true, is plainly murder as well.'

'Interesting.'

'What is?'

Norton shifted uncomfortably next to me. I remembered his instruction to say little and engage less. Fredriks was clever.

'The way you comment on the probability of your wife's death being murder – *apparently*. There are some interesting *apparently* photographs in there as well ...' *Shit, so they'd found the suitcase as well.* 'Some curious activity seems to have been going on recently, Mr Juste, and you seem to be at the centre of it. And we also seem to have a lot of people here,' he waved his hand languidly towards the collection of birth certificates and deed poll paperwork, 'who have more than one identity. That is very strange. We're usually only one person at a time, aren't we?

In name and appearance, unless they're you.' He pushed a newspaper cutting alongside the other papers. The report of my 'confession' in court when Danny's case was dismissed.

'I told you that you wouldn't believe me.'

'And I think that is the one thing that you are being open and honest with me about, Mr Juste. I don't.'

'Are you charging my client?' Norton butted in then, studying Fredriks morosely. Fredriks pursed his lips and the duck re-emerged from behind the crocodile smile.

'All in due course, Mr Norton. There are a few more items for us to look into first. Such as who you might have cremated recently in place of your wife, and why you did that.'

I only just managed not to choke. Christ – how had he come up so quickly with precisely the scenario I was still struggling with? Someone must have told him! I glanced sideways at Norton, but dismissed the notion as ridiculous. He was on my side – and apart from that there was no way Norton would land himself that far in the shit on my behalf. He rearranged his long face into one of shock and surprise, and I did the same.

'As far as I know I cremated my wife, Detective Chief Inspector Fredriks,' I replied at length, as frostily as I could. Norton helpfully jumped on the band wagon then.

'That is an offensive and potentially slanderous accusation, Detective Chief Inspector Fredriks. It is also extremely distressing for my client who is still suffering from the strictures of grief. Wouldn't police time be better spent on actually finding Mrs Juste's killer than on harassing her widower?'

'The principle is rather, is Mrs Juste actually dead?' He selected a red-tagged photograph from the pile and placed it prominently on top of the others. It was one of the annotated pictures of the dummy in the road, with notes about car angle, deflection of the body out of the pathway of the vehicle and where blood would gather. 'Normally forensics would do this kind of research *after* the event. DNA testing could confirm what you say of course, but it seems you, or someone close to you went to a great deal of effort to check out the logistics *before* the event, Mr Juste. As I said – curious activity.'

Norton picked the photograph up and scrutinised it. He frowned and turned to me, icy non-reactiveness lost to genuine surprise.

'Lawrence?'

'There is also a rather large insurance pay-out awaiting allocation with regard to your wife's death, Mr Juste. So where is your wife?'

Fredriks' voice was cool and controlled but I could hear the undercurrent of excitement running beneath the calm. So that was it. That was why Jaggers had remained in the background so long. He knew he didn't need to do anything once all of this found its way into the police's hands. I hadn't set up a policy on Margaret's life, but no doubt he had. No doubt he'd also waited for enough of the evidence that could damn me to surface before he primed his missile to deliver the initiatory blast. Had he known about the contents of the parcels then – even if he hadn't sent them? Or were they merely circumstantially useful.

'I didn't kill my wife, or my sister, or the unfortunate victim in 1988. Nor have I been party to faking my wife's death. If you care to check with the coroner, you will find that I personally visited her on the morning of the funeral to ensure they had all the necessary evidence in terms of samples and identification to ensure that my wife was indeed my wife and that we'd be able to use it in the event that we found the vehicle that killed her. She checked with the lab whilst I was there and assured me they had. That is not the action of a man attempting to pass another body off as his wife. DNA test as much as you wish. That is all I have to say for the time being. If you're going to charge me, then do so. If not, then let me go.'

Norton shushed at me agitatedly but I ignored him. Fredriks eyed me speculatively. He would have to check first. He hadn't expected that at all. Thinking time. That's what I needed – and to get to Margaret. She was the key. Somewhere, out there, I suspected she knew all the versions. She had to be found and persuaded to share them with me. My head cleared properly for the first time since the mess had begun to unfold around me. Treat it like a brief, Heather had said – and Fredriks spreading the information out as he had suddenly turned it into that.

'Mr Juste, please don't plan on going anywhere for the time being. I'm sure I will have further questions for you in due course.' He bundled all the paperwork together and prepared to leave. I watched him, trying to categorise and record it in my mind as he shuffled the piles into one that now I wouldn't have direct personal access to anymore.

'I have a question for you, Detective Chief Inspector Fredriks, if I may?'

He looked up from gathering the paperwork together, surprised. I sensed Norton's agitation beside me.

'If it's possible, I'll answer it,' Fredriks replied cautiously.

'Where did you acquire the items of paperwork from that weren't in my home?'

'I don't think I said they were from anywhere in particular, did I Mr Juste?'

'No, but to me it's clear they are from a number of sources. My home is one of them – and I know which items they comprise. The drawings were mainly from Danny Hewson's room at the children's home in New Southgate. I saw them there when he went missing and I left Miss Roumelia, his social worker, in charge of them. The items are colour-coded so I assume the coding relates to the source. As there were four colours in use there are at least two other sources.'

'I can see why they say you are a force to be reckoned with in court, Mr Juste.' He bit his bottom lip and studied the papers in his hands. 'You are right, 'he added after a while. 'But if I told you the sources, you might take it upon yourself to go and visit the said sources too, mightn't you? Then you might be accused of witness tampering, and I really don't want to lead you into trouble, do I?'

He put the folder back onto the table and gave it a gentle push. The papers slid out from it and spread across the table like a pack of cards fanning. He waited. The tape recorder continued to whirr. His sidekick made to stop it but Fredriks held up his hand and shook his head imperceptibly. I looked at the displaced papers. It must have been a lucky break that they encompassed all sources as they did. Fredriks couldn't have planned it that way if he'd tried. Mine, red-tagged, clearly included Sarah's treasure box items as well as the parcel I'd been sent. Danny's – black tagged – were the drawings I'd already seen. The green tag was attached to a witness statement dated 1988. The shock ran through me like a surge in the national grid at that. He'd already pulled the file from the archives then. I strained to see the witnesses name. *'John Arthur Wemmick. Connection to deceased – Employer.'* The silence in the room was deafening. The remaining page turning at right angles to the Wemmick statement was tagged yellow. The other as yet unidentified source. It was the list from Kat's parcel. The shock arced and earthed.

'And you only have a warrant for my place so anything else has been volunteered to you?'

'That is correct sir, or is already in the public domain.' He shuffled the papers back together and the list from Kat's parcel slid out of sight. 'Interview terminated at,' he looked at his watch, 'fifteen-thirty-six.' He raised his eyebrows, and I decided Donald Duck was a pretty smart mallard. He was sending me off to do his detective work for him. 'Be in touch soon,' he added. I stared at him, but it was purely coincidence, not another bombshell.

Norton bustled ahead of me after we'd completed the formalities of signing out with the sergeant on reception. He rounded on me once we were outside.

'What the hell was all that about? And what about the DNA testing? They'll find out if what you told me you – and Fredriks it seems – suspect about that not being her body is true. '

'He was giving me enough rope to hang myself with to save him the effort. And the DNA – what or who are they going to use as a frame of reference?'

'Dental records,' he reminded me with finality.

'With a cremated body? They still can't compare unless they took a cast.'

He shook his head, worriedly. 'I don't like this at all, Juste. And what *were* the other sources? It was all too quick for me. I couldn't work them out.'

Odd that for me it had felt like extreme slow motion; the fanning papers, the brightly coloured tags, the scrawl of the name across the witness statement, and the rolling out of the list of names on the page from Kat's parcel. I could have almost been back in her poky little lounge, acutely aware of her breasts almost touching my back as she pressed up behind me to read over my shoulder, breath warm against my neck, musky perfume invading my senses and making them buzz and blur with desire. I dragged myself back to the present moment. A Mata Hari indeed. Maybe that was her dual role. Did Mata Haris need to be kept safe – or could they swim against the tide quite effectively all on their own?

'The 1988 murder enquiry notes and Kat Roumelia – Danny Hewson's social worker.'

'The one Heather told me you've been banging?'

'Well I might have put it more politely myself.'

'I don't think Heather thinks very politely about the association, and if she's just pushed you headlong into a pile of shit by volunteering something to the police that makes you seem implicated in any of this, I fully agree with her summation of the young lady.' He paused, presumably waiting for my demurral. 'We'll need to go through all of this very carefully, Lawrence. They may have let you go for the moment, but you heard what the Detective Chief Inspector said – they'll be back for more. I've got a client at four-thirty so I can't go though it with you now, Promise me you'll go home or to Chambers and we'll reconvene on this tomorrow morning. I'll decide if I can still help you then. Don't hang yourself with that rope in the meantime.'

'There are still a couple of things I want to check up on whilst I'm still on the loose but I promise to go straight home after I've done that.'

He looked uncertain. I put on my court face. He seemed more convinced by that. 'OK, but for God's sake don't go and see the woman.'

I watched him head off down the road towards his car. It was parked about three along from mine. Christ, I'd been promising to go straight home to more people recently as a middle-aged man than I had ever as a child. The Austin Healey beckoned to me with all the wiles of a woman but I resisted until I knew Norton was well out of the way. His walk and posture belied his abilities. There was no doubt he was the best even though he appeared to be lugubrious and ineffectual. It was a facade designed to fool his antagonists. Fredriks had probably dismissed him as a puppet practitioner, put up by me to front proceedings whilst he and I danced around each other, but Norton's reconvening tomorrow would certainly take me harrowingly through the mill in preparation for any future onslaught from the police. It behoved me to take him as seriously as Jaggers or the police, and it focused me nicely. Priorities shifted again. First was to determine who was on which side. Second was to get myself off the hook. Then I could revert to the original quest: find out what the hell Margaret was up to.

Of the two women I wanted to talk to, there wasn't a hope in hell of pinning Margaret down at the moment, but Kat … I checked my watch. It would take me about an hour to get to Kat's offices in Morden from here. That would time my arrival for roughly the end of office hours. If I missed her there I'd simply keep going over to Kilburn. Somewhere between the two I should find her. I was even revved up enough for Mrs Tooley if necessary.

I arrived earlier than anticipated and revised my plans accordingly. I prowled the side roads between the centre of town and Morden Hall Road on the lookout for Kat's car. Better to catch her away from the office building itself where she would have back-up to call on if she wanted to avoid me. Down a quiet side road was less easy for evasion. I struck lucky in Blanchland Road. Her grey Nissan Micra was parked about a hundred yards in from the junction with Bristol Road. It made sense. The office building was only a ten-minute walk away. I parked up four along from her and waited.

She swung along the road about ten minutes later. Even knowing she'd deliberately betrayed me didn't detract from the physical reaction even just seeing her produced in me. My stomach clenched and I could feel the strings of desire straining my thighs and buttocks. As she drew closer I studied her features, telling myself I didn't still want her. It was a lie. The bruised plum mouth still tempted me and with barely any effort I could imagine the feel of her lips on mine and the heat of her breath in my mouth. It was lust – pure and simple – but what man can resist lust? The only way to deal with it was to let the rush come and go, and as it ebbed, remember the biting shock of realising she'd voluntarily handed over to Fredriks what could potentially ruin me after solemnly promising not to. There could be no doubt. She knew the possible outcome of what she'd done. It was plain on her face as I slid out of the car and she to a halt in front of me on the pavement. The lithe sway of her body temporarily didn't tempt me.

'Lawrence!'

'Kat,' I ended her name with an inflection on the consonant at the end. It sounded guttural – almost a snarl.

'Gosh. What a lovely surprise. How did you know I was here?' She recovered quickly, but not quick enough for me to see the ripple of panic across her features before they settled into playful mode.

'A lucky guess.'

'Oh. Well. Are you on your way home?'

'Over here? Why would I be on my way home in Morden, Kat? I came to see you. I expect you thought I would be busy?''

'Busy? No. Well.' She hesitated. 'That's even better. Shall we go for a drink or something then?'

'I suppose social niceties could play a part in this. I'm not a criminal – despite what some might like to make me out to be.'

She stopped, still four or five paces away from me. 'That was a significant statement, wasn't it?'

I laughed dryly. 'Yes – and a good description of what I'll have to make soon. I've just come from Chelsea Police Station.'

'Oh. And I've got some explaining to do then, haven't I?'

'You have had for some while now, I believe.' I laughed again. 'Although I do rather wonder with you whether one explanation just leads on to another lie, and then the explanation for that leads on to the next –

ad infinitum.'

'I don't lie.' She was genuinely affronted. 'Like I said before, there have been times I haven't been able to tell you everything, and then that looks as if I'm lying.'

'As you wish. Would you like to explain the most recent one then? The telling me you won't hand anything on to the police and then promptly doing just that. Perhaps you also suggested Margaret wasn't the body in the coffin too? You could also include a fuller explanation of your rather curious and enigmatic relationship with my wife. Have you seen her recently, by the way?'

'No, I haven't. I've already told you that and I was telling the truth.' She was huffy and it made her look all the more sultry. Her eyes flashed at me, dark and dangerous. 'She didn't explain what she was doing, just asked me to help – in return for helping me with Alfie.'

I lounged against the driver's door of the Austin Healey. A passer-by with their dog tempered our argument by walking between us, muttering an apology. The dog peed against the lamppost nearest Kat and she took a step back. I launched myself to standing, anticipating her running away, but she merely watched man and dog meander into the distance, then swung back round to face me. I attacked before she could open her defence.

'So why did you give everything to Fredriks?' I asked when the dog walker was far enough away to be out of earshot.

She sighed. 'I didn't have much choice. When they followed up on Danny's disappearance from the home the dorm parent told the police about the drawings. Then they asked me about them and I had to hand them over. That led to them wanting to know if I knew anything else that might throw light on him vanishing the way he did. They made me feel I'd be culpable if I said nothing, and this is my job at stake here. They came to see me at home the second time and I'd left the parcel on the table. The drawings were on the top. I couldn't very well refuse them looking and then I had to explain the connection.'

'You were supposedly putting it in the drawer of your cupboard when I left.'

'Was I? I must have got it out again then – to try and figure it out.'

'And what theories did you share with them?'

'Which one would you like me to have?'

I laughed aloud.

'Touché. There are rather a lot of them flying around aren't there –

but most of them latterly seem to involve me and blackmail.'

'I might have said a bit about Win, and how I thought he could be involved – but surely that would help you, wouldn't it?'

'It probably rather depends on how he might be involved as far as they are concerned.' Fredriks' question about which the real criminal out of the perpetrator and the persuader would be had made it clear landing the crime on Win wouldn't necessarily clear me of culpability. Nor did I believe Win was guilty of anything other than stupidity and bad judgement. No, I knew who was probably guilty of the murder all those years ago, however appearances made it look on the evidence available. That potentially also put them in the frame for Kimmy's murder, but I had absolutely no evidence to prove it. 'Did you mention blackmail?'

'No.'

'Not at all? Or that you thought something was missing?'

'Well, I had to tell them about that.'

'Precisely what?'

'The certificate like the one you had in your package.'

'So you remember it?'

'Oh yes, but it definitely wasn't there later so someone did take it, didn't they?' She looked vindicated.

'Is that what you said?'

'What?'

'That a certificate like the one I'd received was missing?'

'Yes, but nothing else.'

'That was more than enough, Kat. You effectively told them I'd received something similar and they came looking for it. Of course, as you know, my package contained substantially more.' I didn't add that Sarah's box and Margaret's suitcase completed the icing on the cake. My grumbling gut was warning me in the same way as Norton had. Say little, engage less.

She put her hand over her mouth in a creditable approximation of surprised horror. 'Oh my God, how stupid I am!'

Once upon a time my male ego would have blinded me and I would have accepted that the luscious little Kat had simply made another error of judgement. Pretty, naive, vulnerable little Kat. The stereotype she relied on would have set me up and I would have damned myself before I damned her. Don't pick on her. Forgive her because she knows not what she does. Now, the acid-lemon comments I'd winced over recently ate away the sweet stuff of the stereotype and left me considering what was really underneath the candy coat. A young woman who lied at will, lived part of my wife's double life alongside her whilst claiming loyalty to me, and now teased information out of me so she could blithely pass it on to the police. *Not stupid at all, Kat. Very, very clever. Or very, very dangerous.*

18: The Demise of Truth

One wonders sometimes whether fashioning the truth into an acceptable form which enables life to continue satisfactorily is more important than the truth at all costs. Inevitably I ended back at Atticus in debating that question. Had he supported truth at all costs? He'd supported fairness and equality, but perhaps that was slightly different. If he had, would not all of the truth have been revealed and Boo and Jem hounded until their lives were broken and indelibly altered for the sake of a truth which ultimately did no-one any good? Atticus understood the *essential* truth to be revealed – sufficient to allow justice to be done yet still be able to continue life fairly and in a principled way. I kept coming up against the same hoary reasoning in relation to almost every issue I was facing currently.

If the 1988 murder had been pinned on the wrong man, but he was now dead, how would it serve to upend all our lives in order to reveal the real perpetrator? If Danny's father was unnamed on his birth certificate, how would it serve him to know a family connection potentially as unwelcome as the devil in heaven? And if Margaret was 'dead' because she wanted to be – whatever her reasons might be – what point was there in resurrecting her? I could make cases for alternates to all these truths, but I couldn't get past Kimmy's death. If I failed to bring her killer to justice because I didn't want to face who it might be, then the demise of truth – for whatever perceived good – would surely be hard on my heels all the way to hell. And if one truth had to be an absolute, then so did they all.

Why did I seek to avoid that truth? The answer was unpleasant; because Kimmy's killer could be one of so many people I now held either in fear, or alternatively, held dear – and increasingly both in some cases. Jaggers, Margaret and even Win all *could* have had a hand in it. There was also an outside chance that Kat was involved either as Margaret's puppet, or hand-in-glove with so many of my pursuers I didn't know which of them I was evading next because of her. How far might Kat's role in helping Margaret extend? Did it include murder? The same with Win. He claimed to have been ousted from the mock-up of Margaret's 'death' right at the last minute, but who then had completed the task? And how could Danny have drawn such detailed and discomfiting images as those depicting Kimmy's death, if he hadn't been present to see the murder for himself? That either made him part of the heady mix of murder, or very much at risk. Love and fear paralysed me. Yet I had to do something. Fredriks wouldn't wait for his puppet to take the stage for much longer, and I'd rather choreograph the dance on the end of my strings than have someone pull them for me.

There were two people I decided were paramount to locate before Fredriks hauled me back in. Danny and Margaret, but how I was even going to locate Margaret was as much a mystery as Margaret herself. The possibilities were all tumbling through my mind as Kat went through her paces, apologising, excusing, explaining; artfully wide eyes and seductively posed limbs intent on appealing to my baser nature. I listened half-heartedly. I'd heard it all before but this time she failed to convince me. The stakes were too high. Impulsively I decided to start there and then with the source of the black-edged cards. I slipped back into the car and slammed the door. She stopped mid-sentence and came over to rap on the car window, Heather and Fredriks' style. I reluctantly wound it down.

'I thought you wanted to talk?' She leant on the edge of the open window and her body heat burned me up.

'No, I wanted explanations, not discussion.' I turned the key in the ignition and the car revved, sending a glut of blue fumes out the back. I hoped the exhaust hadn't blown. She waved the fug away with a frown.

'I wasn't discussing anything. You're never satisfied, Lawrence. One minute you're giving me the Spanish Inquisition and the next you're just driving away as if it doesn't matter.'

'It does matter, Kat. That's why I'm driving away. I've heard what you have to say and now I have to do something with it.'

'Like what?'

'Like find out the truth for myself if you're not going to share it.'

I left her open-mouthed and confused in the middle of the cracking pavement on Blanchland Road. I watched her receding figure in the rear view mirror as I drove back towards the junction. She remained stock still watching me drive away. Mirrors – one reflecting the other. But mirrors reflect the opposite image, even though the reflection might appear to be identical. The reverse. And that was how Kat worked largely – on the reverse reaction. Challenge me and I backed down – I had right from the first time we'd met in the interview room. Anger me and instead my curiosity was piqued. Lie to me with an abject apology and I accused myself of the same thing, rather than criticise her. But latterly the psychology had faltered – since she'd felt undermined, first by Ella, and now by – I couldn't answer that last one. By something that was making her irritable, and unable to hide it from me hence the nice/nasty cop routine – but she wasn't a cop.

That caused me to pause. Or was she? The unexpected absence when I'd turned up to look at the parcel with her at her request, the supposed intruder and the open window they'd escaped through and the air of abandonment to the house; they all told an odd tale. Even belligerent Mrs Tooley irrationally difficult about me waiting on the doorstep could make sense from that angle. The last thing you want when discretion is key is someone hanging around. And the wardrobe full of clothes for all kinds of roles? They were redolent of another set-up too. Indeed, I doubted very much any of the clothes were really Margaret's. A little creative thinking on Kat's part to deflect me off on another fool's errand whilst she reeled in the evidence for Fredriks. No, she was more than an innocent bystander forced to hand over evidence. She was either too close to the police for comfort, or I was becoming as paranoid as Mary. It would explain everything, including the sudden swoop on me. Kat had told Fredriks what to find and where to find it. If Fredriks' next move was imminent, and Win was right in his reading of code, the little hanged man really *was* me.

Oh God, how stupid I was! I double-backed to the social services office Kat had said she worked at on London Road. There was a car park alongside, now steadily emptying of cars as the offices cleared. It was five-ten. Their opening times said 9am to 5.30pm. Old school. I marched through the double doors, listing in my mind the anomalies. She hadn't known Danny was back in care when Kimmy was murdered, yet she was his social worker. She would be one of the first of the various authority figures orbiting him to know. She hadn't displayed the concern about it I'd expected of her, because she wasn't concerned. She'd been allowed to take Danny's drawings away from the children's home, but surely they should have been retained as evidence when he was reported missing – unless they were being removed for the police themselves. The notice board pronounced that Social Services were located on the second floor, the cross-services Children and Families Metropolitan Police/DSS liaison unit was on the third and DSS fraud was on the ground and first floors. I approached the bored receptionist, fiddling with paper clips and marking time until five-thirty.

'I have an appointment with a Miss Katherine Roumelia about a client of mine.' I swept my business card in front of her just long enough to see *QC*, but not the name. 'Is she located on the second or third floor, please?'

The receptionist looked languidly on her list. 'Err, third now, but I know she's already gone home. I saw her leave about half an hour ago. Do you want to leave a message for her?'

I exclaimed in annoyance, and pulled out my diary.

'My mistake – the appointment's tomorrow. I'll come back then.'

Yet it didn't quite hold together completely to put Kat hand in glove with the police if she was also working with Margaret. And Margaret definitely wouldn't be hand in glove with the police. The discovery disposed of one mystery simply to be replaced by another. What then really was Kat's role, and who was Margaret aligned to? Not Kat, after all perhaps, because Kat had also received a parcel – a prompt.

And that took me back to the black-edged cards again – my tormentor's favourite medium of delivering my torment. One had been posted to me at home, another to Chambers, and my sister, Emm had received one too. The others had been hand-delivered, but the ones that had been posted would have a post mark on them. There had been another card. What had been on it and where was it?

I racked my brains as I edged along in the rush hour traffic. We slowed to a halt as the lorry in front suddenly decided to change lanes, simultaneously blocking both off as he manoeuvred. The white van next to me decided to switch at the same time and cut me up just as I was about to pick up speed. I rammed my hand on the horn but the noise merely grated raw nerves as the driver gave me the V through his open window. Irritation with the grindingly slow progress boiled over. It was claustrophobic wedged between lorry and van. My head shut down with my lungs. I wanted space to breathe and think.

On a whim I swerved off at the next exit and wove my way through the suburban backwoods until I picked up signs for the All England Tennis Club. Wimbledon Common. The nearest wide open space I could think of. Once I was clear of the town centre itself and heading up the hill to Wimbledon Village I put my foot down. Opening the throttle, its satisfyingly throaty purr vibrated along the gear stick. Travelling from my hand and up my arm, it completed its journey in my brain, and began the process of rattling my head too. Enjoying the sense of power after frustration I romped into a side road on one edge of the common, parked up, locked up and set off. I was in the land of money here. The Austin Healey would be revered – if noticed at all – amongst the other vintage, luxury and expensively polished vehicles the gentry of Wimbledon parked outside their elegantly understated shacks.

Wimbledon Common always reminded me of another world – far away from the smog and grind of the city. If you walk to its centre, the lake nestles amongst woodland and scrub, surrounded by a network of trails and pathways. Flasher ground at night or at twilight, but by day a haven for walkers, solitary peace seekers and lost souls like me. Ironically I'd taken Margaret walking across it not long after our first informal drink together and she'd begun the job of convincing me of her suitability as a wife by seeming to appreciate its gentle banishment of time and pressure as much as I. Later when we'd started to be a couple and had frequented formal events together, if we found ourselves anywhere nearby in the daylight, we generally finished off with a walk on the common. Here I felt the nearest to her that I'd felt since she'd 'died'. I can't say it was odd I hadn't felt the urge to go there before. If anything it was somewhere I'd deliberately avoided in my irritation with her. Today felt different. I needed her, and the sensation was strangely comforting.

Before I got too far in, I rang Heather, hoping the signal on my cell phone would hold out. I was probably no more than a couple of hundred yards along a path leading towards the lake but the common was already working its magic. As I waited for her to pick up, I allowed the late afternoon sunshine to tease away the knots in my neck, sending fingers of sunlight through the trees to stroke my head, shoulders and neck. They flickered out a message. Not SOS. *Slow it down, slow it down, slow it down.* I stopped under a tree and looked up into the rippling branches overhead, shimmering like shoals of brilliant green fish in an azure sea. Margaret would have painted it – or wanted to take a photograph so she could paint it later. She was the artist of the two of us, not that I'd taken much notice of her efforts – too abstract for my liking. A simplistic blend of line and colour intended to impart a complex message I couldn't understand.

'*Imagery, Lawrence – what idea does the impression give you? There's a message in everything.*' I'd seen no message – just swathes of colour. '*A message in a bottle, obviously,*' she'd called ruefully after me when I shook my head and took myself off to my study and the brandy.

Heather answered sharply.

'Lawrence, what are you up to now? You promised William Norton you'd go home but I've been ringing there intermittently for the last hour and you haven't, have you?'

I could picture her, hand on hip, head to one side, lips pursed. I was glad she was in Chambers and I was on Wimbledon Common.

'I will be in a while, Heather – and I haven't gone AWOL even though I have hopefully permanently lost Ella. I've specifically rung you to report in, amongst other things.'

'Oh,' she sounded appeased. 'What other things?'

'The black-edged card.'

'What black-edged card? The funeral notice?'

'No, but exactly the same style. It arrived the day you told me about your parcel. I think you'll find it in the top drawer of my desk.'

'Oh my God – what now?'

'Just look for it, please?' I tried to sound as ingratiating as I could. Hard when you know you're talking to a cross between the ice maiden and the queen of all bitches and she won't believe anything you say to her if it's nice. Shame Heather didn't know she was OK really, underneath the sub-zero exterior. I waited as she went off to find it, listening to the birdsong on the air and watching the breeze gently ruffle the branches above me. They mimicked the rustling on the other end of the phone. I smiled at the surreal mirror-imaging that was going on right now. Me, seeking peace and clarity amidst the whispering leaves and fresh breath of nature; Heather delving amongst the dry roots and stifled gasps of the past. For a while I almost lost myself as solitude and peace descended. Her voice was too loud when she came back on.

'I've got it. It was under some envelopes. Who's it from?'

'That was going to be my next question. Can you look at the postmark? It was on my desk when you dumped all the stuff out of your parcel on top of it but I'm sure it came through the post.'

'It's franked.'

'Does it have an address imprinted with the franking?'

'Probably but it's too indistinct to read.'

'Damn, I thought that's what I remembered.' I tried to visualise it. It had been swallowed up by my shock at Heather's parcel. 'Thanks Heather. Could you turn it over and tell me what it says again?'

She sighed, but read out singsong, *'Costs such a lot to stage a story, doesn't it? I think I will have to look into financial funding first. People so often presume only to get caught out when the bottom line is drawn – like curiosity and the cat. Be in touch soon – J'*

'Does it sound clumsy to you?'

'Obvious,' she corrected, 'as in obviously hoping you'll contribute.'

'But that alliteration?'

'Hang on.' It went silent.

'Heather?' There was no answer. My gut rolled. What was happening that I couldn't see? I imagined the police arriving and silently leading her away, or Jaggers slipping a bag over her head and it filling with the steam from her breath as she gagged and choked. 'Heather, what's going on? Are you all right? Heather!'

'Keep your voice down, will you? You're deafening me. I've worked out your franked address.'

I heaved a sigh of relief and reigned in paranoia. 'What is it?' I asked trying to keep the unevenness from my voice.

'FFF. That's what you meant by clumsy – *financial funding first.* You'd say get financial backing. And I threw an old FFF envelope away only this morning. They're celebrating five years of finding families. I'm invited to the festivities. I thought I would go actually. I've got these new Jimmy Choos which would look just perfect with … But you don't want to know any of that, do you? Actually, hold on.' It went silent again but this time I controlled my imagination and concentrated on the shivering leaves and the fleeting sunlight dribbling through them. 'You've got one too. Same franking anyway. So are you going home now?'

'Yes. And thanks Heather. For everything.'

'Don't thank me. Repay me – or the partnership account. Do I have to ring to make sure you're actually where you say you're going now or can I trust you?'

'You can trust me.'

'Huh, I'll ring you anyway.'

The phone clicked and clarity was restored, but not peace. FFF. I rang Emm.

'Hello you. Have you just spoken to Jill too?' She sounded excited.

I was taken aback. 'No?'

'She got the other half of my drawing through the post today. It's got an address on the back of it.'

'Christ. What is it?'

'It's somewhere in the city. I wrote it down and was going to ring you but one of my customers actually bought something today – well, half the shop in fact!' That explained the high spirits.

'Well done.'

'I'll say! You know who she reminded me of though – weirdly.'

'Who?'

'The girl Kimmy used to be friends with when she was a teenager. Not spitting image, but very similar. Blonde. Probably coincidence since I've got it all on my mind because we were talking about it. Made me think about similarities. Had you noticed how Danny doesn't look at all like Kimmy? Or his dad.'

We were heading into dangerous waters so I steered her back to the address. She went off to find the address and reeled it off when she returned. I wasn't surprised. It was FFF's.

'And that was on Jill's part of the picture?'

'On the back, yes. The front was just a picture.'

'What of?'

'Well, actually more of a pattern. I can't really describe it. You should pop over to see her. Thursdays are her late nights. She'll be at the salon until about eight.'

I looked at my watch. I wanted to visit Danny too and visiting would probably finish by nine in the children's wards but it would be wasted if I didn't see what kind of picture Jill had – especially since it supposedly came directly from Danny.

'How do you know it's the other half to yours, Emm?'

'It's numbered – one, and the edge is torn too.'

'You know that black-edged card you thought I'd sent. Have you still got that too?'

'Possibly. In my drawer.' I apprehensively remembered the state of Emm's drawer.

'I'd really like to know if it had a postmark on it.'

'OK. I'll go and have a look and ring you back. I need to close up anyway. Can't have customers walking into a half-empty shop.' She giggled gleefully.

I retraced my steps back to the car whilst I waited for her to ring. I might as well make my way over to Jill and the mysterious half-drawing in the meantime. It was already nearly seven and time was running out on me to see Danny as well as get to Jill. I could hardly dash in, insist on seeing the drawing and then leave without any social niceties. I was still potentially persona non grata to Jill, even if Emm had belatedly given me her stamp of approval. She rang back as I reached the car.

'It says *Finding Futures for Families*, and it's the same address. How odd. Do you know it?'

I pictured the wide glass reception area and prim-faced receptionist.

'Yes, thanks Emm. I've been there once.'

'OK, and I've rung Jill and told her to give you the drawing and to chat another time. I thought you might need to get on with things. She's doing extensions so she says that's fine by her.'

I had a lurid picture of Jill stretching her legs out across the hairdressing salon like they were pieces of stretchy elastic. It turned out to be hair extensions, painstakingly wound into the recipient's own hair to create length. I watched fascinated for a few minutes after Jill handed me the piece of paper, marvelling at how the young woman with the buzz crop on one side was transforming into the siren with Rapunzel locks on the other.

'Wow,' I commented.

'Yeah, extreme,' the young woman replied.

'Expensive,' Jill mouthed at me over her head and grinned. 'Good luck deciphering that,' she said aloud. 'Emm's explained. Catch up when you can. What's good for Emm's good for me.'

'Thanks,' I said, surprised at the well of emotion that suddenly wanted to flow from me. Was this what they meant by familial love? I didn't know either woman well, and one barely at all, but acceptance because of 'family' seemed to give me unequivocal acceptance by them in all other ways too. It was a phenomenon I was seriously going to have to revisit soon.

Emm was right. The drawing was a pattern. Completely random it seemed, and filling one half of the paper only, drawn in linear style. It wasn't at all childish, but it was childishly adult. The more I looked at it, the less convinced I was that Danny had drawn it, or indeed any of the drawings. At least I could ask him now. I laid it on the passenger seat and studied it intermittently as I drove, making it to Great Ormond Street Hospital with twenty minutes to spare before visiting finished. As I marched through its sweeping entrance and thought about the last time I'd been here with Kat, I suddenly realised I had no idea which ward Danny was on. It had been Elephant then, but he'd been undergoing tests. His admission now was more to monitor him after his unexplained absence.

I made a beeline for the receptionist on the desk inside the main doors. She was in her early twenties but looked tired and fed up, flicking listlessly through screens on her monitor searching for his name, only to come up with a blank.

'You're sure he's here?'

'I was told he was.'

'Are you a relative?'

'Ye-s.' She noticed my hesitation, and stopped scrolling.

'Well, I can't find him on our current lists – unless he went home today. The system updates overnight. Sometimes patients who've been sent home during the day end up in cyberspace when they're discharged, until the system reboots.'

'Not particularly helpful when you're trying to locate someone,' I commented caustically.

She gave me a look that said I was pushing my luck.

'It's not my fault,' she replied at length. 'And who says we're not all in cyberspace most of the time? Do you think we exist simply because we're recorded on a system, or are where we say we are because that's what a computer says?' Her face broke into a grin and the weariness left it. 'Sorry, this is only my part-time job. I double as a philosophy and ethics undergrad in my other life. We're on existentialism at the moment. I'm beginning to question everything concrete in favour of the imperceptible. You might not even exist, other than to ask me this question – and if I can't answer it, maybe you'll just disappear. '

It was an interesting idea and one I would otherwise have been inclined to debate with her under other circumstances but I suspected she was politely telling me to piss off.

'Clever,' I acknowledged. 'So even if he's not on your system now, where might he have been if he was?'

I leaned across the desk, court-room style as I did when I was about to cross-examine. She made a little noise in exclamation.

'You're that bloke, aren't you? I saw you in the papers last week. Bit of a stir over a boy they charged for mugging an old lady when he couldn't have done it and then someone stabbed in your kitchen.'

'Yes. It's the boy I'm enquiring about now.'

'Oh, that's different. He'd be in one of the generals if it was for observation only. Caterpillar or Bruin Bear I'd suggest. So, who did it then? The stabbing, I mean.'

'I'm sorry. That's for the police to find out. You've been very helpful, though, and as I'm now going, I didn't ask you any of this, did I?'

'Yeah, right – I get it. No, I've never even heard of you either. Bloomin' existentialists – what do they think we are? Mad?'

I gave her a little mock salute and found the lifts. Caterpillar and Bruin Bear wards were on levels four and five. The lifts were on both sides of the corridor. Up on the left and down on the right. There was no waiting around for a lift up at this time of the evening – just before departure rush hour for visitors. I called it and it arrived almost instantaneously – convenient because now I was really clock-watching. The sounds and smells were the same wherever you were, antiseptic twang mixed with old sprouts. It reminded me of the children's home and the lingering aroma of Sundays when roast dinner of a sort was a treat. I'd usually spent the day before on floor scrubbing chores and the smell of disinfectant took at least two days to dissipate. My Sunday dinner therefore tasted much like the hospital smelt – hardly a treat, more a treatment, but at least it had been better than the tasteless slop of the rest of the week. I was unlucky on Caterpillar Ward, but the receptionist on Bruin Bear knew who I was talking about straight away.

'But he was discharged earlier on this evening.'

'To cyberspace,' I murmured.

She looked at me strangely. 'No, to a relative. May I ask your connection to him?'

'I'm his uncle, Lawrence Juste.'

'Oh, then it must have been your wife he went home with, Mr Juste.'

'My *wife*?'

She reached behind her to some filing near the reception desk, and pulled out a blue card folder with Daniel Hewson written across one edge in large capitals.

'Yes.' Flipping the cover open, she read aloud. '*Discharged six-twenty to Margaret Juste, Aunt. ID seen.* And she left you this.' She handed me a black-edged card and the blood froze in my veins.

The boy's under rosemary's cloak. Forget the hemlock and concentrate on the herb. Put on a different skin to see.

Be in touch soon - J'

The little hanged man in the corner was complete. Signifying the end for me, no doubt – and Danny was with Margaret? But did that make him safe – or even more at risk than ever?

19: Companion Rats

I didn't know where to go next. Kat and the police were my last choice, and possibly more or less one and the same, it would seem. That left just Heather and home. Or possibly a third choice; family. Win, Emm – or even Binnie, although I wasn't sure why I included Binnie in the possibilities. She'd made it clear I was unwelcome, and yet something still made me feel I could trust her. *Play it safe.* I discounted Binnie for the time being. I needed to work out why my instinct was working the way it was – and as I was only too well aware, it wasn't particularly reliable at the best of times. Going home would give me nothing – not even the contents of the parcel or Sarah's box now, other than being able to read Margaret's letter which Fredriks surprisingly hadn't seemed to have found. Maybe because I hadn't told Kat about it, but I now wondered whether it would contain anything more than recriminations for my failings throughout our married life. She'd led me a merry dance so far – the letter was likely to merely be another step in it. Going home would also put me under Fredriks' spotlight and I had little doubt the press would now be waiting to see how well I became illuminated by it too. So there it was. I had to rely on my least reliable prop: my big brother Win. The rat who'd left me in the sinking ship as a child, and who I'd deserted as an adult. Companion rats. Perfect.

His card had found itself a niche in my wallet now, sunken amongst the old credit card receipts and parking slips I hadn't yet disposed of – hidden. I had to face it. I needed his help but I was ashamed of him, and that shamed me too. I went back to my car and sat in it for a while without doing anything. It was surprisingly quiet for a hospital car park. Perhaps most of the visitors had already gone. It was still light but fading towards that half-grey that presages night – gloomier still in the dingy lighting of the multi-storey. Dirty yellow staining dour grey. I'd never liked this half-state time of the evening – neither the vibrancy of the day, nor the mystery of night. I pulled Jill's drawing out and spread it across the steering wheel. I should at least try to decipher it before I made contact with Win. He would deflect me completely with his brash urgency to *do something* – however unwise. Now was the last opportunity to break the code before the train of thought in my head became even more derailed.

At first it seemed to be a complex series of random doodles, cleverly wrought and intensely imaginative, but devoid of logic. The longer I studied it the less random it became. Inside the coils of repeating pattern it was a trompe l'oeil; Escher-like. One face divided into two, and merged into another form, which in turn flowed into a new branch of what could be a tree if you held it far enough away. Close up it merely looked like a series of arcs – stylised code for bark. One face was awake and the other asleep. Around the tree coiled the serpent with its demon's head. Open mouthed, it staring stonily after the dwindling lines trickling away from its mouth to merge with the tree. Its serpent's tail doubled back on itself and wound inward around the two faces which centred the pattern, and there I was back at the start again. Studying it in more detail I began to see how it worked on its various levels. On one there was the two-headed entity – sleeping or watching. On another there was the age-old reference to the serpent in the Garden of Eden, coiling around the tree of life and tempting Eve into sin. The serpent eventually transformed into a gargoyle, intent on diverting the life-flow away from the two-faced body and into the tree. Sin upon sin, repeating and reinforcing its damage. On yet another level it was obvious the objects linked to tell a tale, or explain a mystery.

Without Margaret's card I would have thought it to have been created by an unsound mind; definitely not Danny's work – far too complex and disturbed. But I knew it wasn't. It was highly and specifically focused – for me. And the stylised depiction of the individual elements was very much at one with the other drawings. That led to only one conclusion – the other drawings weren't Danny's either. Some other budding Michelangelo had both been present at the scene of the crime, or crimes, and wanted to tell the story. Who?

Not Jaggers. He wouldn't want to tell the tale unless it would incriminate me whereas the evidence was now piling up against him. Not Kimmy. She couldn't have created this kind of masterpiece even if she'd been alive – and she was very much dead. Not Win. I didn't even have to rationalise that. All the other protagonists in my little saga discounted themselves – Kat because she was a cop, or as good as – and Heather because I couldn't believe she was involved, other than because of bad luck and me. There was only one person left – and one explanation. Margaret. Margaret was re-telling the tale for me; the tale of an old murder, inextricably linked to a brand new one.

I had all the answers just as Margaret said. Not currently in my possession but I could remember enough to piece them together nevertheless. I guessed it had started more than twenty years ago – with three girls who knew each other at school. Kimberley Juss, Maria Flowers and her twin sister Margaret. How or why they'd got to know Jaggers was mere speculation – and maybe not even relevant – perhaps via Kimberley and Win, or some other connection I hadn't come across yet. Both Kimberley and Maria had got themselves pregnant and both had fallen foul of Jaggers, although possibly in different ways. The photograph of the ring in the package sent to me implied Jaggers had killed Maria Flowers, but not why. Maybe that too was irrelevant. Both children had been born, and one had died. For both the father was 'unknown' so their parentage was deliberately being hidden – Danny's probably for reasons very obvious to me. Baby Flowers – who could tell – other than that his mother was already part of the murky world of the Wemmicks, according to Win.

I knew then partially what had bothered me about the birth certificates. They were both intended as precursors to another set-up. Possibly Kimmy had tried to foist a paternity claim on Jaggers but been foiled. How, I wasn't sure. Blood typing? Genetics? And Baby Flowers too maybe, as part of some plan Maria and Margaret were plotting between them. There seemed to be an awful lot riding on paternity just recently – mine and Win's included. In fact if I'd been creating a Venn diagram, overlapping the corresponding elements, it would be so heavily weighted towards paternity suits the Family Court would be booked up for years to come. Win had started it all with the curved ball involving me and Kimmy, but the more I thought about that night at the party, the more certain I was that the woman I'd had draped all over me couldn't have been Kimmy, in any guise. Or more that I simply *wouldn't* have slept with someone like my sister whatever name she gave me and however drunk I'd been. I just wouldn't. My one-night stand had been with someone else, and conveniently used by unscrupulous manipulators enjoying the bad joke. In other words Win's claim was a red herring. And the doctored birth certificates for myself and Win? Maybe they were red herrings too. Twisting the knife a little deeper whilst deflecting my attention from the real issue at the bottom of the pile of shit – a complicated will and a demand for the return of its bequest. Like all things evil, money was the root cause of this problem, but not the love of it – the need for it.

Fuck! It was all so simple and yet so ridiculously complex. Twisted strands that needed fresh eyes to see them unravelled – like breaking a code. And now the vague understanding for the marking of the passages in *Mockingbird* burst on me with overwhelming clarity.

Code. They all contained part of a code telling me what to do.

I needed three things. My blood test result to finally dispel the hold Win and his games currently had over me where Danny was concerned, the will to determine precisely how far out on a limb I could go in public and Margaret. To get any of them I had to come right out in the open. No more playing it safe. Playing it very unsafe indeed. Ironically, they also required me to go home – the very thing I'd discounted. It might no longer house Sarah's box or the evidence parcel I'd been sent, but it did house something else that I was going to need to prove that I was innocent of at least one murder – the way to reach Margaret. The letter in her vanity drawer and the numbered keys may be red herrings too, but there was something else there that definitely wasn't. The book. I had a code to crack and a campaign to plan, and home was the only place to deploy my troops from.

I called Win.

'Ay up – what's happening then? That hoity-toity cow at your place told me you been taken in – but if you're out and about again you ain't been charged yet, then?'

'Were you expecting me to be?'

'We-ell.' His heavy breathing steamed up my handset even with him absent. 'They're gonna charge someone and it's either you or me. I'd rather it were me, funnily. At least you could get me off. Dunno what I could do to help you.'

'I do. You can come over to my place straight away. You're going to be my eyes, ears and getaway man – but don't let anyone see you. The hacks will be on me like a pack of wolves after this.'

It occurred to me afterwards that he wasn't in the least bit curious or argumentative, which in itself was curious. At the time, I was merely thankful he didn't waste time arguing. My twenty-four hours had dwindled to no more than twelve now, and I wasn't sure if that was going to be enough. I beat him back by fifteen minutes and had checked the mews was clear by the time he arrived. I'd already deciphered the code and written the note.

'Rosemary will have to abandon her blue cloak and come out into the open. To honour the dead, and get justice for the living, Juste memories are not enough. Find your funding at basement level first.'

I wrote it on one of the black-edged cards I had left over from the funeral. The other reason I'd needed to go home. A little dramatic irony to ease the way. Win arrived, loud and ripe, and disturbing the twitching curtains at six despite my caution. I ushered him in and took him to the kitchen. To my mind the chalk marks could still just about be seen on the floor, no matter how hard anyone scrubbed at them.

'Right, first – Kimmy.' I indicated where the smudged outline had been. 'Who was here that day, Win?'

'How'd I bloody know?' He wiped his mouth on the back of his hand. He was sweating.

'Oh, you do. You know a whole lot more than you've been telling me. Who was here and why?' I waited. I knew he would break eventually. I just didn't have eventually. I had approximately eleven and a half hours by my reckoning.

'It weren't me.'

'I know it wasn't you. I would never suspect you of killing your own sister, but I think you know who did and you're shielding them.'

'She were difficult at times – Kimmy. Bipolar – you know that now.'

'And she became difficult that day? Who with?'

'I don't know. She wouldn't tell me – just that she were going off to get her dues. That's what she said. *I'm owed for this little lot. If Peter won't pay me, Paul will.'*

'And who were Peter and Paul.'

He was reluctant and I couldn't be certain why.

'Win, I need to know. Kimmy has been murdered, I'm about to be charged with it – and if I'm right, you're prime suspect number one for Margaret's 'death'. They've found the suitcase and they think it was a put-up job; that I had her killed for an insurance pay-out. That suitcase makes you quite probably the hit man. What we have no proof of – is that Margaret is still very much alive somewhere. If I'm under arrest for Kimmy's murder I can't help get you off, can I? You have to tell me what you know now. All of it.'

'OK,' he rubbed his mouth and chin again. 'It could be the Wemmicks.'

'Jaggers and Margaret together?'

'Yeah.'

'In partnership.'

'That's the problem. Until recent, I'd have said no, but now … she wanted justice, see? Revenge for her sister. But Kimmy insisted on going to see her because she thought she were owed something – even though I said to keep a low profile. I didn't like Kimmy going to your house. I mean, why? Margaret were meant to be dead, so why tell Kimmy to come here? I told her not to go. Didn't know who she might be going to run up against if it weren't Margaret. Thought it were a trap so I followed her. Well, it obviously were, weren't it? We argued. She told me to go or else. I left. I should have stayed.'

'And have you spoken to Margaret since?'

'No, I can't. I don't know how to get hold of her.'

'I do.'

He stared at me as if I was crazy.

'How?'

'I've worked it out from the book and cards she sent. She knew I hated corners turned over in books and that I automatically flatten them out when I find them. That made me open the book and read the text. At first I read out of curiosity, then I realised her messages were referring back to something *on* the page. The cloak changing the colour of the flowers on the rosemary bush meant I had to translate what was on the page and see it differently. Being in another's skin was to see an alternative viewpoint – that is, what I was being told wasn't necessarily true. The sin was to kill a mockingbird.'

He made a face at me.

'What the fuck's that all mean?'

'Mockingbird is a metaphor for innocence – Jonno. The mockingbird singing is telling the truth. Margaret's got all the evidence and Danny's with her. *The boy's under rosemary's cloak.*'

'OK,' he shrugged. 'So you're the demon detective now as well as the bastard barrister. That still doesn't tell us how to get to her.'

'No, that was on the back of the drawing Danny gave Jill. *Financial funding first.* Get it? It was in the first message and the card Emm got asking her to visit Danny was franked FFF. Margaret didn't want to be found, she wouldn't, but she's made it very clear where to look.' I thought about what Heather had said. 'Or at least on one particular night. They're having a party to celebrate five years in business soon and Molly

Wemmick is bound to be there.'

I called Heather.

'Where are you?' She sounded sharp.

'Home, as instructed.'

'Oh, OK – so what are you ringing me about? Do you know what the time is?'

'Late – much later than you'd think. That FFF event, when is it exactly?'

'Why, are you escorting me?'

'I'd never be able dress stylishly enough to complement your Jimmy Choos, Heather.'

'Haha! Funny – but true.'

'But I think I have an angle on Margaret – where I might find her. And by the way, be careful what you say to Kat Roumelia.'

'Even funnier – does the blind man now see?'

'Yes – that she's a snitch.'

'What?'

'I think she's linked to the police, somehow.'

'Oh my God – so all that nonsense about her brother and that dodgy case – it was all to set us up?'

'I don't know. If it had been then I would have expected the police to have moved on us by now. Have you had any problems with anyone?'

'Only you.' It was amused, but icy. 'But that's taken as read now, isn't it?'

'Yes, Heather.' I felt much as I had done when Miss Liddell reprimanded me. The likeness of Heather to her was excruciatingly close at times. 'But that FFF party?'

'Oh wait a minute, I'll find the invitation.' I waited, imagining the seconds of my freedom trickling away down the phone like sand through an hourglass. Win settled on the same stool Danny had sat on at the breakfast bar, stomach protruding from the gap in his shirt where the buttons had pulled apart, the effort to hold things together just too much. The contrast between him and his nephew was extreme – much like the dissimilarity between us; brothers, yet worlds apart in attitude, life and looks. I watched his gaze sweep the room, taking in the pristine emptiness Margaret had artfully created. He made a face. He didn't like it much. Ironically I found I now did – despite my preference for the traditional. The clean lines were satisfying in an unsatisfying way, and a relief from the tortuous complexity of everything else in my life. My mind wandered as I waited and enjoyed Margaret's joke. Even here she'd made our world appear plain, straightforward, *obvious*, whereas it was anything but. It was an insight into my wife's mind I'd never comprehended before – dry wit. Routinely, she'd made the complex appear simple – yet here she was now making the simple unbelievably difficult. That too was telling me something, but I couldn't figure out what.

My gaze ended up on one of the disconnected security screens she'd had fitted. They were linked to the burglar alarm – also disconnected. Her idea had been to connect the whole system to miniature cameras in every room after one of our neighbours was cleared out shortly before her refurbishment plans were completed. In the end it had never been properly switched on; some problem with the circuit which would require all the wiring to be redone. It could work in the kitchen, my study and the hall without the rewiring but at my insistence Margaret had turned it off when I complained it was like appearing on TV in my own home. The neighbour's break in had later turned out to be a scam and blown out of all proportion – a DVD player and a few pounds, not the family silver.

Heather came back on the line, breathless and sounding surprised.

'I can't believe I was so stupid,' she exclaimed. 'I misread the date. It's tonight.'

'Tonight? I thought you said it was next week.'

'No, I said the invitation came about a week ago, but it's actually for tonight. Do you really want to go?'

'Not publically, but you do. Put on your Choos and get over here. I've got a delivery for you to make.'

It was now almost seven. I had to factor in enough time for Heather to change and choose her shoes – at least an hour – and deliver the note. I added '10pm' to the card. The security screen winked green at me. Irritating. Like a lot of Margaret's ideas.

'So what are you doing?'

'I'm throwing a different kind of party and you're delivering the invitation.'

20: The Pit

The back door was indeed a back door – a lower ground back door, or more accurately the basement door. I knew FFF had one. I'd seen the button for it in the lift when I'd wandered the building, found Molly Wemmick's office and first made the connection between my wife as her alter ego, Molly, and my sworn enemy, Jaggers. Margaret would know that. I had little doubt she knew everything I'd been doing ever since she 'died'. On that basis she'd also know what this door would look like to me. My worst nightmare come true. In fact all my nightmares in one, because I also knew precisely where I'd seen this particular door so recently. It was in the picture that Danny had given Emm. Not the children's home door after all but virtually a duplicate of it – shiny and new. Had someone reached into my head and pulled out my vilest memories to recreate them in a modern-day horror story? If they had, who better to do that but Jaggers, or my wife?

It was lost on Win. He didn't seem to remember at all – or maybe he simply didn't associate new with old. And now my busy brain was back to questioning what I thought I'd resolved. If Danny gave the drawing to Emm, surely he'd drawn it? Therefore were there two artists after all?

'Fuck.'

'Yeah, how we s'posed to get in then? It's locked.'

'That's not what I was swearing about, actually – but you're wrong.' He gawped at me as if I was talking another language. 'Doesn't it remind you of anything?'

'A fucking locked door.'

'A *particular* fucking locked door that only *appeared* to be locked.' He frowned. I could see the pattern of thoughts shifting in his head and reforming, jumbled and nonsensically, into nothing. 'Well, it seemed to be locked to me, but it wasn't. Just wedged so I couldn't get out.'

'Oh, *that* fucking locked door.' We eyed each other. 'Sorry.' I was struck again by the odd correlation between us. My life had supposedly been intellectual and legitimate, his brutish and lawless, yet we stemmed from the same root and were now part of the same bloom – the sickly sweet smell of death and decay that the scent of arum lilies always reminded me of.

'It'll open the same way, I think. It's intentional – the similarity.'

'Tricky bastard.'

I wasn't sure if that was aimed at me or the owner of the door, but Win plainly remembered after all. He looked around edgily before working his charm. The back of the building looked out on to a slip road orbiting the building itself so visitors could drive in and out without stopping, or filter off to the small dedicated car park at the rear controlled by a red-painted barrier. Tonight the car park's dozen or so spaces were crammed to overflowing with expensive looking vehicles, but otherwise there was no overt activity. The party was in full swing inside. The road leading to the FFF building had been lined with cars too. Presumably more party-goers, but again it was otherwise deserted. Not so unusual given it was an office building in a land of office buildings. Nothing residential, but the sense of desertion outside in contrast to the dynamism inside was eerie – like two worlds were operating in tandem and we'd been stuck in the one frozen in the void. 'All clear?' he asked. Impatience ground into me like broken glass.

'Just do it.' The sooner we were in and I was facing my nemesis the better. An ending was long overdue – whatever it might be. Heather had the card and instructions to give it to one of the event managers to pass on to the female host urgently *'with compliments'*. I hoped Molly Wemmick would have occasion to check her guest's compliments promptly.

Win wrenched the handle sharply anti-clockwise and lifted the door bodily off its hinges. The locked door unlocked. He dropped it back down onto its sprocket and the door opened easily.

'Still got the old magic,' he commented complacently, giving the door a little kick to keep it ajar. His shoe left a scuff mark on the door, like an arrow pointing *this way*. He stood aside and gestured for me to go first. *Thanks for nothing.* It led into a gloomy passageway lit only by a bare bulb overhead. My imagination started to work overtime, but at least it was light of a sort. There had been none in the cellar when I'd been 'initiated' at the children's home, just dank black fear.

I moved cautiously inside and Win pulled the door closed behind us before I could stop him. Claustrophobia enshrouded me in a heavy blanket of panic.

'Open it again!' I hissed, gasping for breath. It wasn't that the light had gone with its closing, or the rats appeared. It was escape that had been lost. I felt the prickle of sweat all over my body, and the frenzy of hysteria begin to take over.

'Why?' He grimaced at me. 'If it's open security will check it out. Gotta look like nothing's happening to get away with this kinda stuff.' He peered closer at me. 'You losing it, little bruv?'

In the shadows I couldn't detect whether his face was sympathetic or mocking. His voice was expressionless, half whisper.

'Bad memories – you know that.' I struggled to regain control, conscious that I had to lead and Win follow. I gulped in air and clenched my fists the way Margaret had shown me. *'Throw it away, Lawrence. If you don't need it or it gets in the way of what you're trying to do, simply throw it away. Get rid of it.'* I'd throw all this crap away if I could, Margaret, but you're the one who's dumping it on me. How do I throw that away?

He sounded contrite then. 'Sorry, didn't think it would still make that much difference.'

I mentally threw away the first anxiety grenade. The panic exploded against the passage wall and I walked past it, careful not to be caught in its fallout.

'Come on, let's just get this done.'

'Who you after – him or her?'

'You cautioned against confronting Jaggers, and I agree. It's Molly Wemmick and Danny we want. Danny must be here with her – or she'll be able to tell us where he is. Finding him safe is our prime objective, getting information out of her our next one.'

'Molly Wemmick – you mean she ain't your Margaret?' He looked incredulous.

'No, she is my Margaret, but tonight I think she's playing her other role.'

We edged along the corridor until we reached another doorway. I'd blitzed the walls along the way with my mind bombs, razing as my much of my fear as I could but the reservoir remained full nevertheless. We positioned ourselves either side of the door. It looked the same as the outer door, but more worn. More like the door in Danny's picture.

'What now?' Win hissed.

'We need to check it out,' but I couldn't. I'd entered the beast. Now it threatened to devour me. I froze, remembering the dark and the cold and the splash of the imagined rats, dropping into the water and swimming toward me; an army of gnawing dread.

'You want me to.' It wasn't a question, it was a statement. 'I guess I owe you that.' He didn't wait for a reply. He completed the same manoeuvre as on the outer door and disappeared through the gap. This time there was no light. Pitch black with merely a small penlight beam piercing the density. He had a torch. Why hadn't I thought of that? Idiot!

'Is Danny in there?' I knew the answer would be no. Margaret might be enigmatic but she wasn't sadistic and nor did I think she wanted any harm to come to Danny. Quite the reverse in fact.

'No, but I tell you what is.' He directed the thin stream of light at a table and chair. 'Come and have a look.' I edged to the door and strained to see what he was talking about.

'Describe it.'

'Your parcel maker's gubbins,' he announced. 'Got a pretty handy forger here by all accounts.' It went quiet and the beam faded to a faint glow as he trained it on to some other items on the table. From where I stood I could only make out a collection of what looked like blocks, a pile of black-edged cards off to one side, and an open box next to them.

'So, you've come to join the party after all?'

I swung round and found myself face to face with worse than my nemesis. Jaggers. My only conscious thought before the dark engulfed me was that I'd been wrong about coming out in the open and that Win had set me up after all.

***

I woke to the bite of iron around my wrists and ankles, and the cold of stone against my back. Heavy chains restrained me. I could see nothing. The suffocating midnight of the place was all-encompassing with no artificial moon to light it. And where was Win? Bastard. I shouldn't have trusted him – family or not. I eased myself away from the wall, every inch of my body aching. I winced as heavy chain chafed raw skin. My chest screamed pain. Ribs broken? My head buzzed with a swarm of angry bees determined to escape through my skin, stinging angrily as it refused to release them. Rats were the least of my worries now. I laughed wryly – a half-cough that tasted of blood. My front teeth ached and my lips were tight with dried spittle. The mumbled groan from alongside me made me freeze with disbelief. I cleared my throat of cloying sputum. It sounded like I was drowning and my ribs roared in protest at the convulsions needed to do it. I could taste more than feel the tears sliding down my cheeks as I heaved and gasped until my voice grated through the barrier.

'Win?' A mumbled sound of pain filtered through my confusion in reply. I repeated his name until he grunted back.

'Another fine mess you got me into, Stanley.'

I wanted to shout with laughter at the incongruity and the relief. Something we had in common at last – a sense of humour that withstood disaster, and trust. He hadn't betrayed me.

'My turn ... say ... sorry ... now,' I croaked back.

'Too ... right. So bloody ... say it!' He paused and groaned again. 'Fuck ... that ... hurts!' More silence, then his voice echoed hollowly in the dark again, suddenly strong and belligerent. 'Jesus ... Christ. I'm in chains here! Fixed to the wall! This is a bloody dungeon!'

I shifted to take the weight off my arms, which throbbed as much as my ribs stung now the blood was flowing back into them. The more I talked the easier it became even though my chest ached with the effort.

'Any ideas ... how are we going to ... get out of here?'

'How the ... fuck should I know? Where is here anyway?'

I concentrated on controlling the pain in my ribs as the bees moved down to swarm inside my arms, delivering a million pinpricks to the second with their stings. Blood trickled into closed veins and collapsed capillaries as the minutes ticked away. The bees must have eventually punctured a hole in my skin big enough to escape because the pin pricks subsided to a dull ache as ligaments stretched and muscles tensed. Other senses kicked back in once the pain receptors abandoned their zeal and dumbed down in response to my attempts at control. It wasn't wet in here, but musty-smelling. Stale. It was silent in the dark. No patter of feet, rustle of bodies or chatter of teeth at least. Just silence – and Win's muted grumbling – or maybe conscience had me imagining that.

'I don't know. Are you OK?' I managed in return, how much later I don't know. Time lost meaning in the oblivion of pain.

'Do you fucking think I'm OK?' he replied. I debated repeating that I was sorry. When I'd ridden us both into this on my creaky white charger, I hadn't given a thought to the possibility of danger – only confrontation and conclusion. For once I'd led and Win had followed, and it had been a crap decision. 'Nothing's broken, at least,' he added after a while. 'And we ain't in the basement of no fancy office building now. I know where this is.'

'Where?'

'The club.'

'The club? You've lost me now.'

'The Gargoyles club. He had this idea once about a play dungeon – for the kinky bastards who wanted to be tied up and whipped. I didn't fancy it much – too sick. After Jonno, I was out anyway. I left him to it. I just did the collection jobs for him – and the clean-ups, whilst I bided me time. I heard tell he did the dungeon anyway, but I thought it were only a rumour.'

'That would mean we've been moved – how far?'

'Gargoyles is Soho. Not far. Explains why I feel like me legs have been broken though. We must have been chloroformed to get us here. That's why your mouth feels like a camel's crapped in it. Mine does, anyway.'

'Shit! Now I'm not going to be able to get hold of Margaret.'

'Jesus – you ain't gonna be able to get hold of anyone if we don't get outta here!'

He subsided to hostile silence and I peered into the gloom, hoping my eyes would get accustomed to it eventually.

'So what's the plan, Brains?' He asked after a while.

'I might have to work on that for a while.'

I tried to estimate how long we'd been there, and conscious. At least half an hour, surely? The dark was as dense as when I'd first opened my eyes – so much for that idea.

Win laughed humourlessly. 'Yeah, well, don't take too long.'

'What else was on that table? In the box, I mean.'

'Didn't get the chance to look. You yelped like a puppy and then he was on me.'

'Damn! That was evidence. We could have shown it to the police to prove who was behind all of this.'

'Christ mate, you gotta be alive to show the police anything,' he reminded me. 'You really think that's part of the plan? Last time I read any dungeon stories this were about the time the bloke copped it.'

'If Jaggers was going to kill us he would have simply done so – not chained us up down here. Someone will start asking questions after a while – Heather Trinder, for instance. Then there'd be attention directed at his businesses, and he wouldn't want that. No, this is to frighten us – and maybe find out something.'

'Like what?'

'Who's playing on my team, perhaps? Or what Danny has been saying.'

'So where d'you reckon Danny is, and what does he know?'

The cold finger of fear joined the heat of pain in my ribs. If Margaret wasn't behind this, and Jaggers was, then I didn't want to think about where Danny might be.

'We need to get out to find that out.'

'C'mon then. Let's go.'

'Ha-ha!'

'I mean it. You had all these clever ideas about finding Margaret and talking to her. Get her on the blower, why don't you? She can come and get us out!'

'Don't be so fucking stupid.'

'I ain't the fucking stupid one – you got us in, you get us out. If you reckon she'll help, try it.'

'How exactly?' I was coldly sarcastic, whether I was responsible for our predicament or not. 'I'll just give her a call, shall I? Hey, Margaret, I'm a bit tied up at the moment so perhaps you could come and get me out of a fix? Oh, sorry – I didn't explain properly. I'm in a dungeon somewhere – probably in Soho. Sorry that's not really your usual kind of place to visit.'

'You prat! Although …' He went silent again. I ignored him whilst I tried to cudgel my already battered brain into working. 'Actually, that ain't such a stupid idea. Ring her.'

'What?'

'Ring her. Fuckin' stupid dick! You're rich. You must have a mobile phone. If she's been trying to get you to react, bet you she'd answer if you rang her.'

I was about to let rip with a tirade of derisive mockery when I realised, ironically, what he said might be the makings of a plan. I ground my left hip against the wall and abandoned it as quickly.

'It's gone. Must have been taken when they brought us here. Now what?'

'Now we're fucked.'

How many hours of freedom were left to me? None, however many the police or the black-edged card might have allocated me.

'Christ, I've made a mess of everything.'

'Don't get maudlin' on me. I can do without that.'

'But I have, Win. I let you down as a kid and I've done it again now as an adult. I've let Danny down too. Jesus, I'm a failure!'

'Jesus and me are your father confessor! Shut up will you? Everyone makes mistakes. Even when you try not to. Summat don't go your way, or someone has it in for you. You can't sort that. Shit happens. Live with it.'

'But I'm the cause of the shit. Especially where Danny is concerned.'

He snorted. 'You want to shoulder all that blame, go ahead, matey. You don't even know the truth for sure yet. And Kimmy had summat to do with it too, remember?'

'What do you think happened, Win? With Kimmy – after you left?'

'I think some evil bastard knifed her, that's what, and I've got me suspicions who.'

'Jaggers?'

He didn't reply. The footsteps in the passageway silenced him. The door swung open and our fate was silhouetted in the doorway.

21: Mirror Image

'So you followed the trail. I always loved that story; Hansel and Gretel – brother and sister. So apt now. The brother causes all the trouble until they are locked up and awaiting the witches pleasure. Then the sister saves the day.'

'And which are you, Margaret?'

She laughed – a light, amused trill. 'A little of all of them, I guess.' She stepped through the doorway and flicked on the light. From pitch dark, a cold harsh white light flooded over us. Not exactly as I imagined Molly Wemmick would look now, but close. The blonde wig, teeth more protuberant behind fuller lips, chin more prominent – my wife, but bolder and more edgy. She had the box from the basement under her arm. 'Including the witch,' she laughed. 'Now, if I let you go, my cover will be completely blown. So you'll have to deal with the fall-out from your alternative form of release if I organise it. Is that a deal?'

'I think I need some answers first.'

She moved all the way into the room and pushed the door gently shut behind her. The light spilled on her head and cast her lower face into shadow. Her smile had a touch of the grimace to it.

'I don't think you're in a position to barter, actually, Lawrence. What do you want to be – dead or alive?'

'Oh, for fuck's sake, quit arguing and just get us out of here, will you?' Win interrupted. 'Have your lover's tiff some other time.'

Margaret laughed again. A tinkling sound like water over stones as a stream ran downhill.

'Well said, Win.'

'At least tell me where Danny is then?'

'Does that matter?'

'Yes, it bloody does!'

She put the box down in the middle of the room.

'He's fine.'

Maybe to irritate me, she released Win first. He stretched painfully and cursed as she came to stand in front of me. She pulled the false teeth out and smiled. She was immediately more Margaret. 'I can't take the rest off. Takes ages to put on. I'll have to remain the lantern-jawed heroine,' she joked.

'Very pretty,' I sounded sour and liked the fact.

'No, not at all. Quite ugly, really but it's enough without being too much.'

'Did you go on a spree in Emm's shop like that?'

'She told you?' She smiled and her small pearly teeth shone luminous white in the fluorescent light. 'Bit of fun – and it was getting boring not being seen.'

'She didn't know it was you – but she said you looked familiar.'

'Like my twin.' I raised my eyebrows. 'Oh, no. Not my real one – as you've probably gathered by now.'

'Yes, I had got that far.' I rattled my chains meaningfully.

'Oh yes – so dead or alive then, Lawrence?'

'Alive preferably, and not being manipulated.'

'I'm sorry about that. It was the only way.' She unlocked the manacles attached to the chains and watched me laboriously remove myself. 'But you've been doing a bit of manoeuvring yourself recently, I believe.'

'You were dead.'

'What difference did that make? Don't widowers usually grieve – at least for a week or two – before finding a replacement?'

'Why was it the only way?'

'Don't change the subject.'

'I'm not. I want to know.'

'Would you have dug up your dirty past if I'd asked you to, even for justice?'

I couldn't answer that, but she already knew. I was ashamed.

'It's over now anyway, with Kat. I'm more destructive than a train wreck. But I'm sure you don't really care.'

'Do I care? It's up to you what you do when I'm dead. It's what you do if I'm alive that matters.'

'So now we've got that cleared up, are you alive or dead?'

'I don't know. I haven't decided yet. Maybe that's up to you?'

'Up to me? That's a tall order, Scout. Would it matter which I opted for?'

Her eyes widened in surprise and I looked into them properly for the first time. Dark, bottomless pools – and not brown, as I'd always thought. A deep mossy hazel, sharp in the harsh light, reflecting me back at me. Mirror image. She smiled.

'Not quite, but I knew you'd work that out eventually.'

'I'm not sure I have completely, but I have a bad feeling I might be about to.'

'I'm not Scout – but you do need to be Atticus. Is that so bad?'

'Like you, I haven't decided yet.'

'You'll have to tell me when you do, then. I'm going to have to disappear again now.'

She stepped away from me and unexpectedly I felt the sense of loss her death had failed to produce in me.

'Disappear? Why? And where to?'

'If you want to, you'll be able to find me again – when you've worked it all out. In the meantime, your time's run out about the same time as mine.' She produced a mobile phone from the beaded evening bag over her arm and clicked the speed dial. 'Hello, yes I want to report a disturbance at the Gods and Gargoyles club in Soho. No, no name.' She clicked the phone off. 'Upstairs, there's about to be an interesting little addition to John's *guests*. The police. And unfortunately you'll have a little explaining to do, my love. But I'm sure you're up to that. *Atticus.*' She winked and gently caressed my raw cheek before starting back towards the door. 'John won't know whether I let you go, or the police did this way. Don't let them forget that.' She gave the box a gentle kick.

Win was already waiting impatiently by the door, rubbing his head where a dark bruise extended across his cheek bone and was beginning to black the other eye to make a pair. At least he was symmetrical now.

'Wait, Margaret!' My progress was slower, broken ribs prohibiting speed or sharp movement. 'How did you know we were down here?'

She looked amused. 'I'm a little bird – with a bird's eye view.'

'A mockingbird?'

'Whatever you want, Lawrence. Just don't get fooled by every song you hear.' And she was gone, soft blue dress floating after her like wavelets playing up the shore and then running away again.

The other party-goers joined us mere minutes later – Fredriks and his sidekick, still sweating.

'An unusual place to find you, Mr Juste, and maybe not quite in normal party-mode.' He eyed my bloody lips and hunched posture, after taking in the manacles and chains behind me in one sweeping glance. 'Or perhaps you are? But fortuitous anyway as we have one or two things more to discuss with you.' He swung round and nodded charmingly to Win. 'And you, Mr Juss. Maybe you'd *both* like to accompany me down the station?' Win opened and shut his mouth like a goldfish and then gave me a disgusted look, before acceding quietly.

Fredriks moved further into the room and came to a stop in front of the box.

'What's in this?'

'I don't know. It was in the basement of the FFF building where Heather Trinder from my Chambers, is attending a party tonight.'

'Hers, or yours?'

I laughed painfully. 'Neither.'

'So why is it now here? With you?'

'I don't know. I imagine it will be self-explanatory when you open it.'

He raised an eyebrow at me. 'The reason being?'

'A mockingbird told me.'

He shook his head sadly. 'I'll make sure the doc sees you down at the station,' but he nodded to his sidekick anyway.

Norton was waiting for us when we arrived at Chelsea Police Station. It was past midnight.

'I'm impressed,' I commented. 'Above and beyond the call of duty. How did you know?'

'Your girlfriend rang me and left a message.'

'Kat?'

'No, I don't think that was the name – more like a bird – finch? I thought that was probably her surname. Heather told me it was an odd one.' I laughed aloud then, even though it hurt; more than anything had ever done before because I'd been such a fool.

'Yes, she's an odd one.'

Win was put in a separate interview room whilst a local GP attended to me and pronounced me fit to be questioned. After he'd finished with me he wandered off wearily to examine Win, and was replaced by Fredriks and his man. It had suddenly turned cold – or maybe it was the way I felt. I shivered as Fredriks displayed all his wares on the interview table again. He signalled to his sidekick – DS Jewson, I learned then – to locate a blanket for me and I sat swathed in regulation blue trying to not merge with it as I waited for the ice core inside me to thaw.

Fredriks opened with, 'A strange turn of events, Mr Juste. We had an anonymous call to say that there was a disturbance at the club you attended tonight and that someone we were interested in was there. We turn up and there you are – in a room with chains and manacles, somewhat dishevelled and providing us with yet more unusual items of evidence. Maybe you would like to talk us though events?'

He was lying. I'd heard exactly what Margaret had said in the call, but if he wanted to play games, I could play them with the best. I'd spent the last few weeks learning the rules.

'I think I probably need someone to talk me through them too, to be honest.' Norton nudged me. I ignored him. He was trying to help but as he had no idea what he was helping with all he was likely to do was hinder me – and hurt my ribs. 'Can I see what is in the box?' The box from the table in the basement sat temptingly to the side of the interview room table now.

'By all means. I think we'd all like to see inside it, wouldn't we?' He donned surgical gloves and took the lid off the box. And there was the fall-out Margaret had warned me about. He silently placed them in evidence bags and laid them out across the table. A clear plastic bag, misshapen and with a length of rope still tied around its open end. Norton stared at it uncomprehendingly but the pit of my stomach turned over. Next to it were my blood test results, then a disposable camera with half the shots used, and finally a bloodied knife.

'So, Mr Juste, can you help me with these?'

The only item I had eyes for was the blood test results. 'May I look at that?' I indicated the curling slip of paper, dated the day after Danny had first been taken into hospital and I'd visited him. The results that had supposedly been lost or contaminated – I couldn't remember which now. Fredriks picked them up carefully and handed the bag to me. I spread them out flat on the table, the hieroglyphics meaning nothing to me other than for one. The haemophilia gene. The faulty Y. I had it too. My blood ran cold. The jigsaw was still missing a vital piece but I feared it would be what I'd been desperate for it not to be. The forensics lab would have Kimmy's blood work. How could I ask for it to be tested?

'This is important to you?' Fredriks asked.

'Yes, but not in relation to my sister's death. In relation to her life – and her son's parentage.'

'Oh?'

'It gets very complicated.'

'I like complicated,' he smiled his duck smile.

'In preparing Danny Hewson's defence we discovered he suffers from haemophilia. But both parents need to have contributed a faulty gene to his biological make-up. There is no such problem on his father's side, so maybe his father isn't who we've always believed him to be. It's more of a personal issue for me because his mother was my sister, but it would also be helpful to establish who else in the family may be at risk.'

'Ah, I see.' I hoped not, or my well-kept secret was about to become part of a police investigation. 'So if his father is possibly not his father, who is?'

'Well that's another problem. And it's tricky because we can't now get the answer from Kimmy – unless forensics would be prepared to release a sample of her blood to follow up some leads I have been given privately – for the family.'

'Why do you need her blood to do that? Is there some doubt she is his mother?'

'No, but ...' It hit me like a train then. I spouted some crap about splintered families and needing to ensure facts were accurate before announcing to a child one of his parents might not be who he thought they were. He seemed to buy it and agreed nonchalantly to ask forensics for a report on Kimmy's genetic structure, in case it might have a link to her death, but his sideways glance at me afterwards told me he wasn't fooled. I suddenly found I didn't need the blanket after that – I was hotter and sweatier than DS Jewson.

'And the rest?' He indicated the other bagged items.

'Have you tested any of it for fingerprints or blood?'

'We are about to. I suspect it is your sister's blood on the knife, don't you?'

'I imagine so.'

'And the bag?' I shrugged. 'Did you know your sister suffered from epilepsy?'

'No.' That surprised me. Why hadn't Win said so when we found the bipolar diagnosis in Sarah's box?

'We'd assumed the suggestion of hypoxia from her colouring was due to the fact that she appeared to have suffered an epileptic fit on or just before death. She'd swallowed her tongue. One wonders now if we perhaps misread the situation. No doubt the knife could have fingerprints on it. Whether we'll get anything off the bag, who knows.'

I assumed Margaret had done her job properly if she was laying the trail to Jaggers.

'Then the sooner you test both, the better? And develop the photos, one assumes?'

'Indeed. And I will have more questions for you shortly, I expect. In the meantime, I am asking that you remain here.'

'Are you charging my client, DCI Fredriks?' Norton seemed pleased to have a role in the proceedings finally.

'No sir, I am asking for co-operation. Do you want me to charge him?'

Norton looked morosely at me. 'Do you want him to charge you?' he asked sarcastically. Yes, he was a cute cookie. He'd worked out the rules of the game too. I shook my head.

'Then, no DCI Fredriks, Mr Juste is happy to co-operate, but please bear in mind his distressed physical state after the anonymous assault on him.'

Fredriks turned to me.

'Oh, I assumed that was as a result of a disagreement with Mr Juss. Is that not so, then?'

'No, we were both attacked.'

'In the basement, or at the club?'

'In the basement.'

'And may I ask why you were in the basement?'

'I was given to understand my nephew might be there.'

'Danny Hewson?'

'Yes.'

'Why?'

I shrugged.

'Kids – maybe he didn't like being in hospital. I'm not really sure, DCI Fredriks, but I was concerned about him.'

'And his parentage,' he said flatly, smiling.

'Yes.'

He pursed his lips.

'I see. I'll be back in due course. Interview suspended at one thirty-five am.'

I didn't even attempt to explain to Norton and I don't think he wanted me to. He was operating on the same basis as I'd explained to Danny once – need to know. I drank the disgusting instant coffee the duty sergeant brought us and fell asleep, arms resting on the table, head resting on my arms. It was the only position that eased the pain in my ribs. I don't know what Norton did, but he was still sitting bolt upright alongside me when Fredriks reappeared at eight forty-five. He laid down on the table a set of results with similar hieroglyphics to my own, a forensics report on the knife and another on the plastic bag.

'Such dedicated people, these forensic guys. And such interesting results. Shall we talk about them and I'll tell you what I think they mean?'

22: Genesis

So there I was, going back to court – this time defending my brother against a murder charge. The knife was apparently covered in his prints, the blood on the knife was Kimmy's and the bag and knife almost certainly comprised the joint murder weapons. My nosey neighbour at number six had also helpfully identified him as visiting at about the time of Kimmy's death. I was off the hook because the insurance policy was belatedly found to have been cancelled before Margaret's death. I suspected Margaret's helping hand at work there and silently thanked her.

'OK Brains, now you got to get me off,' Win instructed when he was charged. Norton closed my case file as he opened up Win's. I held the phone away from my ear for a full ten minutes whilst Heather vented at me about sending her on a wild goose chase to a party which was a non-event since the fabled Molly Wemmick, aka Margaret, didn't even appear – although she did get to show off her Jimmy Choos. She also ranted and railed against me for taking Win as a client, but this time I was adamant.

'I owe him and he's family, Heather. It's the one useful thing I've learnt recently. Look after your own.'

'He's barely that,' she retorted.

'He's absolutely that,' I replied. 'Whether I like it or not.'

And there it was – I'd finally done it; claimed my family for my own – whether it was a desirable claim or not. I sat in my study savouring a brandy – slowly this time, and considering the last forty-eight hours. The rollercoaster of solving the riddle of the notes and the identity of the sender, the physical punishment resulting from our visit to the FFF offices and a night spent alternating between the cells and being questioned by Fredriks and his sidekick had knocked the stuffing out of me, but I was still too wound up to sleep.

It was surreal – all of it was surreal. Three months ago I'd been sedately, if unsatisfactorily married, at the peak of my career and anticipating the ultimate accolade, the judge's mantle. Life had been steady, measured and secure. Now it was uncontrolled, alarming and dangerous. Just touching the still tender red rings around my wrists from the manacles in the Gods and Gargoyles dungeon playground was enough to make my heart race with fear again. Or maybe it was partially to do with Margaret and the odd response she'd prompted in me when she'd rescued us. Not quite anger and not quite relief. And she was different too – not quite the woman I'd married, and not quite not.

The brandy warmed the back of my throat and deadened the rawness that still lingered from whatever they'd used to drug us. I tracked its pathway down my gullet and into my stomach, settling in a molten pool there. Gradually it had the desired effect: torpor followed by drowsiness. I must have drifted, half-in and half-out of sleep, and in my dream I was talking and laughing with an unknown woman to unknown companions. I knew them – but they were strangers too. Familiar faces I couldn't remember, and just when I thought I did, they transformed into someone else and the process of identifying them started all over again. In the background a little green light winked at me and I knew if I could get to the green light and turn it off I would know who everyone was and what they were doing there. I woke to find myself slumped over the desk with a blinder of a migraine starting, complete with zig-zag visual disturbances and flashing lights. The brandy hadn't done its work after all.

I pushed the dregs of it away from me and stumbled upstairs to bed, sliding under the covers without even taking my shoes off. It was only the annoyingly insistently ringing somewhere that eventually roused me hours later. I lay rigid for a while, disorientated and sore, before I placed where I was and that the ringing was the phone downstairs. I was tempted to duck under the covers and ignore it. The effort of facing another day of problems and confusion was almost too much, but trying to turn over and burrow into the duvet aggravated my ribs. The combination of the phone starting up again and what felt like a knife stabbing in my guts persuaded me to heave myself upright. I waited long enough for my head to steady and stumbled downstairs to catch the caller just as they were about to ring off.

'Lawrence! I wondered where you were. I didn't think you could have been off on another spree after the last few days, although you do have a habit of surprising me recently.' I held the phone away from my ear. Heather, bless her – but not today. Today I just wanted to be left alone, even though I should have been up and working on Win's defence – such as it was. She descended into a tinny rattle on the other end of the phone.

I breathed in and out deeply several times, trying to convince myself I was up to the task of engaging with her. I wasn't. '… and Danny's back.'

'What?'

'I said Danny's back. Just wandered into the children's home large as life first thing this morning, pretending he didn't know what all the fuss was about. Said he'd wanted an adventure – it was boring in the children's home.'

'Christ! Why didn't you tell me earlier?'

'I've been trying to. I've been ringing since Norton told me. At least your brother's not being charged with kidnapping now.'

'Was he going to be?'

'He seems to have been involved in just about everything else so why not? Fredriks needs to have someone to throw the book at since you've got yourself off the hook for the moment. What have you been doing?'

I looked at my watch. It was two-thirty in the afternoon. Jesus, what a state I was in. I caught sight of myself in the hall mirror and cringed. Hollow-eyed, grey complexion, rumpled, creased and with a heavy five o'clock shadow. Even Win must look better than me.

'Sleeping Heather, really. Is Danny all right – no harm come to him?'

'Yes, he's fine apparently – just saying nothing – other than wondering where you are. Fredriks probably is too. Norton's spent the morning there and Fredriks is in fine form. You should be down there – and then seeing to the boy. Maybe he'll talk to you. He's been told about his mother but he seems to have almost disregarded that. You're the only one he's asked for.'

I made the appropriate response and escaped further castigation by suggesting I got going instead of wasting time on the phone debating my failings. Heather was huffy but it did the trick. I struggled back upstairs, showered, shaved and made a fairly decent stab at looking the consummate professional even though inside was a mix of exhaustion, confusion and apprehension. I didn't know what to expect when I arrived at the station but Fredriks seemed to be in conciliatory mood. Maybe playing both ends against the middle in case I decided to complain about my treatment the night before. He even let me take a copy of the report on Kimmy's blood work home, but for the time being insisted on keeping the evidence he'd acquired from my home, Heather's and Kat's. I was allowed copies of the parts that belonged to me. The rest I could have access to as evidence to build the case for the defence. Norton was still with Win so I left them to it. It was a cop-out but I hadn't the energy to face either of them for the moment. Tomorrow. Tomorrow I would have my head together again.

I met Kat on my way out of the police station after collecting the paperwork. It was an awkward meeting. There was too much unfinished business on both sides. She was also officially part of the investigation into Danny's removal from Great Ormond Street, even though he was sticking to his story that he'd simply run away. Danny seemed the best way to build bridges whilst I figured out what to do next, and whether Kat still came into the equation.

We lingered awkwardly on the steps to the police station, politely bandying olive branches.

'By the way, you don't look shit today.'

I laughed.

'Thanks. I don't feel like shit for once – just *shit upon*.'

'Ouch. Do you accept apologies?'

'How?'

'Coffee – apologies to be given over ...'

'OK.'

'There's a good place just round the corner from here.'

'Of course – your patch. That's why you're always able to turn up so quickly and conveniently on my doorstep.'

She looked embarrassed.

'Not always, but sometimes – and I wasn't lying about everything.'

'No, I know I definitely looked shit most of the times you told me so.'

She looked as if she was about to give me another icy retort but I was smiling. We continued to the coffee shop in silence and settled into a corner. Neutral ground. I ordered two coffees and we surveyed each other cautiously across the table. The salt, pepper and small vase of pinks carefully positioned to hide the spillages of earlier customers provided the barricades for us.

'So what are you really, Kat?'

'Danny's social worker. But his case isn't straightforward, is it? And I have to bear in mind what else is happening to affect the welfare of the child so I ended up in a dual role: part social worker, part police liaison. Neither of Danny's parents were whiter than white and Danny seemed to have become involved in something that might be a more widespread problem. The mugging gang. It started with me simply keeping the police informed about progress when he started talking to you. It seemed harmless then – and useful – to help them track down who was taking advantage of a minor for criminal purposes. The trouble was, you started telling me things that implied there was more to it than that and I was getting pulled into the thick of it.' She hesitated. 'Then they started talking about having another look at Alfie's case since it had been defended by your Chambers and you seemed to be at the centre of the maelstrom. He may be in the wrong, but he's still my brother, and he's finally started to get his life back on track. Got a job and a flat – even got a girlfriend. I couldn't do that to him, so I agreed to be the police eyes and ears about anything to do with Danny and his case – and that of course was mainly you, especially after Kimmy was killed. But if you're innocent, Lawrence, there's nothing to worry about, is there?'

'People generally see what they look for, and hear what they listen for.' I grinned ruefully. 'That's a quote, by the way – from *To Kill a Mocking Bird*. Tom Robinson was innocent but because he was black he was seen as guilty anyway. It doesn't always work the way it should, Kat.'

'I'm sorry. I didn't mean to cause you any trouble. You must know that, Lawrence.'

'What's done is done. Let's move on from it, shall we?'

She gestured to the packet of photocopies next to me on the table.

'From FFF?

I was about to ask how she'd guessed but then realised she must know most of what was happening apropos me and the case from Fredriks and her involvement so far. She had to in order to tease out of me the kind of information he was looking for.

'Only some of it. Mainly copies of the package sent to me personally, although I'll need all of it for Win's defence eventually.'

'Are there are things relevant to Danny in there too?'

'Yes.'

She gazed at me, intent. 'So therefore also relevant to you personally?' I nodded. 'Can I ask about them?'

'Why do you need to know? I'm a potential suspect, not a potential partner now.'

'That's not true. It's just complicated.'

I thought about Margaret and little blue rosemary flowers; and Kat and bruised fruit. Yes, emotions were complicated – too complicated for me to draw any conclusions about right now. I didn't answer but opened the parcel and laid the blood work report on the table between us nevertheless. She leaned toward me to decipher the hieroglyphics of my sister's genetic make-up and I breathed in the smell of her skin. It had the usual effect on me.

'What does it mean?' she asked eventually. I turned the report round so it faced me.

'Basically I'm not Danny's uncle.'

'But?' She looked at me wide-eyed, as she took that in.

'But nothing. I'm not his uncle. There's no link between me and Kimmy and Danny.'

'But Kimmy was ...'

'My sister.'

She shook her head, frowning.

'So you mean Wilhelm Johns *is* his father then?'

She'd missed the point. I didn't make it for her.

'That's something we would have had to have asked Kimmy – when we could.'

'You mean we'll never know?'

I shrugged.

'Unless she's left a convenient explanation somewhere.'

'And Win's not your brother.'

'Oh God, yes! He's my brother all right. That's obvious.' She looked mystified. 'To me, at least.' I sighed. 'We're too alike not to be. I can see that now.' She obviously wanted me to elaborate, but if she couldn't see the behavioural similarities, I wasn't going to make a study of them for her. After all, somewhere along the line, she was potentially the enemy, as well as the ally.

'So what are you going to tell Danny?'

'The truth.'

'He'll be devastated.'

'The truth is often devastating, but it's better than a lie.' She looked shamefaced. 'He already knows Kimmy is dead. That was pretty devastating too, but he's survived it.'

'Not because of that – because you're not his uncle.'

'Well, things can be complicated, like you say. I don't have to be his uncle to care.'

I didn't explain what the report really told me, with my now growing familiarity with genetics – and which she'd seemingly entirely missed. It wasn't so much that I wasn't Danny's uncle – it was more that my sister wasn't Danny's mother.

***

Later on that day I explained to Danny as gently as I could about Kimmy's death, but nothing else.

'Why'd you have to tell me that, Mr Big?' His lower lip pouted and the belligerent street kid was pitifully absent. I hadn't liked the street kid persona, but he'd had guts. Danny needed guts more than ever to survive now. I explained as gently as I could that I wasn't his uncle, but nothing else. I wanted to ask him to drop the nickname. It reminded me of gangstas and spats with black shirts and white ties, but I hadn't the heart. Ten years old was too young to be an orphan – let alone face the weight of your parent's misdeeds. 'How'm I ever going to go home now? It were all going to be alright before. Now it ain't.'

I thought about that for a long time before answering. It wouldn't have been all right. None of it had been all right for a very long time. Maybe it would be – one day – although Danny wouldn't be able to see that right now. Perhaps in about forty years' time.

'Because we have to be able to live with the truth, Danny. To do that we have to face the truth and then learn how to accept it and make it part of our lives.'

I thought of everything I'd found out so far. Yes, we had to live with the truth, even if it was unacceptable to live with.

'But how'm I going do that?'

'I guess we'll have to work on it together.'

***

'Thanks a lot!' Kat greeted me with when she delivered Margaret's stored boxes and the contents of the wardrobe to my house later that week.

'For what?'

'For not telling me about Kimberley. I've read the medical report now. Why didn't you put me straight when we were talking about it?'

'Because that was my reading of the situation, but I'm no expert. Now you've had the expert's opinion.'

She twisted her lips in an expression of irritation.

'Why can't you ever just be straight with me?'

'Why can't you? You and Margaret...' I indicated the pile of boxes. She ignored that and turned her attention to Heather, hovering in the study doorway behind me. Whilst I prepared the case for Win's defence

217

Heather had become my self-appointed warden in place of Ella. There was no arguing with Heather but there seemed, strangely, to have been a truce called between her and Kat.

'So what do you make of it all with Margaret?' Kat asked Heather very deliberately. Heather put her mid-morning coffee down on my desk, ignoring my anguished look at the ring it was making.

'She's a manipulative bitch,' Heather replied, smoothing her perfect hair. 'And trouble.'

'Danny thinks she's an angel – or that's the way he draws her.' Kat commented. 'What about you Lawrence?' It was more pointed than one of Heather's shoes.

'It's complicated,' I replied. They both waited for me to elaborate, Kat more intensely than Heather. When I'd told Heather this was all about me and my past, I'd been almost correct. It was certainly all about *the* past, but not just mine. 'OK, she's a mystery,' I concluded eventually. One I knew I would find out a lot more about in time as I prepared Win's defence. The black-edged card I'd received this morning confirmed that.

'Guilt is relative, whereas justice is not. But to achieve one it's necessary to shoulder the burden of the other. You can share my name if sin is acknowledged. The way to do it is already there. You only have to look for it.

Be in touch soon – J.'

The boxes and the unopened letter in Margaret's vanity drawer upstairs were going to be an education, but I knew who 'J' was now. Justice – however she might appear in corporeal form.

23: Finch

When Heather and Kat had both gone, I slowly and painfully arranged the boxes around the walls of my study. Fredriks sent a PC over with Sarah's box later on in the morning and I added it to the barricades, without wanting to open any of them. Norton was taking the lead with Win's case whilst I recovered, so the pressure was off – marginally – in order for me to research what I could to help the case. An unhealthy languor had descended on me now the truth seemed to be about to besiege me from all sides and I wondered whether I really wanted to know what it was. I wandered out the kitchen and sat at the breakfast bar, imagining the chalk line – now long since polished away – of Kimmy's body on the slate floor.

With surprise, I realised the languor wasn't slothfulness or the desire to avoid the truth. It had its roots in sadness. My sister's death now finally made me feel wretched, and sorry for her loss of life. Perhaps it's easier to regret someone when they are no longer there to confront you, or make your life difficult. Perhaps when their supposed crimes against you are removed they seem more palatable and their absence more to be lamented. I hoped it wasn't merely that – relief that I hadn't committed incest and a reprieve from having the crime laid at my door. I hoped it was sentiment I was feeling; genuine sorrow for a wasted life, albeit one I hadn't cared about whilst she was alive. At least it would define me as a man in making, not an emotionless block.

I let the rest of the morning and early afternoon pass indeterminately, drifting through the rooms of the house, trying to imagine Margaret back in them or what she had been thinking as she designed the décor of each of them. They should tell me something about the psychology of my enigmatic wife and now – where I'd been entirely indifferent to it in life – I was infinitely intrigued by it since her death and resurrection. But try as I might, I couldn't fathom her. The rooms remained as I'd always viewed them – stylish, sparse and inscrutable. Perhaps they weren't a window onto Margaret but onto the role she'd been playing in my life. A non-permanent one that didn't require personal investment, although that didn't explain the now uncovered hidden agenda for us to adopt Danny. You didn't plan to adopt a child with a partner you had no intention of remaining with.

By mid-afternoon I had to accept that the answers weren't on the walls, but in the boxes that I'd created walls out of – in my mind and in my study. I wondered if that was another twisty little Margaret analogy, like Mary had intimated. 'Twisty, twisty,' she'd said when I'd visited. My wife had a distinctly twisty turn of mind. She'd turned everything on its head and with it, all of my mental boxes too, so they had no choice but to empty their contents into the general mêlée of questions and answers to be married together. Procrastination had to stop. I made my last port of call our bedroom and the vanity unit drawer with its unopened letter and numbered key. Time to know all Pandora's secrets. I took them downstairs and placed them next to the jam jar containing the rosemary, now wilting because the water had evaporated and I'd forgotten to top it up.

Where to start?

I started with Sarah's keepsakes box because it was the smallest and I didn't want to open the letter. I wouldn't normally have admitted to superstition but opening a letter only to be opened in the event of death now seemed like asking for trouble, given how precarious her safety might currently be. I undid the bundle of papers and spread them across my desk. They were the same. Fredriks might have looked through them but he hadn't removed any of them. Margaret Flowers must have become Margaret Green in 1989 in order to present herself as such to me. That seemed the most likely explanation for the original name change. Retaining the name of Flowers would have made me suspicious. So, then she'd not wanted me to make the connection between her and her murdered sister, but now – through Sarah's keepsake box and the parcels of evidence she herself seemed to have sent me – she did. Strange – but very relevant. I moved on to the other papers and the forlorn little death certificate for baby Flowers – her sister's child. I idly worked out the age. He – it recorded – would have been ten now. The same age as Danny.

The figures danced in front of my eyes. I knew then what had really bothered me about the certificate the first time I'd looked at it. Stupid prat – how could this child be born to Maria Flowers? She'd died a year earlier. And Kimberley had a child registered to her who wasn't hers, but she'd definitely been pregnant at the time, according to Win and Jill and Emm. So her child must have been the one stillborn!

The pieces of the jigsaw suddenly all started to fit together with alarming ease. Danny Hewson wasn't Kimberley's boy – he was the child Maria Flowers had supposedly given birth to. But Maria Flowers wasn't alive when Danny was born, so someone else had given birth to him. Maybe someone who wasn't lying when she registered him as born because she was *'present at birth'*. I sat, alternately furnace-hot and ice-cold, stunned by the unbelievable possibility that Danny Hewson could be my wife's child.

When incredulity gave way to logic I began to question how and why.

Why? To cover up his origins. Or maybe to keep Danny or Margaret safe.

But who from?

The latter seemed obvious, more because of my natural inclination to hate and fear him: Jaggers. They clearly knew each other ten years or more ago – the photo on his desk proved that, whether their familial relationship was fact or fiction. Could *he* be the father then? He would have to have the faulty gene too. There didn't seem to be any evidence of it in his family history. Jaggers had joined in his share of fights at the children's home with gusto and never been the worse for them. Judge Wemmick had died from a heart attack, but when he'd had a minor fall when I'd been there once, he'd barely bruised, and the small graze on his cheek had healed within days.

No. It wasn't conclusive, but there was still another far more likely candidate than him – or two of them. Wilhelm Johns had also been keeping company with the Flowers girls, via Kimmy and Win, and then there was Win himself. He'd denied being the father of Kimmy's child, but this wasn't Kimmy's child. I thought about that for a while longer. It was only surmise since there was no proof who mother *or* father were, but the perplexing coincidences were coalescing into an extremely suspect mix. It still didn't answer why Margaret and Danny might need to be kept safe, but if that *was* the case, I had a sneaking feeling Margaret would be making sure I knew before too long.

I set all the papers aside and toyed with the small perfume bottle Sarah had kept. I wondered sadly what precious memories it had evoked for her when she was alive. I sniffed at it and knew. Ma. It smelt of Ma. I could remember her wearing it so clearly it made me wince. Rare for her to wear perfume, or even to get dolled up enough to warrant wearing it but whenever we kids had been christened – unheard of not to if you were Catholic, whether you were devout of not – Ma dressed up and dabbed on her perfume from the only small bottle of perfume she probably ever owned. I could even remember loitering in the bedroom doorway, watching her dab it onto the tender part of her neck just by the collar bone and the scent filling the room the day Jill and Emm were to be christened.

Memories. I was back to where I'd started the day after Margaret had supposedly died, and the ones of the day we'd been taken to the children's home which had started this descent into oblivion. I didn't want to remember but I had to. Sarah's keepsakes box was telling me that. I put the perfume bottle down, eyes smarting, and spread out the birthday cards Sarah had obviously treasured and I'd not looked at before. They covered a number of years, from when she was about sixteen onwards. The first one was from the man I assumed she'd married – the name was the same as the others had mentioned in relation to her. He'd died some years before in a road accident, apparently. Like Margaret hadn't.

There were more cards from him, sporadically spanning the intervening gap and then there was one from Win, making contact when Sarah was twenty-five. The little note inside told her in his characteristically bad grammar that he was keen to reunite the family, and nestling inside the letter was a photo similar to the ones Win had showed me. All ten of them grouped together, including Mary; but not me. So that had been true. Win had been instrumental in bringing them all back together. All of them, but not me. Why not me? No-one had even attempted to contact me. Suddenly, from me denying them, it seemed as if it could have been the other way round. That stung. I put the letter and photo down and examined the feeling. I was offended – upset. I'd been deliberately excluded by them, not the other way round.

I put everything back in the box and closed it up, angry and hurt. I toyed with Margaret's letter but still couldn't bring myself to open it. The rejection had left me too raw. The brandy bottle sounded the usual plaintive refrain it always did at times like these. I was about to be weak and abandon the aspiration to join humanity I'd embraced as I'd mourned Kimmy's death earlier when the walls seemed to bend and reality shifted.

I stared, wondering if was going mad, or my recent excesses had caused permanent brain damage, but the sensation of everything moving around me was real. As my eyes glazed with concentration the front wall exploded at me, spraying fragments of brick, plaster and glass across the room as the window shattered. I tried to duck behind the desk as the room blackened but the car drove straight through the study window and everything seemed to speed up to an incredible pace. The car obliterated window, desk, stacked boxes – and almost – me, before it shuddered to a halt. It wedged against the splintered desk with Margaret's boxes bulldozed ahead of it. I sat in the middle of the carnage like a freeze-frame, the noise ringing in my ears and the dust making me gag and cough. When I recovered my breath sufficiently to speak nothing came out even whilst the words thundered in my head.

Fucking hell, fucking hell, fucking ...

'... hell ... What's happening?' I whispered. 'What's happening?' My head buzzed and swam. I tried not to pass out but I couldn't get my voice above a whisper.

As the dust settled inside, shouting and screaming slowly drifted in through the gaping hole that had been my study wall. The brickwork grumbled and settled, spewing small bits of debris from its gaping wound.

'Hey, hey – here! Over here ...' A voice filtered through the hole in the wall that had been my home.

'Jesus! Anyone in there?' The brickwork's blown to shit!'

'Watch it! It could go in anytime.'

'Someone call the fire brigade.'

'Already done. Anyone in there?'

'It's Lawrence Juste's place. Poor man ...' It was the old biddy from number six. I recognised her voice from the few times she'd acknowledged me on my way in and out of the mews. I giggled hysterically and it sounded like a baby's whimper.

'Hellooo. Anyone hurt in there?'

'Me, me – here – me.' I was back to childhood and hurt, crying for Ma, and she was sweeping me up and cuddling away the pain and the tears. I sobbed like an infant as the unseen voices called and instructed, manoeuvred and steadied the crumbling bricks and plaster.

'Brace that. Here – use this bit of wood. Stop the window going. Hello?' He burst through the rubble like the car, and still I was crying.

'Are you all right? Christ – there *is* someone in there – and he's trapped. Get help!'

The car had nudged the desk and me right up against the back row of Margaret's boxes stacked between the bookcase-lined back wall and the rest of the room. I and my chair were tightly wedged between them and the desk, air sucked from my lungs by the force of the impact. The stink of petrol filled the space like the rosemary had. Through the dust-storm of exploded plaster and brick fragments I could see the car was my own beloved Austin Healey, now mangled and defunct. There was a body in the front seat, collapsed over the steering wheel and spraying blood at the crazed windscreen like someone had turned a hose on. I wanted to puke, but hadn't even the breath to retch.

I struggled to extricate myself and the desk crumbled around me into a serrated arrow of splintered wood pointed at my gut, waiting to impale me. My ribs screamed with pain as I pulled in my stomach and pressed my back hard against the chair to put as much space between me and its deadly tip. That gave me a mere extra half-inch before it pierced me like a warrior on a lance. The smell of petrol made it hard to breathe and my head swam but at least it curtailed the sobbing. Jesus, one spark and she would blow. I thought I could hear myself yelling but no-one seemed to hear. The undulating wail of sirens and shouts for help made it past the wall of debris but they didn't bring any more help with them. My would-be saviour had already ducked out again on smelling the petrol.

Sarah's box was still balanced on the cracked edge of the desk top, teetering gently from side to side as the wood shifted, creaking angrily. The letter fluttered flirtatiously at me next to it, trapped under the box by one edge but agitating as the box rocked, only to be pinioned again as the box settled back on top of the key. The blood spray had stopped and the windscreen was now a patchwork of red and clear, with the blood congealing in the crazing and running in rivulets down the unbroken sections. Beyond it, the body trailed tragically across the steering wheel, one arm flung up against the dashboard and allowing the hand to appear to gently caress the windscreen with its blackened finger tips. It was a woman's hand, and as the blood trickled away I realised the finger tips weren't black. They were clutching a small blood-sodden card, with the black edge protruding beyond them. Through the panic and petrol fumes I struggled to focus on it.

'Remember I always win. Next time she'll be real.'

'Here, mate, you all right?' A light shone suddenly through the haze and straight into my eyes, blinding me. It transformed the dust storm to a dirty yellow fog accompanying a fireman. 'Hold still and we'll get you out. Got to be quick though. There's sodding petrol everywhere.'

I thankfully let him and my rescuers take charge. They freed my legs first. My lungs clogged with dust as I gasped in air once the desk spear was removed, but still I couldn't see anything. I started coughing. The box dropped onto my knees and with it a fluttering white bird and its shiny jewel – the key. Mary had come to save me with her origami. I laughed crazily.

'Come on then mate, let's be having you. Mind the glass.'

I stumbled to my feet and felt hands pulling me through the now disintegrating wood of the antique desk I'd cautioned Win about leaving a ring on with his dripping coffee mug. The little white bird fluttered with me and we lurched past the blood bath that was my car. I paused as I passed the door, mentally grieving for a past I'd never had – car or no car – and noticed the body was a tailor's dummy, brown wig askew and plastered half across the dummy's face with blood. It was wearing a red and black dress patterned like tyre tracks on a blood spattered road.

'Margaret …'

'No, it ain't a real person, but someone don't like you much, do they mate?' The emergency services operative commented, steadying me as I climbed through the remnants of my front wall.

'My book.' I made to go back.

'No book's worth it, mate. Buy another one.'

The fireman led me across the mews as the rest of his team doused the wall of number five and the adjoining houses. I sat against the front wall of number six opposite, marvelling at how someone had managed to steer my car along the narrow mews and aim it so perfectly at my study window with sufficient force to destroy it. The same fireman came over and helped me up after a while, directing me to the entrance to the mews where an ambulance had parked up.

'Come on mate. Best get a bit further away, just in case. Awful lot of petrol leaking in there and you need a once over too.' He left me in the ambulance, having my blood pressure taken and muttering replies to the paramedic's questions until he seemed content enough to allow me to sit on the stretcher in the back whilst he watched the proceedings outside.

I rested there, folded in on myself, Sarah's box on my knees and Margaret's letter and the key clutched in my hand, registering the message I'd just been sent. Kimmy had been first. Margaret – and probably me too, would be next, unless … I didn't know what the 'unless' was, but I could guess. My opponent was getting tired of playing and wanted to finish the game. I felt strangely detached, like I was watching but not present. It wasn't all of the message though. The rest of it followed about five minutes later when number 5, Atherly Place Mews, Chelsea partially collapsed in on itself as the car exploded and the fireball scorched where I had been sitting just minutes earlier.

'Hope you're insured, mate.' The paramedic commiserated with me. 'You won't be seeing any of that little lot replaced in a while.'

End of message.

But not from my 'J' – she was justice.

And if Margaret had styled me Atticus Finch, then now I had a message to send back.

24: Puzzle Pieces

Heather collected me from the back of one of the ambulances sent out to deal with the carnage – of which there was a lot in bricks and mortar, and luckily none in flesh and bone. I was smoke-grimed, and my teeth were still chattering with shock but I was determined not to be admitted to hospital for observation. I was surprised by the lack of human injury, assuming that Jaggers would have had little concern for who or what got damaged in order to get his message across. I briefly wondered if I could have been wrong about the identity of the sender but almost immediately dismissed the thought. We had reached end game, and it was merely luck that the end game hadn't damaged anything but property – yet.

Heather greeted me jauntily with, 'I'm always coming to your rescue, these days, it seems, but you didn't have to blow your house up to get my sympathy.'

I was going to tell her that the joke was in extreme bad taste, until I realised she was a godsend. Not a divine one, but a very human godsend. Her immediate support proved she really was on my side. She also came up with the suggestion we should use the disaster to petition for a postponement of Win's case, giving me more time to prepare, and making it impossible for Fredriks to hound me for information I hadn't yet decided if I should make available without appearing to be callous. It also meant it was difficult for Kat to approach me, unless officially, and that was a relief too. With my emotions already so scattered, I didn't need her to diffuse further what few solid principles I'd been struggling to reassemble. My wife was still alive, and it was becoming rapidly apparent I might owe her more than lip-service to the role of husband. I insisted on keeping hold of Sarah's box – having put Margaret's letter and key inside it; guarding it like a pit bull guards its territory. I might even have gone so far as snarling when the paramedic tried to prise it away from me before Heather arrived, before descending into hysterical giggles. It was that which nearly got me admitted. God bless Heather for her pragmatism and pout.

'Take me home, Mummy,' I replied instead, grinning inanely at her. The paramedic gave Heather a look that said she was mad to be taking me on, but thrust the forms confirming I voluntarily refused treatment at me to sign and then let us go.

I sat in her pristine champagne BMW convertible, making the cream leather seat filthy, and clutching my box, silly grin still tacked to my face to keep my teeth from chattering again. The strange detached feeling was starting to wear off, to be replaced by the jitters. Everywhere – stomach, chest, hands, legs. Everything wanted to shake and I had to hold myself rigid to stop it.

'They told me about the "body" in the car – was it meant to be you?'

'No; Margaret, I think. But the message is much the same, whoever it was meant to be, isn't it?' We sunk into a tense silence. Me, more tense than her as the jitters intensified.

'Are you sure you're all right?' she asked after we'd stop-started all the way through the Hammersmith lights and I'd jumped at every one of them.

'No, but there's not a lot I can do about that. I just need a shower and some clean clothes, and then I've got some thinking to do.'

'Are you sure? You've just had a pretty terrible experience – and your house ...'

The edgy silence settled between us again as realisation began to join the jitters. My house, my car, my life – oh, my God – nearly my life.

'Can you pull over? Quickly!' Heather cast an odd sideways look at me but swerved over to the kerbside as the car behind her hooted angrily. I wound the window down and puked violently out of it and onto the kerb, uncaring of who was passing by. Then I slumped back against the seat and closed my eyes.

'Great. Any more where that came from?'

'Fuck off! I've just nearly been blown up.'

'I didn't mean it that way.' She sounded gentle, more like Ma would have done and I wanted to cry again.

'I'm sorry, Heather. It's shock.'

'I know. But I'd better move on before someone makes a fuss about the mess on the pavement though – if you're OK for a while?' She slipped the car into gear and pulled away smoothly. Tears slid down my face but I didn't try to stop them this time. 'It's all right.' She added. 'No-one but me can see and I'm not looking.'

We drove on in silence until my tears eventually stopped and I wiped my eyes so I could look out of the window at the passing street scene. We reached Oxford Circus and the traffic piled up. She started commenting acerbically on the female shoppers' fashion sense – or lack of it, the ridiculousness of current fashion trends, the shop windows, the volume of shoppers – anything – a steady stream of words that slowly brought me back to the realm of normality. She ended with, 'Well I can arrange the shower, but I don't think you'd look too good in any of my stuff. We'd better do some shopping on the way home, hadn't we?'

She kitted me out like I was a school kid being prepped for their first day, ordering me to stay where I was in the chain store and *don't move.* My ability to do anything seemed to have been lost with my home so I didn't. She created another kind of barricade to the one that had been consumed by fire mere hours earlier – a mound of shirts, underwear, trousers, jeans, and even pyjamas. I allowed her to until we got to the pyjamas.

'I don't wear them,' I protested.

'You do in my spare room,' she retorted and added another pair to the pile for penance. I'd allowed her to convince me to leave Sarah's box locked away in the boot of her car for this trip. We were an odd enough couple as it was without me clutching my box like it was a comforter. I was relieved when we got back to the car and it was unmolested. Heather threw the bags full of my new image in the boot next to it whilst I grabbed it back out and pressed it to me.

'It's not going anywhere, Lawrence – other than where we're going. And what's so important about it anyway?'

'It's my link to Scout.'

'Oh my God – I'm taking you to the hospital after all.'

'Scout is a code name, Heather – Margaret's. She's the one who's been sending me the messages, and all of us the evidence parcels.'

She rammed the brakes on and pulled over, this time half-mounting the kerb. Lucky there were no pedestrians nearby, but I doubted that would have bothered Heather.

'Why didn't you tell me that earlier?'

My head cleared a little. This was something I could do – explain what I knew.

'I did – or at least about the evidence. I've been trying to figure out the messages as I've been going along, but you knew about one, at least. I asked you to find it for me and tell me the address on the franking, remember?'

'But that was from FFF.'

'Exactly – and somewhere under their umbrella is Margaret – playing God knows what game, but it's a dangerous one.'

'I think you'd better start from the beginning, Lawrence – and this time, don't leave *anything* out.'

So I did – the whole story, including precisely how I'd persuaded Lord Justice Wemmick to finance my studies, who I suspected might have been responsible for Maria Flowers death in 1988, and who Maria's sister was. She already knew the accusation levelled at me over Danny's parentage so the last confession to be made by a dying man had already been made, even though I had no intention of dying just yet, but I added the newest twist on that score.

'I think Danny's Margaret's son – not Kimberley's. The blood results prove he's not Kimberley's, and Maria's son was registered as born a year after she died, so that couldn't be right. Kimmy was pregnant at the time but I think the child that died was Kimmy's, and Danny – although he was registered as Kimmy's – is really Margaret's child.'

'Whew, so they swopped, and muddied the waters by using Maria's name?'

'I believe so.'

Heather whistled appreciatively. 'It just keeps getting better, doesn't it? So we've moved on from the possibility of you being – or not being – his father now, have we? Replaced a mystery with another mystery? You think *Margaret* is Danny Hewson's mother?'

'Possibly. And his father's identity is going to remain a moot point, I suspect.'

'Although presumably not one involving you if Margaret is his mother?'

I shook my head, unsure I knew even the right answer to that.

'But I can't be sure of any of it without a blood test, or an admission.'

She grunted but surprised me with her calm. I'd expected her to do what she'd once threatened to do to me if I complicated matters any further – macerate me.

'Well neither of those is likely – unless you ask the coroner to use the blood samples they kept from Margaret's post mortem.'

'You're overlooking one thing.'

'What.'

'Margaret's post mortem wasn't on Margaret.'

'Oh God, no! I'd forgotten that. So how are you going to sort this? And that asshole Wemmick? This is his doing?'

'It would seem so. He wants the money back – the judge's money that the trust created by the will gave me, remember?'

'So bloody give it back to him then! I thought that was a given. '

'I can't – he's just blown most of it up and Margaret and Jeremy have co-opted the rest between them.'

The, 'oh my God' was muffled this time. For only the second time ever since I'd known her, Heather looked beaten, head in hands.

'Well, we'll have to find a way to get it back then,' she said at last. 'Or to make him lay off you permanently.'

'And how do you propose doing that?'

'I don't know – but I know a woman who might.'

'Who?'

'Your not-so-saintly wife. What did you call her?'

'Scout.'

'We'd better ask her to call on the whole Red Indian tribe to help us too then. It's high time she did something to help sort this mess out instead of keep adding to it.'

'Not that kind of scout.'

She ignored me. 'How did you get in touch with her last time?'

I laughed. 'I didn't. You did. That card I gave you to take to the FFF party, remember?'

'Shit!' Heather's expression was a picture – best not described.

It wouldn't be that easy this time. I'd sent her a message and she'd responded because she'd wanted to – a little like the oracle at Delphi. It answered because it had something to say back. If there was no reason for Margaret to reply she was hardly going to come out of the shadows when Jaggers had just made it so clear what would happen if she did, however much help I needed. I had to have a damn good reason to tempt her into the light. I sighed. Twisty-twisty, like the cap on a bottle, sealing it all in. I might as well hope for an answer to a message in a bottle thrown into the sea as hope for her help here. This was one party Margaret was definitely not coming to.

Bottle.

Twisty-twisty.

I echoed Heather's shit, but in my head. Aloud, I laughed like a maniac as I scrambled to tear the lid off Sarah's box whilst Heather watched me as if I'd finally gone completely mad. I fished around in the box until I found the photograph. Kimmy, Maria Flowers and her sister Margaret. I peered at it, trying to bring into fine focus the tiny images. I couldn't, but the effort did wrench the hazy memory free from the crevasse of denial it had been wedged in until now. Maybe it was the explosion that had finally shaken it loose. No, it most definitely hadn't been Kimmy I'd slept with. The miniscule and apparently insignificant memory now detonating in my head confirmed that. The memory that had sent me scrabbling in the box of the young woman I'd bedded, and later, ironically wedded, without realising we already had a very intimate and specific reason to be so inextricably linked. The young woman who hadn't been able to unscrew the cap off a bottle, and thus manoeuvred her first introduction to me.

'I broke my arm skiing, and it's never been any good ever since. Could you?'

I opened the bottle for her, and there the memory drifted away again, except for the fact that I remembered sneaking away from the hotel room the next day, too hung over to exchange pleasantries, and hoping she didn't wake before I left.

Jonno, Win and I *all* had the faulty gene. Mixed with correspondingly faulty code on the mother's side any of us could have produced Danny, but it was clear to me, given who I believed his mother to be, who the only realistic candidate could be.

Me.

So here was the way to draw Margaret out: Danny – but if claiming Danny also meant damning him and Margaret to join me in perdition, what good was integrity if you were too dead to savour it?

'I take it a card wouldn't work a second time?' Heather asked glumly.

I shook my head, mind still struggling to comprehend the enormity of what I'd just worked out. I answered almost automatically whilst my brain processed the idea.

'But I need answers somehow, Heather. I need to know how to nail Wemmick but still get myself off the hook. How I can set the record straight without crucifying us all? That also means I have to know for sure who killed Maria Flowers in 1988.'

'Rosemary Flowers, you mean?' I stared at her. She sighed. 'OK, let's go back to basics without Margaret. I'll make it easy for you – although God knows you don't deserve it – or me. Rosemary Flowers: Maria was her stage name. I've been doing a bit of research. Her real name was Rosemary Clare Flowers. Her sister was Margaret Ann Flowers. The sister disappeared off the scene shortly after Rosemary – Maria – was killed. At the time it was assumed that she was avoiding the press coverage, which if you recall was pretty rancid, given how badly mangled the body was. You reckon that your sister Kimberley was hanging around with her at the time too? I couldn't find any record of that, but then they did like their aliases, didn't they.'

'Where did you get all of this, Heather?'

'Archives. After you implied we'd all been involved in a cover up I thought I'd better find out what had really been going on at the time.'

'And what had?'

'What I'm telling you now. After the inquest the girl, Maria, was apparently buried quietly somewhere near the coast – odd name that I can't remember offhand at the moment but it'll come back to me. The culprit was supposedly your pal, Wilhelm Johns, who would never say what or why he'd done it. There was nothing to go on apart from circumstantial evidence which was more than damning at the time. Fingerprints on the murder weapon, timing right, her blood on his clothes, no motive; but everyone started on about it being a crime of passion and then no motive was needed.'

'I know all this – it was what I prosecuted the case on. It was too pat though, wasn't it? And the fact that we were just handed it without even trying was even more suspect. But aside from that, I've got the case folder – or did have – in my desk at home, and it had something else in it that had been planted in there since. A segment of nail that I think might have been Margaret's.'

'I know.'

'What? How?' Now my head really did spin. The case file hadn't been out of my possession since this had all started. I'd seen to that with so many opportunities for the media to latch onto it. Heather may have said she would see what else she could find out about the Johns case, but that had to have been from other sources.

'You're not the only one who can have secrets. It's not a privilege solely reserved for guys, you know.' Her mouth twisted in a wry grin.

'So what's your secret, Heather?'

'That case Margaret got me to defend for Alfie Roumelia, and your asshole Wemmick kicked up about?'

'Yes?'

'He made a wrong move when he did that. Got too big for his boots, maybe? He wrote me a longhand note, and I kept it. I was so pissed off with him at the time I wanted to think of a really scathing reply but needed time to do it so I put it in a plastic wallet and kept it. I never got round to the reply because this all kicked off instead, but when I checked through the Johns notes – in your desk drawer at the time – I noticed the handwriting similarity straightaway. I've had it checked against Johns' statement by a handwriting specialist since. They were written by the same person – and it's pretty difficult to write anything when you're dead – as Margaret found out.'

'Meaning he falsified the evidence against Johns?'

'Oh, more than that! I've been *very* busy whilst you've been swanning around playing off-screen lover with your little social worker, and secret agent with your wife. There was one unidentified print on that murder weapon, but it was written off as not worth pursuing since everything else against Johns was so conclusive. It was the same one that was all over that letter I was sent, and that bag they found discarded at the murder scene. It was also on the bag they found at your house after your sister was killed, but has yet to be identified. I got Norton to show me the file before they closed it on you. Well, I needed to know how badly you were going to burn us.'

'So did you plant the finger nail clipping?'

'Oh, for God's sake Lawrence! No, I don't plant stuff. I even buy my herb garden ready-potted. But someone did, perhaps as a clue, or an anomaly; hoping you'd figure out it was Margaret's – the colour was more signature than her handwriting, after all. That meant at some stage *you'd* also wonder how it could get there – even as blind as you've been. Who do you think that might have been?' The sarcasm was unmistakable, as well as who she meant. 'I got in on the act much later when I was starting to wonder just how much of the case I was going to have to solve for you because you were too immersed in your fascinating family background. What with that and the little social worker I realised then I'd have to get on it for you since you weren't. And by the way, the case folder you think got burnt in your desk was a copy I got Louise to make. The original is in *my* desk drawer – just in case.'

'Jesus, Heather. Don't get me wrong, I'm very grateful, but is anyone completely what they appear to be?'

'No, Lawrence – and God help you if you haven't realised that by now.'

'So where do I go from here? Even with the leverage you've turned up on Jaggers I'd have to get to Margaret to tell her about it, and we still need the rest of the evidence she claims to have to nail him completely.'

'Why is Margaret's codename Scout?'

'Her cryptic messages. I may not have understood them completely but they're to do with my love of a book. *To Kill a Mocking Bird*. Scout is the young narrator who learns how to see through the pretence to gain a better understanding of people and principles. There was also a bit in one of the messages about rosemary and hiding under a blue cloak, which gave the herb an alternative name – Rose of Mary.'

Heather's eyes widened. 'Oh she's smart, your Margaret, isn't she?'

'Why?'

'Picking on something close to your heart.' She laughed. 'It's an allegory, Lawrence. The cloak and the rosemary too. Yes, her sister's name was Rosemary so she was playing on it but it's also a metaphor for hiding behind a bloodline – blue blood – or behind appearances. I remember reading *To Kill a Mocking Bird* too. I reckon Margaret is telling you to look at a bloodline and see what is being hidden behind it.'

I shifted uncomfortably. This was getting very close to another awkward confession I might need to make, processed or not.

'She uses lots of allegories, Heather. The cards for instance. They're her little way of teasing me.'

'Maybe, but it's more than that – this is about what was going on before Danny was even conceived. Who else has an ambiguous pedigree?'

'Well, Margaret, and her sister Rosemary. Jaggers too – John Wemmick, I mean. When he was at the children's home with me he was John Arthur Green. Now he's John Arthur Wemmick. How did he suddenly switch families?'

'Maybe he didn't. Maybe they're all the same family and Margaret has been playing the same game you have?'

'You mean they really *are* brother and sister? Wemmicks?'

'Or Greens.'

'But if they're Greens, how can he force the issue with old Judge Wemmick's will?'

'He couldn't, if there was someone around to contest it. But there isn't, is there? You said George Wemmick, the father, is in Dubai and in his dotage – who else is there? Margaret, if she had any say in it, maybe – but if Margaret is in hiding – under Rosemary's cloak ...'

'But Rosemary's cloak isn't real, is it? It's a euphemism. Playing dead: hiding under the blue cloak of death ... *to be read in the event of my death.*' Heather stared at me. It was no good. 'I guess there's one more relevant confession to make then.' My real death bed one.

She opened and shut her mouth several times before saying, 'I should have known! You tricky bastard. You and she are made for each other. Why didn't you tell me before?'

'I just have – and before you hang me, I've only just figured it out.'

She burst out laughing. 'I said you were blind – or in this case, blind drunk! Congratulations, Daddy – the press will have a field day with that but if you do it right you might still come out of the manure they grow them in smelling like roses! So there's your next party invitation. '

'Funny!' and then, 'oh fuck, Heather – I've probably had all the answers all along. I've just been too arrogant and pig-headed to read them.'

I opened Sarah's box and took out Margaret's letter.

25: Patchwork People

It was all in there, as I'd thought. She must have been watching me with such amusement these last weeks as I ran around like an idiot trying to find a reason for her coercing me. She'd raised all the questions, and given me all the answers only to force me to confront myself. She'd been offering me a chance to find out about her and her son because she couldn't get me to bother any other way.

'Forgive those who have sinned against you, they say...

Well, the sinner is my brother – John Arthur Green, who I didn't actually meet until I was fifteen and he was twenty-seven. And there is no forgiveness to be had. He's the one who killed the mockingbird.

Our father managed to shield my sister and me from him until then. We were his second family and John is my half-brother, taken into care because he was so wild when he was young and our father was suffering from severe depression after his first wife's death. Dad died quite young – he was a haemophiliac, you see – like Danny. Mum withered away from grief shortly afterwards. They were always so inseparable, and there were Rosemary and I, just fifteen and all alone. When our brother appeared to claim us it seemed like heaven had answered our prayers. We didn't know then it was quite the reverse and we'd just met the devil.

We already knew your sister, Kimmy, from school, but through her we also came to know your brother Win, and through him and John, Wilhelm Johns – Jonno. I suspect now that John only found out about us through Kimmy's connection to Win. John called himself 'a businessman'. His business was – is – the Gods and Gargoyles Club. Kimmy worked there when she was old enough. She introduced Rosemary to it, and she and Rosemary became even closer whilst I got excluded. In many ways I didn't mind. I didn't want to be connected to that place. I hated it, but I had nowhere else to go. By the time she was eighteen, Rosemary had taken to John's nightclub like a duck to water. She was always more gregarious than me. She was Maria there – much more interesting than

Rosemary. She'd been calling herself Maria privately for a while anyway.

When Rosemary started actually working at the club – dancing, and then stripping – so did I. My job was in accounts because I have a head for figures and administration, not a body for desire. In my spare time I immersed myself in reading and studying to shut it all out – both Rosemary and I have always been veritable encyclopaedias if tested. But things got steadily worse.

There were drugs around and I suspected Rosemary of taking them but couldn't prove anything. Kimmy too. Then there were the parties – wild ones, for the night club's clientele. It was after one of these that Rosemary first became unwell. She was pregnant. To begin with she wouldn't tell me who the father was. I assumed it was one of the punters. I was wrong. It came out after a terrible fight one night that it was John. I stormed out, but I still had nowhere to go so I had to go creeping back eventually. I vowed then I'd get my sister and myself away from him somehow. I never got the chance. The next wild party they had, things got too wild.

Of course as she was pregnant and an autopsy was likely because it was a suspicious death, John had evidence of her pregnancy hidden. He did it in the brutal way everyone read about later, but I had evidence – which you've seen. I used it to keep myself safe for as long as I could by holding it over John, but in the meantime he wanted control of the club back. Win and Jonno were partners – John hadn't had the ready cash to buy it outright, you see. His clever little plan? Set up Wilhelm Johns with the suspicious death and get himself off the hook. That ousted Jonno because of the criminality clause too, and left only Win to deal with. He figured Kimmy could be used there someday. A nice fait accompli and I was still trapped, but not forever...

The success of that little scheme produced in John an assumption of invincibility and his ideas became wilder and wilder. He'd come across you again by then – through Win. He decided to set you up with Jonno's prosecution so you'd be in his pocket without even knowing it and then tap into you later. I watched you and your quiet determination in court and decided you could be the one to help me. You had your own little party afterwards to celebrate the victory and I took a leaf out of my sister's book as the consummate party girl. You ended up with me – and Danny. You don't remember because you were too drunk, but even that worked in my favour when we met officially later.

I couldn't let anyone know about Danny. It would make me – and him

– far too vulnerable. Remember the only thing keeping me safe was that evidence I held over John. If he'd known I had a weak point he could manipulate, the game would be over. Worse still, Danny has a genuine claim to the Wemmick estate, and John would never allow that. It would spoil his fun altogether. My great grandmother was the real Molly Wemmick, you see, and my grandmother was Molly's illegitimate daughter. No-one publically acknowledged her, but the claim is real nevertheless. That was how John first got the idea to assume control of the Wemmick's empire. It was an ironic joke. The family had otherwise died out bar 'Uncle George' – and us – so John could assume control relatively easily once he'd found a way of manipulating 'Uncle George'. Some nasty little secret he'd dug up, I guess. I decided I might as well acquire another name to add to my own whilst I played along; Molly Wemmick – in honour of my unacknowledged roots. My own little joke!

I confided in Kimmy because there was no-one else to go to, and she was pregnant too – and worried – at the time. Being pregnant is death to a career as a stripper, so the only way was down for her. She went to Win for help and he agreed to hand over his share in the club in return for John setting her up securely. John won again. Win's a big softie really, despite the hard man front. Kimmy lost her baby and was afraid what Win would go back on the deal when he found out, but I still had a child I needed to hide. We agreed then to make the switch, with her looking after Danny as her own, and me keeping the stillbirth to myself and providing the cover for her to do so. She wasn't the best bet for a substitute mother, of course. She's bi-polar – in case you didn't know. When she takes her medication she's fine. When she doesn't ... But she promised me she would play it straight and I had no other options. Anyway I enjoyed the irony of John protecting the one thing he would otherwise have harmed. I found myself a husband too – you. John loved that. More irony, and my place as intermediary was assured.

For Kimmy, though, the arrangement was only ever agreed to out of expediency. After a while, she forgot to take her meds and her condition became uncontrolled. That was when I knew I had to step in again. By then John's schemes had become even more grandiose. He set up FFF to launder money but I saw it as a way to get to Danny. Through it I devised the scheme to adopt him, and it was all going well until Kimmy got into trouble with John again. Unbeknownst to me, she'd been borrowing money from him and not repaying it. By then money was one of John's hang-ups – so worried everything was going to blow apart after a couple of dodgy deals went wrong. He needed the money back. She couldn't pay it. He remembered you – and the money you got from Judge Wemmick's will. You were Kimmy's brother. You could repay it – and more. That is the crux of it all, and where everything started to unravel. He used Danny against Kimmy as he would have used him against me – except of course she didn't care. I had to do something. The something was pulling you and your past into the open to make you react.

The rest – as they say – is history. Your brother Win hates John for what he did to Jonno. He's a rough but easily led man, so easy to use. So are the rest of your family because I've known them for years – and their foibles. Apart from Win, only Sarah and Binnie made the connections, but they've never interfered. The risk to Danny prevented them, but I had to fake my death for the next part of the plan to work. You were still resisting action. Without me there you had to make the running. John wants the Wemmick's money and you're the only one who can give it to him. I, as your wife, would get caught in the crossfire. As Molly Wemmick, I could be his sister, and – so he thinks – his ally. The intermediary again.

I have all the evidence you need to prove John's guilt. It's safe in a deposit box and you even have the key. You just need to find and open the box. It doesn't take courage to tell the truth. It takes courage to live it.

If you're reading this letter it's because somehow all my planning has backfired and I really am dead – not just pretending – so I need you to do my work for me. You'll know where the instructions to find the safety deposit box are, if you think carefully. It's the main thing we've always had in common; twisted roots. Take courage, Lawrence. I know it was always your intention to. I haven't watched the reverence with which you handle that copy of 'To Kill a Mocking Bird' you've had for donkey's years for nothing. Now is your time to close the book and complete the story.

Your wife,
Margaret

***

She met me on Fulham Broadway, far enough in public view to be 'safe'; anonymous enough in the milling pedestrians all intent on their own business for us to be intimate. A card did work in the end. Left in every library and bookshop copy of *To Kill a Mocking Bird* I could find. It was returned through the post 'from Scout', with a time and place to meet.

'So you've worked out whole game, then?'

I shook my head. 'No, but the letter asked me to make a stand.'

'And you read the letter?'

'I had to.'

'Even though I'm not dead.'

'We're all dead, Margaret – the old us. You gave us no choice in that. But it's fitting we make a stand together now. I need your help – and you need mine.'

'Tell me what you're standing for first.'

'Justice for a mockingbird.'

She studied me, then smiled. 'You have my help then.'

'And you know how to achieve it?''

'I have an idea, but you'll need to trust me. Will you?'

'And who would I be trusting today?'

'Margaret Juste, if that's who you want me to be?'

'And tomorrow?'

'The same.'

'For Danny's sake, I don't have much choice, do I?'

'That was the general idea.' She paused. 'But it won't be easy, you know. John's a dangerous enemy and Danny's our vulnerability.'

'Why did you send Emm to see him?'

'The past casts long shadows. It was time she walked into the light too. Danny was one of her shadows. But I also wanted her to check on him whilst I couldn't. Ironically, of all of you she was the only one I could trust at the time. Historically she had an axe to grind so she had to play it straight down the line or be under suspicion herself if she didn't. She would have worked that out. She's smart.'

'And not devious.' She made a little bow as if in thanks. 'But why not trust me?'

She smiled. 'You're too close.'

'To the problem?'

She shook her head, laughing.

'To the patchwork. Did you know, the Quakers have a special way of depicting the major events in their lives? When their children are born the wife starts to sew a quilt. When their family is complete, so is the picture, and they spread the quilt across the marital bed and thank God for what they've created.'

'I have noticed your inclination to manipulate inconsequential literary and cultural information for your own ends,' I replied dryly.

She grinned. 'Like the letter says, Encyclopaedia Britannica – that's me. But this isn't inconsequential at all, Lawrence. Danny is the quilt, don't you see?'

I did, but adjustments took time and patience, like patchworks – and justice.

'You're a manipulative bitch.'

'And you're an arrogant sod.'

'What happened to your no swearing rule?'

'I'm a patchwork woman.'

She moved closer and leant towards me so I could smell her skin and hair. Unexpectedly my head spun.

'I guess now we'll have to learn how to be patchwork people together.'

The sensations the kiss created were strange; aggression, anger, relief – and intense passion. She frowned and touched my lips in surprise, eyes questioning. Then she kissed me back and all ambiguity was sucked away and replaced by a maelstrom of unexpected longing. I held onto her giddily until she pulled gently away, smiling.

'*I* can't come out into the light just yet, Lawrence. There's still too much at risk. *That* will have to wait.'

'For how much longer?'

'Just until.' She smiled and I wondered again how I'd overlooked her attraction all these years.

'And will you be OK, in the dark?'

'I have Atticus Finch looking out for me.' She smiled, and touched my lips lightly with her fingers. They smelt of herbs. 'And you still have work to do – on John.'

'I understand. But how can I reach you if I need to?'

'I devised the game, remember? I'll find you.'

A car hooted and made us both jump. A dark Merc rounded the corner, windows blacked, like the one that had shadowed me on my way home from Kat's.

She took a step away, allowing a passer-by to slip into the gap between us.

'I must go. No-one must see us together yet. The evidence is all in the box. Sarah put it there for me. You've got the key.' And she was slipping away from me, merging with the crowds.

I called after her. 'Where? Where is it?' but wasn't convinced she'd heard.

The car slid alongside the kerb and a shiver of fear trickled down my back. I could just see her shake her head before a group of tourists engulfed her. Her voice floated back to me through their waving cameras and backpacks, a lilting tease.

'Under Rosemary's cloak. I'll be in touch soon,' and she was gone.

I dodged the Merc and the crowds and slipped shakily into the mouth of Fulham Broadway Tube station. The Merc pulled back into the traffic and edged along as if looking for something – or someone. I knew who it was, but he hadn't found either of us, or our mockingbird tale yet. And nor would he if Atticus had his way. There was evidence and a way to stop him now. In the ruins of my collapsed life and dismembered past there was the possibility of a future – for Margaret and Danny and me. As my brother Win's namesake once said, it wasn't the end, or even the beginning of the end, but the end of the beginning [2] One we now would have to begin and end together. A re-sewn and re-worked patchwork – almost complete.

Bibliography:

1. Opie and P. Opie, *The Oxford Dictionary of Nursery Rhymes* (Oxford: Oxford University Press, 1951, 2nd edn., 1997 p. 149).
2. From a speech at the Lord Mayor's Day Luncheon at the Mansion House, London, 9 November 1942 (Copyright © Winston S. Churchill, *The End of the Beginning*, London: Cassell, 1943, p. 265), renewal copyright Randolph S. Churchill 2009.

The Patchwork Trilogy

PATCHWORK MAN

Have you ever met a patchwork man?

Lawrence Juste is one. The QC with a conscience - privileged, reputable and emotionally frozen. The perfect barrister.

But Lawrence hasn't always been who he is now. When he is glaringly in the public eye after his enigmatic wife is killed in an apparently random hit and run, he could do with his hidden past surfacing like a hole in the head.

Unfortunately the past has a way of finding its way back to you, just like betrayal. His dead wife has helpfully left him a sinister resume of his, and she just keeps adding to it...

Patchwork Man is the first book in the trilogy.

PATCHWORK PEOPLE

The second book in the trilogy.

Lawrence Juste QC has already had to face the public appearance of a long lost and criminally inclined brother, the renewed attentions of a boyhood bully, threatening to ruin him professionally and financially, and the machinations of his dead wife apparently keen to do the same. What else could go wrong?

Plenty.

It seems it can only end one way for Lawrence - disaster; unless his dead wife can help...

PATCHWORK PIECES

Patchwork Pieces is the third and final book in the trilogy.

It seems Lawrence Juste's life is so disassembled it would take a miracle to put it back together without losing himself in the process. And even then the picture wouldn't be pretty. Murder. Blackmail. Revenge. And the living dead. It sounds like fantasy. In reality its fate, and the past finally catching up with not only Juste, but anyone who's ever cheated, lied or betrayed alongside him.

It's going to be one hell of a party when the patchwork is completed...

About D. B. Martin

D.B. Martin writes adult psychological thriller fiction and literary fiction as Debrah Martin, as well as YA fiction, featuring a teen detective series, under the pen name of Lily Stuart.

You can find more about her work and sign up for updates on forthcoming publications on www.debrahmartin.co.uk and www.lily-stuart.co.uk.

Printed in Great Britain
by Amazon.co.uk, Ltd.,
Marston Gate.